DESCENT

A Stone Mountain Mystery

Kristina Stanley

DESCENT
A Stone Mountain Mystery #1

This is a work of fiction. Names, characters, places and incidents either are the product of the author's imagination or are used fictitiously. And any resemblance to actual persons, living, dead (or in any other form), business establishments, events, or locales is entirely coincidental.

www.KristinaStanley.com

FIRST EDITION Trade Paperback

Imajin Books — www.imajinbooks.com

July 25, 2015

ISBN: 978-1-77223-095-6

Cover designed by Ryan Doan — http://www.ryandoan.com

Praise for DESCENT

"In this impressive debut, Kristina Stanley weaves a vivid, chilling tale of jealousy, secrets, and betrayal in a close-knit mountain ski village. Like its likeable young heroine, Kalin Thompson, DESCENT is both tender and tough." —Barbara Fradkin, award-winning author of the Inspector Green Mysteries

"Murder rocks the competitive ski world in Stanley's layered tale with enough suspects to keep readers guessing until the last chilling chapter." —Brenda Chapman, author of the Stonechild and Rouleau Mysteries

"From the first line, you're strapped into a Stanley novel. Just turn the page, hang on, and enjoy the ride." —Garry Ryan, award-winning author of the Detective Lane Mysteries

For Mathew: He who is my life.

Acknowledgements

Mathew is the person I need to thank first. His unending belief in me and his support of my writing journey kept me writing.

My friends for life who read, reread, commented and commented again: Liliana Conn, Michael Conn, Adrienne Cristelli, Janice Janczyn, Sue Kreiling, Debi Sarandrea, and Melanie Wagner.

For medical advice, cheers go out to Dr. Rama Behki.

For his mischievous suggestion on how to tamper with a binding, a shout out to boot fitter and Calgary firefighter Billy Stewart.

To George Duncan for his expertise on ski lift operations.

To Tony Trimble for his legal advice.

I would like to thank Humber School for Writers through which I received feedback from Joan Barfoot and Mary Gaitskill, and Garry Ryan for his support and mentorship through Crime Writers of Canada.

And of course, thank you to Cheryl Kaye Tardif and Imajin Books for believing in me.

CHAPTER ONE

Day One: November 28th

Death swept up the mountain and across the frigid snow, giving no warning, no threatening growl, just spreading tendrils, searching for a victim while Stone Mountain Resort buzzed with energy, unaware of the impending doom.

Kalin Thompson gunned the engine of her snowmobile, forced its skis over a mogul, and sped toward the summit of the Alpine Tracks run. The Holden ski team owned the race course for the next twenty minutes, and when the local team finished, Kalin planned to ski the gates, just for one run, just for the adrenaline rush.

Her sled hit a patch of ice and slid toward a chairlift tower. She gripped the handlebar and leaned left, edging around the structure, brushing the metal side with her ski pants. Damaging equipment five days into being the director of security at the resort would not impress her boss. She regained control and drove toward the summit. Exhilarated by the ride, she skidded to a stop beside Ben Timlin and let out a whoop.

Giving her a wink that could seduce even the coldest of hearts, Ben said, "Enjoying yourself?"

Kalin glanced around and checked that no one was looking in their direction. She leaned over the handlebar, their ski helmets thudded, and she kissed Ben. "I am now."

At the starting gates, a super-G racer sliced his skis backward and forward, leaning hard on his poles in an aggressive stance, anticipating the signal to launch. Frozen breath exploded from his lungs as he waited for the skier ahead of him to clear the course.

Kalin undid her helmet's strap and pulled her neck tube over her chin. "How's the training going?"

"Not great. I'm surprised Coach Jenkinson hasn't cancelled the session."

"Why?"

"More than half the racers either slid off the course or fell. One sprained his ankle."

"Snow injection?"

"Yup, the course is a skating rink."

Stone Mountain's one hundred and fifty-six-person chairlift covered five meters per second from the bottom of the Alpine Tracks ski run to the summit, and the lift clanged around the unloading station, dropping skiers and their gear several meters from where Ben and Kalin waited. Kalin counted the last of the team members arriving at the summit. Six skiers still had runs to conquer before she could ski.

Only razor-thin ski suits protected the racers from the elements. Kalin blinked, and her eyelashes frosted together. She pinched her lashes between her index finger and thumb, melting the ice. *Was Ben cold too?* She laughed at herself for worrying about her boyfriend. His high-tech ski patrol jacket, filled with first aid and safety gear, protected him more than adequately from the sub-zero temperature.

Ben nudged the skis strapped to the back of Kalin's snowmobile. "You can't ski today."

"Is that a dare?"

"The racers are having a hard time. It's too dangerous."

Listening to advice about being cautious was not Kalin's strongest asset, but Ben's expression told her she couldn't win this one. Still, if no more racers fell, she'd try to talk him into going.

The signal blasted, and the racer between the gates shot his legs backward, his head and shoulders forward, and burst over the start line. He tucked his curved poles around his sides, bent his knees and rounded the first gate. His elbow whacked the second gate, but he kept his balance. He picked up speed, skirted the third gate, and the timing screen showed he clocked ninety-four kilometers per hour. His edges cut the ice and held firm.

Super-G, a cross between giant slalom and downhill, required a minimum of thirty-five gates and was different from the downhill in that a skier didn't get a practice run before a race. Each skier had one chance and skied to the extreme.

Rounding the fourth gate, the racer pressed hard against his edges, but instead of power transferring to the snow, one boot released from its binding. The racer flew into the air with speed. He swung his arms forward, not fast enough to break his fall, and his head slammed into the ice packed surface.

Without taking his eyes off the skier, Ben simultaneously turned the key in the snowmobile ignition and spoke into his radio.

The racer's limp body rag-dolled down the steep descent. He plowed over the fifth gate, flattening the pole to the ground. The orange safety netting lining the side of the run stopped him from sliding into the forest.

Ben drove his snowmobile toward the fallen skier, and Kalin followed on hers.

Pandemonium erupted. People from every direction ran to the racer.

"Stand back." Ben pushed through the crowd and squatted. The racer lay face-up with his body twisted in the netting and his neck turned in an unnatural angle.

The skier's goggles hid his facial features, but with the temperature below zero, Kalin should have been able to see his breath.

Ben made eye contact with her. "You better go tell Reed."

CHAPTER TWO

Four days earlier... November 24th

Kalin spotted Tom Bennett, the director of security at Stone Mountain Resort, sitting with his wife, Ginny, at a table near the fireplace in the Mountain Chalet Restaurant. She had a few moments before Ben was due to appear and stopped to say hello.

"Any security issues with race training today?"

Ginny answered for Tom. "It's our anniversary. Thirty-four years, so Tom is taking the night off."

"Congratulations." Kalin shook Tom's hand. Sweat covered his palm, slippery against her skin. "I'll leave you two alone."

Tom clenched Kalin's hand, pulling her forward.

"Ginny—" He released his grip and slumped sideways. Kalin leaned across the table. Her fingers touched the fabric of his sweater, but she missed grabbing his sleeve. His head hit the slate tile with a smack.

Kalin launched around the table and collided with Ginny at Tom's side. She knelt beside him, checked for a pulse on his neck and found none.

"Get the AED," Kalin called to the bartender, who stared at her with unblinking eyes.

With her heart rate picking up speed, Kalin pointed toward a set of swinging doors and hoped he couldn't see her hand shake. "The defibrillator. It's hanging on the kitchen wall." She kept her eyes on him until he turned toward the equipment.

A server hovered nearby. Kalin cleared her throat to steady her voice. "Call 911 and then security. Wait, not security. Call ski patrol."

"How do I find ski patrol?"

Kalin tossed her phone to the server. "Call 911 first. Ben's is the last number dialed. Call him second. He's already on his way here."

Ginny leaned over Tom, her reading glasses swinging from her neck, and shook his shoulders. "Tom. Tom. Answer me."

Kalin grabbed Ginny's hands. "He needs CPR. Step back. Okay?" Precious seconds were lost as Ginny got herself under control. Kalin blew two breaths into Tom's mouth, ignored the sour aroma of recently eaten garlic, and began the count of thirty compressions.

While she pumped his chest, one of the servers gently placed a dishcloth on Tom's bleeding forehead. After three rounds of compressions, sweat pooled at the bottom of Kalin's spine. Out of the corner of her eye she saw Ginny crouched beside her, rocking to the beat of her chant, "No. No. No." *Tune her out. Just keep pumping.*

Kalin let out a breath when Ben pressed his palm between her shoulder blades. She stopped pumping at the end of a compression cycle and shifted sideways, giving him space to access Tom. She braced her hands on the top of her thighs, tucked her chin and took a moment to calm herself. She clenched her fists and shoved herself off the floor. Dirt from the slate tiles covered the knees of her jeans, and she absently wiped them, leaving sweat marks on the denim.

Ben dropped his toque and ski gloves on the tile and kneeled beside Tom. He cut Tom's cable-knit sweater and the white T-shirt he wore underneath, exposing his torso, and shaved two patches of grey chest hair. He placed electrode pads on Tom's chest and waited for the AED to analyze his heart rhythm. "It's recommending a shock."

Kalin pulled Ginny away from Tom, keeping her arm around Ginny's shoulder. "Ben knows what he's doing."

"I'm clear. You're clear. Everyone's clear," Ben said. After the initial shock didn't establish a normal rhythm, the AED repeated the shock two times.

Ben turned his attention away from Tom and toward Kalin.

"Keep going. I'll empty the restaurant." Kalin resisted a surge of grief and turned to the bartender. "Stay with Ginny."

The restaurant manager came out of the back office.

After taking in the scene around the room, Kalin approached the manager. "I need you to help me empty the restaurant."

"But people are still eating."

The conversation had ceased, and all eyes were turned toward Ben and Tom. One man held his fork midway between the table and his mouth. A woman clutched a napkin to her face.

"No one's eating anymore. Offer a voucher or a full refund. Whatever it takes to get people out quickly. They'll understand. Get your staff to help. It'll keep them busy."

Kalin returned to Ginny. "Has Tom been sick?"

Ginny wrapped her silk scarf around her shoulders and chest as if trying to hold herself together. "He had a cold that turned into walking pneumonia, but he's better now."

"Is he taking any medications?"

Ginny shook her head, and her dewdrop earrings swung from her lobes. "He's going to be okay, right?"

Ben performed a second round of CPR with the tick-tock of the AED's metronome timing the compressions, but Tom's vital signs remained absent.

No one answered Ginny.

Ginny squished Kalin's hand. "Kalin?"

"I don't know."

The paramedics arrived. One pulled a stretcher, and the other carried a defibrillator.

"How'd you get here so fast?" Kalin asked. Stone Mountain Resort was nestled between two peaks in the Purcell Mountain Range at twelve hundred meters above sea level and was separated by eighteen kilometers of rough highway from the nearest town of Holden, British Columbia.

"We were at the resort on another call." The paramedic glanced at the staff guiding patrons to the door or closing bills. "We'll load and go, and treat during transport."

The paramedics lifted Tom onto the stretcher and wheeled him toward the exit. Ginny hung on to Tom's ankle and followed them toward the ambulance.

Kalin's eyes roamed the restaurant until she found the server who had her phone. She called her boss first. Gavin Reed was also Tom's boss and the president of Stone Mountain Resort. "Tom Bennett collapsed in the restaurant. I think he had a heart attack." She took a calming breath while Reed spoke, then said, "He's been taken to the hospital. Ginny is with him." She finished the conversation and turned her attention back to the people in the room.

With the last of the restaurant's patrons cleared from the room, the servers, bartender and manager huddled together in front of the fireplace. The flames licked and danced around the wood, emitting a campfire odor. Two of the women cried, and the rest of the group sat in silence.

Ben joined Kalin, tucked her hair behind one ear and rested his palm on the back of her neck. "You okay?"

Kalin allowed herself the luxury of a full-body hug. She snuck her arms underneath his ski jacket, buried her nose in his brown, curly hair and breathed in the scent of his shampoo. Instead of answering, she nodded, and his stubble scratched her cheek.

She removed her knee length tunic-cardigan and folded it over the nearest chair. Using her thumb, she scrolled through the address book in her phone and called the counselor the resort kept on retainer. After she finished the call, she joined the employees.

"This is a lot to take in. The resort's counselor is on her way. She'll lead you through a debriefing. If any of you feel like talking, in a group or alone with her, she'll be here in half an hour."

"Is he dead?" the bartender asked.

Kalin pressed her lips into a combination of a frown and a smile, an expression she knew made her appear empathetic. "I don't know. Gavin Reed is going to meet Tom and Ginny at the hospital. He'll call me when he knows something."

"He didn't look good," one of the servers said.

"No. He didn't." Kalin addressed the manager. "Why don't you take everyone to a conference room and wait there?" The Mountain Chalet Restaurant sat at the base of the ski hill, a five-minute walk from the administration building that housed Kalin's human resources office, the accounting team and conference rooms. Distancing the employees from the scene would be good for them. Kalin wanted to distance herself too. *But not yet.*

"Who's going to clear the tables?" the manager asked.

"Ben and I can do that later. Don't worry about things here. It's more important your team gets a debrief session."

Kalin called the director of lodging and explained the situation. "Who do we use to clean blood and body fluids?"

Instead of giving her the information, he offered to contact the specialized company and get the cleaning done. With that taken care of, she couldn't put off the next call any longer. She phoned Fred Morgan and told him the news. She heard his intake of breath and stayed silent for a moment. Fred, the manager of security, had reported to Tom for twelve years.

"How many security officers are on duty right now?" she asked.

"Two."

"They need to be told. Do you want me to meet with them, or do you want to come in?"

"I'll come in. Thanks for calling ski patrol and not security. The officers are close to Tom. They would've had a tough time treating him."

Alone in the restaurant, Kalin and Ben sat in silence waiting for her boss to call with an update. All that remained of the tragic event were the remnants of Tom's shirt, latex gloves and tiles stained with blood.

CHAPTER THREE

November 25th

Kalin's boss expected her in his office at eight-fifteen to talk to her about Tom Bennett's death. Probably about her breach in protocol. The experience of treating a colleague had left her exhausted, and after she'd locked the restaurant and gone home, she'd stumbled into bed. She hadn't had time to process what the death of a director meant and wasn't sure if she was about to be reprimanded.

She snowshoed to work, wearing a fleece top underneath her ski jacket and thermal underwear beneath her ski pants. She entered the administration building and traded her winter boots for hiking boots. Once inside her office, she dropped her headlamp and bear spray on her desk.

After hanging her ski jacket on the hook behind her door, she walked to Gavin Reed's corner office. The sun rising over the Purcell Mountains pulled her attention outside and away from the photos of Reed's son ski racing. Ian Reed in action dominated the interior walls.

In a nervous habit, she tightened the elastic holding her shoulder length hair in a ponytail. She fluffed her bangs using her fingertips. She'd learned there was no point in straightening her hair before her trek to work. She could ignore a little bit of frizz and curl in order to stay fit.

The early morning exercise had pulled her out of her funk from the night before but meant she'd be wearing her ski clothes for the day. A quick sniff at the armpit of her fleece. All good. Who wants to stink in front of the president?

Reed stood and greeted her. Neatly dressed in a button-down shirt and ironed jeans, her six-foot-two boss angled his neck to look down on her, and she straightened her back, making herself taller. When she turned fifteen, she'd shot up like a fast growing poplar tree to five-foot-ten, towering over the boys in her class, making her anything but popular. After all the teasing she'd taken, she discovered she found shorter men attractive. *Lucky Ben.*

"I'm sorry about Tom," Kalin said.

"Thank you for everything you did last night. I hear you performed exceptionally well. Ginny said you took charge and asked me to pass on her thanks."

Generous, considering Tom died. Kalin had been scared and performed as if she were on autopilot. Both the hospital and the ambulance dispatch center were in Holden. In a snowstorm, the drive could take over an hour, and for that reason, first-aid training for managers was mandatory. That training had pulled Kalin through the night before. "How is she?"

"As well as can be expected. Have a seat."

Kalin sat in a chair opposite from Reed, and the leather seat creaked. "Was it a heart attack?"

"Sudden cardiac arrest. The doctor evaluated the AED data and will debrief Ben today. When she's ready, I'll ask Ginny what help she needs." Reed cleared his throat. "Tom held a key role, and I know this sounds harsh, but we have to fill his position immediately."

As the human resources manager, Kalin was in charge of recruiting. To her, it did seem heartless to post Tom's position right away. *Thanks for your years of service, sorry you're dead, but we need a new security director.* She gave herself an imaginary slap. She was being unfair. Reed had a resort to run. Ski race training had started, and she was sure he had things to worry about other than security. "What about Fred Morgan?"

Reed scratched the back of his neck. "I don't think he's ready. He hasn't shown the required leadership skills." Reed must have seen the look of surprise on her face because he tempered his comment. "He's very good at his job, but he's not a forward thinker. He's knowledgeable about security, and he manages his team well. I just don't think he can strategize at the level I need."

Kalin couldn't argue with Reed's assessment. Fred was solid, but he did tend to focus on immediate issues. "Okay. I'll update the job description. I'm sure no one's looked at it since Tom filled the role. After you've approved it, I'll post it on the relevant sites."

"That'll take too long. With the resort opening in three weeks, I need an immediate solution."

"I can try a head hunter."

"I was thinking an internal hire."

Mentally, Kalin ran through the list of managers at Stone Mountain, but before she came up with a recommendation, Reed spoke.

"You've done an excellent job managing HR. I've seen significant improvements in the department since I moved here. I'd like to combine human resources and security into one group and promote you to director."

Security patrolled the premises, answered alarms and investigated thefts. They were first responders to anything requiring the police or paramedics. Kalin thought of the team as a mini police force, which would make her a mini police chief. "I'm flattered, but I'm not sure I have the experience."

"I don't think that's true. You handled the situation last night perfectly. I've talked with the other directors, and they agree you're a good choice. Fred knows the day-to-day details and can help you with that."

Only if he doesn't resent me. "I'm really not convinced I'm the right person." Kalin wasn't sure she wanted the promotion. She'd moved to the British Columbian interior eleven months ago, and with her HR background she excelled at her current job. The HR office opened five days a week, meaning she didn't work nights or weekends. She had a solid team in place. It was a sweet setup. In contrast, security operated around the clock and would cause a significant lifestyle change, but maybe it was a choice of moving her career forward or having a personal life.

Reed interrupted her thoughts. "You broke protocol by calling ski patrol instead of security."

"I know."

"You made the right call. That's the type of quick thinking we need in a director. HR and security are both about dealing with people. Your leadership skills are more important than specific security knowledge."

Maybe. HR dealt with staff issues. Security dealt with guest issues. Both could be difficult, but security issues were more likely to end up in the media or in dealings with the Royal Canadian Mounted Police. The power and excitement of the position tempted her, but without relevant experience she might fail.

Reed continued to pressure her and explained her new compensation package.

"How much time do I have to decide?"

"I'd like to know right now."

Kalin had the fleeting thought she should discuss this with Ben, but it's not as if they were married or even engaged. This was her career and her decision. And it was a lot more money, so Ben would have to suck it up and go along with her. "If I accept, I have one request. I'd like to promote Monica to the HR manager."

"She's too young."

"She's twenty-two, but she's been in her role since she was nineteen. She knows the department and is good with people. Since most of our employees are in their early twenties, they relate well to another young person, and I think she's ready."

"With both of you still here, you have time to post and recruit for the job."

"I'm not sure about that. We aren't fully hired for the winter. We have a new staff housing building to bring on line, and if I have to focus on security, I'd like Monica to take over my role. We can hire a replacement for her much easier."

"Okay." Reed gave a curt nod. "You can promote her, but it's your responsibility to make sure she succeeds."

CHAPTER FOUR

November 26th

"Are you nervous?" Ben asked.

Kalin tugged her quilt around her bare shoulders and opened her eyes. "Yeah."

Two days had passed since Tom Bennett died. Reed said he'd speak with Fred Morgan first and then announce Kalin's promotion later in the day.

After Reed had given her a total of ten seconds to decide, she'd accepted the job. At thirty-one, she was the youngest executive on the director team, and that was too cool to resist. Ben hadn't been thrilled she'd taken the promotion without talking the decision over with him, but he'd come around to the idea after she'd convinced him the change wouldn't affect their lives much. She just hadn't defined *much*.

Ben stood beside their bed in their one-bedroom suite with a towel wrapped around his hips and dripped water on the carpet. His thick hair rested flat against his scalp, hiding his curls. "You'll be great."

If his half-naked body didn't distract her from being nervous, nothing would. And she liked to be distracted. "Have time for a longer shower?"

Ben's eyes crinkled, and he gave her his best I'm-the-hottest grin. "Rain check? It's twenty to eight. Can you walk Chica?"

At the mention of her name, their yellow Labrador thumped her tail and pressed her head further into Ben's pillow.

From where Kalin lay, she could see the hairline scar that etched Ben's lower jaw. Kalin had flexible hours, but Ben didn't, and his boss expected him at the mountain operations building by eight. "I'll take her to work with me."

"You'll be a star as a director, so don't be nervous." He lowered himself to the edge of the mattress and sucked her lower lip.

She wrapped her arms around his back and pulled him close.

"I gotta go, but save that thought," Ben said in a husky voice.

She buried her nose into his muscular neck and took a deep breath.

He pressed his lips onto hers, gifting her with a second kiss. "I really gotta go." He dropped his damp towel and sauntered across the bedroom.

She luxuriated in the sight of his butt, muscles hardened from a lifestyle of backcountry skiing and snowshoeing, while he ambled to his dresser and searched for thermal underwear.

He winked at her before he left the room, and she whipped down the quilt and flashed him. She listened to him laugh all the way to the end of the hallway.

Ben was thirty-one, a senior ski patroller and the deputy chief of the Stone Mountain volunteer fire department. He had a history of making the rounds with the women. Each season he'd charmed his way to a new girlfriend or two or three. A feminine sigh of disappointment had crossed the resort when Kalin moved in with him.

She'd heard the gossip that he'd only had one girlfriend for longer than a few months and that he wouldn't stick with Kalin. Well, he hadn't had her before, and she didn't care what other people said. She intended to keep his heart. She stuck her tongue out and blew through her lips in Chica's direction, and Chica wagged her tail.

After a quick shower, Kalin slipped into jeans and a scarlet V-neck sweater, topping the outfit with a cream jacket cropped at the waist. Her single accessory was a chunky leather belt. Ski attire on her first day as a director didn't seem appropriate.

She filled a thermos with coffee, shoved a strawberry yogurt into her jacket pocket, stepped into her winter boots and opened the door. She jumped back, startled. She hadn't expected to find a blonde Goddess on her doorstep. "Oh…"

"Does Ben Timlin still live here?"

Crap. This was not how she wanted her day to start. "He does. He's not home right now."

"You must be his new housemate."

Ten centimeters of fresh snow blanketed the driveway, and Chica left paw prints as she bounded across the drifts. Kalin kept her eyes on her but let her run. "Not exactly."

The Goddess gave Kalin a thorough examination and pouted. "Then who would you be?"

Instead of taking in the snow covered peaks visible from her ground floor suite, as was her custom before taking off for work each day, Kalin eyed the Goddess in return, taking in her tanned skin, her mascara covered eyelashes, and her full lips painted with expertly applied lipstick, and wanted to gag. "Kalin. And you?"

"Vicky Hamilton."

The women stood face-to-face, and sweet perfume wafted toward Kalin. She waited for the Goddess to make her move. Kalin knew who she was. The only woman Ben had spent more than a few months with, and her stomach curdled.

"Do you have his cell number?"

Kalin pasted on an insincere smile and shook her head. "He doesn't like me to give that out. Can I give him a message?"

"I'm sure he'll want to hear from me."

"Maybe. Give me your number, and I'll let him know you dropped by." She would never let this woman enter the home she shared with Ben, and she would never pass on her number. Ben was *her* firefighter, ski patroller, mountain man hero.

Beside the Alpine Tracks lift shack, Ben prepared a rescue sled, getting ready to ascend the mountain. The icy wind brought the scent of pine trees, a scent that reminded Ben of spring skiing, and the official winter season hadn't even begun yet.

Amber Cristelli's raised voice grabbed his attention, and he glanced in the direction of the loading station. He tried to stay away from the drama that occurred at the resort. Not his thing. But sometimes, he got caught up in it.

Amber stood in front of the four-person detachable chairlift that carried skiers to the top of the Alpine Tracks ski run, the run assigned to race training, and her job was to ensure each racer had a pass. "I said don't touch me."

Steve McKenzie, a twenty-year-old racer from the Holden team, poked Amber on her shoulder, pushing her backward. He towered over her, leaning forward, and his quads bulged against his red and yellow race suit.

Ben left the rescue sled, zipped his ski patrol jacket, made sure his name tag was visible, and clomped in his ski boots to Amber's side. His ski pants rustled as he walked. "Hey. What's going on?"

Both McKenzie and Amber turned toward him. Amber was the type of woman men wanted to rescue. Her hair fell in curls, bouncing around her pink earmuffs and onto her shoulders. Her rounded cheeks had the healthy glow of red apples. Ben had the urge to take care of her in the same way he'd take care of a lost puppy. Kalin called this his chivalrous side.

North American and European ski teams rented ski runs during the weeks before Stone Mountain opened to the public. The teams were training for World Cup and NorAm events. The racers brought with them coaches, fitness trainers, tuners, ski equipment and huge egos—and the huge egos were always a challenge for ski patrol.

Ben touched his radio and decided against calling for backup. His boss was thinking of moving to Calgary, and Ben wanted to be the next ski patrol manager. He could handle McKenzie on his own.

McKenzie jerked his head in Amber's direction but didn't touch her again. "She won't let me up the lift."

Amber gestured at McKenzie with her scanning gun. "He doesn't have his pass."

"Where's your pass?" Ben asked.

"In the tuning room with my jacket."

Ben ignored the sneer of superiority on McKenzie's face. Not intimidated by the height difference, Ben squared himself to McKenzie. "You'll have to get it."

"This is a joke. I need to make my training run." He pointed to his race suit. "Obviously, I'm a racer. She knows who I am. She's just being a bitch."

Ben kept his cool. "Don't talk to her like that."

"I know why you're doing this," McKenzie said to Amber.

Amber stuck out her tongue, showing off her tongue piercing, and crossed her eyes as Ben stifled a laugh.

Jeff Morley hovered behind them, wearing the same color race suit as McKenzie. "Let him up or move out of the way. I have to get up too."

"You have your pass?" Ben asked.

Jeff dangled his pass in front of Ben's nose.

"Scan Jeff and let him on," Ben said to Amber.

The scanner beeped, sounding like a *Star Wars* light-saber, when she ran the reader across Jeff's pass, and he winked at her. She stepped aside and let him slide by.

McKenzie skate-skied around Amber and sat on the chair with Jeff.

Without hesitating, Ben pushed the emergency stop-button. "Off the chair."

"Fuck you, asshole."

Ben grimaced but kept his tone calm. "I'm not restarting the chair until you get off."

The lift attendant came out of the shack with a radio in his hand. "I've called security."

"Don't make me miss my run. Just get off." Jeff pushed McKenzie, forcing him to stand. "Get your shit together."

Howard Jenkinson skied toward Ben, with his unzipped Holden team jacket flapping at his sides, and slammed to a stop inches from Ben's feet. "What the hell is going on?"

Jenkinson had been the coach of the Holden team for the last eight years. He'd succeeded in getting one skier on the Canadian Olympic team and was grooming Steve McKenzie for the same glory.

With McKenzie a couple of meters from the chair, Ben restarted the lift.

"This racer…" Ben turned toward McKenzie. "What's your name?"

Amber giggled when Ben didn't give McKenzie the satisfaction of letting him know he knew his name. McKenzie's ego was on fire, and Ben wasn't going to stoke the flames.

When McKenzie didn't answer, Ben said, "This racer poked Amber and swore at me."

"Is that true?" Jenkinson asked McKenzie.

McKenzie pushed his goggles onto his helmet, and an innocent expression morphed onto his bearded face. He shook his head.

"When she wouldn't let him on the lift, he poked her hard enough she almost fell over," Ben said.

"Why the hell didn't she let him up?" Jenkinson asked.

"He doesn't have a pass," Amber said.

"Let him up now. He needs to train."

Two security officers arrived and positioned themselves on either side of Jenkinson.

"What is this? You're not having security kick us out of here," Jenkinson said.

Ben straightened his back. "He needs a pass."

Jenkinson removed his toque, and the sun glinted off his hairless dome. A vein pulsed across his temple as if straining to fuel his anger. "We pay for the run. It's ours to use."

"You may have paid for it, but that doesn't give him the right to abuse our employees. Amber's job is to protect the racers by keeping everyone else off the hill."

"McKenzie's on the Holden team. Stop pretending you don't know who he is."

"That's worse. He should be setting a good example. How do we know you didn't ban him from training? If he doesn't have a pass, we have no way of knowing he's authorized, and he's not skiing until he apologizes to Amber."

"The conditions are perfect today. You have no right to make him miss his training time."

The snow making team had been operating the snow guns since mid-October, and the hiss generated as the snow blew over the runs created the first of the winter buzz. McKenzie would miss the best conditions and that would cause problems.

The two security officers edged forward, and Ben blocked the entrance to the lift.

Jenkinson glared at Ben for a moment as if memorizing his face. "You won't be working here long." He pushed with his poles and skate-skied to the edge of the maze and out of sight.

Gavin Reed slammed the phone into the cradle. His son, Ian, hadn't made the cut on the Holden ski team. His wife would be furious, and he understood why Ian had waited until this morning to break the news. Reed decided he would ask Coach Jenkinson for a favor. Ian's times were fast enough to make the Olympic team, so Reed suspected Ian hadn't made the team because he wasn't a local.

Reed had moved his family from Fernie, a competing ski resort two hundred kilometers south of Holden, to Stone Mountain the previous spring, and locals still treated him as if he was an outsider and not the president of the largest employer in the area. Power came with his position, power he intended to use. He called to his executive assistant and said, "Please get me the number for Coach Jenkinson."

Gertrude filled his doorway with her heavyset frame. "He's in the outer office. Would you like me to bring him in?"

He gave a tight nod. He removed his gym bag from the guest chair, making a space for Jenkinson. He rolled his high-back chair to the table and rested one hand on the cool leather.

Jenkinson strode into the office and stopped inches from Reed. "I guess you know what happened."

Reed stepped away from Jenkinson, whose ski jacket smelled sour as if sweat from the fall season festered in the material. "That depends on what you're talking about."

"I thought since you asked your secretary for my number, you wanted to talk with me about the incident at the lift. Ben Timlin didn't call you?"

Gertrude mumbled, "Executive assistant to the president, not secretary," and Reed knew Jenkinson would get no help from her in the future.

"About what?" Reed asked.

"The girl checking for passes wouldn't let Steve McKenzie up the lift."

Even though confident the ticket checker would have had a good reason, Reed had to hear out Jenkinson. Coaches always needed to be heard. "Why not?"

"He didn't have his pass. What kind of jackass move was that? Everyone here knows who he is. I want him to receive an apology from her, and I want him to be able to ski whether or not he has a pass on him."

McKenzie was a hero with the locals, but he was also competition for Reed's son. "I'll need to talk with the ticket checker and hear her side of the—"

"This is not about her. This is about our best skier being denied his training run. I don't care what the ticket checker says. You haven't been here long enough to know how important this is."

Ignoring the insult, Reed steeled his voice. "How many spots are left on the team?"

"What?"

Reed was pleased he'd surprised Jenkinson with the change of subject. "How many spots are left on the team?"

"None. What does that have to do with anything?"

"My son just called me. He said he didn't make the cut."

"And?"

"And...I'd like Ian on the team."

"That's not possible. I'd have to kick someone else off."

"He skis as fast as McKenzie."

"Your son pissed off my brother-in-law."

What trouble had Ian gotten into again? "I've no idea what you're talking about."

"My brother-in-law's the Fernie coach."

"I get it." Reed's expression turned cold. "I'll see if I can get some time with the ticket checker in the next day or two. I'll call you once I've done that."

"You can't be serious."

The two men eyed each other. Six-foot-four and lean, Reed hovered over Jenkinson's stocky build. Reed, a fond user of sunscreen, had only acquired one wrinkle in the shape of a lightning bolt beside his left eye on his otherwise smooth skin. Jenkinson had deep crevasses the sun couldn't reach when he squinted, leaving white lines slashing his skin across a dark tan. The warrior paint of a mountain man. Reed carried a smile he knew how to use. Jenkinson's frown preceded anything he had to say. But both men were used to a position of power and getting their own way.

Jenkinson caved first. "The best I can do is put Ian on the team as backup. He can train and travel with them. If someone gets injured or quits, he can take the open spot. If he's fast enough."

"I'll inform the ticket checker McKenzie gets up the lift with or without his pass."

"I want you to call whoever is in charge of security and tell him to keep his grunts away from McKenzie and me."

"What does security have to do with this?"

"They came to the lift and forced us to leave. They had no right."

"I'll talk with security."

"You better. Ian's spot on the team is not guaranteed. And I want Ben Timlin fired."

Without hesitating, Reed said, "I'm not going to fire Ben."

"If you want Ian on the team, you will."

"Ben's one of our best ski patrollers. I need him. It's not negotiable."

Jenkinson pressed his lips into a thin line. "Fine. We have a deal." He strode from the room.

Reed opened a window, letting the frigid air clear the stink out of the room, and said to Gertrude, "Please get Kalin Thompson in here."

CHAPTER FIVE

November 26th

"We've got a problem," Reed said to Kalin the moment she crossed through his doorway. "Come in and sit down."

Without speaking, Kalin entered and sat. Reed seemed agitated, and she waited for him to say what was on his mind. She pulled at the bottom of her cropped jacket and shifted in her seat.

"Coach Jenkinson has made a complaint about the security team."

Kalin wanted to look away from the intense stare of his husky-blue eyes, to look at the family photos that filled the corner of his desk or out the window at the spectacular view of the Purcell Mountains, but she forced herself to maintain eye contact. "Who's he?"

"The coach of the Holden ski team. You need to know the local players. In your new role, it's not acceptable for you to be unaware of who he is."

Harsh. Her first day as the director of security, and she was already being reprimanded for something as inconsequential as not knowing who a local was.

"Two of your officers were called to the lift today to deal with an altercation between Steve McKenzie and a ticket checker."

Kalin's stomach tightened. She performed well as the human resources manager, and she liked being good at her job. What made her think she could take on security? Mini police chief sounded cool. But really, what did she know about running security at a ski resort or the politics that came with the position? "Did security do something wrong?"

"They intimidated Jenkinson and McKenzie."

McKenzie dated Kalin's friend Nora Cummings. Small town connections drove her crazy. If she sided with security over McKenzie, she sided against Nora. "They must have had a reason."

"That doesn't matter. I want Jenkinson and McKenzie to be left alone."

"Regardless of what they do?"

Reed clenched and unclenched his jaw. "They're too important around here."

She would do as he asked even though the instruction seemed wrong. Until she got a handle on running security, she'd have to take direction from Reed. So much for getting on Fred's good side and having him support her promotion. She hadn't even met with him yet. "I'll notify Fred."

Kalin needed to speak to Fred about her promotion, but with the added complication of telling him about Reed's instructions for the security team, she'd rather avoid the meeting altogether.

As she walked along the administration building hallway, Kalin called Ben. "Can you talk?"

"Yup. I'm in the dispatch hut."

She stopped at her office, picked up Chica and walked toward the lower village, skirting the gondola. "I just met with Reed. You won't believe what happened."

"Is he pulling McKenzie from the hill?"

"How do you know about him?"

"I was at the lift this morning. I stopped the chair and made him get off." Ben explained what had happened.

"Reed never mentioned you were there."

"Shit. I wonder if that means I'm in trouble. Jenkinson threatened to have me fired."

"Reed's not going to fire you for doing your job."

"Man, I hope not. I don't get what Nora sees in McKenzie."

Chica strained against her leash, and Kalin yanked her back, encouraging her to heel. "Me neither. Reed's authorizing him to ski without a pass."

"You're kidding. What about Amber?"

Kalin clomped down the metal stairs that connected the upper and lower village, and snow dropped between the grids with each step. The cuffs of her jeans were frozen by the time she hit the path. "She'll have to accept it. It gets worse. He told me to instruct the security team not to interfere with the coach or McKenzie. Fred will hate that. We haven't even talked about me being his boss, and *this* is my first directive."

"He'll be cool. He knows Reed."

"I didn't even argue. I should have told Reed I couldn't agree." Requiring special treatment for anyone was the wrong message to give to the security team. Maybe once Reed had more time to think about the situation, she could talk him into changing his mind.

"I don't think you want to counter Reed on the first thing he asks you to do as a director. Just tell Fred what happened."

Fred's office was tucked between the general store and The Creek Side Restaurant, and the balcony gave the security team an unobstructed view of the street. "I'm outside his office now. I'll call you later."

"Hey, don't forget about my rain check."

Kalin smiled and disconnected the call. She'd rather look forward to a rendezvous with Ben than think about the Goddess being back at the resort.

The open layout of the security quarters contained Fred's office, the security team's meeting room and workspace. Kalin sat at the conference table. Her ankles were freezing, and she wanted to take off her boots and wet socks. Chica trotted along with her and settled at her feet.

Kalin imagined a similar meeting space could be found in any police station. Despite the meeting topic and her crappy exchange with Reed, she was excited about being the mini police chief. On the wall was a BOLO—Be On The Lookout—list that contained names of people at the resort who security wanted to monitor. Thieves, drug dealers, stalkers. The BOLO list was her responsibility now.

"Thanks for seeing me," she said.

Fred grabbed a dog treat from a desk drawer and joined Kalin at the table, sitting across from her, his back stiff. He placed the notebook he used to keep track of details squarely on the table. Kalin saw him sneak a treat to Chica, and she liked the kind streak that tempered his serious nature. His hair, cropped short in a military style, framed a square face that he often kept expressionless, and she had a hard time reading him.

"I'm sorry about Tom," Kalin said. "How's the team taking his death?"

"They're okay. They're a tight group."

"Reed approved closing security for the day of Tom's funeral."

"What about first-aid?"

"Ski patrol can handle anything that comes up in the village. If there's a big issue, the RCMP can assist."

"The team will like that," Fred said. "Thank you."

"Reed told me he spoke with you."

A fleeting smile crossed his face. "He did. Congratulations on your promotion."

"Thanks. I wasn't sure how you'd feel about me being your boss. Tom had a lot of experience."

"I'm fine with it."

Kalin needed Fred's support. He had the training, and every member of the security team respected him. Even though he hadn't asked, she felt the urge to explain. "With the season starting so soon, Reed wanted the role filled quickly. Your duties won't change. The only difference will be that you report to me instead of Tom."

Fred jerked his chin in a quick motion as if he was nodding but couldn't quite bring himself to fully agree with Kalin's explanation. "Okay."

"Is this going to be a problem?"

"Who's the new HR manager?"

Kalin let it slide that he'd ignored her question. She guessed he needed time to decide if her promotion would be a problem or not, and telling him about Reed's decision regarding the altercation at the lift was not going to help. "I've promoted Monica Bellman."

A squeak of air escaped from Chica, and Kalin hoped a gaseous emission wasn't about to permeate the room.

"Good choice. She deserves the job." Fred waved one hand in front of his face and pressed his palm over his nose. "You've got to be kidding me. That's rancid."

Kalin couldn't help but laugh. Her laugh was contagious, and Fred joined her.

Chica stared at Kalin with her brown eyes as if saying, "And what are you going to do about it?"

Kalin opened the nearest window. "It's like she knows what she's done."

Fred chuckled. "What do you feed her?"

"It must have been something Ben gave her. I'd never do that to her."

After the air cleared, and they stopped laughing, Kalin spent half an hour talking about logistics. For the first couple of months on the job, she wanted to be included in the weekly security meetings. She wanted a weekly debrief from Fred personally, without the rest of the team present. She asked him for each team member's latest performance reviews. She intended to know each security officer. Reed was not going to catch her off-guard again.

A puddle formed beneath her feet as the ice melted off her jeans and water trickled into her boots. "There's one more thing."

Fred waited.

"I spoke with Reed earlier today." Kalin described her meeting with Reed and the outcome.

Fred grunted. "Have you met Coach Jenkinson?"

Kalin shook her head.

"He's not the kind of guy who can be intimidated. Who was the skier?"

"Steve McKenzie."

"Something else is going on. There's no way, with those two together, anyone from security intimidated them."

"Reed asked us to give them special treatment. No matter what they do, they're not to be bothered by security."

"You agreed to that?"

"I did."

Fred stared at her with flat, grey eyes. "So the first thing you do as director of security is change a rule I've had in place for years. There is no special treatment for anyone." His voice was polite, but his expression told her he was suppressing anger.

"I didn't agree with him, but he gave me no choice."

"Does this have anything to do with Nora?"

"What do you mean?"

"You're friends with Nora. Nora dates McKenzie."

"I'm going to forget you said that." Back to the small town connections. Who her friends were was not a secret. But to say she'd let her friends influence her decisions at work, well, that was just wrong.

After driving down the mountain with Ben and dropping him at the grocery store, Kalin hustled into the drugstore in Holden and stopped abruptly when she spotted Nora Cummings. The nineteen-year-old stood in an aisle, staring at a home pregnancy test.

Kalin reversed direction and turned out of the aisle before Nora saw her. She picked up her birth control pills from the pharmacist and strode toward the cashier.

Nora turned into Kalin's aisle. "Oh…"

Kalin kept her eyes away from Nora's hands. Short, black hair that stuck out at odd angles topped Nora's five-foot-one, hundred-pound frame. As usual, Nora wore cargo pants tucked into work boots, and Kalin guessed she'd bought her parka at an army surplus store. Dressed in her puffy ski jacket, skinny jeans and leather boots with a heel, Kalin knew she looked elegant by comparison even though she felt like a giraffe towering over Nora.

Nora's sparky personality attracted Kalin. Despite their age difference, they were friends. The problem—Nora dated Steve McKenzie, and he didn't like to socialize with anyone other than skiers and coaches. "Ben and I are going to a movie tonight. Wanna come?"

"Thanks." Nora moved her hand behind her back, hiding the test. "But I've got too much going on. I'm tuning for the Holden team and preparing the rental shop for the season. My boss is letting me prep the shop at night."

"That's good news. Does that mean you're Steve's tuner again?"

"Yeah." Nora grinned. "We're both stoked. Hey, wasn't today your first day as a director? How was it?"

"Harder than I thought it'd be."

Nora grimaced. "Because of Steve at the lift?"

Kalin wondered what version of the story had circulated throughout the resort. "You heard."

"Sometimes Steve's..." Nora shrugged as if that explained everything.

"Don't worry about it. It'll work out." Kalin paid, placed her purchases in a cloth bag, gave Nora a quick wave and bolted.

She idled her truck in the drugstore parking lot and watched the exhaust glow in the reflection of the store lights. She turned the temperature to max and held her hands over the vents while she waited for Ben. She still hadn't mentioned Vicky Hamilton to him. Maybe the Goddess would disappear in a puff of smoke. She distracted herself from that thought by people watching.

Nora's cousin, Donny, rolled his wheelchair across the snow-filled parking lot and got into his van. Kalin was always impressed with the way he managed the winter conditions on his own. The door to the drugstore opened, and her boss's son, Ian, scooted across the parking lot. She hoped he hadn't seen Nora with the test. That juicy detail would spread quickly.

The passenger door opened and Ben hopped inside. He checked the clock on the dash. "We've still got time. Let's go."

Kalin drove forward out of the parking space and pushed the pregnancy test to the back of her mind.

CHAPTER SIX

November 27th

Ben arrived at the base of the Alpine Tracks ski run at eight twenty, ten minutes before the Holden team racers were due. He expected a clash if one racer didn't need a pass and the others did. Guest services had assigned two ticket checkers to scan passes, and he recognized Amber Cristelli but not the other.

Ben was pissed off Reed hadn't reprimanded McKenzie for pushing Amber. Instead, Reed had given Kalin a hard time about her security team. Why uphold the rules if the president didn't have the guts to hold firm? But Ben took his job seriously, and he'd take the flack whether the president backed him or not.

He straddled his snowmobile and spoke into his two-way radio, letting the patroller on the hill know he'd be up in twenty minutes. Before he drove to his assigned position along the course, he wanted to make sure McKenzie didn't hassle the ticket checkers.

"Hey, handsome."

Ben recognized Vicky's voice without looking in her direction. "Hey."

"That's all you've got for me?" Vicky slipped her hand inside the neckline of his jacket and turned him toward her. She pressed her lips onto his. "Mmmm."

Ben backed away. The feel of her lips hadn't changed, and his heart hammered against his ribs. "What are you doing here?"

Vicky played with the zipper of her cream ski jacket, raising and lowering the tab seductively. "I've moved back. I thought we could get together later."

Ben forced his eyes away from her naked fingers. "I have a girlfriend."

"I met her. She doesn't strike me as your type." Vicky laughed. "I can see by your expression she didn't tell you I stopped by yesterday morning."

"What did you say to her?"

"Nothing, so stop worrying. I just asked if she could tell you to call me. I guess she didn't pass on the message."

A maze of poles and ropes guided skiers to a single entry point at the chairlift, and Kalin strode past the far side in the direction of the Mountainside Café. Ben liked the way she walked with purpose. Her mixture of curves and muscle was sexy as hell. He loved the dimple that appeared on her left cheek when she smiled, and how her nose wiggled when she talked. He'd never met a person with one green eye and one brown eye before. Sometimes he couldn't believe she'd chosen him. She was definitely his type, and he desperately hoped she hadn't seen Vicky kiss him.

Vicky sucked her lower lip between her teeth, a gesture Ben remembered well, and hooked her finger underneath his jacket collar. "You never looked at me that way. Don't tell me you're actually in love."

Ben had thought he'd been in love with Vicky. She'd worked in ski patrol, been on the volunteer fire department, skied like a demon and was gorgeous. On the surface, they'd been a perfect match.

McKenzie clomped through the maze entry with his ski boots undone. He wore his racing suit and balanced his skis on one shoulder. He stopped a foot in front of Ben and sneered at him.

"Do you want something?" Ben asked.

"Nope. Just making sure you understand how to treat me." He grinned at Vicky. "Hi, babe. You're back."

Ben nudged Vicky away from him. He wanted to punch the smug smile off McKenzie's face and maybe break his crooked nose, but his job with ski patrol was too important to risk just for the satisfaction of hitting the jerk. "Good luck training today."

"That's more like it." McKenzie dropped his skis and snapped into the bindings. He shoved with his poles and sped around the ticket checkers without glancing in their direction.

Jeff Morley tried the same maneuver, but both checkers blocked his path. Amber held the scanner in front of him. "I need to see your ski pass."

"Why does McKenzie get on without one?"

"I gotta go," Ben said to Vicky and then strolled over to Jeff. "The president of the resort has decided McKenzie is not required to have his pass on him. The rest of the skiers are."

"That sucks. If he doesn't need one, I don't."

"Dude, I agree with you. Talk to the president if you want to complain. Otherwise, show your pass."

Jeff straightened his back and puffed his chest. He exhaled in one long breath and laughed. "Oh shit, who cares?" He held his pass in front of Amber.

While she scanned his pass, she asked Jeff, "Do you know what time Donny gets off work?"

"My brother? Why?"

Amber reddened. "I want to ask him about tuning."

Jeff placed his hand on her shoulder and squeezed. "Sure you do. He gets off at seven." He winked and skied toward the chair.

"You have the hots for Donny?" Ben asked Amber.

Amber didn't acknowledge him, and Ben followed her gaze to the edge of the maze. "What are you looking at?"

"McKenzie's girlfriend. I applied for a ski tech job in the rental shop, but Nora told the manager I didn't have enough experience."

Nora Cummings stood at the edge of the lift maze. *Holy shit.* Ben kissed his ex girlfriend.

She watched Steve talk with Ben and then get on the chair. Every one called him McKenzie, but not her. McKenzie sounded distant. Jeff Morley, her high school sweetheart, got on the lift behind her boyfriend. Awkward, but she couldn't do anything about that. But what should she do about Ben? Should she tell Kalin? She'd bumped into Kalin at the drug store when Kalin was on her way to a movie with Ben. They hadn't broken up. So what the hell?

She watched until Steve's chair disappeared from view and then scampered to the tuning room.

Nora found Charlie Whittle, the Holden team's head tuner, in the back corner. Donny Morley, her cousin by adoption, worked at the next table.

Charlie kept his eyes on the edge of the ski he filed but motioned with his head to a pair of skis leaning against the wall rack. "The skis behind the table need to be done."

"Those aren't Steve's."

"He's using his Rossignols this morning. I already tuned his skis from yesterday in case he needs them later."

Nora put on her white apron over her dark green sweater and wrapped the ties twice around her waist. She was the tiniest tuner in the room.

Ian Reed's tuning station was empty. Ian resembled Charlie with his red hair and freckles. Charlie looked more like Ian's dad than Gavin Reed did. If Charlie wasn't partially bald, the birthmark above his left temple would be hidden, and she bet that underneath his beard, he was probably good looking for a guy his age. "Where's Ian?"

"Ian resigned. He started training with the team this morning."

At least she wouldn't have to work side-by-side with the jerk anymore. "You're kidding. I thought he didn't make the cut."

"I guess Jenkinson decided they needed extra back up. You know what the conditions are supposed to be tomorrow?"

"A skating rink if it's true Reed approved another run injection." A special hose injected the Alpine Tracks run by squirting water beneath the surface, making the snow fast and hard, and Nora knew exactly how Steve liked his skis for the conditions. Too bad she was tuning someone else's skis.

"It is. He gave the go ahead during the coaches' meeting yesterday afternoon."

Nora and Charlie chimed together, "You need to train on ice to race on ice," and they both laughed. When Nora had busted her knee during a race at the age of fifteen on an injected run, her racing career had come to a smashing halt. She'd moped for the rest of the season, but her adoptive mom, Lisa, had talked her into tuning. Nora considered herself a talented tuner because she'd raced herself and understood what a skier wanted from a set of skis.

Nora grabbed the skis Charlie wanted tuned first. She was starting her second season as a ski and board tuner in the resort's rental shop. She loved her job but couldn't resist the chance to tune for the Holden race team. The ski teams, not the resort, hired the tuners, meaning she had two jobs for the next couple of weeks. Steve's spare time dropped to nil when he trained, and so she might as well work.

She placed a ski on the tuning bed. The repetitive motion of scraping wax off the ski bottom gave her time to think.

She'd met Steve when he'd been dating her best friend, but Rachel had been so much more than her best friend. She'd been her adoptive sister, Lisa's real daughter. Nora squashed that thought. Lisa had chosen to adopt Nora, and Nora was her real daughter too. Lisa had given Nora her first ski lesson, her first tuning lesson and her first driving lesson.

After Rachel died, Steve and Nora had spent time together, consoling one another. In a couple of months they would celebrate their first year of dating, and they were getting serious.

Steve was ambitious and sometimes that affected the way he treated people. She believed he hid a good person underneath his gruff exterior. He loved her. He'd said so. It was a trip hanging with him, and she could follow him to the Olympics as his tuner. She put her hand on her flat belly and wondered what a baby meant for their future.

"Hey, Aunt Lisa," Donny said.

Nora followed Donny's gaze and spotted Lisa leaning elegantly against the tuning room doorframe. Nora waved her over.

Lisa approached Nora's station and asked, "How's Jeff doing today?"

"I haven't heard yet. They're on the mountain now. What are you doing here?"

"I wanted to see what my favorite people were up to." Lisa reached forward as if to brush a strand of hair off Nora's forehead and stopped midway. "The gallery was quiet, and I missed you guys."

After losing Rachel, Lisa needed to see her just to make sure she was okay, and Nora always humored her. "You might be able to see Jeff ski if you head to the lift. He does like an audience."

Lisa touched Nora's cheek with the back of her fingers. "Good idea. I'll see you later."

"Come back afterwards. There's something I want to tell you."

Nora watched her leave and picked up the scraper. At the tuning station beside her, melted wax hit the floor, and the pungent odor made Nora nauseous.

"What's up?" Donny asked. "You're all pale."

"Nothing." Every time Nora worked with Donny tuning skis, he in his wheelchair and she standing, she knew she'd been lucky only her knee got busted. Donny hadn't been so lucky.

"Excuse me," she said to no one in particular and ran. She flung open a bathroom stall door and vomited. Morning sickness really sucked. How was she supposed to hide her pregnancy if she kept running for the toilet? She rinsed her mouth and returned to the tuning room.

Donny gave her a questioning look, and she shook her head.

"What's with you?" Charlie asked.

"Nothing. I must have the flu, or it's something I ate."

Charlie frowned.

"What?"

"I didn't expect this from you."

"Expect what?"

"Coming to work hung-over."

"I'm not. I didn't drink anything last night. Really, it's just the flu." Nora couldn't imagine not being part of the tuning team. Tuning was her life. If the morning sickness continued, she might have to tell Charlie she was pregnant.

CHAPTER SEVEN

November 27th

Ian Reed hunched over the dinner table, glancing between his mother and his dad. His dad might be the president of Stone Mountain, but his mother held the power at home. She had something to say, and as usual, she was going to wait until they finished eating dessert.

The table was set with matching tablecloth and napkins. The candles circling the centerpiece gave off enough light to eat by but also the sickly sweet scent of incense. Any passerby who witnessed the scene would assume the family was enjoying an intimate dinner. Appearances were everything, or so his mother always told him.

Susan Reed held out her hands to Ian and his dad. It drove Ian crazy his mother had turned religious and now they said grace before every meal. Ian watched her as she prayed. Her brown hair with blonde highlights hung straight until it curved underneath her chin. She wore a shade of lipstick that matched her rose blouse. She looked perfect— plastic perfect.

Ian wore a Holden ski team sweatshirt. His wet hair created a damp spot around the back of the collar. He didn't care. He'd bought the sweatshirt right after the coach invited him to train with the team. The aroma of bison steak brought his stomach alive, and Ian resisted the temptation to scarf his meal.

"Coach Jenkinson came to see me this morning." Ian wouldn't tell his mother he'd only been asked to train with the team. A spot had to open up for him to compete, for what team ever finished a season without an injury? He'd be an official member soon. He'd make sure of that. And then his mother would be proud.

His dad smiled and nodded his approval at him.

His mother finished chewing a mouthful of bison steak. She placed her knife and fork on the edge of her plate, careful not to leave stains on the tablecloth, and held Ian's gaze. "We'll talk after dinner."

Ian felt a blush creep across his cheeks. "I thought you'd—"

"I said we'll talk about this later. Finish eating."

Midway through dinner, a cat rubbed against Ian's calf. He glanced below the table, and a black and orange cat arched its back and purred. "Who's this?"

His mother's face softened. "Maxine. We're going to foster her until we find a good home."

His mother had a weakness for cats. She'd drive hours to deliver a cat to a new home. She put in more free time at the SPCA than any other volunteer did. At times, they'd had as many as four cats living with them. Ian believed her care for the cats was genuine and not something she did for appearances, so he helped her take care of them. He kinda liked the cats.

The three consumed the remaining food in silence. He wished his mother wasn't such a great baker. Then maybe they could skip dessert and get straight to the issue.

After she'd eaten the last morsel of homemade apple pie and taken her final sip of tea, his mother said, "I know your father spoke with Coach Jenkinson."

"What's she talking about?" Ian asked his dad.

"I asked Jenkinson to give you a spot. Your times are as fast as McKenzie's. He's not the only Olympic hopeful in this town. Even if the spot's only to train with the team and not race, you never know."

"Okay…" Ian understood why his mother was unhappy.

"You should've been able to do this on your own. Your father can't bail you out every time you get into trouble."

His mom referred to his disgrace at Fernie. Ian had been on the Fernie team and managed to get himself kicked off midseason, all because of the coach's daughter.

"You're nineteen. If you don't do this now, you'll never make the Olympic team. After your lack of points last year—"

"That's because I didn't finish the season, not because of how fast I skied."

"Don't interrupt me, and don't let me down this year. Steve

McKenzie is your main competition. I expect you to knock him out of the running."

"I'm only training with the team."

"You need every training run to be better than his. Did you ski instead of tuning skis today?"

His mother changing subjects was never a good sign. The less he said, the better. "Yes."

"That must have been inconvenient for your boss."

"Charlie was great. He said he was happy for me and that they'd be fine." Either she wanted him to be on the team or she didn't. How could he ski and tune at the same time? Just once, he'd like to please her, make her happy like one of those stupid cats did.

"I don't want you burning any more bridges. You've done enough of that already."

"I thought you wanted me on the team. It's not like I'd get another chance if I said I couldn't start right away. Charlie knows that."

"I hope so."

Around eleven o'clock, Ian heard his dad's footsteps pad along the hallway toward his bedroom door. His mother must be asleep. Otherwise, his dad wouldn't have come. The bedsprings squeaked when his dad sat beside him.

"You'll do great," Reed whispered.

"Why is she like that?" Ian had his suspicions and wondered if his dad would fess up.

"Your mom has high expectations of everyone, including herself."

Nope. Not going to fess up. "If she wasn't so hard on us, maybe Melanie wouldn't have run away."

"You don't know that. Don't blame her for your sister's problems. Your mom wants the best for you. Get in a few good runs, and she'll come around. She loves you. She isn't good at showing it, that's all."

Ian knew his mom loved him. He even understood why she'd changed. Sort of. He just wished she could get back to the way she used to be. He missed his smiling mom. Maybe if he made the Olympic team, she'd snap out of her unhappiness.

Jeff Morley arrived at his home in Holden and snuck into his garage. What filled his vision was not his downhill mountain bike hanging on the wall nor the bench covered with tuning equipment, but the van designed to be driven with a wheelchair secured where a driver's seat should have been. Their aunt bought the van for Donny since their parents didn't think Donny was worth the investment. The van consumed half of the garage and dripped melting snow onto the cement.

Aunt Lisa was his mom's sister and was the generous one in the family. She adopted Nora when Nora's mom died and brought her from Toronto to Holden. Jeff had fallen in love with Nora when he was fourteen years old. Man, he'd been serious for his age, and he'd pined for her until they were in the last year of high school and she finally agreed to go out with him. His biggest regret was what he'd done the night of his prom. That had started the path to Donny's car accident.

Jeff set his ski boots on the boot dryer and hung his poles on a hook. He stacked his helmet and goggles on the shelf beside the garage door. He ran a cloth along the full length of the bottom of each ski. He checked for any scratches, slid his fingers along the edges feeling for nicks, and once satisfied set them in the rack for Donny to tune later. He leaned his skis against the wall and grabbed a mop. Taking his time, making sure he didn't miss a spot, he cleaned the floor.

McKenzie had beaten him in the training session on the Super-G course by thirty one-hundredths of a second. No matter how hard he trained, he couldn't beat the guy.

The door to the house banged open and a stream of light made him squint. His father stood, a halo surrounding his head, and Jeff surprised himself by laughing at the image of his dad looking like an angel. An angel of all things. He touched a bruise on his thigh and inwardly cursed.

Jeff's white-blond hair matched his dad's. On the outside, Jeff was a younger version with a square jaw and a pug nose. He knew girls fell for his Nordic appearance. Too bad his mom hadn't searched deeper. On the inside, he guaranteed himself, he would never be anything like his dad.

"What the hell is taking you so long?"

"I—"

"Did you do what I asked?"

Yeah. Like I had the fastest time just because you asked. He stepped away from his dad and placed a ski between them.

"Are you threatening me with that?"

"No, I need to wipe the bottom. Coach said to keep them dry."

"You were fastest then."

Jeff shook his head and studied imaginary water spots on the floor.

"Coward. You can't even speak."

"I know I've disappointed you. I'll do better next time."

"Damn you. If you want to make the Olympic team, you need to be first."

Being an Olympic skier wasn't Jeff's dream. That dream belonged to his dad. His dad worked at the paper mill, and he'd been bragging for years about how his sons were going to make him rich. Donny might have.

A month previously, on his twenty-first birthday, Jeff decided this would be his last year competing. He wanted to go to university and make something of himself. He didn't plan on spending his life working in a factory, and it's not as if skiing would provide a good enough living if he wanted Nora back. He missed her. He wanted her to move away with him. Nora had been dating that McKenzie bastard for almost a year, and pretending he was okay with their relationship was killing him.

Before the accident, Jeff's brother had the talent. Donny was two years younger and had always been faster than Jeff. After the car accident, their dad had taken a wall's worth of newspaper clippings and burned them in the fireplace. His first words to Donny had been, "What the hell am I going to tell the guys at the plant?"

The townspeople of Holden had collected money and bought Donny an F1 custom-made sit-ski with Harley-Davidson shock components and a set of lightweight outriggers. They'd presented the gift to him, smiles all around, photos being taken. That night Jeff had heard Donny in his room, crying. He hadn't gone to him but wished he had. The sit-ski sat in the back of Donny's van, gleaming the way only brand new equipment can gleam as if waiting for Donny. Someday, maybe.

Jeff's dad took a step toward him, bringing him back into the present.

"Dad, please."

"Don't be a sissy. You need to take what's coming."

"I have another training run tomorrow. I'll do better." Jeff's eyes stung and he blinked, knowing he couldn't cry in front of his dad.

"You can't guarantee that."

Donny maneuvered his wheelchair into the doorway. "Dad?"

"Stay out of this."

"Mom just drove up."

Their dad respected their mom. It was his one good quality. As far as Jeff knew, he'd never hit her. His dad tried to make her happy, but she just couldn't be. When she was around, Donny and Jeff were safe. Otherwise...

His dad broke into his thoughts. "I'll be waiting for you tomorrow, and you can tell me personally how much you beat McKenzie by."

The second Nora entered Steve's rental unit, he yanked at the top button of her army-green sweater and pressed his groin into hers. She'd changed into the low cut sweater because a view of her cleavage, even though small, turned him on. Using his hips, he shoved her ass onto the side table that rested in the corner of the entryway. She wrapped her legs around his butt and let him kiss her.

Steve took what he wanted when he wanted, and she almost gave in. He smelled of athletic sweat, a manly smell, a smell that excited her. Ignoring the building heat of desire, she turned her head away from him. "Hang on a sec." Nora laughed at his eagerness. "You can undress me later."

He pulled her face toward his. "What's with you?"

She placed both palms on his chest. "Stop. I need to tell you something."

He slipped his tongue along the edge of her ear, and a shiver ran down her spine. "We can talk after."

"Please."

Steve sighed and made imaginary quotes with his fingers. "Okay. I can see you need to talk."

Steve wasn't much of a communicator. Action was his thing, but she had to tell him. She'd been daydreaming about their wedding day, and the picture hadn't included a ginormous belly. They needed to get married before she started to show.

She kicked off her army boots. Her cargo pants hung low on her still-flat belly, exposing a slice of skin. "I have some happy news."

"Did Charlie put you on permanent?"

"Figures your first thought would be about me tuning your skis."

"You're talented. I like the advantage you give me."

She couldn't help herself and was flattered. He didn't give praise often, so he must be in a good mood. The timing was right. "Can we sit?"

"Wow, this must be serious."

Nora followed Steve into his living room, buttoned her sweater and snuggled beside him on the couch. Her throat tightened, and all of a sudden, she couldn't speak.

"You're being weird. Since when can't you talk?"

"I thought I knew how I was going to tell you this, but…"

"Can you get to the point? We've got better things to do."

Nora swallowed hard, straightened her back and said the dreaded words, "I'm pregnant."

"Are you sure?"

"I think so. I took a home pregnancy test, and the result was positive. I haven't seen a doctor yet. I wanted to tell you first."

Steve pushed himself off the couch and paced in front of the coffee table. Workout equipment crammed the room, ski magazines with articles about him littered the table and photos of him crossing the finish line covered the walls. Everything in the room screamed pay attention to Steve McKenzie.

Nora followed him with her eyes. He wore a corduroy shirt over a white T-shirt, hanging outside loose jeans. Bruises from his ski boots covered the tops of his bare feet. His black hair, buzzed within a centimeter of his scalp, left pale skin shining through. His body indicated agitation. He just needed a little time. She'd been shocked at first too. She'd been thinking about the baby for days, and he'd only had moments.

He rubbed his thumb over the bend in his nose. "It's early though. Right?"

Nora's stomach cramped. He couldn't mean an abortion. She'd had the same thought but briefly. Once he realized the child was his, he wouldn't want her to get rid of the baby. "A few weeks, at the most."

"We were careful."

"I know."

He stopped pacing and his back went rigid. "It can't be mine."

He couldn't know. She'd made that mistake once. Just once. Her eyes brightened with tears. She'd dreamt about him proposing, telling her everything would be okay, that they'd be a family. How dumb could she be? "Of course it's yours."

"I doubt it. I made sure of it. Who else have you been with?"

"I love you. Why would you say something like that?"

Steve glared down at her in the same manner he used with people he thought were beneath him. "This is not what I want."

"It's not what I want either, but—"

"Then get rid of it."

"We can manage together."

Steve shook his head, and an eerie calmness settled on him.

Nora backed into the corner of the couch.

"Time for you to go. This has nothing to do with me."

"You don't mean that."

"I would never have a child with you."

"Please."

"I know who you slept with. He told me he only slept with you to get at me. As if that would affect my skiing."

Nora shook her head.

"Don't look so surprised. The baby's not mine. I don't want to see you again."

Nora bolted from the room without grabbing her jacket. The cold air slammed into her face and bare neck. She didn't care. She ran until she couldn't suck any more air into her lungs.

Nora pulled her cell from her backpack and called Lisa, her adoptive mom, her safe place. She tucked her fingers inside her sleeve and pressed the phone tight against her head, blocking the wind as best she could.

In a voice just above a whisper, Lisa said, "Hello."

Nora flopped onto a snow bank, and her rear end sunk in the snow. Darkness surrounded her. She was invisible. She didn't matter. If only she could melt like a snowman in spring and disappear. Without her winter coat, the cold air stung the bare skin exposed by her low cut sweater. The sweater she'd chosen for Steve. How could he kick her out? Didn't he care at all about her?

Lisa cleared her throat and spoke louder. "Hello?"

Tears froze on Nora's cheeks before they reached her chin, and she didn't bother to wipe them away. She sniffed and her nostrils stuck together, freezing into place. The cold air took away her sense of smell. At least Steve's scent lingered no more. "Lisa, it's me. Where are you?"

"I'm at the Morley's. My sister and I needed to talk." Lisa hesitated. "It's late. Are you okay?"

Nora could imagine Lisa and her sister hiding in the Morley's garage, trying to talk privately. Men were creeps. Her shivering began with a slight shake and then grew into a tremor that wouldn't stop. "Steve just broke up with me."

"Oh, baby, I'm sorry. Did you tell him?"

Nora fisted a ball of snow and threw it at the nearest tree. Smashing against a lodge-pole pine, the snow sprayed in all directions. The sound of Steve's head hitting the tree would be more satisfying than snow hitting bark. "I did, and he kicked me out like I've never meant anything to him." *Like I'm a piece of garbage.*

Lisa groaned and then asked, "Do you want me to come over?"

"No, I just want to go to bed and never wake up." Nora wished she hadn't said that to Lisa. The words must have terrified her.

"Don't say that. I'm on my way."

CHAPTER EIGHT

Day One: November 28th

Ian Reed left the administration building and heard boots crunching on snow before he saw McKenzie. The sun hadn't risen yet, and the only light came from a nearby streetlamp.

"What were you doing in the tuning room so early?" McKenzie asked.

What he was doing at the resort was none of McKenzie's business, so he lied. "Finishing some work for Charlie."

McKenzie shoved his hands into the pocket of his jeans. He wore his own ski jacket, not the team jacket, unzipped and flapping in the breeze. The jerk must be on his way to change into his race suit.

"I've got news for you. The bitch is yours," McKenzie said.

"What are you talking about?"

"I dumped Nora last night. You can have her."

Ian was offended and couldn't say why. It's not as if he'd treated Nora well either. "Nora's not a deck of cards you can trade around."

McKenzie stepped closer to Ian, breathing in his air space. "She's got a surprise for you, and you deserve it."

Ian turned back to the tuning room just to get away from McKenzie. He'd been excited about putting on his racing suit but didn't want to spend another second with McKenzie. He had plenty of time to change before the training session started.

"Don't you want to know what the surprise is?"

Ian opened the outer door. "Not really."

"Fine. I'm sure she'll tell you eventually. I talked to Coach yesterday."

Ian stopped mid-step. "So?"

"I told him if he wants me on the team, he has to kick you off. It doesn't matter that your dad's the president, Coach will side with me."

"I doubt it."

"When I tell him about you using Nora to get at me, that you've been trying to bring me down for months, he won't want you anywhere near me. I'm his dream. Enjoy your last day training."

Without saying a word, Ian stepped through the outer doorway and returned to the empty tuning room. No way would Jenkinson kick him off the team if his speed made McKenzie seem like a snail. Ian's career depended on the next training session, and he would deliver. McKenzie was finished.

The signal blasted, and the racer between the gates shot his legs backward, his head and shoulders forward and burst over the start line. He tucked his curved poles around his sides, bent his knees and rounded the first gate. His elbow whacked the second gate, but he kept his balance. He picked up speed, skirted the third gate, and the timing screen showed he clocked ninety-four kilometers per hour. His edges cut the ice and held firm.

Rounding the fourth gate, the racer pressed hard against his edges, but instead of power transferring to the snow, one boot released from its binding. The racer flew into the air with speed. He swung his arms forward, not fast enough to break his fall, and his head slammed into the ice packed surface.

The racer's limp body rag-dolled down the steep descent. He plowed over the fifth gate, flattening the pole to the ground. The orange safety netting, lining the side of the run, stopped him from sliding into the forest.

Dead. A Holden skier was dead. Kalin was sure of it. No breath escaped from his lips. His neck twisted at an odd angle. Kalin would never forget the image. She just didn't know whose image was frozen in her brain.

She returned to her office with Ben's words, "You better go tell Reed," echoing in her mind. After chasing Ben on her snowmobile and reaching the downed skier only seconds behind him, she'd known the Holden skier was seriously injured. She'd left the race course without thinking about what Reed would want to know. Not exactly director material behavior.

She'd found Reed in his office and told him a skier from the Holden team crashed after he rounded the fourth gate and Ben was treating him. Reed had been angry she hadn't waited at the scene long enough to find out who the skier was or if he was actually dead. All she'd told him was she thought he was dead. She didn't mention she'd almost hit a lift tower while driving her snowmobile to the summit.

She grabbed the back of her office chair and leaned on it for support. How could she not have asked who the skier was? Before she had a chance to sit behind her desk, her cell rang.

"Can you come meet me?" Ben asked in a voice that sounded rough, as if he had a cold.

"Where are you?"

"Mountain Side. Steve McKenzie's dead."

Nora was crazy about McKenzie, and Kalin's heart ached for her. The pregnancy test. A baby. Poor Nora. "I'm on my way."

In a rush to leave her office, she forgot her toque and mitts. By the time she reached the café, her ears were frozen. She pressed her palms over the sides of her head and was glad she didn't have pierced ears. Imagining metal in her lobes made her feel even colder. Mad at herself for thinking about her ears, instead of Nora who was about to be crushed, Kalin entered the Mountain Side Café.

She found Ben slouched over a table, clenching a Styrofoam cup with both hands. He pushed a coffee in her direction. The café, with its cedar chairs and tables, hardwood floors and mustard walls, exuded a welcoming atmosphere. The gloom on Ben's face did not match the decor.

He blinked several times. "There'll be an investigation."

"That's okay. You did everything right." The aroma of coffee tempted her, but she moved her cup out of the way and caressed his forearm. "Has anyone told Nora?"

Ben rubbed his hand over his eyes and breathed deeply. "I'm not sure."

"What happened after I left?"

Ben pulled his sweater over his head and piled it on the chair beside him. Sweat ringed the neck of his fire department T-shirt. He clenched his fists, and his biceps flexed against his sleeves. "I administered CPR until we got him down to the ambulance, but—"

"But nothing. You treated him well."

"He was at full speed. Everyone's talking about run injection and that the run was too icy."

"I need to call Reed and tell him the skier was McKenzie."

"He already knows."

"He needs to be told run injection is being blamed. Who else knows McKenzie's dead?" When he was with her, Ben wore his emotions on his face, but he controlled them in front of others. He was barely keeping a blank expression, and she knew what the effort cost him.

"William and I were in the clinic when the hospital called. He told Coach Jenkinson. I don't think the other racers know yet. I feel like a shit. I pretended I didn't know who McKenzie was. I tried to ban him from skiing." Ben's face paled, and Kalin could tell his mouth had gone dry.

"You couldn't have known. Should we tell Nora?"

"I can't say anything. I'll mention her to Jenkinson. He should probably tell her soon. I'm sure she knows something's going on."

"What happens now?"

Ben shrugged. "We wait until we're told how to handle this. I don't want to be responsible for a media leak. I'm sure Jenkinson wants to talk with McKenzie's family first and then the team."

"Can you leave after the patrol debrief meeting?"

"I think so."

Kalin held his hand. When Ben was low, he needed to move. Sitting still and drinking coffee was not going to help him. "Let's get Chica and go snowshoeing."

Nora burst into the café, wild eyed, with her jacket and winter boots undone and her tuning apron hanging below her knees. She ran to Kalin and Ben. In between breaths, she asked Ben, "Is Steve okay? No one will tell me anything."

Kalin stood and tenderly guided Nora by the elbow. "Sit with us."

Nora shifted her gaze between Kalin and Ben and squeezed Kalin's hand. "It's bad, isn't it?"

"He fell rounding the fourth gate," Ben said.

"I've heard that already. You were there, so just tell me."

Ben's softened voice was barely audible. "I don't know how to say this…Steve died."

"No way. Not Steve."

"The hospital called."

The café had gone quiet when Nora entered. Kalin took in the scene. Gazes were hastily averted, but the other patrons were all straining to hear. "Let's go somewhere we can talk privately."

"This can't be true." With her elbows on the table, Nora rested her face on her fingertips and tears ran down her cheeks. She sat, uncharacteristically still, and Kalin and Ben gave her a moment.

Kalin tugged at her to stand. "Come on. Let's go to my office."

Reed's office door slammed against the wall and Coach Jenkinson barged in, kicking the door when it bounced back in his direction.

"I'm on the phone. You'll have to wait."

"I'm not waiting." Jenkinson grabbed the phone from Reed's hand and hit the end button. He tossed the phone on the table. "I need to speak with you. Now!"

Gertrude hovered in the doorway. "Should I call security?"

"Get out and leave us alone," Jenkinson commanded.

"Apologize to her."

Jenkinson's nostrils flared, and he took several deep breaths, getting himself under control. "I'm sorry for the outburst."

"We're fine, Gertrude. You can close the door," Reed said.

She fussed with the pockets on her oversized sweater and hovered.

"It's okay."

"I'll be right outside."

Jenkinson was under stress and was aggressive by nature, so Reed held his body pumped, ready for action but controlled. "I'm sorry about Steve McKenzie."

Jenkinson pointed a stubby finger and held it inches from Reed's face. "This is your fault."

Uncomfortable wet spots developed in the armpits of Reed's dress shirt, but he did not step away. "What's my fault?"

"Don't play innocent. McKenzie's accident." Spit stuck in the cracks, where Jenkinson's lips joined, and he darted his tongue into both crevices.

"How can it be my fault?"

"The team is going to sue the resort. Your run techs made the surface too icy."

If Jenkinson hadn't looked distraught, and very capable of violence, Reed would have laughed. "That's the first time you've complained about fast conditions. How many times have you complained the conditions were too slow?" Reed waited while Jenkinson clenched his fists, then opened them.

Jenkinson didn't answer.

"I can think of quite a few. You specifically asked for the run to be injected." Reed had discussed the early season conditions with the run techs. Warm temperatures, or rain during the fall season, could cause run closures. To ensure the run stayed open, during the training weeks, the snow required injection. Every minute the run remained closed the resort lost money.

The coaches had pressured him to inject the run to allow the racers to train on conditions similar to what they would compete on. Injection had been good for the resort, and for the teams, and meant the racers achieved high speeds on the icy conditions.

"McKenzie wasn't wearing his pass," Jenkinson said.

"What does that have to do with anything?"

"The pass carries the resort's release of liability statement. That won't look good in court."

"Why are you trying to blame someone for the accident?"

"Someone has to pay for what happened to him." Jenkinson wiped his mouth on the back of his hand. "Don't think this guarantees Ian a spot on the team."

"We had a deal. Ian's times are as fast as McKenzie's, and now there is a spot. I expect you to honor the deal and put Ian on the team." Reed's first thought, which he wasn't proud of when he'd heard McKenzie died, was Susan would be happy.

"Do you know how many skiers crashed during our training session?" Jenkinson asked.

"No, but I think you do. You could've stopped the training at any time. I believe McKenzie skied late in the session. It was your call to pull him if you thought the conditions were dangerous."

"What? You think this is my fault?"

"I think Super-G is a dangerous sport and people get hurt. I don't think it's anyone's fault."

Jeff Morley opened the garage door, not caring if the motorized hum notified his dad he was home, and hit the light switch. He could see from the emptiness on the left side that Donny was out. The grey cement sparkled as if it were brand new. A spotless garage floor was an unreasonable expectation from an unreasonable man. His dad used it as a way to get at Donny, as if Donny paralyzed himself on purpose.

Jeff would never forget how he'd almost ignored his cell on the night of the accident, but something made him answer. He'd been drunk, screwing some girl at a party. He left her sprawled on a bed and bolted for the hospital.

He found his mom in the emergency waiting room with her knees pulled to her chest, slowly rocking. She must have been on duty because she wore her nurse's uniform. His mom was tall and thin, just like Aunt

Lisa, but the way she sat curled into herself made her look small, vulnerable even.

"Mom? Is he okay?"

His mom sat but remained hunched. "I don't know."

"What happened?"

"The car hit a tree. Rachel's hurt too."

Rachel Hudson was his cousin, and he thought of his aunt. "Did you call Aunt Lisa?"

"I can't."

Jeff ran his hand over his mom's back, trying to soothe her. He should have been the one driving Donny home, but he'd been too focused on some girl he didn't know, too worried about his own problems with Nora, to bother with his brother. He looked over her shoulder at a blank wall, avoiding eye contact with his mom. "I'll do it. We need to call Nora too."

His father hadn't shown his face at the hospital, and Jeff wished he'd stayed away for good.

Three years had gone by since that horrible night. If Nora hadn't dumped him after the prom, he wouldn't have been fucking that girl, and Donny wouldn't have been in the car with that asshole. And now the asshole was dead. Very satisfying.

Jeff paced the garage. His boots squeaked on the floor. He wanted to move out, but the problem was Donny. He couldn't leave him there to deal with their dad on his own. Next year he'd figure out a way for Donny to come with him, assuming the university accepted him.

Aunt Lisa had helped him with the application process, but he'd hidden his dream from his parents and Donny. He planned to wait until he was accepted to tell Donny. He didn't want to get Donny's hopes up, but he was too excited. He might tell him soon.

Once touring started, they'd both be out of Holden for a while. All Jeff had to do was keep in the top three on the team, and the coach would let him race. He had a better chance now with McKenzie dead. Too bad Jenkinson had let Ian Reed on the team. Jeff guessed having a dad who was the president of the resort helped.

Jeff stopped pacing at the back of the garage and placed his skis in the rack. He'd had the fastest time today. That should keep his dad from exploding like an avalanche.

The side door to the garage opened. "Well?"

"I was fastest." Jeff placed his boots on the boot dryer and hung his poles on a hook. He was about to toss his helmet and goggles on the shelf except his dad stepped in front of him.

His dad picked up a wrench from the counter and tapped it against his thigh. "You think you're such hot shit. You couldn't beat McKenzie. He had to crash for you to get the fastest time."

"You said I had to be fastest, and I was. It's not my fault he fell." Jeff kept an eye on the wrench, not really believing his father would hit him with the metal tool. He fisted the strap of his helmet, resisting the urge to swing his arm. One strong bang on the head, and his dad's life would be over. Of the many versions of this daydream, the sound of the helmet smashing against his father's head was the most satisfying. The thought of his mother stopped him. She depended on their dad, and Jeff didn't think she could survive without him. "I finished the run when most of the team didn't. That counts."

"Where's your brother? He should be home by now."

Not long after Donny's accident, their father started to refer to Donny as "your brother." Jeff hadn't heard his dad say Donny's name since he'd lost the ability to walk.

"With so many crashes, he's probably tuning tonight."

"I phoned your so-called coach. He was too busy to talk to me."

"That's not my fault."

"What was your time?"

"One minute thirty-three forty-three."

"That's still not good enough." His father stepped forward. Jeff stepped backward, keeping an arm's length from his dad.

"You coward. Don't move away from me."

Jeff kept his eyes on the wrench, ready to protect himself. "You don't know, do you?"

"Know what?"

"McKenzie's dead."

Jeff's dad smiled and hung the wrench back on the hooks on the cork board.

CHAPTER NINE

Steve McKenzie had been dead for only one day, and already reporters laid siege at the bottom of the Alpine Tracks run. Kalin recognized two local reporters. The third reporter wore a *Calgary Herald* jacket. All three shouted questions at the ticket checkers.

Security officers arrived and herded the reporters back, forcing them out of the maze.

Kalin spotted Ben and joined him beside his snowmobile. His eyes strayed below her neckline, and he grinned. Ben must have been injected with extra testosterone when he was born. She shoved his shoulder. "Get a grip. I'm wearing a ski jacket."

"Yeah, but I know what's underneath. Can you get off early today? Maybe I can remove that jacket before I go to fire practice."

"Nope, but I'll be happy to remove your fireman's uniform when you get home." To say his turnout gear was a turn-on was a gross understatement, and she'd have no problem taking it off him later.

Ben winked. "Promise?"

She turned and stood shoulder to shoulder with him, not quite touching but enjoying the sensation of his presence. The lift hummed as it carried racers from the German team to the top of the run. Kalin recognized Edwin Bucher, their top skier, from his photos in ski magazines and wished she had time to watch him ski. Finished with their training session, some of the Holden team skiers milled around the bottom, waiting for their coach. Snippets of conversations about speed reached Kalin, but the skiers seemed subdued.

"Do you think we should do something about the reporters?" Ben asked.

"No. My security guys can handle the three of them."

"I need to tell you something."

With the last of the Holden skiers through the gates, Coach Jenkinson skied to the bottom, making tight, precise turns. After he skidded to a stop, spraying loose snow, one of the local reporters approached him, and for a change, Jenkinson wore a welcoming smile.

"Hang on. I want to hear them." Kalin stepped closer to Jenkinson.

"What caused the accident?" a reporter asked.

"You heard how many skiers fell. The run techs over injected the snow, making the run an ice rink."

"Why didn't you cancel the training?"

Jenkinson's eyes froze along with his smile. "The resort didn't get the injection right. They're at fault."

"Who's going to replace McKenzie?"

Ian Reed stood close behind Jenkinson. He gripped the top of his ski poles and leaned forward on his skis, looking intent on hearing the answer.

Again, with a frozen smile, Jenkinson said, "He's been dead twenty-four hours. Ask me in a week."

Kalin watched security move closer to the reporters and imagined the story to come. There would be a description of run technology and then a hint Stone Mountain was at fault. She'd better brief Reed after she met with Fred. "I gotta run. Fred wants me to watch the video of the crash. Can we talk later?"

Ben rested his hand on her shoulder for a second as if he wanted to say something and then changed his mind. "See you tonight."

Leaving her security officers to handle the situation, Kalin pulled her jacket tight and strode to Fred's office. Her throat ached with the beginnings of a cold, and her jeans felt brittle against her thighs. She didn't know why she sometimes forgot to wear thermal underwear. Too preoccupied she guessed. And who wouldn't be? She was about to watch a video of a man dying.

Kalin entered the security office and found Fred Morgan and William DeWell sitting at the conference table. "Is that the video?"

As ski patrol manager, William was Ben's boss. He wore his ski patrol jacket and ski pants. He'd tossed his toque and mitts on an empty chair, and his mud-colored hair looked as if he'd run his hand through the curls many times. He paused the video on the computer screen. "We got confirmation he broke his neck."

Kalin avoided staring at the spot where William's earlobe should be—the lobe he'd lost to frostbite. "That's really sad."

Fred swiveled in his chair and faced her. "I think it might have been more than sad."

"What are you talking about?"

"Here, watch this." Fred played the video for Kalin. The footage showed McKenzie skiing the Super-G course. He skied around a gate and launched out of his skis onto his head. "Do you see what I mean?"

Kalin had never seen a video of someone dying before. She felt oddly detached as if what she watched wasn't real, except she knew it was. "Not really."

"I see that his boot released from his ski for no reason. He didn't catch an edge. He didn't hit another gate. It's like he stepped out of his binding." Fred raised his thick eyebrows at her and waited as if expecting her to understand.

"Show me again." Kalin watched the accident a second time. This time the crash wasn't as shocking, and she could focus. "Could his binding have come loose when he hit the earlier gate?"

"I doubt it." William shook his head. "It would have released then."

"You think it was a gear malfunction?"

"Maybe…"

"Maybe what?" Kalin asked.

"Reed's concerned about the resort being sued," William said. "He asked me to review the video to see if it showed anything that proves the resort wasn't at fault. After watching the video several times, I thought Fred should see it before I talked to Reed."

"You guys aren't being clear."

William reversed the video to just before McKenzie fell. "Watch his right foot."

Kalin did as instructed.

McKenzie skied around the gate, and the heel of his ski boot lifted effortlessly out of the binding.

"You saw his boot release?" William asked.

"I did."

"I think his DIN setting was too low." DIN were the initials for the German standards institute, and the amount of force required for a boot to release from a binding depended on the DIN setting.

Kalin turned to Fred, who said, "I asked one of the guys to get his skis from the patrol room."

Kalin stood. "There are reporters nosing around, and Jenkinson's blaming the resort for McKenzie's death. Let's keep this quiet for now.

Make sure the skis are secured, and then we'll update Reed."

Fred shook his head. "I'll take care of the skis. You're the director. It's your job to deal with Reed."

Kalin was sure William noticed the tension between her and Fred. Trying to distract him, she asked, "You want to come?"

On their way to Reed's office, Kalin phoned Gertrude and asked if they could meet with Reed in fifteen minutes.

"What do you think we should tell Reed?" William asked.

"Exactly what you told me but maybe a little more direct." There were times when Reed smiled a lot, and she suspected he had a side to him that didn't show in the office, but this wouldn't be one of those times.

They entered Reed's outer office, and Gertrude motioned for them to go straight in.

Once seated, William glanced at Kalin, and she interpreted that to mean he wanted her to fill Reed in on what they'd found.

"This must be serious if neither of you want to say anything," Reed said.

"William, Fred and I have reviewed the video of Steve McKenzie's fall. There's definitely something odd about it." Kalin looked to William. "Maybe you could explain."

William straightened and after a moment said, "The video shows McKenzie's boot disengaging from his binding. There's nothing unusual about that. What is unusual is he appears to have stepped out of his binding without resistance. He didn't catch an edge or hit anything." William stopped talking and let the information sink in.

"You have a theory?" Reed asked.

"I think his DIN setting was too low."

"That doesn't make sense. He'd know what his DIN setting should be. Don't the racers check that before skiing?"

William shifted in his seat. "You'd think, but if he had a regular tuner, he might not worry about it."

"Are you saying his tuner made a mistake?"

"It's possible."

"Where are his skis now? I want them examined."

Kalin took over from William. "Security is picking them up from mountain ops and taking them to the security office. Fred will keep them locked until we decide what the next step is."

"Tell him to give the skis to the RCMP. If a tuner caused this, we want to be sure. I don't want to hamper an investigation into the tuning team. The resort is not at fault." Almost as an afterthought, Reed asked,

"Who is his tuner?"

You mean who was his tuner. It wasn't easy when someone just stopped being. Nora must be devastated, and if Kalin could shield her from being investigated, she would, but Reed could find out easily enough, so she might as well give up her name.

"Kalin, who tunes his skis?"

"His girlfriend, Nora Cummings."

RCMP Constable Miller found Ben in the employee change room. "Can I speak with you in private?"

Ben glanced at the curtain bisecting the room shared by ski patrol, ski school and lift attendants. The other side was allocated to female employees. He didn't know if anyone occupied the area and half expected Vicky to jump out unannounced and kiss him again. He pulled his sweater on and led Miller to an adjacent room used for storing uniforms.

"This will have to do. I don't have an office." Ben and Miller knew each other because of the interaction between the fire department and the RCMP. Miller was a good cop. At thirty-four, Miller had kept himself in shape, and the only sign of his age was the hint of grey at his temples.

Miller's Kevlar vest added bulk to his broad chest. He stood erect, three inches taller than Ben, with his RCMP cap tucked under his arm and a notebook in his hand, and chuckled. "It's fine if you can ignore the smell. I need to ask you about the skiing accident."

"Sure." Ben was glad Kalin had called him about her meeting with Fred earlier in the day. The RCMP must be taking the DIN theory seriously. Having a girlfriend in the know was handy even if she did tend to get herself into trouble.

"Is this the first death you've dealt with while on duty?"

"No. Why?"

"You seem composed. That's all. You were first on scene with Steve McKenzie?"

"I was. Is something going on that I should know about?" Ben examined his actions from the moment McKenzie fell until he handed him over to the paramedics. He hadn't made a mistake. He was sure of it.

"Did you see him fall?"

"I did. I was on my snowmobile at the top of the run watching the racers train. It's part of the contract for renting the run, ski patrol being on the hill during training, I mean."

"Can you describe what you saw?"

"Sure. He was fast. He slapped the second gate with his arm, cleared the next and fell rounding the fourth gate. He hit the ground head first and rolled into the safety netting. His body was limp when he rolled, and I assumed he was unconscious. When I reached him, his vital signs were absent."

Miller wrote in his notebook and then asked, "You treated him?"

"William, my boss, arrived. We followed protocol. Stabilized his neck, initiated CPR, and got him down the hill. The paramedics waited at the base of the run and took over once we reached them. Did someone complain about how I handled the scene?"

"Is it usual for William to actively patrol?"

"Not really. We're short staffed. We won't have our full team here until the season starts. The other patroller on duty was treating a sprained ankle. Our contract with the team requires us to have two patrollers on the hill during each training session."

"Was McKenzie the only skier to fall?"

"No. I was surprised Coach Jenkinson didn't postpone the training. I'd say over half the team didn't finish. The guy with the sprained ankle fell a couple of runs before McKenzie."

"Did you touch McKenzie's equipment?"

"Just to get his ski off him."

"Did you alter any of the settings on either ski?"

Ben had put the heel of his hand on the back of the binding still attached and pressed hard to release the boot, but he hadn't looked at the DIN setting. "No."

"Did anything seem unusual about the fall?"

Ben thought a moment. "Not really, but I was at the top of the run, four gates away."

"Did you see anyone touch the ski that came off?"

"I was focused on McKenzie. I'm not sure who brought it to the ski patrol clinic."

"Alright. If you think of anything else, give me a call."

Miller's standard-issue black boots echoed on the cement floor and before he reached the outer door, Ben called out, "There were people taking pictures."

Ben arrived at the fire station half an hour before fire practice was scheduled to begin. The hall was empty, and the quietness of the place gave him time to think. He walked through the lounge. The four Ikea couches were vacant, but after fire practice they'd be full of firefighters watching the forty-two inch flat screen TV and doing their best to empty the beer fridge.

Ben entered the adjoining kitchen, turned on the coffee machine and headed for the locker room to change into his turnout gear. He opened his locker, and the door blocked his view to the shower room. He stripped off his shirt and hung it on the silver hook.

"I see you still come to practice early," Vicky said.

He stood still, hiding behind the locker door. *What the hell?*

"Are you going to come out from behind there? I won't bite."

Ben lowered his chin to his chest and sighed. He eased the door shut and turned to face Vicky. "What are you doing?"

Vicky stood before him wearing half of her turnout gear. "I asked the chief if I could rejoin the fire department. He said yes."

"That's not what I meant." Ben threw a towel at her. "Cover yourself."

The towel dropped to the tile floor in front of Vicky's feet. She tucked her thumbs underneath the suspenders and snapped them against her bare skin. "You used to like the way I looked in my turnouts."

"I told you I'm seeing someone."

"That never stopped you before. What's a little romp with me? Before anyone gets here. No one will know."

Ben was at a loss for words. He had to get rid of her, and do it fast. Vicky bit her bottom lip and tilted her head. Her blonde hair draped across her shoulder, and a familiar line of freckles dotted her collarbone.

"I won't tell your girlfriend. There's a big comfy couch in the lounge."

Ben's feet felt as if they'd been crazy glued to the floor. He couldn't seem to move away from her. "As I remember it, the last thing you said to me was, 'Don't come near me again.'"

Vicky seductively worked her way a few steps closer to Ben. "That's history. I made a mistake. But that doesn't mean we can't rectify the situation. Come on. Remember how much fun we used to have?"

"I remember you broke my heart."

"Since when do you have a heart when it comes to women? Don't pull that on me."

The outer door to the fire station creaked open.

"Anyone here?" Fred asked.

"You need to go," Ben said to Vicky.

Instead of taking the hallway back to the women's locker room, Vicky left by the door to the lounge.

"It's my lucky day," Fred said.

"Not yours, stud. Someone else's," Vicky said.

Fred poked his head into the locker room. "Hey."

Ben raised his hands, palms facing Fred. "Nothing happened."

"Not my business."

"Fuck. She surprised me." Why couldn't it have been someone other than one of Kalin's employees? He had to tell her about Vicky soon, but he just didn't know how.

CHAPTER TEN

Nine p.m., and Ben still wasn't home from fire practice. Kalin paced the living room, picking at a tissue as if it had committed some offense and needed to be destroyed. Earlier he'd wanted to talk to her. What if he wanted to get back with Vicky? What if he was with her now?

"Grrr," she said to Chica, and Chica wagged her tail. Kalin's cell rang, distracting her from her dreadful thoughts. Constable Miller asked her to meet him in her office. She slipped into jeans and a sweater, and without using a brush, pulled her hair into a ponytail. She scribbled a note for Ben and grabbed her Jeep keys. Chica followed her, but Kalin shut the door to the garage before the dog pushed through.

Kalin met Miller outside the administration building, unlocked the door and motioned for him to follow. "This must be important if you couldn't wait until tomorrow."

She flipped the switch to the main hall light, illuminating enough of the floor to expose her office door. A red exit sign glowed at the far end of the hallway.

"Thanks for coming in so late. I've just finished interviewing and need to ask you a few questions. I could've waited, but I want to talk with you about one of the resort staff and don't want the rest of the employees to have any insight into the investigation. Gossip seems to travel fast."

Kalin laughed. She'd never heard Miller put together a string of words that long. He seemed almost nervous. "That's a bit of an understatement." She led Miller into her new office. "You've had a long day."

"I have. You changed offices?"

Her office was a third of the size of Reed's, but the carpet wasn't worn through to the floor like in her old office, and the chair was new. There was even room for two guest chairs and a small side table. "I've been promoted. I'm the director of HR and Security now."

"Congratulations. You should meet the rest of our team. Security often interacts with us."

"I'd like that." Kalin wondered if the other constables were all as good looking as Miller. Maybe the ability to charm female suspects was an RCMP prerequisite.

"Can you pull Nora Cummings' file?"

"I can, but I'm not sure I should. I have to follow the privacy laws when it comes to employee information. Why do you want to see her paperwork?"

"You know she was Steve McKenzie's girlfriend?"

"I do."

He removed his RCMP cap and tucked it underneath his arm. "I can go through official channels, but that takes time. I'd like to eliminate suspects quickly. If Nora had nothing to do with McKenzie's death, then I won't use any information from the file. If it turns out she did, I'll ask for the file officially."

"Are you saying she set his bindings incorrectly?"

"I'm not saying anything. I'll do a background check on anyone close to McKenzie. It's standard procedure."

"What does it mean if she accidentally set the DIN wrong?"

"She could be charged with manslaughter."

Kalin's stomach tightened. She asked Miller to wait while she retrieved Nora's file from the HR file cabinet. Nora might have made a horrible mistake and set McKenzie's bindings to the wrong number. She was Kalin's friend but also an employee, and right now Kalin felt the less she knew the better, so she wasn't going to ask Miller for any more information on Nora. She didn't want to have to lie to her.

"Do you know Nora well?"

"We became friends over the summer. Ben employs her as a fly fishing guide."

"Then you were friends with McKenzie too?"

"I didn't know him at all. He hung with racers."

"Were McKenzie and Nora close?"

"I think so, but I only know what she told me about him."

"What was that?"

Kalin thought a moment before responding. "She liked tuning his skis and was excited about race training. She didn't like that he was snobby about who he hung out with. She wanted him to hang with her friends too. I got the impression she believed they had a future together. I don't know what else to say."

"Did you ever see them fight?"

"No, but I didn't see them together. Nora never said they fought."

"Anything odd about her?"

Revealing Nora bought a pregnancy test was too much of a betrayal. "Not really," Kalin said.

Miller looked at the file Kalin hugged to her chest. "How about if I just read the file? I won't take it with me. Will that make this easier for you?"

She'd known Miller for almost a year, and she trusted him. Although unethical for her to show him Nora's file, she wanted to help with the investigation. Besides the file put Nora in a positive light. The security team needed the RCMP's cooperation, and she didn't want to do anything to mess up the relationship Fred had developed with them over the years. She passed Miller the file and watched his face as he read. He removed a pen from his front pocket and wrote in his notebook.

"What are you writing?"

"Her social insurance number and birthdate."

"This is lame." The bar was quiet, no one was dancing and Ian Reed was sick of drinking beer. "I need a joint."

He tugged on Monica's arm, pulling her toward the door. Monica grabbed her ski jacket and put it on over her cropped sweater. Ian snuck a glance at her belly button piercing before she zipped up.

The rest of the gang followed, and they milled outside the bar without a plan. The full moon illuminated the lift station. "Let's climb to the top of the bull wheel," someone suggested.

"We can't do that," Monica said.

One of the women shoulder bumped Monica. "You're not going to turn boring just because you're the HR manager now, are you?"

"No, but we really shouldn't go up there."

"It's not that high. Come on. It's not like the lift is operating or anything." Ian climbed the fixed ladder that led to the top of the Alpine Tracks lift station. His boots knocked snow off the rungs, clearing the way for the others.

The group of eight sat cross-legged, taking up most of the steel surface. Someone lit a joint and passed it around the circle. The fog of their breath, mixed with the smoke, created an eerie atmosphere.

Dizzy from the mix of beer and marijuana, Ian leaned back onto his elbows. A round of giggles hit the circle, and he wasn't sure what everyone was laughing at, but he laughed too.

"I like your smile," Monica said. "Don't look so shocked. I'm not hitting on you. You racers have such big egos."

Ian rolled his eyes.

"So I guess you get an official place on the team," Monica whispered to Ian.

"You never know with Jenkinson. I think he hates me."

"Why would he?"

"I did something stupid, and his brother-in-law has it in for me."

"What did you do?"

Ian glanced at the others sitting nearby. "Nothing I want to talk about."

"Come on, I'll share if you do. They're all too stoned to hear us."

The cold from the steel surface seeped through Ian's jeans and he shifted, moving closer to Monica. "What've you ever done that's stupid?"

"You heard about the Bingo game last year?"

Ian chuckled. He'd heard. He knew only women competed but men took advantage of the rules, and wished he'd been at the resort to take part. A guy he'd talked to had gotten a lot of mileage out of the game. The first girl who slept with Ben Timlin got an automatic win. Otherwise, squares were marked off based on where a woman had sex. The riskier the spot, the more squares marked off. Maybe the game would happen again this year.

"I almost won," Monica said.

"No way."

"Yup. Not that I went crazy or anything, but I got four squares crossed off for one time."

Ian pushed himself off his elbows and looked at Monica. "There weren't many things four squares were awarded for."

"I'm not proud. I was on the gondola with McKenzie. There were guests in the next car. Doing the dirty where guests could see you was the trick. We screwed the entire way from the lower village to the upper village. McKenzie never said a word. Walked off the gondola and didn't speak to me again. I stopped playing after that. I hated him." Monica's eyes widened. "I didn't mean that."

"Don't worry. Not many people liked McKenzie, but who wants to say that now?"

"What did you do that was stupid?"

Ian checked to see if any of the others were listening. They were all too busy with their own conversations, so he told Monica about sleeping with the coach's daughter in Fernie and getting kicked off the team. He left out the part about the pregnancy and his regret at suggesting the abortion.

Monica held out her little finger to Ian. "Pinkie swear never to repeat our secrets."

He twisted his finger around hers, and they made a pact. Ian blinked at the flashlight beaming in his face.

"Security. Get down from there."

"Oh shit," Monica said. The group stepped down the ladder and stood with hanging heads.

"Dude," Ian said. "You don't need to report this."

The security officer hesitated as if thinking about his options, but as soon as Ian heard Kalin's voice, he knew the guard would follow protocol.

"Report what?" Kalin asked.

The officer gave her a quick update.

"He does need to report this. Monica, can I see you for a moment?" Kalin turned without saying more. Monica looked wide eyed at Ian. "Sorry," he mouthed at her. She frowned and followed Kalin.

CHAPTER ELEVEN

Early the next morning, Kalin hesitated at Reed's office door. Her eyes perused the photos of Reed's son that plastered his walls. The theme: ski racing. The pictures catalogued Ian's skiing accomplishments.

She cleared her throat to get Reed's attention. "You wanted to see me?"

"Come in." He motioned to an empty chair. "I'm not happy."

Kalin lowered herself, placed her phone on the table and asked, "With me?" *Crap.* He'd heard about Monica being on top of the lift station. She'd convinced him Monica was the right person to be the HR manager. At least Ian had been with her. If he reprimanded Monica, he'd have to do the same with Ian.

"I know you're new at this, but it's your responsibility to ensure our premises are secure."

Kalin didn't know what to say, so she remained silent. She assumed he meant new at being a director. Less than a year ago, Kalin had relocated to Stone Mountain with the intention of staying a year. By the end of the winter, she'd fallen in love with Stone Mountain, with her job and, best of all, with Ben. Now, she couldn't imagine leaving.

"That doesn't just mean making sure the doors are locked, although that's important. It also means keeping people under control."

Still hoping he wasn't talking about Monica, she played dumb. "I'm not sure what you're getting at."

He slapped the *Calgary Herald* on the table. The paper was open to the sports section. Kalin read the headline he'd highlighted. *Stone Mountain Run Injection Causes Death.* Reed gave her a moment to read the article, which wasn't as damaging as the heading. A newspaper story wasn't what she'd been expecting. Maybe he hadn't heard about Monica and Ian.

"I understand the media was at the lift yesterday, and you let security officers handle the situation."

Kalin nodded, and a lump wedged in her throat.

"You have certain responsibilities as a director. You cannot allow junior staff to give statements to the media. Yesterday, you should have taken control of the situation and spoken to the reporters yourself. If you didn't feel comfortable making a statement, then you should have brought them to me or to public relations, but you should not have let them wander around talking to anyone they wanted."

Kalin had been a director for four days and wondered if she'd made a mistake accepting the promotion. Reed expected her to be an expert at everything already. "I'm sorry. Security was escorting the journalists away from the lift. I thought it would be okay."

"But you didn't stick around to make sure."

"I hadn't realized they would write something that damaging."

"The paper is wrong. Dangerous conditions didn't cause McKenzie's fall. The RCMP confirmed someone sabotaged his equipment."

Kalin took in the implications of his statement and asked, "Someone murdered him?"

"Yes."

She understood why Miller had dragged her into the office last night to get Nora's file. His story about trying to prevent gossip was bullshit. He must have already known McKenzie was murdered, and he suspected Nora. She wasn't sure how Reed would feel about her giving Miller access to an employee file and decided not to tell him. "Do they know who did it?"

"No. Not yet anyway."

"It's hard to believe. Who would want to kill a ski racer?"

"I have no idea," Reed said, sounding impatient.

"Does the RCMP think it's one of the racers?"

"They haven't said. Do *you* think it's one of the racers?"

"I don't know. Who knows about this?"

"The coaches all know. They've been asked to tell their teams, but to try to keep everyone from talking about it."

"That's impossible." Kalin couldn't believe she hadn't already heard about the RCMP's declaration. The news would spread like a virus from one mouth to the next. This was too big a story. Monica probably knew, but she'd been hiding from Kalin all morning.

"I agree, but instruct your team to only talk among themselves."

"What happens now?" Kalin asked.

"What do you mean?"

Kalin's thin knit sweater felt unbearably warm, and her skin prickled. "Will race training be cancelled?"

"The teams want to continue training. The RCMP agrees it's best. They need time to investigate. Without training, the skiers will leave the area."

"Don't McKenzie's teammates need time to grieve?"

"I'm sure they do, but not one of them wants to miss any training. Their careers are on the line. Jenkinson cancelled training for the day of McKenzie's funeral. This is a lot to take in, but I need you to focus. I expected the skiers' equipment to be secure. You need to work on that," Reed said.

"I need some time to come up with a plan. I haven't been involved with the race training." *Lame. Definitely lame.*

"I understand, but I want to make sure you're clear on your responsibilities going forward."

Kalin nodded even though she was anything but clear. "Do you know how his equipment was sabotaged?"

Reed tapped his pen on the table's surface and sounded as if he was practicing his speech for reporters. "The RCMP hired an independent expert who examined the binding. The outer cover was removed. The internal mechanism that sets the DIN was fixed to a low setting and then the cover was put back on. Whoever did this knew how to set the DIN low enough that the binding would release when McKenzie was skiing, but not so low that it would release before he picked up speed."

"Didn't the murderer take a chance McKenzie would notice the setting was wrong?"

"The indicator on the outer display was glued to his normal setting. If McKenzie checked the display, he would have seen the needle set to the correct number. We know his bindings were tampered with. What we don't know is how someone accessed the tuning room or his skis. I want you to find out how that happened before the RCMP figure it out."

"I'm not really—"

"You have an experienced security team at your disposal. Use them."

"Okay." She wished she'd started out better with the security team. Fred wasn't openly hostile, but he wasn't going out of his way to help her either. She'd have to work harder at gaining his trust but wasn't sure how. Luckily, she'd supported security at the lift and taken the officer's side over Monica's. She hadn't pressured him to look the other way. She couldn't afford another divide between herself and the security team.

"I also want you to make sure the tuning room can't be accessed by someone without the authority to do so."

She'd come to the meeting thinking the worst thing was if Reed had found out about a party on the lift station. She never imagined they'd be talking about murder.

CHAPTER TWELVE

How am I supposed to do what Reed wants? During the ten minutes Kalin loitered in the entryway of the tuning room, she counted twenty-five people who entered or exited and only recognized a few of them. The room took up three quarters of the ground floor. A foyer lay between the tuning room and the stairs to the first floor. To access the foyer a person either had to use the exterior door to the administration building or the stairs from the second floor where her office was located.

Files scraping metal buzzed through the room, and the odor of melted wax accosted her. Four teams used the large space. The tuners, engrossed in their task, didn't pay attention to the other teams. None of them noticed Kalin examining them. It was unnerving that every person she evaluated could be the one who killed McKenzie. Anyone could enter or exit the room during operating hours without drawing attention to themselves.

Kalin wandered through the room, trying to appear casual. She caught snippets of conversations, but the voices lowered as she neared.

Donny Morley sat in a wheelchair while he tuned a ski, and Kalin's breath caught. The way his head tilted to one side as he concentrated and the way his blond bangs drooped across his forehead reminded Kalin of her late husband, Jack. She'd never noticed the similarity before. The last time she'd seen Jack, his head had been tilted at just the same angle as he oiled the chain on his bike. Two blocks from their apartment, a car hit him and didn't stop. The police never found out who killed him. Experience told her the cops might not find out who killed McKenzie either.

Monica sidled up to Kalin, jolting her out of her memories. "Hey."

Kalin kept her eyes on the tuning room and her voice civil. "I wondered when you were going to talk to me."

"I'm sorry about last night. I don't know what I was thinking."

"Here's the thing. I convinced Reed you were ready for this position. I can't have you getting into trouble on resort property even if you were off duty."

"I know. It won't happen again. Did Reed say anything?"

"I think you got lucky. He's distracted right now. Maybe he won't read the security reports today. You put me in an awkward position. Sticking me right between security and HR, and making me choose." If Constable Miller hadn't called Kalin and asked her to meet him, she never would have seen Monica and her gang on her way home, and maybe security wouldn't have reported the incident since Ian was Reed's son.

"I'm really sorry. Thank you for not telling Reed. I heard McKenzie—"

"Now is not the time. I've got too much to do."

Monica blushed. "Okay. I'll be at my desk." She turned and bolted for the stairs.

Kalin recognized Charlie Whittle, head tuner for the Holden team, and stopped at his station. In his late forties, he'd kept half of his red hair. Freckles dotted the other half of his head, and a birthmark in the shape of a scythe lay above his left temple.

He glanced at her. "Can I help you?"

She introduced herself as the new head of security. "I've been asked to secure the tuning room and would like to get your ideas on how best to do that."

"You're taking over Tom's job?"

"I am."

"Tom was a good man. Do you mind if I work while we talk? I've four more sets of skis to tune before I can go home. My wife gets annoyed when I'm late." He shrugged as if apologizing for her.

"Not at all. Do you live in Holden or up at the resort?"

Charlie ran a file along the side of a ski and tested the results with his palm. Apparently not satisfied, he slid the file again. "Holden, when I'm not traveling with the team."

"What time do you usually finish work?"

"By seven. Although it could be later if one of the skiers did serious damage to their skis."

Kalin canted her head in the direction of the tuners. "Do the others finish at the same time?"

"It depends on how many skiers had runs, how many runs and how hard they were on their skis."

"Any idea how often someone would be here after seven?"

"Not a clue."

"Who locks up at the end of the night?"

"The last person to leave. There's really no security if that's what you're getting at. We've never had a problem before. Just the techs, skiers and coaches enter this room. No one else has a reason to be here."

Except the person who killed McKenzie. "Would you notice if someone, who didn't belong, was in here?"

"Maybe not." He scratched his beard with his fingernails. "I'd probably notice if someone was tuning skis who shouldn't be."

"Is the equipment left here overnight?"

"Sometimes. That depends on where the team is from. Some of the locals like to take their skis home at night. The racers aren't supposed to take skis to their hotel rooms but some do anyway."

"Did McKenzie keep his skis here?"

"He had the spot in the corner."

Kalin looked in the direction Charlie pointed. McKenzie's ski jacket still hung where he'd left it on the day he died. "I think we should limit access to the room and have a lockup procedure. I'd like to put a plan together and run it by you before I show it to the rest of the group. Would you mind helping?"

"Not at all. Everyone's in a bit of shock right now, and anything we can do to settle them will help."

"I'll get back to you." It occurred to Kalin that Charlie could be the guilty one, just as well as anyone else in the room, but she needed his help if she wanted the others to support a new process. She'd have to risk his involvement. But right now, her stomach demanded attention. Time for lunch.

Kalin's stomach growled. The walk from the tuning room to the cafeteria took her five minutes and by the time she arrived, her throat ached from the cold. She didn't have time to be sick. Food! She needed food to keep her healthy. She breathed through her nose and her nostrils stuck together. The *Farmer's Almanac* had predicted a cold winter in British Columbia and, so far, the weather supported the forecast.

Kalin reached the cafeteria and stomped on the metal grate, clearing snow from her boots and waiting for the sliding glass doors to open automatically. She entered and let warm air breeze over her cheeks.

Cedar timbers stretched across the vaulted ceiling. The walls, constructed of glass from floor to ceiling, displayed a spectacular view of the ski hill. Skiers and employees crowded the room. Cutlery clinked, talking mixed into a blur of voices, and equipment scraped over tile. The sounds of life.

A mixture of aromas—cooked pasta, grilled meat and something sweet—drew Kalin to the buffet. Dishes heavy on carbohydrates and protein covered the table and most racers helped themselves to large portions. Kalin took a small square of lasagna and grabbed a side salad. She spotted Ben sitting at a corner table with two other ski patrollers. He may be an inch shorter than she was, but he was still the hottest guy in the room. He waved her over.

Ben shifted his chair, making room for Kalin, and stood when she arrived, taking her tray and placing it on the table. She sat, and Ben reached over and pulled her clip from the back of her head. Her hair fell loose over her shoulders. "Way sexier."

She glanced sideways at him, and he pressed his thigh tight against hers.

"It's cold out." Kalin rubbed her hands together and then wrapped her fingers around her mug of tea. She didn't want the others to know why her cheeks had gone red. "You guys getting enough breaks to warm up?"

All three patrollers laughed.

"She never takes off her HR hat. If the racers can take the cold in their polyester race suits, I think we can stand it," Ben said.

"I know. You people are tough. What's the talk about McKenzie?"

"There's a rumor circulating that he was murdered and his bindings were damaged on purpose. Have you heard anything?" Ben bit into his burger and sighed.

Racers' skis, duffle bags and poles were haphazardly spread on the tiles. Melted snow created a sea of puddles. The skis that weren't on the floor were leaning against the wall outside the cafeteria entrance. No one paid attention to the equipment, which begged the question of how often McKenzie had left his gear unattended. She didn't want to talk in front of the other patrollers, so she didn't answer Ben. Instead, she waved her hand in the direction of the gear. "If it's true, why isn't anyone worried about the safety of their own equipment?"

Ben raised one eyebrow. "Do you think they should be?"

She shrugged. "Who's being gossiped about?"

"Just who you'd expect. Other team members or competing teams. Someone who wanted McKenzie off the circuit. And obviously Donny Morley."

Jeff Morley sat in his truck and turned the heat to high. He'd had a good training session, but now his quads ached. He'd looked for Donny before heading home, but couldn't find him. He'd have to catch a ride with someone else.

His cell rang, and he checked the display before answering. "Hi, Aunt Lisa."

"Have you talked to Nora today?"

Jeff used to talk to Nora every day until McKenzie stole her away. Even after they broke up, they still spoke. The car accident had brought them closer, *as friends* Nora liked to say. Unfortunately, the crash had brought her closer to McKenzie too. He didn't get it. "I've been training all morning."

"I'm worried about her. She says she's fine, but…"

He understood his aunt's anxiety. She lost her daughter, and Jeff suspected she felt guilty about not preventing Rachel's death. Nora was the only daughter, even if she was adopted, Aunt Lisa had left. "I'll call her."

"That would be good but don't pressure her. Just be her friend."

"I am her friend. Don't worry."

"I need you to keep an eye on her and make sure she's okay."

Jeff couldn't count the number of times he'd wanted to bash in McKenzie's head. He didn't know what Nora had seen in him. His initial euphoria over McKenzie's death had diminished. He'd wanted the guy out of Nora's life. Not dead. Well, he was certainly out of her life now, and Jeff intended to take advantage of his absence.

The passenger door opened, and Vicky Hamilton's sweet perfume entered before she slid in.

Now here's a pretty face. "I saw you were back. Nice try at the lift with Ben."

Vicky pushed her jacket hood onto her shoulders, and the fur trim of the hood blended with her blonde hair. "Shut up."

"How come you left Whistler?"

"That didn't work out."

Jeff chuckled. "I heard. So did everyone else here. I guess sleeping with your boss at work wasn't the best idea you've ever had. Is it true his wife fired you?"

"Really, shut up. So what do you know about this Kalin chick?"

Jeff laughed and shook his head. "You thinking of getting Ben back?"

"Don't laugh. She hardly seems his type, so give me the dirt on her."

"I don't know her."

Vicky angled her legs toward Jeff. "But your precious Nora does. She must talk about her."

"News flash. Nora dated Steve McKenzie for the last year."

"Holy shit, you're kidding."

"Nope. Anyway, you don't stand a chance. Kalin lives with Ben. They have a dog. I've heard they're serious."

"I thought you didn't know her."

"It's a small town."

Vicky slid across the seat, flipped her hips, placing one leg on either side of Jeff's legs. She pressed her groin against his and planted her cold lips on his throat.

"It's cold. Colder than cold." Fred zipped his security jacket tight under his chin and stretched his knitted toque low over his ears. Kalin and Fred crossed the snow-covered sidewalk and entered the foyer beside the tuning room.

Vicky Hamilton sashayed toward Fred, wearing a cream ski jacket that showed off her curves. Kalin's stomach tightened at the sight of the Goddess.

Vicky leaned forward and kissed him on the cheek, letting her gloss-covered lips linger.

Fred blushed and stepped back. He cleared his throat. "You know Kalin?"

"We've met." Vicky gave Kalin the same once over she'd given her the first time they'd seen each other. "I've rejoined the fire department."

That's just great. If Ben didn't already know Vicky was back at the resort, he would soon.

Vicky placed her hand on Fred's bicep and caressed his arm. "Next time you see me at the fire station, I'll be wearing all of my turnout gear. Not just the bottom half."

"Enough," Fred said.

Vicky winked at Fred and wiggled her ass out the door.

Kalin wanted to ask what that was about but couldn't bring herself to articulate the question.

"Is it true McKenzie was murdered?" Fred asked.

"Yes." Kalin filled him in on her conversation with Reed.

"When we watched the video, it crossed my mind that someone killed him," Fred said. "I didn't really believe it though."

"Me either. Let your team know, but make sure they understand they're not to talk about the investigation outside the group." The ice on Kalin's neck tube melted, and she pulled the soggy wool over her head and shoved it into her ski jacket pocket. How did the Goddess look so glamorous in the cold weather? Kalin was just too practical.

"They'll be discreet."

"After I met with Reed, I hung out in the tuning room for a while. Too many people have access. We need a system to keep track of people. I was thinking about the scanning equipment used at the lifts."

"What about it?"

"We could issue a card to anyone who should have access to the room. If we scan the cards at the inner door, we only have to control one entry point."

"Not bad." Fred surveyed the area around them. A moment passed before he said, "I see two issues. One, how do we know who should or shouldn't be in the room? And two, who's going to pay someone to stand there every day?"

"I'll pull Amber Cristelli from the lifts. Guest services assigned two people to check tickets after McKenzie caused a scene. Obviously, that's no longer required. We don't need any extra scanning equipment. Most of the scanners won't be in use until the season opens." Kalin nodded at Charlie Whittle, who dribbled wax on the bottom of a ski. Burn marks scarred the cuffs of Charlie's sweater, and wax droplets peppered his jeans.

"Let's go in and talk with Charlie about who should be given access to the room."

Nora stood at the tuning table beside Charlie's and checked the bottom of an iron with her thumb. Her untamable hair stuck out in every direction. The apron she wore was two sizes too big, and she looked like a kid playing a grown up game.

Kalin explained her idea to Charlie. Fred stood by her without speaking, either acknowledging her senior rank or being unhelpful. He'd never lost his military stance with his erect posture, straight legs kept hip distance apart and hands clasped behind his back, and she thought he looked a lot more like the head of security than she did.

Charlie scratched the birthmark on his head. "I guess we could reduce the number of people who need to be in here. The technicians all require access, but the racers don't really. Someone has to bring the equipment in and out for us, but each team could allocate a person. Let me talk with the coaches, and I'll get back to you."

Fred and Kalin left the tuning room.

"Did you notice Nora watching us?" Fred asked.

Kalin couldn't have missed the intensity of Nora's green eyes. There'd almost been a physical connection. "Not really."

"She was very interested in what we were saying. I'm surprised she's back working already. I thought she'd take time off."

Kalin led Fred away from Nora and any thoughts he might be having about Nora accidentally killing McKenzie.

"About lunch today." Kalin placed her steak knife and fork on top of her empty plate. She loved the way Ben grilled steak, but that didn't mean he'd get away with flirting at work.

Ben gave her a lopsided smile, the one he used when he tried to be cute, and moved from the dining room table to the living room, dropping his dishes on the kitchen counter with a clang as he passed by. "I knew you were going to bring that up. I thought maybe I'd get lucky and you'd forget."

Kalin followed him to the couch. She'd moved in with Ben and Chica the previous winter, sharing the bedroom in their seven hundred square foot suite. Tendrils of warmth spread from the fireplace, and Chica found a spot as far from the hearth as possible and leaned against the sliding glass door.

"Don't think for one minute your smile is going to get you out of this. Playing with my hair at work is not professional."

"It's a ski resort. Nobody cares."

"I care."

"Okay, city girl. You win. I won't touch your hair at work, but I can't make that promise at home." Ben jumped across the couch, wrestled her down with his bulk and used a pillow to mess her hair. By the time he finished, static had taken over, and her hair stood on end.

"Much better. I like my women wild." He caressed her cheek. "Your face is hot."

"I think I have a fever. I don't have time to be sick. My throat's been bugging me since yesterday."

Ben lay on top of her, resting his weight on his elbows. "Are we going to talk about Vicky or just avoid the subject?"

"You know she came by?"

"She told me."

The sting of jealousy picked at her. "When did you see her?"

"She came to the lift the other day when I was getting ready to head up the mountain."

"Is this going to be a problem for us?" *Please say no.*

"That depends on how you take this."

"Take what?"

"Before I could stop her, she kissed me."

Kalin shifted out from underneath Ben. "On your lips?"

"Yes."

"Those are my lips."

"Are you mad?"

"Did you kiss her back?"

"No."

Chica woofed, startling them and ending their conversation. Ben peeked over the back of the leather couch. Kalin smoothed her hair.

Nora Cummings stood on their patio, peering through the sliding glass door at the back of their suite, with the forest looming behind her.

Ben waved her in. He leaned into Kalin and gave her a quick kiss. "You have nothing to worry about. You look great, and these *are* your lips."

Nora slid the glass door open, dropped her ski jacket and mitts on the floor and stepped out of her boots. The slight scent of pine followed her into the room.

"Look at Nora's hair. It's always crazy. You don't need to keep yours so—"

Kalin pushed Ben out of the way. "What's wrong?"

Nora's eyes were puffy, and the skin below her nose was raw. "They think I killed Steve."

"Who thinks that?" Ben asked.

Nora flopped into the leather armchair, filling half the seat, and folded her knees to her chest. "Fucking Constable Miller and his cop buddies."

Ben sat across from her on the couch, and Kalin tucked in beside him. "Why?"

"Because I didn't tell them Steve and I broke up."

"I didn't know you did. I'm sorry," Ben said.

"Why does Miller think you killed Steve?" Kalin asked.

"We broke up the night before he died."

"That's a bit of a leap." Unless the RCMP thought Nora told McKenzie about the pregnancy test, but Kalin didn't know if Miller knew about the test. She argued mentally with herself about whether to admit to Nora she'd shown Miller her file and decided not to.

"I guess because I didn't mention our breakup when they interviewed me the first time. I was upset and didn't think it mattered. Miller asked questions about the morning of the accident, where Steve was, where I was, but he didn't ask about my relationship with him."

Nora's cell rang. She glanced at the call display. "Hi, Lisa." She turned her back to Kalin and Ben. "No. I'm okay. Sorry about the message. I'm at Kalin's. I'll call you later." Nora pressed the end button and shrugged. "I left her a bit of an emotional message."

Nora was tight with her adoptive mom even though she didn't live with her anymore, so Kalin wasn't surprised Nora had called Lisa first before coming to her. "Did they accuse you or just ask questions?"

"Obviously, Miller didn't arrest me or anything, but he asked about Steve's skis. He wanted to confirm I tuned his skis the night before he died and not Charlie. He asked if I'd tampered with the DIN setting. Can you believe that? If I didn't, like did I notice anything odd about the bindings?"

"How did he know you and Steve broke up?" Kalin asked.

"Ian Reed told him. I have no idea how he knew. I didn't tell Ian, but it was the first thing Miller asked me about today. I can't believe he thinks I killed Steve. I loved him."

"The cops have to investigate. They don't know you," Ben said.

"You're on their side?"

"I didn't mean it like that. Only that they have to consider everyone. I know Miller. He's a good guy."

"Who would want to kill Steve? I still can't believe he was murdered." Nora twisted in her seat and faced Kalin. "Can't you help me?"

"How?"

"You're the head of security now. Maybe you could find out what happened, or at least let me know what the RCMP is doing."

"The RCMP won't tell me anything."

"Kalin, please. People talk to you. They like you. Maybe you could just ask around a bit. I can't stand the stress. What if it was something personal? What if the person who killed Steve has something against me too?"

"Do you really think that's possible?"

"I don't know what to think."

"You're asking me for something I can't do."

CHAPTER THIRTEEN

Kalin held a scanning gun with her arm extended above her head and noticed her deodorant had failed. She lowered her arm a bit. "This is the same type of scanner we use at the lifts," she said to the tuners and coaches occupying the room. Charlie had done his part, and given her a list of who should be allowed in the tuning room, and helped her get everyone together in the conference room. Her part was to persuade everyone to follow her process.

"Each of your ski passes has been updated to access the tuning room. Amber Cristelli will monitor the door." Kalin had chosen Amber for the role because she'd shown she could stand up to the racers when she'd refused McKenzie access to the lift.

Amber stood and smiled at the audience.

"She'll scan your pass as you enter or exit the room. If you don't have your pass with you, you won't be allowed in." Kalin spotted a hand raised near the back corner. "Yes?"

"Do we have to do that every time we come and go or just at the beginning and end of each shift?"

"Every time. The goal is to know who is in the room throughout the day."

"What's that going to do?" the same person asked.

"It should deter anyone from tampering with equipment."

"You think the athletes are in danger?" another person asked.

Kalin had no idea but wanted to keep people calm. "No, I don't. Because of what happened to Steve McKenzie, the president of the resort asked me to secure the tuning room. He wants to be proactive and improve our process. The room will be locked during off hours, and no one will be given access." Kalin heard the authoritative tone in her voice and felt like a high school teacher lecturing students. And lectures rarely worked.

Several of the technicians groaned and exchanged eye rolls.

"That's not going to work. What if we need to get in at night?" a technician sitting near the front asked.

Kalin rested her backside on the edge of the table at the front of the room, hoping to appear more relaxed and part of the team. "The room will be open from seven to seven. If you don't already have a ski pass, please go to the guest services desk and get one. Also, I'd like each of the coaches to inform the racers they'll no longer have access unless they are escorted by their coach."

As the tuners and coaches cleared the room, snippets of conversation reached Kalin, most of it grumbling. Nora smiled at her on her way out. At least she didn't resent the new process and maybe she wasn't angry about Kalin refusing to help her.

Kalin put the scanner and presentation material in her backpack and was about to leave when she heard a throat being cleared.

"Hi, Donny," Amber said and hovered for a moment.

"You can go if you want," Kalin said to Amber.

Amber's smile lingered on Donny until she turned toward the exit.

Donny watched Amber until she was out of sight and then propelled himself forward. "Can we talk a minute?" Fingerless gloves adorned hands that led to muscular forearms. He rotated his chair, stopping beside the nearest table.

"Sure." Kalin sat beside him, and while she waited to hear what he had to say, she wondered if he'd seen Nora at the drugstore on the night she bought the pregnancy test.

"Do you really think there's no danger to anyone else?"

"You should be asking the RCMP that kind of question. My role is not to investigate the murder. It's to secure the ski equipment." Kalin guessed Miller had already interviewed Donny. There was no way Donny wasn't a suspect, and she swallowed hard. "I'm not sure what you want me to do here."

"My brother's on the team. I guess I want some reassurance."

Kalin knew of Donny's brother Jeff because he used to date Nora. They'd broken up before Kalin met her, and he didn't hang around Nora as much as Donny did. "Why?"

"What if someone is targeting racers? Or someone's trying to take down the Holden team. Everyone knows Jenkinson wants to send another skier to the Olympics."

"Hey, what's up?" Nora found Lisa on her front porch, waiting in the dome of her outdoor light. Lisa bounced her lanky frame from one foot to the other, like a prized racehorse waiting to break through the gates.

"Today's Rachel's birthday," Lisa said.

Nora ran to Lisa and hugged her. *How could I forget?*

"Come inside." She dragged Lisa by the hand and pulled her through the doorway. Her cramped one-bedroom suite was all she needed. For now, anyway. Lisa had helped her find the place and decorate the interior. One of Lisa's paintings hung in the entryway. She'd painted Nora ski racing, using her signature vivid colors, and given the framed canvas to Nora as a fourteenth birthday present.

By the time they settled in the living room, the kettle whistled. Nora made herbal tea. One sugar and a splash of milk for Lisa. Black for herself.

Nora had been too preoccupied with her own problems to remember Rachel's birthday and that the day always threw Lisa into a depression. Rachel had been her best friend and had accepted her as a sister, and Nora should have remembered, no matter what. "I wish I could make you feel better."

Lisa sipped her tea, and the mug tinkled when she placed it on the glass coffee table. "I keep expecting it to get easier. I watch the clock all day, waiting for the moment she was born. She should still be here with me, not…I should have stopped her."

"Oh, Lisa." Nora hugged her with her small body, folding inside Lisa's arms. "None of us saw what she was planning."

"It feels like yesterday. I don't know what I'd do without you."

Sometimes it did seem as if only days had passed since Rachel died. The night it happened, Donny had still been in the hospital recovering from the car accident. Jeff, Nora and Lisa were visiting him. They'd started a routine of playing Euchre in the evenings. Jeff and Nora agreed to put their differences aside for Donny's sake. She had a hard time pretending she wasn't angry with Jeff, but Donny had become her adoptive cousin when she was two, and she loved him.

No one thought to worry about Rachel. They all focused on Donny during the weeks following the accident. They'd been playing cards for an hour when the RCMP entered the hospital room, solemn faced, and asked to speak with Lisa. Nora waited with the guys. Donny whispered Rachel's name as if he knew the news was about her. Lisa's sobbing confirmed something bad had happened.

Lisa returned to the hospital room, her face the color of the curtain surrounding Donny's bed. "She's killed herself." And they'd all known who *she* was.

Nora never understood why Rachel committed suicide. The accident paralyzed Donny, not Rachel.

Forcing herself back to the present, Nora tugged a photo album from underneath the coffee table. "Let's talk about happier times with Rachel."

Nora and Lisa had been through the ritual before.

Lisa traced her finger over a photo of Rachel and Nora taken when they were two. "That's the day we moved to Holden. I was so excited to have a new home with you girls and to get away from Toronto."

In the photo, the girls stood on the top step of the veranda in front of Lisa's house. They held hands and smiled for the camera. Lisa never made Nora feel like less of a daughter to her than Rachel was. Years ago, Nora stopped asking Lisa why she didn't have any pictures of her birth mother. All Nora knew was Lisa adopted her after her mom died and before that, they'd been in art school together.

"My life would have sucked if you hadn't adopted me." Nora flipped the page. "This is one of my favorites." The photo showed Rachel standing sandwiched between Donny and Jeff, before Donny had been paralyzed. Lisa's sister was the boys' mother. Nora wasn't related to them by blood, and although there had been resistance when she started dating Jeff in high school, the subtle pressure against their relationship had died out when they'd gotten along so well.

"I remember that day too. Jeff was teaching Rachel to drive, and she frightened both the boys. Rachel said they screamed like babies."

"That was a good day."

The next photo showed Nora and Jeff, standing in the school gym, dressed for their high school prom. She thought she still glowed from the night before, thought she must have looked different. The night before the prom had been their first time. The night before the prom had been the start of the end.

"I haven't even asked how you are." Lisa smoothed Nora's hair. "Your hair has its own personality."

"Sorta like me." Some of Nora's friends complained about their hair, but Nora liked her own hair. Her hair announced her personality. If someone didn't like the unpredictable way it stuck out in odd directions as if it didn't know where to settle, they wouldn't like her. At least, that's what she told herself.

Lisa was beautiful. Her hair, the color of a sandy beach, hung straight, reaching below her shoulder blades. Combined with full lips and rounded cheeks, she was a knockout. No one would ever confuse Nora with being Lisa's daughter by birth. Rachel had inherited her mom's beauty. Nora would never be considered beautiful, but she didn't care. She looked how she looked.

"Have you decided about the baby?"

"Not yet. There's something I have to do first."

CHAPTER FOURTEEN

After an hour-long snowshoe, Kalin and Ben returned to the trailhead at the entrance to the resort. Using their headlamps for light, they'd taken Chica for a night hike. Kalin pretended she wasn't sick, hoping the exercise would drive the flu out of her system.

Kalin removed her toque and pulled her hair off her sweat-soaked neck. "I don't think people know how great Stone Mountain is at night. I bet most guests ski all day, but never come out in the dark."

Ben punched her shoulder. "You're such a jock. Who else wants to be active twenty-four-seven?"

Ben and Kalin were hidden in the shadows, the resort's lights not quite reaching them. Ben pulled her to him and pressed the entire length of his body against hers. "Let's go home. I can think of something else to get rid of your energy."

"Don't you ever think of anything else?"

"No, but neither do you."

Kalin leaned into him, resting her head on his shoulder, and swore she could feel the warmth of him through her snow pants.

"You're perfect for me," Ben said.

"Ditto." She eased him away, bent and undid the strap holding her boot. She stepped out of her snowshoe and reached for the strap on the other one.

Ben did the same and undid his strap, lost his balance and bumped Kalin's hip with his. Surprised, she pushed back into him, knocking him over and falling beside him. She landed on her stomach. He rolled her over and lay on top of her. He pressed his lips against hers and explored her mouth with his tongue.

Delicious. The heat from his mouth on hers countered by the iciness of the snow on her neck sent a shock of pleasure through her body.

He tossed his gloves aside and unzipped her ski jacket. He slid his hands underneath her sweater. "Nice sports bra." He nipped her ear, chuckling, letting her know he was teasing.

Chica barked and took off.

Ben rested his forehead on Kalin's. "Figures." He zipped her jacket and pulled her to her feet. "I guess we have to get her."

Over his shoulder, Kalin spotted Nora. She almost yelled to her when she noticed Nora was in an animated conversation.

"Turn and look," Kalin said.

Ben sighed and let go of her. "I wonder who she's talking to."

"She's arguing with someone. Should we go over?"

"I don't think we have a choice. That's where Chica went."

Chica bounded across the snow, wagging her tail, rushing to Nora.

Ben and Kalin followed Chica.

Ian Reed stepped out from behind Nora. His eyes darted between Kalin and Ben. The light from above shone on the band of freckles crossing his nose. His strawberry blond hair snuck out from underneath his toque. Ian was her boss's son and had been partying on the top of the lift station with Monica, and now he was here with Nora. He sure seemed to get around.

"Is everything okay?" Kalin asked Nora.

"Sure. We're just talking. You know Ian?"

Ben and Kalin nodded

"I heard you made the Holden team," Ben said. "That's sweet. Usually only locals get admitted to the circle of Coach Jenkinson. You must be good."

"Thanks." Ian glanced at Nora. "I gotta go." His winter boots crunched on the packed snow with each step he took away from them.

Kalin watched his back disappear into darkness. "What's going on?"

"Nothing really," Nora said, but her frown contradicted her words.

"Come on. We'll drive you home," Ben said.

They dropped Nora off at her place and continued in Ben's Ford F-150 along Black Bear Drive.

"Did you know Nora and Ian were friends?" Ben asked.

"I've seen them talking a couple of times, but Nora's never mentioned him. They tuned together before Ian got on the Holden team."

"It's weird, them fighting. Maybe Nora thinks he had something to do with McKenzie's death."

Kalin shifted, and her ski pants caught on a slight tear in the leather seat. "Why would you say that?"

"I heard Ian didn't make the team then he gets on as backup, and the next day McKenzie dies."

"Meaning?"

"Meaning he wouldn't get to compete unless someone left the team," Ben said.

"You're not seriously saying Ian killed McKenzie just to get an official spot."

"Why not? Someone killed him, and with McKenzie out of the way, Ian could take the top spot, not just an official one."

Kalin played with the zipper on her ski jacket. What if Ian had killed McKenzie? It was possible. Her gut told her to talk to Nora in private. Maybe she'd tell Kalin what was going on with Ian if Ben wasn't there. "Can you drive me back to Nora's? I want to talk to her. I'll meet you at home later."

Ben wiggled his eyebrows. "I'd rather you come home."

Kalin laughed. "Do you actually think the eyebrow thing works?"

"It seems to with you." Ben made a U-turn and headed back toward Nora's.

Kalin knocked on Nora's door. Each time she exhaled her breath froze into tiny clouds in front of her face. She circled her lips, blew out and failed at creating cloud rings. Instead a cough erupted from her throat.

The door opened a crack, and Kalin saw one of Nora's green eyes. Nora recognized Kalin and opened the door wide. "Where's Ben?"

"He took Chica home. I need to talk to you about something. Can I come in?"

"Of course."

Kalin deposited her boots and jacket in the front hall and followed Nora to the kitchen.

"Want some hot chocolate?"

Kalin's body ached, and the thought of a warm drink comforted her. "That sounds good."

"So what's up?" Nora removed dark chocolate from the refrigerator and dropped a square into a saucepan. Using a wooden spoon, she stirred the chocolate as the sweet substance melted.

"Yum, real chocolate."

"I like to make it from scratch. Lisa used to make cocoa for me when I lived with her." Nora waited until the chocolate melted and a smooth layer covered the bottom of the pan. She measured two cups of milk and dribbled the white liquid over the chocolate while she continued to stir.

"How are you feeling these days? Any better?"

"I'm fine. Well, as much as you can expect, considering…"

Kalin inhaled deeply, enjoying the scent of the melting chocolate. "What was going on with Ian?"

Nora concentrated on stirring the milk into the chocolate. "Nothing."

"We could see you were fighting with him. You can trust me. I'm your friend."

"I know. It's nothing really."

"Are you hiding something from me because I said I wouldn't tell you what the cops are up to? They won't tell me anything about the investigation."

"I'm not hiding anything. Can you pass me two mugs?" Nora pointed toward the cupboard on the other side of the kitchen.

Kalin passed the mugs to Nora. "Were you arguing because you think Ian had something to do with Steve's murder?"

"What?" Nora dropped one of the mugs with a clang on the granite counter top, but Kalin grabbed it before it rolled over the counter's edge. "Why would you ask that? What do you know?"

"Slow down. I don't know anything new." Kalin took the saucepan from Nora and filled the mugs with the steaming cocoa. "Come on. Let's sit." She moved to the kitchen table and Nora followed.

"I thought you were fighting with Ian because you suspected him."

"No. It's something else." Nora placed her mug on the table and sat opposite Kalin. "Ian has nothing to do with Steve."

"Ben mentioned Ian was on the team as backup but someone would have to leave the team for him to compete."

"No way. You think Ian killed Steve to get a spot on the team? That's crazy."

"What if Ian didn't mean to kill Steve but just injure him? That would get him off the team. And Ian must be under a lot of pressure from Reed."

"Dude, you couldn't be more wrong."

"Here's the thing. Whoever killed Steve is probably willing to kill again if they think someone suspects them. It doesn't matter if they meant to kill him or not."

"I can't believe this."

"It's not something to fool around with. The RCMP will figure out who killed him. Let them do their job."

"My talking to Ian had nothing to do with Steve."

"Then what was it? We could tell you were fighting with him."

Nora wrapped her delicate fingers around her mug. "Okay. I'll tell you, but promise you'll keep it secret. Not even tell Ben."

"Of course."

"I'm pregnant."

"What does that have to do with Ian?"

"You don't seem surprised."

"I'm not. Remember the night we bumped into each other in the drugstore?"

"Sure," Nora said.

"I saw the pregnancy test." Kalin had seen Ian leaving the drugstore that night and wondered if he'd seen the test too. Nora's cousin Donny had also been at the drugstore.

Nora smiled at Kalin. "You didn't say anything."

"I thought it was your own business, and you'd tell me if you wanted to."

"Have you told anyone?"

"No, of course not. What does this have to do with Ian?"

Nora blew the top of her hot chocolate, cooling her drink before taking a sip. She set the mug on the table but left both hands wrapped around the ceramic sides. Without taking her eyes off the mug, she said, "I think the baby is his."

"Oh."

"Yeah, I know. It was one time, and it was a mistake."

"Are you sure it's not Steve's?"

"I wish, but Steve and I were careful. Ian and I weren't. It just happened. I don't know what I was thinking. Ian has a way. It was over before I knew what I was doing. Steve slept with Amber, and I guess I was trying to get back at him. Ian was an easy way to do that."

Oh, shit. Kalin had just hired Amber to monitor the tuning room. Now she had a motive too. "And now you have to walk past Amber every time you enter the tuning room. That's gotta be awkward."

"It sucks. I couldn't believe it when you picked her for the job, but what could I say, really. And to make it worse, I think she has a crush on Donny. She's always flirting with him. I hope he doesn't like her too."

"I had no idea about her and Steve," Kalin said but didn't add she would have hired her even if she'd known. She couldn't pass on a person for a job because of a wild personal life since that would seriously reduce the number of job candidates in a ski resort.

Nora pressed her palms against her eyes. "I'm such a fuck up."

Kalin rested her hand on Nora's shoulder. "No you're not. Is that why Ian was so angry tonight?"

"He said he didn't believe me and even if it was true, it was my problem, not his. Stupid me."

"You're not stupid. You trusted him, that's all."

"Speaking of trust, do you know Ben's old girlfriend is back at the resort?"

"Yup. He told me the bitch kissed him."

"Oh thank God. I've been so worried. I saw her do it and didn't know what to do."

Kalin laughed. "Everything's fine. You don't need to worry."

CHAPTER FIFTEEN

Kalin scanned a tuner's pass and let her enter the tuning room. Aches traversed her body, reminding her she was sick and that she shouldn't have gone snowshoeing last night or let Ben ravage her. She ignored the shivers and waited for Amber to return. Amber, who'd slept with McKenzie. Amber, who might have killed him.

Donny rolled his wheelchair toward Kalin, and she scanned his pass. "This your new job?" he asked.

"Amber needed a break." Kalin hadn't planned to relieve her until lunch, but Amber had called and said she needed a few minutes. Since security of the room was important to Reed, Kalin wanted to make sure the process worked, and guarding the door also gave her an excuse to watch the tuners for a bit.

"What do you think of the new process?" Kalin asked.

"Seems a little late to do any good, but I guess it'll keep the gear safe."

"How's everyone doing?"

He motioned inside the room with his coffee cup. "The tuners you mean?"

"Yes."

"Okay, I think. Nora seems uptight, but I guess you'd expect that. Charlie's grumpy. He's pissed Ian left the tuning team and he's short staffed. Coach Jenkinson storms in and out of here like his ass is on fire. He's a jerk to begin with, but now, he's yelling at everyone. Tune faster, do a better job, whatever."

"Can anyone else on the team match McKenzie's times?"

"Ian Reed. But Jeff's a close second. Ian hasn't been on the team long enough to be a favorite. Jenkinson's a talented coach, but he picks a favorite and works with that skier the most. Once he picked McKenzie, he ignored the rest of the team. Now, he'll focus on Jeff, and I bet his time improves."

Kalin could tell Donny was proud of his brother, and instead of being jealous Jeff could still ski, he cheered for him.

"Hi." Amber returned and took the scanner from Kalin. "Thanks."

Amber fussed with her big curls and gave Donny a timid smile. "How's tuning going?" she asked Donny.

"Busy. I'd better get back."

The two women watched him wheel himself to his tuning station. McKenzie's ski jacket caught Kalin's attention. Had he meant anything to Amber? Did Amber know Nora had found out about her sleeping with him?

Amber rubbed her index finger under one eye and then the other. "Is my mascara okay? My eyes water when it's this cold."

"Not a smudge. Have any trouble today?"

"Mr. Reed wanted in the room. I didn't know he was the president, and he didn't have a pass. I told him he couldn't come in."

"What'd he do?"

"He was cool. He thanked me for doing my job well, told me who he was and went in."

"I'll get him added to the list. Anything else?"

"A cop came to see Donny. I made him wait while I got Donny, and they left together."

"I'm going to get you a notebook, and I'd like you to keep track of anyone who wants in the room and doesn't have a pass."

Ian Reed waited near the bottom gates of the training course. He'd had a fast run and wanted to compare his time to Jeff Morley's. Jeff was good but not that good, and Ian intended to blast ahead of him in the standings. He leaned on his ski poles, taking a deep breath, coughing as the cold air entered his lungs.

Jeff should be coming down soon.

While Ian skied, his mind focused and was occupied with what his body needed to do. Standing here, unwanted thoughts of Nora bothered him. He couldn't be sure the kid was his. He couldn't be sure it wasn't. He didn't want a baby and hoped Nora had taken him seriously when he'd told her to leave him out of her mess.

He'd blown his season last year because of a stupid girl. At least

Nora wasn't the coach's daughter. Who'd believe her anyway? She wouldn't want anyone to know she'd cheated on McKenzie. If someone found out she was pregnant and the baby wasn't his, they'd suspect Jeff was the father. He was always sniffing around her. A person would have to be blind to miss how bad he had it for Nora. But what if the baby was Ian's?

Jeff flew through the finish line and slammed to a stop beside Ian. His smug expression told Ian he'd had a fast run. Ian had dreamt of being an Olympic athlete since he was eight years old. He started skiing at six, and by fifteen, he was part of the Alpine Canada regional junior elite program. At seventeen, he'd been accepted into the national development program. He was old enough now for a shot at the World Cup team. He'd blown last year and wasn't going to let that happen this year. He'd train harder, make himself better, whatever he needed to do. He planned to own the NorAms this season.

"Did you get your time yet?" Jeff asked.

"Nope. I was watching you ski."

Jeff glanced sideways at Ian.

"Maybe I'll learn something," Ian said. "Come on, let's go up. We've got time for another run before the employees get the hill."

They skated to the lift entrance, showed their passes and plunked on the chair. Leg cramps and cold muscles would increase their times and both accepted the blanket the liftie offered.

Cold seeped from the chair into Ian's Spyder suit, and he shifted his lower back off the seat. He wished they'd had a chance to see their times. He'd give the next run everything he had. Jeff wouldn't know what hit him. Ian was the better skier. This was just an off day.

"So does Donny tune your skis?" Ian asked.

"Yeah. Why?"

"I've never seen your gear in the tuning room. I figured he tuned them at home."

"We've got a sweet set up in our garage."

"Doesn't it bother him?"

"Tuning my skis?"

The chair rumbled by a lift tower, and snow dropped onto Ian's blanket. He knocked the clump off his leg. "I'd think it would be hard."

"The accident happened a long time ago. He decided he wanted to tune skis."

Ian continued rattling Jeff, hoping for an advantage. "Just seems like it might bother him, you skiing on the team when he was better than you."

"Donny isn't like that."

"Maybe Donny wanted McKenzie off the team. Give you a better chance. Ever think of that?"

"Fuck you. Maybe you killed McKenzie. You weren't good enough to get a spot, and the day after you're on the team, McKenzie gets murdered."

"Maybe Donny finally had enough of McKenzie and offed him. He must have hated the guy."

"You're an asshole."

Ian ignored Jeff and tried a different angle. "How come Donny doesn't ski? That sit-ski must have been expensive."

The chair bounced into the unloading station.

"Back off." Jeff pushed off the chair and skied down the exit ramp toward the training gates.

Amber stood beside the tuning room waiting for the tuners to return from lunch. She'd learned each tuner's habits. At the start of the day, Charlie was usually the first one in, followed shortly by the rest of the tuners. He ate lunch in the tuning room, paper bagging his meal. The others ate in the cafeteria. Amber memorized every tuner's name and chatted with as many of them as she could, mentioning she had tuning experience. She'd get a tuning job somehow. No matter what others at the resort thought about her, she'd prove she was good enough.

She sipped hot chocolate and licked whipped cream off the edge of the Styrofoam cup. The aroma of cocoa always reminded her of skiing with her mom. The squeak of wheels on the laminate flooring announced Donny's arrival. She lowered the zipper of her pink fleece top.

"Hey." His eyes seemed to see right into her. Why did men always have long lashes and women needed makeup to get the same look? She rubbed under her eye, wiping away a mascara smudge that wasn't there, and tugged at her bangs as if she could make them straighter with her fingers.

"How was lunch?" She was so not cool.

"The usual." Donny shrugged. "I'm not a big buffet fan. Didn't you get a break?"

"Not yet. I hope Kalin comes soon. I'm starving."

Donny pulled an energy bar from his pocket and offered it to her. She didn't like them. They tasted like cardboard flakes, but she accepted the snack, leaning forward to give him a better view. "How's the tuning going this morning?"

Donny's eyes didn't stray below her neckline. "You ask a lot about tuning. You interested?"

Amber livened. Most guys were attracted to her body, but she was picking up a vibe that Donny was different, and she might have to try harder to get his attention. If they spent time tuning together, they'd have something in common. "I wanted to tune at the rental shop but didn't get the job. Not enough experience. Maybe you could teach me?"

"Not during race training. But after maybe."

"Great. How long have you been a tuner?"

"My Aunt Lisa taught me after…well, since I've been in this chair. Are you going to ski during the employee session?"

"I wish. I gotta stay here." Amber bit the corner of her lip and tasted strawberry lip gloss. "Can I ask you something?"

"Sure."

"How come you don't use the sit-ski?" Amber had noticed the ski designed for a paraplegic in the back of Donny's van but had never seen him use the equipment.

Donny lifted his eyebrows and held eye contact with Amber. "People don't usually have the guts to ask me that."

"Oh…I didn't mean to be rude, but don't you miss skiing?"

A gentle smile eased across his face. "I didn't used to. I mean I try not to think about what I've lost, but this week I've been wondering if maybe I should try." Donny watched snow fall outside, and Amber watched Donny. The blond stubble on his angular jaw countered the soft bangs swooping across his forehead, but his eyes are what drew her to him.

"Maybe I could help you." *Because I know so much about using a sit-ski. Not.* "I'll trade you that for tuning lessons."

"I'll think about it. I'm not sure who's getting the better deal, though." Donny wheeled toward the tuning room, leaving her to mull that over.

"Dude, I need to scan your pass."

CHAPTER SIXTEEN

Kalin wanted to forget about the murder for a couple of hours and met Ben at the edge of the maze gates at the entrance to the Alpine Tracks chair lift. About thirty employees hung in the area waiting for the go ahead from the liftie. Every few days during race training, the employees were given an hour to ski along the edge of the run. With the center injected, and set for racing conditions, the surface was too dangerous for non-racers. Kalin listened to the lively chatter and laughter. This was a good day.

Getting to ski before the season opened was a perk Kalin used for recruiting, and she made Ben wait with her until the last employee sat on the lift. Ben and Kalin snagged a four-person chair to themselves and snuggled in the middle.

"You sure you feel well enough to ski?" Ben asked.

"I told you, I'm not sick."

"You are too. You're just taking enough cough medicine to hide it."

"I am not, so stop bugging me."

Ben put his arm around Kalin's puffy ski jacket and pulled her closer. "Did you hear Reed has decided to stop injecting the run? Last night was the last time."

"I was in the tuning room when he told the German coach. The guy was pissed. He said Reed had no right."

"What's the point of stopping the injection? Dangerous conditions didn't kill McKenzie."

"Reed said he didn't want the liability." Kalin clanked her ski boots together, eager to get skiing. "Too much scandal already, I guess."

Kalin and Ben disembarked and skied through a mogul field along the side of the run. Her knees compressed and decompressed as she attacked each mogul. She expertly followed Ben, turn for turn, and suspected he skied hard just to compete with her. He zagged off the run and into the trees. *If he thinks he can lose me that way, he's mistaken.*

She kept right on the back of his skis, inches from him, hooting to keep the pressure on. He turned back onto the run and tucked the flats to the bottom. She reached the maze a second behind him, out of breath and exhilarated.

"My boot's bugging me," she said between deep breaths.

"It's probably not adjusted right. Let me see."

Ben bent and pulled the leg of Kalin's ski pants above the top of her boot. His hands were warm on her calf, and she felt heat rise through her belly. The memory of him naked beside her that morning was fresh. *Jeez, control yourself.*

Ben tugged at the top of her sock. "Your sock's bunched up in your boot. You need them smooth or the ridges will give you a bruise."

"I know that," Kalin said, adding a bit of sass to her voice.

Ben raised one eyebrow at her. "And what? You forgot how to get dressed?"

Kalin nudged his shoulder, pretending to push him off balance. "I was distracted."

"Yeah. You were."

With one foot connected to her snowboard and the other pushing against the ground, Nora did the snowboard shuffle to Kalin's side. "Yo, can I go up with you? Or do you want to be alone with the hot guy?"

The chair clanged around the bull wheel and into the loading station. Without waiting for an answer, Nora joined them on the chair.

Ben leaned around Kalin, resting his forearms on the safety bar, and spoke to Nora. "How are you guys doing with Ian race training instead of tuning?"

Nora's face reddened, and Kalin wasn't sure if it was from the cold or from Ben referring to Ian.

"We're doing okay. It helps to be busy."

Ben's phone jingled. He handed one glove to Kalin and shifted his hip sideways to get the phone from his pocket. Their helmets thudded against each other.

Kalin slid closer to Nora to give Ben space, and while he spoke on the phone, she said to Nora, "How are you?"

"I'm okay. It's just that…I can't believe he's gone."

"Me neither." Kalin checked out Nora's stomach. "I'm glad you came out, but should you be snowboarding?"

Nora banged her board against Kalin's ski. "Shush."

"He can't hear us, and he doesn't know."

Nora squeezed Kalin's wrist. "Thanks."

"If you need us, you can come over any time. You know that, right?"

"I do."

"What do you think of the scanning process?"

"It keeps people out of the room. Without interruptions, we have more time to focus on what we're doing. I kinda like it, but every time I see Amber, I feel like gagging. Donny's been a bit off his game. I've had to redo a couple of skis before Charlie noticed there was a problem with them. And you should see the way Amber flirts with Donny. What a slut. He's way too good for her."

Donny was like a little brother to Nora, not just a cousin, and her natural instinct would be to protect him. Funny Donny said Nora was off her game too. "What's wrong with Donny?" Kalin asked.

"I don't know. He seems freaked by Steve's death. He keeps asking if the cops suspect anyone. Like I'm going to tell him they suspect me."

Suspects. People Kalin knew were actual suspects. She pinched her nose between her thumb and index finger. Her elbow rested on the conference table in the security office. She hadn't had time to eat after the employee ski session, and her stomach growled, telling her she was ready for dinner. Food would have to wait. "I'm not sure what to do next."

"Are you asking for suggestions?" Fred asked.

"I am. Reed wants me to figure out how someone accessed McKenzie's gear. Constable Miller doesn't want me interfering with the investigation." Kalin wanted Fred to understand the difficult position she'd been in. That she had a boss too. The security team hadn't been compromised by Reed's decision to give Jenkinson and McKenzie special treatment. Something much worse had happened. "What would you have done?"

"Pardon?"

"If Reed asked you instead of me to give special treatment to someone."

"I wouldn't have agreed."

"Are you sure?"

"I'm sure." Fred paced in front of the table. His black leather boots creaked with each step. "Let's make some lists. Who had access to the tuning room? When was there an opportunity to access McKenzie's gear?"

"I'd like you to print a list of everyone that's been in the tuning room since we started controlling entry." Kalin craned her neck to keep him in her sights. "Can you stop pacing? You're making me dizzy."

"Sorry." Fred sat across from her. "I'm not sure what that list would tell us."

"I don't know, but I thought we should at least know who the people are. It'd be interesting to see if there's anyone who should have access now that's staying away from the room."

Fred went to his computer, pulled up the list and hit print. While the printer hummed, he said, "What about motive? Any ideas?" He grabbed a marker and went to the empty Be-On-The-Lookout list.

Kalin stretched her tired quads. Every year she promised herself she'd be fit for early season skiing, and every year she ended up sore. Maybe next year. She thought about Fred's question and said, "Let's start with the obvious. Donny Morley."

Fred wrote Donny's name at the top of the list. "I'm not sure he's obvious. The accident was three years ago. If Donny was going to kill McKenzie, you'd think he would have attempted something before now."

"What about someone who didn't want McKenzie racing?"

"Jeff Morley was the second fastest skier. At least until Ian Reed got on the team. What do you think about him?" Fred wrote Jeff's name on the board.

"I don't know him well enough to have an opinion, but I guess he has a motive. Maybe the combination of McKenzie being the faster skier, dating Nora and hurting Donny was too much for him." Kalin thought about Nora. Would McKenzie abandoning her when he found out she was pregnant be motive enough? Could she have lost control? Kalin didn't feel right telling Fred about Nora's pregnancy.

"Rumor has it McKenzie split with Nora the night before he died. Maybe she killed him." Fred wrote Nora's name below Jeff's.

"I've seen her angry, but enough of a temper to lose control and commit murder? I don't think so." Kalin remembered Nora's face when she'd been arguing with Ian. Maybe Ian had hit on Nora to get at McKenzie. "What about Ian Reed? He wanted a spot on the team, and he must be under pressure from his dad to perform. I can't imagine Reed was too happy when Ian didn't make the first cut. Pretty embarrassing to be the president with a son not making the local team."

"I called a friend in Fernie and asked about Ian. He told me Ian was kicked off the Fernie team mid-season last year," Fred said.

"Did he say why?"

"He said it's gossip, but the rumor is Ian got the coach's daughter pregnant and dumped her."

Kalin wasn't going to tell Nora this. "Nice. Did she keep the baby?"

"No baby was ever seen. Everyone assumed she had an abortion. Ian missed half the season because the coach wouldn't let him ski again. The coach happens to be Coach Jenkinson's brother-in-law."

"Maybe he's desperate this season. So this is gossip too, but I heard McKenzie slept with Amber Cristelli while he was dating Nora. That might give Amber motive."

"Or Nora." Fred wrote Ian and Amber's names underneath Nora's.

Kalin hadn't meant to put more focus on Nora, just the opposite actually. "There's also Charlie Whittle, the head tuner. He had access and knowledge, but I don't know what his motive would be."

"We can't forget Ben. He'd been giving McKenzie a hard time." Fred added Charlie and Ben to the list.

Kalin tried not to be annoyed by his comment, but the emotion was hard to suppress, and her voice came out harsher than she wanted. "You can't be serious. You know Ben."

"I don't really think Ben's the guilty one, but the list needs to be complete."

Kalin let Fred's insult pass, not wanting to insert another wedge into their already tense relationship. "There are also the other ski teams. That seems a bit off the mark but possible. Have you talked with Miller since you gave him the video?"

"No. He's gone quiet. I don't know what the RCMP are up to."

"There's always the possibility they're investigating someone we haven't thought of."

Fred picked up the list from the printer, and together they examined the names of everyone who'd been in the tuning room since McKenzie's death.

Kalin shoved the papers away, and they slid across the table. "This tells us nothing."

By the time they finished talking, darkness had descended, and Kalin grabbed her headlamp from her backpack. On her way out, she curbed the temptation to erase Ben's name from the list.

Kalin arrived home and found Chica alone and prancing to get outside. Her meeting with Fred had gone longer than expected, but Ben should've been home to take care of Chica. The Goddess crept into

Kalin's thoughts and she pushed her out. No way was Ben with her.

Chica raced through the door, brushing Kalin aside, and squatted in the nearest snow. Kalin wanted to crawl into bed and nurse her cold but instead reached inside and snagged Chica's leash. "Let's go."

Chica wiggled her body and wagged her tail with genuine dog exuberance, and Kalin clipped the leash onto her collar.

She trudged through the snow, sticking to the tire tracks to make walking easier. Her phone rang four times by the time she fumbled it out of her jacket pocket.

"Constable Miller here."

"What's up?"

"I need to ask you where you were from four p.m. the day before Steve McKenzie was murdered until the next morning when he got on the hill."

Kalin stopped walking. "Am I a suspect?"

"I'm just trying to place everyone."

"I worked until five thirty. I was with Monica Bellman until we closed the HR office. I walked home. Ben and I took our dog for a walk and then spent the night in. I was at work by eight thirty the next morning."

"Okay. Have you spoken to Ben this afternoon?"

"No. He's not home yet. Why?"

"No reason. Thanks."

Weird. She shoved her phone back into her pocket.

Half an hour later, she stood in the empty driveway. Ben still wasn't home. She called his cell but got voicemail. She texted him and waited. A set of headlights approached, illuminating snowflakes that lazily floated to the ground. The circles of two headlights grew and lit Kalin as they turned by her and into her driveway.

Before Ben got out of the truck, Chica jumped over him and into the passenger seat. "Think she wants to go somewhere?"

Kalin laughed but saw Ben's serious expression. "What's wrong?"

He pulled Chica by the collar and dragged her out of the front seat. "I'll tell you when we're inside."

Ben kicked off his winter boots and left them to drip melting snow in the front hall. He headed straight for the fridge and grabbed a beer. "Want one?"

"Sure. Give me your jacket." Kalin held out her hand to Ben and hung both of their coats.

Before joining Kalin on the couch, Ben shoved a couple of logs into the fireplace and lit the kindling.

"What's going on?" Kalin asked.

"Miller interviewed me today."

"What for?"

"McKenzie's murder."

"That's why Miller called me. He wanted to know where I was from the afternoon before McKenzie died until he fell. At least you know Miller."

"It didn't feel that way."

"I can imagine. He can really go into cop mode. What did he ask you?"

"For fingerprints."

"You were fingerprinted?"

"He said he needed to check my prints against the prints on McKenzie's skis. He also wanted an alibi. I guess you already corroborated it. He probably called you just as I left the RCMP headquarters. I called you a couple of times but got your voicemail."

"I was with Fred. Did you tell Miller what we were doing?" she asked, teasing him, trying to lighten the mood. She warmed at the memory of the evening they'd spent in front of the fire.

"As if. I said we walked Chica after work and then spent the night here. I had to give a timeline of the morning. What time we got up. How long it took me to get to work. Who saw me arrive at work. Lucky for me, William was in when I got there."

"Why do you think he wanted to know all that?"

Ben inhaled sharply.

"Sorry. Stupid question. It's because of the incident with McKenzie at the lift. Fred mentioned it today too."

"Shit. How many people think I killed McKenzie?"

Tension exuded from Ben, and Kalin wished she hadn't mentioned Fred. "I can't imagine anyone believes you're the murderer. Maybe Fred said you're a suspect just to bug me."

CHAPTER SEVENTEEN

"You better come in to the security office," Fred said.

Kalin lifted her phone off the bedside table and checked the time. Seven a.m. "What's going on?"

"Bar fight last night. Some of the racers were involved. Two spent the night in jail. We'll have to decide what to do next."

"Okay. Give me fifteen minutes." Her head ached, and she barely had enough energy to stand, let alone go to work, but in spite of that, she shoved herself upright. *Move your ass, Miss Mini Police Chief.* "What are the roads like?"

"Ugly. The plows haven't been by yet."

Kalin decided she needed to look serious and put on dark blue pants with a matching blouse and topped the outfit with a tailored jacket. She threw on her ski jacket, chose her dressy winter boots and grabbed a set of keys.

Her Jeep was in the garage, and it was faster to take Ben's truck from the driveway. She wasted several minutes scraping snow off the red Ford F-150 but arrived at Fred's office within the promised fifteen minutes.

She blustered into the security office and shook snow off her head. "You left Ben's name on the board." She hung her ski jacket behind the door and ran her fingers through her damp hair.

"I left all the names," Fred said.

Kalin put both hands on her hips. "Ben has an alibi."

"I suppose that's you." Fred smiled, taking the sting out of his words. "Oh relax. I told you I don't think Ben killed McKenzie." He wiped Ben's name off the board.

"So what's going on?"

"Jeff Morley and one of the racers from the German team were arrested. There was a brawl in the bar. We don't have too much time before they get here. I've asked to speak to both of them."

"How come only two were arrested?"

"When the cops arrived, everyone else settled down. One cop pulled Morley off the German guy, and Morley hit the cop. The German took Morley's side and pushed the cop. That's enough for them to spend the night in jail."

"I'm guessing they were both drunk."

"They were."

"Does their behavior warrant banning them?"

"You didn't ban McKenzie when he pushed Amber. I don't see how you can ban these guys."

Touché. "They were fighting with cops."

Fred took a deep breath. "And McKenzie shoved an employee."

A knock on the door interrupted them. Constable Miller stuck his head in. "Morning. I have your two friends waiting in the car. Do you want me to bring them in?"

"Sure. Thanks," Fred said.

Kalin pointed to the BOLO list. "You better erase the rest of the names."

Miller escorted two sullen men into the room and motioned to the empty seats across from Kalin. "Sit here and be polite." He turned to Fred. "You need me here for this?"

"I don't think so," Fred said.

Kalin recognized the top German skier and was awed to be in the presence of an Olympic medalist. Reminding herself not to be a star struck groupie, she examined the men and kept her breathing shallow. Day old sweat and stale beer were the fragrances of choice. When they were alone, with the door closed for privacy, Kalin resisted the urge to open a window and directed her first question to Jeff. "What happened last night?"

"This guy hit me for no reason."

"Das ist nicht…That is not true," Edwin Bucher said. "He hit me first."

Kalin recorded their comments in her notebook. Jeff had a bruise under his left eye, and his shirt was ripped and dirty. Edwin was in about the same condition, except his bruise covered his entire right cheek. For a young man, he didn't have a lot of hair, and his large forehead shined with sweat droplets. His small mouth and thin lips weren't in proportion to the rest of his face. "This isn't going to work if you don't cooperate. Fred and I have to decide what to do with you, and we can't do that if you don't help us."

"What do you mean?" Jeff asked.

"Normally you'd get banned from the resort."

"You cannot ban us. We need to train," Edwin said.

Edwin spoke in a formal manner, and Kalin realized it was the way he spoke English as a second language. Maybe he wasn't nervous at all.

"Then you two better tell us what happened." Fred wore his poker face, and Kalin could see he was in no mood for crap.

"Well?" Kalin said to Jeff.

Jeff swallowed twice and cleared his throat. "He insulted my brother, and we got into an argument."

"What did he say?"

"He called Donny a cripple and said he couldn't possibly tune skis. That's why I'd never win a race."

"Is that true?" Kalin asked.

Edwin had the grace to blush before he nodded.

"Is there a reason you said that?"

Edwin jerked his head in Jeff's direction. "I wanted to get in his skin."

Kalin suppressed a smile at the slip in English. "Then what happened?"

"He hit me. He got so angry. He exploded on me."

"Did you hit him first?" Kalin asked Jeff.

"I lost my temper. It's no big deal."

"I think it is." Kalin pointed to Edwin's face. "You could've broken his cheekbone."

"It is not broken," Edwin said. "I provoked him."

"So this is a competitive thing?" Kalin asked.

Both men nodded.

"It couldn't have been fun spending a night in jail."

Both men shook their heads.

"You're both going to get a warning. I'm not going to ban you, but, and I mean this, any more trouble and I will. Understood?" She glanced at Fred, who remained expressionless. She wasn't sure if she passed or failed his test.

"Yes."

"Yes."

Edwin stood and disappeared in seconds. Jeff hovered.

Fred got up, opened a window and leaned against the sill. His sharp eyes watched Jeff carefully. "Is there something else?"

"My dad can't find out about this."

Odd a man his age would worry enough about what his dad thought and ask for them to be discreet. "We won't tell him, if that's what you're asking," Kalin said.

"I'm asking if there's any way to keep this quiet. You don't know my dad, but he won't deal well with this."

"How are you going to hide the bruise on your face?"

"I'm not. I'll tell him I was in a fight that I won but not about jail. He thinks I spent last night with a girl."

Kalin and Nora collected their meals from the buffet in the cafeteria. Kalin led Nora to an isolated corner, thinking about her morning talk with Jeff Morley. They were early. Not many of the racers had come in from the mountain yet, which gave them a bit of time to talk privately.

"Do you ever tune Jeff's skis?"

"Not usually, why?"

"I'm just trying to figure out how the tuning works for the team."

"Donny tunes Jeff's skis at home. They have a sweet setup in their garage."

Nora seemed agitated, and Kalin didn't want to put any more pressure on her. She'd validated what Donny said about tuning Jeff's skis. No lying yet. She changed the subject. "How are you holding up?"

"I miss Steve. I know we'd broken up, and I was angry with him, but I thought he'd come around. I surprised him. That's all. Now we'll never have the chance."

Kalin empathized when Nora's eyes filled with tears. She knew from experience how much losing someone she loved hurt. "Have you talked with Ian again?"

"It's hard. He won't speak to me. Every time I try, he walks away."

"Are you sure the baby is his?"

Nora poked at her chili with her spoon but didn't eat any. "I'm still hoping Steve's the father."

"Did Ian ever say anything to you about Steve?"

"We didn't talk much. It was one stupid fuck. Nothing more."

Kalin was tempted to tell Nora about Fernie and what Ian had done, but she didn't have the heart. Instead, she said, "Did you ever talk when you tuned skis together?"

"Not about anything important. Ian talks about skiing. Nothing else seems to matter to him."

Steam rose from Kalin's cauliflower soup, and she dipped a buttered slice of bread, soaking it with flavor. Her mouth watered from the aroma before she tasted her food. "He must have talked about Steve a bit."

"Well, yeah. We only talked while we were tuning skis, and he talked about everyone on the team. He knew every skier's times, where they ranked, what conditions they skied best in."

"He didn't talk about Steve more than the others?"

"Everyone talked about Steve more than the other skiers. He was the best."

"How do the racers pick which skis they'll use each day?" Kalin asked.

"That depends on the type of race they're training for and what the conditions are."

"Do they make the decision on their own?"

"Sometimes. Each skier is different. Also, Coach Jenkinson didn't have the same amount of interest in all the racers."

Kalin noticed Nora hadn't taken a bite of her chili yet. She was too busy stirring her meal and answering Kalin's questions. "You don't like the chili?"

"It's not that. The smell is making me nauseous."

"Do you want my bread?" Kalin passed the uneaten slices to Nora. "What about Steve? How did he decide?"

"Jenkinson, Charlie and Steve usually talked about it the night before training. Then I'd be given instructions." Nora nibbled at the bread.

"How would someone know which skis to tamper with? From what I understand, only one pair was touched."

"There's a system. One rack is for skis that are first up. A racer's other pairs are kept in a second rack. The skiers take their skis from the first one."

Kalin still didn't understand how a person could know which skis to tamper with. "Who sets up the rack?"

"Charlie. He's the only one who knows what all the racers want. The rest of the tuners do what he says."

Kalin slurped her soup and burnt her tongue. She ignored the burning sensation and thought about Charlie. He kept coming up as a suspect, but she knew little about him. "Did Charlie have anything against Steve?"

Nora snorted. "Not that I know of. If there was something, I can't imagine what."

"Ian would have known which skis Steve was going to use."

"It's not hard. They're labeled." Nora lifted a spoonful of chili as if she were going to eat but put the spoon back down again. "You really think Ian killed Steve?"

"Maybe."

"He's a jerk, but killing Steve just to ski?"

Ian and Jeff sauntered through the sliding glass doors into the cafeteria. Jeff glanced Kalin's way, with a hangdog grin clear on his face, and she couldn't help but smile back. Despite the fight he'd had with the German skier, she liked him. She liked his brother, Donny, too. For Nora's sake, she hoped one of them didn't kill Steve.

Ian hustled toward the buffet table and weaseled his way in front of other skiers. His posture appeared orchestrated to ensure Nora couldn't catch his eye.

Kalin pointed toward him. "There's Ian now."

"See what I mean. He's avoiding me."

"Is he friends with Jeff?"

"I don't think so."

"You should eat that instead of making circles in it with your spoon."

Nora filled her spoon and ate but never took her angry eyes off Ian.

Nora stomped back to the tuning room, thinking about Jeff. She'd dated him for three years. Why had he kissed someone else so soon after she'd first slept with him? She should have forgiven him. Maybe if she had, Donny wouldn't have ended up paralyzed and Rachel wouldn't be dead. She thought back to the dreadful night of the accident and to one moment when she could have changed everything.

She'd been standing on the back porch at a house party, and Jeff had cornered her. His face was too close to hers, and his breath smelled sour.

"It was one stupid mistake. That's all," Jeff said.

Nora stepped away from him, and the small of her back pressed against the wooden deck railing. "You cheated on me."

Jeff gripped the railing on either side of her, removing any distance she'd put between them. "I know, but—"

"There's no *but*. I told you we're done."

Donny cleared his throat. "Hey, Jeff. Can I get a ride home?" Donny looked at Nora with sympathetic eyes. Being the good guy, he was trying to help her out.

"Sure. In a bit." Jeff stormed through the patio doors and disappeared in a throng of partiers.

For half an hour Nora pretended to socialize. Anything to keep her mind off Jeff. Steve and her adoptive sister, Rachel, were at the front door getting ready to leave, and she approached them to say bye. She had the feeling Rachel had been crying but couldn't ask in front of everyone. Rachel's sandy blonde hair was pulled into a ponytail, making her eyes look tight. Nora gave her a quick hug, and with the height difference, her nose stuck in Rachel's armpit.

Donny interrupted them. "You seen Jeff? I was going to catch a ride with him."

"Nope," Rachel said.

"You guys leaving? Can you drop me at home?" Donny asked.

Steve hesitated.

Donny lightly shoved Steve's shoulder in a gesture of camaraderie. "Come on. It's not out of your way."

"Fine." Steve opened the front door and stepped outside. Donny followed Rachel off the front porch and into darkness. It was the last time Nora had seen him walking.

Why hadn't she offered Donny a ride instead of trying to find Jeff? If only…

CHAPTER EIGHTEEN

At two fifty-nine, Kalin entered Reed's outer office. Her nerves bit at her from all sides. Facing her boss and telling him his son was on her suspect list was not part of her job description, but she'd have to go that far. She just didn't want to. "Is he ready to see me?"

Without pausing her tapping on the keyboard, Gertrude pointed with the top of her beehive hairdo toward Reed's door. "Go on in. He's waiting for you."

Reed sat on one side of the table. He wore ski pants, ski boots and a ski sweater. His cheeks were flushed from recent outdoor activity, and Kalin gathered he'd been checking out the training run. She knew Reed liked to ski fast and liked to be on top of the run conditions.

He pointed toward the chair opposite him. "Sit."

Kalin wondered if she should give him a paw too but did as he instructed.

"Have you cleaned out Tom's office yet?"

Kalin had avoided his office since he died. She knew eventually she'd have to face clearing out his desk and file cabinets, but his memory was too fresh. "No."

"I'd like you to do that. You can stay in your own office or move to his, but we need the space. Did you bring an update with you?"

"I did." She handed Reed two sheets of freshly printed paper. If he noticed the shaking pages, he'd know her nerves weren't under control. "The first page outlines the actions I've taken since we last spoke. The second page is a list of possible suspects."

Reed placed the papers on the table and didn't glance at them.

"Have you spoken to the RCMP?"

"Only about some of what's written there." Kalin pointed to the papers. She'd spent the last hour and a half working on the report, making sure the contents were perfect, and Reed dismissed it as if it were a wad of chewed gum.

"Is there anything you've talked about with the RCMP that's not in your report?"

"Constable Miller asked me for my whereabouts from the afternoon before McKenzie died until he was on the hill the next morning."

"Why isn't that in your report?"

"I didn't think it was relevant. He said he was placing everyone, making sure all stories lined up."

Reed flattened his palms on the table and leaned forward. "That's unacceptable. I expect to be informed about every interaction you have with the RCMP."

Taking his time, Reed read the suspect list. "You haven't included Ben's name."

"He's not a suspect."

Reed eyed Kalin with what she interpreted as suspicion. "I spoke with Miller. He has him on his list."

Kalin jiggled her knees up and down. Where was the conversation going? "When?"

"When did I speak to Miller? Meaning before or after you did?"

"I'm hoping it was before." Kalin shouldn't have been surprised he knew about Miller's call. "Ben has an alibi."

"An alibi from his girlfriend. Now, let's talk about the other elephant in the room."

Kalin picked up her pen, put it down again, shifted in her seat. Reed was going to wait for her to speak. That's twice someone pointed out she was Ben's alibi. She was in a position to prove Ben's innocence, and the way to end the speculation was to figure out who killed McKenzie.

"Ian is your son. I couldn't take him off the list just because of that."

"Yet you took Ben off because he's your boyfriend. What reason would Ian have to kill McKenzie?"

"Well, he did want on the team." And he tried to get at McKenzie by sleeping with Nora. Maybe when that didn't work out, he went one drastic step farther.

Reed laughed. "Is that all?"

"Yes. But—"

"But nothing. Do you know how many kids want on a team? They don't kill someone to get a spot. I think you can remove his name."

Kalin figured she'd get one shot to discuss Ian with Reed. "Did Constable Miller ask you about Ian?"

"Of course he did. He agrees Ian's not a suspect."

Reed's eyes darted from Kalin's, only for a second, and she knew he lied.

"I don't want to see Ian's name printed anywhere. I'm the president of this resort. I can't have it out there that my son is a suspect."

Kalin would keep her own list and one for Reed. Miller wouldn't reveal any information she gave him, and Reed couldn't control her interaction with the RCMP. The wild thought that her boss could be the murderer struck her. Maybe he'd wanted his son on the team badly enough to do something about it. *And maybe I'm crazy.*

"Now let's talk about the others. Why is Nora on the list?"

Kalin hated talking about Nora, but she couldn't pretend Nora wasn't a suspect. Reed probably already knew the answer to his question and was testing her. "She and McKenzie broke up the night before he died."

"A crime of passion?"

"I don't know. I can't believe it was her. Nora's fiery but angry enough to kill McKenzie? I think the murder was premeditated."

"Why do you say that?"

"First the person had to know how to tamper with a binding without anyone noticing. Then he or she had to access the binding and alter the DIN setting. It's not like someone in a rage would do that. I think a person carefully thought about a way to get at McKenzie. Maybe the goal was to injure him, not to kill him."

"Interesting. You do realize Nora had knowledge and access. The RCMP has a witness who saw Nora running from McKenzie's place the night before he died. The witness said she yelled 'I won't let you off the hook.'"

Kalin didn't want to admit Nora was a serious suspect, but the words sounded incriminating. Doubt crept into her mind and she shook it off. "She was angry, but that doesn't mean she killed him."

"So who else?"

"Charlie had access, but I have no idea what his motive would have been. I've listed everyone on the team along with the top skiers from the other teams and all the tuners. Donny Morley, for obvious reasons. Jeff Morley held the number two spot on the Holden team until Ian joined, and he has a temper." *And McKenzie was dating his high school sweetheart.*

"Jeff's a possibility. I read the security report. Jeff could have picked a fight with Edwin Bucher to stop him from competing in the upcoming season. I believe Bucher is the fastest German skier."

Kalin and Fred entered Tom Bennett's office. She had to organize his belongings but felt as if she were invading his privacy. He'd left his security jacket hanging on the back of his door. His winter boots stood in the corner. His skis and poles hung from hooks. Except for the musty smell, the office gave the impression of a man thinking he'd return and go on with his life. *Get a grip.*

Tom's office was in the back of the mountain operations building and too far from the busy action of the administration building, so she decided to stay in her HR office, close to her HR team. She asked Fred to help her go through Tom's office and determine what she needed to keep, what Fred needed and what they should shred.

She rested her ski jacket on the back of Tom's chair and sat. Her jeans slipped against the shiny wooden surface. Photos of his wife and people she assumed were his kids decorated the desk. She wiped dust from the desk's surface with her sleeve and shook her arm. The dust floated through a stream of sunlight coming through the office's single window.

"I guess we should collect his personal items. Do you want to give them to Ginny?" Kalin asked Fred.

"Thanks. I'd like to."

Kalin placed the photos into a cardboard box. She unlocked his top drawer and sifted through the contents. She found a pen engraved with Tom's name and added it to the box. She handed Fred a set of keys. "Here, these must be for the filing cabinets."

"I'll start a pile for shredding. Some of this stuff is in the security office files too."

Kalin called IT and asked for the password to Tom's computer. She turned on the computer and stared at the screen. She had no idea where to start. She called IT back, had them remove Tom's user-id from the security database and asked them to transfer the contents of his computer to hers.

She searched his desk. She pulled a sealed envelope from Tom's bottom drawer. *Charlie Whittle/Private* was written across the top. She held it up for Fred to see. "Should I open this?"

"You probably need to. Everything in this office is your responsibility now."

Kalin considered not opening the envelope until she was alone but decided to use the opportunity to prove to Fred she trusted him and they were a team. She slid her finger underneath the seal and let the contents fall to the surface of the desk.

"It looks like a traffic report from a month ago." Kalin read the document. "Does Charlie have a drinking problem?"

"He used to. His license was suspended about ten years ago. I think he stopped drinking then."

"This says he drove his car into a snow bank, and he had alcohol on his breath."

"Who signed the report?"

Kalin glanced at the bottom of the form. "Tom."

"Are there any witness statements?"

She flipped to the next page. "You won't believe this. There's one from Steve McKenzie. He saw Charlie driving erratically right before he hit the snow bank."

Fred held a file mid-way out of a cabinet drawer and waited.

"Why would Tom keep this sealed in his desk?" Kalin asked.

"Charlie and Tom were friends. Maybe he didn't want Charlie to get into trouble."

"Would McKenzie threaten Charlie with this?"

"I can't imagine why. Charlie was his head tuner. What would he have to gain?"

Kalin called Constable Miller and left him a message.

CHAPTER NINETEEN

"Hey, you awake?" Ben nudged Kalin with his elbow.

She squished her face into her pillow. "No."

"How can you answer if you're not awake?"

She moaned.

Ben leaned forward and kissed the back of her head. "I've got to be in early. I'll call you later." He felt bad about disturbing her when she was sick, but with what was going on he wanted her to know where he was.

After dressing in the dark, he slipped out the garage door. He started his truck, and the headlamps illuminated Chica, standing in the snow, staring at him expectantly. She must have snuck out with him, and he hadn't noticed. He returned her to the house and backed out of the driveway.

The avalanche forecaster had the day off and asked Ben to record the weather and snow conditions. Getting up at five was not Ben's idea of fun, but avalanche forecasting was cool. Besides, Ben wanted to be first choice for the manager role if his boss moved to Calgary, and in order to get promoted he'd have to show he could do more than patrol.

Ben parked his truck beside the mountain operations building, grabbed his gear bag from the back seat and hustled across the parking lot. The lights from the groomers flittered across several ski runs. The groomers were in the latter part of their shift and would finish the lower runs within the next hour. They pushed snow from the whales created by the snowmaking guns, flattening out the runs, prepping for opening day.

A group of people walked from the base of the Alpine Tracks run, heading toward the mountain operations building. The snowmakers were coming off shift. Other than the snowmaking manager, Jason Tober, Ben didn't see the crew often. They came to the mountain, worked the night shift and went home before the daytime employees arrived.

"Timlin. Sup?" Jason raised his fist, and the men gave each other props. Awkward considering the size of the canvas gloves Jason wore. His thick blue jacket hung midway down his thighs. The fur-lined flaps of his hat were tied underneath his chin. A face mask covered the bottom half of his face.

"Avi reports. Derek's off today. What's it like up there?"

"Cold."

"You going to be awake later? I'll be off in time to get in a few runs." Ben and Jason were good buddies, often skied together, and both loved the preseason runs. Because of his job, Jason always found the best snow.

"Yup. We can catch a ride with one of the groomers and hit the bowl. I'll call ya."

A light shining through the glass door of the administration building distracted them. The tuning room was across the foyer from that door, and it looked as if that's where the light came from.

"Did you see who that was?" Ben asked.

"Nope."

"That's weird." Ben left Jason and jogged to the administration building. A pile of snow prevented the lock on the exterior door from catching, and he entered. The door to the tuning room stood ajar. He held the door handle for a moment. *Chicken.*

Ben took a deep breath and entered the tuning room. Even this early, the room smelled of wax. He listened to the silence for a moment. Funny how eerie a room can be when it's empty, and it's pre-dawn, and no one should be in it, but maybe somebody was. "Anyone here?"

"I'm in the back. Come in."

Ben didn't recognize the voice. "Please come to the door."

Charlie emerged from the storage room, wiping his hands on a cloth. "Morning."

Ben stood close to the exit with his body tense.

Charlie scratched the birthmark on his head. "Is something wrong?"

"What are you doing here so early?"

"I had a date with my wife last night. I didn't finish the skis for today."

Without moving away from the door, Ben released the tension in his shoulders and calmed his breathing. Charlie seemed too relaxed to be a threat. "How did you get in?"

"I used my key."

Kalin was not going to like this. "You have a key to both doors?"

Kalin banged her palm against her forehead. She'd been stupid. Fred had been stupid. They'd missed an obvious security issue. She stomped to the resort's locksmith office, preparing her plan. First, she needed to find out who had keys.

Fred should have known about the keys issued to people. Had he forgotten? Did he purposely keep the information from her? Without Fred's cooperation, she might fail as director of security, and now that she was the mini police chief, she wanted to keep the job. She couldn't be a director if she was only responsible for HR.

Located in the basement of the same building that housed the front desk, the locksmith office contained a key-grinding machine. The keys to the hotel rooms were created using a card system, but the keys to the resort's offices and conference rooms hadn't been upgraded and still used metal keys. Kalin knew all this, but hadn't understood the implications. She dreaded telling Reed.

The locksmith was a crusty man in his mid to late fifties with a full head of frizzy hair, thick arms and an unfriendly demeanor. Kalin introduced herself. One quick nod and a grunt from him. *Nice.*

"I know who you are," Ted Brightman said in a husky smoker's voice. By the odor emanating from his person, Kalin figured he still smoked.

"I need a list of people who have keys to the tuning room."

The scowl on Ted's face deepened. "What for?"

"Surely you know what's been going on at the resort."

"I do."

"It's important the room is secure, and to secure it, first I need to know who has access."

Brightman rubbed his beard. "I can't tell you that."

Not the politest employee she'd met. Was he rude to everyone or just to her? She wanted control of the conversation and wasn't going to take any crap from him. "Can't or won't?"

Brightman eyed Kalin from where he sat. "I don't have a list."

"How can you not have a list? How are the keys issued?" *And how could Fred not be on top of this?*

"The locks haven't been changed for years. There's no point in a list."

"I'm not sure I get what you mean."

"Here's how it works. I get an email from a director authorizing me to issue a key. It's up to the director to get the key back when the person should no longer have it."

Kalin ignored his defensive manner and pushed for more information. "Where are the emails kept?"

"On my computer."

"How often do you delete them?"

"I don't. I just read them and do as I'm told."

"Okay, I can sort through your account and find any email asking for keys."

Brightman waved at his computer and slid his chair out of the way. "Do what you need."

Kalin clicked on his email icon. She sorted by title and scrolled to K, hoping to find anything with "key" in the title. She scanned hundreds of emails before stopping and realizing she needed a better plan. Some of the titles included information such as the room or door the key was required for. She glanced at other emails, some without titles and some with a key request buried in the middle of the text. This was going to take a while, and she didn't want Brightman watching her.

On the way back to her office, she called IT and told them what she needed. By the time she reached her computer, IT had given her access to Brightman's. She popped up his email on her screen.

First, she read the emails, checking for people who had access to the tuning room. She created a spreadsheet and entered the relevant data. She cross-referenced her list with names in the payroll system, flagging current and past employees. She expanded her list to people who had been issued keys to the building's exterior door. She bolded the names of people with keys to both doors. One of the names surprised her, and she wasn't sure how she felt.

Two hours slid by, and she was ready to discuss her findings with Fred. She called him and asked to meet in his office. She grabbed a printout of her list and headed his way.

Kalin stopped abruptly when she entered the security office. "How come you're so dirty?"

Fred's black pants were wet and covered with grit. His security jacket, spread on the back of a chair, had a water stain across the back and shoulders. "A guest had a flat. When I changed the tire for her, I slipped and got wet. I haven't had time to go home for dry clothes yet."

"That was nice. We missed something significant for securing the tuning room." She waited until she had his full attention before she continued. "We forgot about hard keys. Here." Kalin handed Fred her printout.

Fred glanced at the list. "Where did you get this?"

"I made it. I went through Brightman's email. I've bolded the names that could be an issue. Brightman doesn't keep track of the keys after he distributes them. I'm not sure what your relationship was with Tom, but I want to be clear on my expectations. I don't have his detailed knowledge. This is the type of information I need you to bring to my attention."

Fred's face reddened, and he kept his eyes lowered as he read the names. "I can't believe I didn't think of this. I'm sorry. We should get the locks changed and issue new keys. That'll secure the room for now. I'll talk with Brightman about getting a recording system in place. I didn't realize it was this bad."

"I hope there wasn't more to it. You can't be forgetting things like this. I know you're not happy about our situation, but you still have a job to do. Until we know who killed McKenzie or how his gear was accessed, you need to think about the tuning room security from every angle. I'll call Miller and give him an update. I want the locks changed by the end of today."

CHAPTER TWENTY

On her way back to her office, Kalin heard a helicopter thundering above the center of the resort. She jumped off the gondola and ran to the hillside. An air ambulance helicopter swooped into the air space above the resort, flew between the Alpine Tracks chair lift and the forest, and lowered over a team of people about three quarters of the way down the run. The chopper blew snow in all directions as it hovered a meter off the ground, nose dipped toward the surface and tail angled toward the sky.

At the base of the run, people grouped and took in the drama on the hill.

The chairs on the lift hung motionless, frozen in place.

Kalin watched the ski patrol team attend to the downed skier. By his posture, she knew it was Ben crouched face to face with the helicopter's nose. He held a skier's head stable. The skier lay in a rescue sled, and another patroller pulled a strap tight, preparing him for transport. Kalin felt pressure across her chest as the unsteady machine thrummed above Ben and the others.

Ben secured the sled to the side of the helicopter. He flattened to the ground and wrapped his arms over his head to ward off the snow pelting him. The chopper blew backward and took off. The thump of the blades echoed between mountain peaks, creating a thunderous noise.

Kalin waited for ski patrol to clear the area and ride down the hill. Ben stopped his snowmobile beside her. She rested her hand on his shoulder. His smile was all the reassurance she needed that he was fine. She resisted touching her lips to his. "What happened?"

"A German racer fell during his training run. He has no feeling in his legs. Might be temporary, but I don't think so."

"Who is it?"

"Edwin Bucher."

"Where are his skis?"

"One of the patrollers probably took them to mountain ops."

"Can you go secure them? I need to talk with Reed." Kalin took off running and raced toward Reed's office.

Kalin burst into her boss's office without asking Gertrude's permission. "There's been an accident."

Reed's expressionless face gave her no hint of what he was thinking.

"Edwin Bucher fell during his training run. Ben thinks he might be paralyzed."

"Slow down. Does he know that for sure?"

"No. Ben told me Edwin had no feeling in his legs."

"Where's Edwin now?"

"He's being airlifted, so I assume it's to Calgary."

"I need to speak with someone who saw the accident. Someone who works here, not someone from the ski team."

"I'll find out who did and send them here."

"Did Ben see him fall?"

"He treated Edwin, but I don't know if he saw the accident."

"I'll call the coach of the German team." Reed made a move to pick up his phone, but Kalin held her hand in the air, motioning him to stop. "There's something else."

Reed left his hand on the phone but didn't dial. Kalin explained the situation with the keys and the gap in her security process.

"Let's hope today was an accident. If not, your lapse in security might have made it possible for someone to access the tuning room."

Ouch, that hurt. If she'd banned Edwin for fighting in the bar instead of giving him a warning, he wouldn't have been skiing and he wouldn't have been injured. Banning him might have caused a media headache but nothing like his crash would.

Reed picked up his cell and had a discussion with the German coach.

Kalin gripped the back edge of a chair to keep her hands still and waited. Her breathing had almost returned to normal.

"That was interesting," Reed said. "The German coach is blaming Jeff Morley for Edwin's accident. He said the fight they had wasn't the first one. Last year, after a race at Lake Louise, Jeff and Edwin got into a shoving match. Jeff fell, broke his wrist and missed some key races. Maybe he's carrying a grudge. Have you already called the RCMP?"

"No. I wanted to speak with you first."

"Call them right away. If today wasn't an accident, Jeff Morley could be the guy."

Kalin returned to her office and called Miller. This wasn't a conversation she wanted anyone to overhear. A portable heater rested in the corner. She turned the knob to high, waited for the rush of hot air and put her hands over the vents. The little heater competed with the draft sneaking through a crack in the window frame. Miller answered on the third ring, and Kalin updated him on the situation.

"The racer was Edwin Bucher." Kalin wanted Edwin's crash deemed an accident. Otherwise, someone was out and about killing skiers.

"How is he?"

"You can probably find out faster than we can," Kalin said. "I think he's on his way to Calgary. Ben said he had no feeling in his legs."

"Did Ben treat him?"

"He was first on scene."

"The same as with McKenzie."

Kalin's pulse raced. She refused to believe Miller considered Ben a suspect. "What are you saying?"

"Nothing. Just thinking aloud. Did he see any similarities?"

"He didn't say. Are you going to question Jeff Morley?"

"Why would you ask that?"

"Because of the fight with Edwin. Maybe—"

"Maybe nothing. You're jumping to conclusions. There's nothing yet to indicate today was anything more than an accident."

Kalin allowed herself a small smile at his conservative policeman approach. He wouldn't speculate with her. "Are you going to check out Edwin's equipment?"

"Of course. Where is it now?"

"I asked Ben to secure his skis in the mountain ops building."

Miller's sigh expressed his displeasure.

CHAPTER TWENTY-ONE

The section of the room allocated to the German tuning team looked as if the area had been abandoned in a hurry. Skis remained in tuning blocks, half-melted wax lay in globs and tools rested haphazardly around the area.

The action in the rest of the tuning room impressed Kalin. Even with the two tragedies, the other tuners hadn't lost focus. The remaining tuning stations were alive with the smell of melted wax and buzz of filing, but the chatter had diminished.

Kalin hesitated at the entryway and stood beside a smiling Amber. Since she'd transferred Amber from the lifts to the tuning room, her attitude had improved. Was her change in behavior due to the visibility and added level of responsibility, or just that it was warmer inside?

Needing to exude confidence, Kalin forced the look of gloom off her face. Edwin's accident scared her, but she didn't want to cause panic among the remaining skiers. She plastered on a smile and asked Amber, "What are you grinning at?"

"Donny."

Kalin couldn't help but join Amber in a real smile. Now she understood Amber's change in attitude. Kalin was getting used to Donny's resemblance to her late husband. Her feelings weren't rational, but the reminder of Jack was part of the reason she liked Donny. She'd loved Jack and couldn't let him fade into her memory. When she first met Ben, she felt as if she were betraying Jack, and it had taken a while for her to give herself permission to fall in love with Ben. "You like him?"

Amber blushed. "It's not like that. He's nice. That's all. I don't know him well."

"But you'd like to?"

"I guess. I asked him if he wanted me to help him ski again. He said he'd think about it."

"That's cool."

Donny lifted a ski and whirled it into place, clearly an expert in handling the equipment. He caught Amber's eye and winked.

Kalin elbowed her.

"Stop, he'll see you," Amber said with laughter in her voice.

Kalin suppressed her thought that both Donny and Amber were suspects, and walked through the tuning room, studying each person and wondering if one of them had murdered McKenzie. The idea she could be in the room with a murderer gave her the creeps.

Charlie Whittle stood in the corner, talking on his phone and shaking his head. Kalin closed in on him.

"Gotta go." He slipped his phone into the pocket of his apron. "I guess you want to talk to me about the accident."

"That and other things." Kalin stared at a ski resting behind the German's tuning table. "Do you know Edwin Bucher?"

"I've seen him around."

"What's Jeff Morley's relationship with him?"

"They're competitors, so it's competitive."

His answer was not overflowing with information. Charlie must understand how serious her questions were and yet he answered as if she were an annoyance. "Does Jeff blame him for missing races last year?"

"I'm not his counselor. How would I know?"

Kalin figured he didn't want to talk about Jeff in a personal way, so she changed tactics. "Has anyone talked with the coach of the German team or their head tuner?"

"I don't know. They both went to Calgary."

She noticed the empty tuning station beside Charlie's. "Where's Nora?"

"She called in sick."

"What's wrong with her?"

"I'm not sure. Yesterday, Ian Reed asked me to tune his skis and not let Nora touch them. I think she might be at home sulking." Charlie grimaced. "Sorry, that was uncalled for. The rest of us have to cover for her, and she's been coming in hung over lately. I didn't expect that from her."

Kalin had promised to keep Nora's secret, so she couldn't stand up for her. "Why doesn't Ian want her to tune his skis?"

"He's spooked by McKenzie's death."

"What does that have to do with Nora?"

"Not a clue," Charlie said.

"Don't be too hard on her. She's going through a lot." Kalin would call Nora later and let her know Charlie thought she was drinking. "Has Fred been by yet?"

Charlie's phone rang, but he left the call unanswered in his apron pocket. "You know, not getting in here after hours is going to be a pain in the arse. How are we supposed to get our job done?"

"How often does a tuner need in here after seven?"

"That depends. I stay late maybe three times a week, and usually I see one or two other people in here."

Donny removed a ski from the tuning block and set it in the rack behind his tuning station. He caught Kalin's eye, but didn't say anything.

Kalin lowered her voice. "Why didn't you tell me you had keys to the building? You know I'm trying to secure the room."

"I needed to get my work done and didn't think you'd care if I came in."

"Were you angry with McKenzie before he died?"

"What's that supposed to mean?"

"He saw you got caught drinking and driving, and I'm wondering what that did to your relationship with him?"

"I think it's time for you to go."

Snow dripped off Ben's ski boots onto Reed's pristine carpet, and he didn't know whether he should move or drip in one spot. He felt as if he were fifteen again and standing in the principal's office being reprimanded for cutting too many classes. He didn't get how Kalin could work with the guy. Ben wasn't even in trouble and yet he felt guilty. Kalin had asked him to tell Reed what he saw, but that didn't mean he was enjoying the experience.

Reed glanced at Ben's boots but said nothing.

Ben used all of his self-control not to shuffle his feet. He'd been asked to get there quickly and hadn't had time to change into winter boots. Sweat formed underneath his ski jacket, and he undid the zipper to cool down. He held his black helmet hanging against the side of his leg.

"I need to know exactly what you saw today," Reed said.

Where should he start? And was Reed looking for mistakes in his work? "I'd been on duty since eight. The run was stable. I mean, not too many racers fell today. Not like the other day."

"You're saying the conditions weren't at fault."

"I don't think so." A second person crashing made Ben sick. He wanted the fall to be an accident, not murder. "Edwin Bucher fell on the bottom quarter of the run."

"Did you see him fall?"

"He shot forward, his right boot ejected from his binding and he landed hard on his back."

"Could you tell if he hit something or caught an edge?"

"No. It happened too fast. The Germans had their video going. I'm sure they caught the accident."

"Anything else I need to know?"

"Constable Miller came to see me. I gave him Edwin's equipment. The cops are going to have their own expert analyze the bindings. Miller was on his way to see the German team when he left me."

"Good work today," Reed said with an almost smile on his face.

Ben stopped by Kalin's office after he finished meeting with Reed. He eased in, shut the door and engaged the lock. Kalin leaned against his chest, and he wrapped his arms around her. Only for her, could he let down his guard. She always knew when he needed her. He hadn't had to say a word. Somewhere along the line, Kalin had become his life. His friends were betting he couldn't hold a relationship together just because he never had before. They were wrong. He wouldn't fall for Vicky's tricks.

Ben reluctantly let go of Kalin and kissed her lips. "I love that you have an office with a door."

She intertwined her fingers with his. "You look drained."

"I just met with Reed, but that's not the reason. I can't shake the look on Edwin's face when he asked me if he was going to be okay. I said yes."

"What else could you say? He needed to hear that."

"What if someone tampered with his bindings too?"

"I've been thinking about that since he fell. I don't want to believe it. That would make me partly responsible. I didn't properly secure the gear, and I should have banned Edwin for fighting."

"You can't blame yourself. I know you hate when I interfere with your job, but I don't want you nosing around about McKenzie or Edwin. It's too dangerous. What if you find out who the murderer is? He could come after you. It's the RCMP's job to investigate."

"I know it is, but Reed asked me to help. I can't ignore what he wants. Nothing bad is going to happen to me."

"You're already stressed out. You're barely home in the evenings.

It's not good for you. Please let this go. Let Reed think you're working on it and that you didn't find out anything. He'll never know."

"I can't do that."

"I know. I didn't actually mean you should." Ben couldn't force Kalin to do what he wanted, but that didn't keep him from wishing he could. He wanted her to understand how important she was to him. Finding a murderer wasn't her problem.

"When can you go home?" she asked.

"Soon, I think."

"Good. Chica's probably ready to go out. I need to meet with Fred and then I want to drop by Nora's. I'll call when I know what time I'll be home."

Ben massaged the small of her back. "Why don't you come home early? I'll keep you entertained."

"As tempting as that is, I have to deal with this."

"Your cold is going to get worse," he said, taking one more shot at persuading her to forget about work for a while.

"Stop worrying."

Ben kissed her neck. "Did I mention I love that you have an office with a door?" Ben opened the lock and headed home.

Disgruntled crossed Kalin's mind when Ted Brightman arrived at the tuning room with the new locks in hand. As a locksmith, he appeared technically competent but oddly didn't seem to care much about security.

Brightman eyed both Kalin and Fred. "I don't know what good this is going to do. When people need a key, I'll get an email and it'll add extra work for nothing."

His attitude bothered Kalin. She worked hard at recruiting the right type of people for the resort. Helpful, friendly, willing to work with others were all attributes she interviewed for and didn't find in Brightman, but he'd come to the resort long before she had, and she'd give him a chance. "I'll make it easy for you. You are not to issue a key to this door unless you get an email from me."

He grimaced. "The other directors won't like that."

"I'll talk to them, and I'll send you an email, so you have my instructions in writing."

"I don't need anything in writing. I do what I'm told."

"I didn't mean it that way. Anytime you get a request for a key, send my email as a response. Then you won't have to take the brunt of the complaints. I will."

"Huh." He nodded as if he approved. He pulled a screwdriver from the chest pocket of his overalls, dismantled the existing lock on the tuning room door and installed the new one with speed. He handed both Kalin and Fred a key and started on the exterior door of the administration building.

"Now what?" Kalin asked Fred.

"What about giving Amber Cristelli a key? Someone needs to open and close the room each day."

The clang of Ted's screwdriver hitting the tiled floor distracted Kalin. She studied both doors for a moment. "I'm not comfortable with that. She's too junior. Can you make it part of the security rounds for a while?"

"Sure. I'll have whoever's on duty meet Amber first and last thing each day. I'll instruct them to sweep the room before they lock the door."

"Charlie Whittle complained about not being allowed in the room during the off hours," she said.

Brightman stopped moving, and Kalin figured he was trying to hear Fred's answer. She lifted her palm toward Fred and shook her head.

Fred waited until Brightman finished with the second lock installation, handed them both a key and disappeared through the outer door. "I talked with him. Interesting that he didn't tell us he had a key."

"I asked Charlie about drinking and driving. He basically told me to get lost."

"I can't imagine he wanted to discuss the subject," Fred said. "Let's keep the room tight until we see what happened to the German skier. Then we can decide if anyone gets in after hours. Besides, the teams are only here for another five days. After that, only the Holden team will be around and this room won't be used for tuning."

Kalin felt the pressure mounting. Reed hadn't mentioned a deadline, but she guessed he'd want to know who killed McKenzie within the next five days.

The next stop for Kalin was Nora's. As she walked, she pulled her neck tube over her nose. The exposed piece of skin between the tube and her bottom eyelashes stung, and she picked up her pace.

Nora answered the door and frowned at Kalin. Her dull eyes were puffy from crying.

"I wanted to check on you. Charlie said you called in sick today." Kalin remembered the deliciousness of being sick as a child, of being taken care of, of having no responsibilities. Sometime during the growing up process that had disappeared and turned into getting out of bed no matter how awful she felt. She couldn't pinpoint the moment the transformation occurred, but she missed lying in bed having her mom take care of her.

"I think I have that flu that's going around," Nora said.

"Tell me about it. Can I come in?"

"I'm really not up to it." Nora leaned tight against the doorframe on one side and pulled the door close to her on the other.

"Did you hear about the accident today?"

"Charlie called me. It's just like Steve."

"I hope not. Is that why you didn't go to work today?"

"No. I just feel lousy."

"Do you know the German skier?"

"It's not that. It just makes Steve's death seem so real."

"Can I do anything?"

"I'm tired. I need to go to bed."

Before she could react, Kalin was staring at the outside of Nora's front door. She might as well go home. She'd wanted to tell Nora Charlie suspected she was going to work hung over, and Nora should clear that up with him before she lost her job, but Nora wasn't in a sharing mood. She hoped Nora had been sick and not doing something else.

CHAPTER TWENTY-TWO

Kalin smelled wood burning when she was a couple of houses away from home and couldn't wait to warm herself in front of their fireplace with Ben. She needed to find a way to balance her personal and professional life. The Goddess hung around the periphery of their lives, waiting for a chance to use her Goddess charms to steal Ben away. Weren't Goddesses known for trickery when it came to love?

Chica bounded toward Kalin the second she was inside, running in circles and rubbing her head against Kalin's leg. Ben rose from the couch, pushed Chica out of the way and hugged Kalin. The glow from the flames bounced off a bottle of red wine and two glasses that graced the living room table.

She hung her ski jacket in the front hall and kicked off her winter boots.

Ben poured her a glass of wine. She wrapped her fingers around the stem and sat beside him on the couch, poking her toes underneath his thigh. He was trying to make up for pressuring her about her job. "I went to see Nora. She wouldn't let me in."

"That's odd. What's up with her?"

"She said she has the flu, but I don't believe her."

Ben lifted his wine as if to take a sip but stopped before the glass touched his lips. "Because?"

"I think she was upset, not sick. Have you heard anything more about the accident today?"

Ben massaged Kalin's calf, and she stretched her legs over his thighs. "Nothing's being released until Edwin's family gets to Calgary."

"Thanks for telling me about the keys to the tuning room. I had the locks changed today."

"No problem."

"I created a list of everyone who's been issued a key. How come you have one? And why didn't you tell me?"

A smile deepened across Ben's face. "You think I snuck into the tuning room and tampered with McKenzie's binding?"

Kalin couldn't help herself and laughed. "Yeah. And your motive is to be the next Olympic Super-G star. I think you better start practicing."

A deep peal of laughter burst from Ben's throat. "Well, it's a relief to finally get that out in the open."

"Should I call Miller and tell him you're guilty?" Kalin's laugh dwindled and turned into a frown. "We shouldn't be joking about this."

"I know. I got a key a couple of years ago. Security was short staffed, and I picked up the extra hours."

"Did anyone ever ask for the key back?"

"No. It's still on my key ring along with the other keys I got at the time. I thought I might need them again someday and didn't want the hassle of getting them reissued." Ben went to the front hall table and grabbed his keys. He sorted through them and held one up. "I think this is the one to the tuning room."

"If it is, you can throw it out. It won't fit the new lock. Do you know what time the overnight snowmakers get off shift?"

"Around five. It depends on how long their debrief meeting is."

"I was thinking I should talk with them. On the morning McKenzie died, maybe one of the snowmakers saw someone entering the room."

"Okay Miss Detective, any chance you can let the cops question the snowmakers?"

"We've been over this before. Reed asked me to help."

"Reed's not the one being put in danger."

Kalin set her wineglass on the table. She didn't want to argue with Ben. She had enough stress at work. "I'm not in danger. I'm just going to ask if they saw anyone."

"I give, but you'll have to get up early." Ben wiggled his eyebrows.

"I know I'm not a morning person, but I can do it if I have to."

"I wasn't thinking about the morning." He wiggled his eyebrows again. "I was thinking we should go to bed early."

Pushing her annoyance aside, Kalin kicked his thigh and laughed. "Nice try with the eyebrows. I'm not going tomorrow. I'm too busy. I'll go the day after."

"Even better. Let me entertain you."

"You're such a dork sometimes. All the girls think you're so cool, but I know the real you."

"I am cool. In fact, I'm Mr. Cool to you."

"Okay, Mr. Cool. Let's see what you have to offer."

Ben picked her up and threw her over his shoulder, firefighter style. "Oh, I'll show you. The question is can you keep up?"

He tossed her on their bed and flopped on top of her.

She lifted her arms, and he pulled her sweater over her head. He used his teeth to unsnap the front of her bra in one quick motion. "Ta da. Not only am I cool, but I'm extremely talented."

"You look like a rooster who just scored."

"I haven't, but I will."

"Told you I'd score." Ben wasn't going to admit to Kalin how exhausted he was. She was a dynamo. He wrapped one arm around her, and she pressed her cheek onto his chest. She flopped her leg over his thigh and snuggled closer. Their quilt lay on the bedroom floor where they'd tossed it, the sheet tangled underneath them, and until he cooled down, that's where they'd stay.

"So are you going to tell me about Vicky and the fire department?"

Kalin's breath tickled his chest when she spoke, and his intense feelings for her frightened him. He didn't want Vicky to screw up his relationship with Kalin. "I didn't know how to bring it up."

"You're going to see her a lot now. I'm not sure how I feel about that."

"Are you mad at me?"

"You can't control what she does."

Ben heard the thumping of Chica's paws before he saw her. She bounded and landed on the bed with them. He shoved her gently back onto the floor. "You're being pretty understanding. I'd be pissed if I were you."

"It's not your fault she joined the department. You can hardly tell the chief not to have her back."

Ben stared out the window and thought about what to say.

"Why are you being so weird about this? Did something else happen?"

Ben nodded and his chin hit the top of Kalin's head. "Sorry."

"Are you going to tell me or should we play twenty questions? Maybe I could torture it out of you." Kalin stuck her finger in Ben's belly button and pushed.

When he didn't say anything, she plucked a couple of his dark chest hairs.

"Okay, okay, I give." Ben took a deep breath. "She showed up at the fire station." He told her what had happened, including that Fred had shown up and seen Vicky half naked. By the time he finished, Kalin was laughing.

"What's so funny?" Ben asked.

"You should hear your voice. And Fred. Boy, he must not have known what to do."

"I can't believe how much I love you. Only you would find this funny."

Kalin's cell rang.

"Are you on call?" Ben asked.

"No, but considering what's going on, I should get that."

"Don't."

"I have to." She walked to the chest of drawers, shaking her butt at him and laughing. Impossible. She was impossible to be mad at when she strutted around naked, which he suspected she knew. She dumped her backpack onto the floor and found her phone among the contents scattered on the hardwood.

"Kalin Thompson." She hit the speakerphone button and sauntered back to Ben, wiggling her hips.

"The police are questioning Ian. What did you say to them?" Reed said.

Kalin stuck out her tongue at the phone, making Ben chuckle silently. "I didn't say anything."

"Did you take Ian's name off all lists?"

Kalin plunked onto the edge of their bed. "Ian's name was on the list of people who had keys to both the tuning room and the outer administration door."

"I told you to keep Ian out of this."

"I understand. But—"

"But what?"

"I can't alter the facts. I gave the RCMP a full list. It's up to them to decide what to do with the information. I didn't single out Ian."

"I don't want you giving anything else to the RCMP without my approval first."

"Okay." After the call, Kalin dropped her cell on the bedside table and placed her forehead on Ben's chest. "That was pleasant."

"He was almost yelling at you. How do you work for him?"

"I think the situation with Ian is too personal."

"You're standing up for him? You shouldn't have answered, and

Reed shouldn't be calling you at home unless it's urgent."

"He's my boss. I can't ignore him. Anyway, I included Reed in the list I gave to the RCMP."

"And mine too. Right?"

"I thought about taking yours off, but it would look bad if anyone ever found out."

"No kidding. Maybe Reed killed McKenzie," Ben said.

"You mean Gavin or Ian?"

"Gavin. I heard he pressured Coach Jenkinson into putting Ian on the team. He'd have known there wasn't a spot and someone had to leave the team for Ian to get a shot."

"I don't believe Gavin murdered McKenzie, but I'm not so sure about Ian."

CHAPTER TWENTY-THREE

Jeff helped Donny into the passenger seat of his truck, stored the wheelchair in the back and slid onto the front seat. He twisted the key in the ignition, increased the heat and turned on the seat heater. "Man, I'm sick of the cold."

"You're such a girl," Donny said, wishing his legs felt cold too. He could only imagine the cold from the leather seats seeping through his jeans to his skin.

Jeff reversed out of the driveway. Their father stood in the front door and scowled at them. "What's with him this morning?"

"Mom had an early shift at the hospital and didn't make his breakfast. I guess he's hungry. Did she say anything about your eye?"

"Nope. Just shook her head at me." Jeff stopped at the corner and waited for traffic to clear. "We should move out."

Donny examined Jeff's face. "Do you mean it?"

"I do. I can't take much more of him." Using the bottom half of his sleeve, Jeff wiped frost off the inside of the windshield.

"What about Mom?" Donny asked.

"He never touches her."

"Not yet. If we're not there, he might."

"Shit. We're going to have to move out sometime. We could try. Besides, I can't see him hurting her. She's the one thing he values." Jeff signaled and turned left out of their suburban neighborhood. "I applied to UBC."

"Why didn't you tell me?"

"I was going to wait until I got accepted, but I think we need to make plans. If I get in, we can both move to Vancouver. UBC has a good engineering program, and it's close to Whistler/Blackcomb. We can still ski…"

Donny slowly nodded.

"Shit. I'm sorry. I didn't mean…sometimes I forget."

With a chuckle, Donny said, "Don't be so sensitive. Besides, I've been thinking of trying the sit-ski."

"Awesome. You should."

"I'm only contemplating it. So UBC?"

"What do you think?" Jeff asked.

"It's great. You want to move out now to see if Mom's safe before we go too far?"

Jeff appreciated Donny didn't ask about skiing. That he instinctively knew Jeff didn't want to make a career of the sport. "Yeah."

"You sure you want me to go with you?"

"Sure. Someone has to work."

Neither said a word until they were ten minutes from the turn into Stone Mountain. The one highway between the resort and Holden demanded four-wheel drive technology in the winter, and the wheels of Jeff's truck held snug to the snow-covered road.

"Have you talked to Nora since McKenzie died?" Donny asked.

"Yeah. Why?"

"With McKenzie out of the way, you could get back together."

Jeff laughed. "You always liked her."

"You were the one glued to her through high school. I thought you'd marry her."

"Yeah, well that didn't work out."

"Why don't you ask her out again?"

"I saw her the night before McKenzie died."

"And?"

Jeff took his time and prepared his words. "I was heading to the parking lot after the bar closed and found Nora sitting in a snow bank. She didn't see me. I watched her for a bit and realized she was crying. It took me a while to persuade her to let me drive her home. McKenzie had just dumped her. By the time I got her home, Aunt Lisa was waiting on her doorstep, so I just dropped her off."

"What a bastard. Did Nora tell him she was pregnant?"

"She's pregnant?" Jeff looked at Donny, and the truck swerved to the right.

Donny broke into a sweat and put both palms on the dashboard. "Watch the road." He couldn't remember much of the crash he'd been in, but he'd never gotten over the fear. His pulse settled only after Jeff got the truck back under control. He kept his hands on the dashboard until his breathing slowed. "I saw her in the drugstore buying a pregnancy test."

"Have you told anyone?"

"No. I found out by accident. I'm not sure she's pregnant. I don't know the results of the test. Besides, I wouldn't gossip about her. She deserves better."

A few minutes after nine, bells jingled when Kalin pushed open the door to Holden's single art gallery. The gallery specialized in local art, and Lisa Hudson had her studio in one of the back rooms. Nora talked a lot about Lisa, and Kalin was looking forward to seeing her.

The last ten days had worn on Kalin, and she thought she deserved a present. Her office had a vacant feel as if she hadn't moved in yet, and her idea was to put local art on the wall, something that showed the spirit of the resort and the mountains together.

Lisa, a lithe woman of about fifty, with blonde hair tied back in a red bandana and wearing a smock covered in a multitude of colors, poked her head out of a side door. "I'll be right there," she said with a smile in her voice.

While Kalin waited, she toured the gallery, getting a feeling for the artwork. She stopped in front of a painting of the Dragon's Bowl.

"Captivating, isn't it," Lisa said.

"You could say that." Kalin tilted her head up to meet Lisa's eyes. She didn't often meet a woman taller than herself.

"You don't like it?"

"I love it, but it's a bit too dramatic for my office. I was thinking of something fun. I've just been promoted and want my office to be welcoming."

Lisa's face brightened. "Nora told me about your promotion. Congratulations."

"Thanks. Nora suggested I come here."

They meandered through the gallery, viewing paintings, but nothing inspired Kalin.

"Come on. I've got others in the back I don't have room to display." Lisa steered Kalin through her workshop, past an easel with a freshly painted canvas drying on it and into a storage room.

"You must have been up early," Kalin said.

"Pardon?"

"The canvas is wet. It looks like you got an early start."

Lisa smiled. "I'm always up early. I do my best work in the morning."

A vibrant painting of two boys skiing filled one wall.

"Wow," Kalin said.

A wide grin, full of perfect teeth, beamed across Lisa's face. "Thanks. They're my nephews."

"It's fantastic. Too bad it won't fit in my office."

"It's not for sale." Lisa pressed her fingers to the bottom corner of the canvas. "That one has too many memories for me."

"Good ones, I would think."

"Until things changed. You must know what happened."

"Nora told me."

"The one on the left is Donny." Lisa traced Donny's face on the canvas with her index finger. "The other is Jeff. They were about eight and ten."

"You captured their excitement. Were they close growing up?"

"They were. Jeff looked out for Donny. After the accident, Jeff was devastated. Sometimes I think more so than Donny."

"Donny seems to cope well."

"He does." Lisa tucked an errant hair under her bandana. "Are you into skiing too?"

"I learned at Camp Fortune. It's a small hill near Ottawa. My stepdad used to take my brother and me." Thinking about her estranged brother made her sad. One day she'd figure out how to repair their relationship. Kalin shrugged. "I've skied all my life. Skiing is part of the reason I moved to Stone Mountain."

"Nora mentioned you were promoted, but didn't say to what."

"I run the HR and security departments."

"That sounds interesting."

"It is. I couldn't believe my luck last year when Stone Mountain posted the HR job on the Internet. It was incredible that I could work in my profession at a ski resort."

"What do you do for security?"

"Not much yet. I just took over the department. It's different from what I expected. Steve McKenzie's death changed the focus on me." Kalin cleared her throat. "Let's look at some paintings."

"I have one I painted last year. Let me show you." Lisa pulled out a canvas that had been hidden behind several others. Painted from the top of one of the Purcell Mountain peaks, the painting showed the Rocky Mountains to the east of the resort. Below the range, Stone Mountain hummed. The action jumped off the canvas giving the viewer a sensation of being part of the scene. She'd used primary colors to make the painting bright.

"I love it. This will be my Christmas present to myself."

"I'll need to frame it for you." Lisa moved with the grace of a ballerina across the workroom, showed Kalin a selection of frames and together they chose one. After they negotiated a price, Lisa said, "It'll take me a few days to get this done. I'll call when it's ready."

Kalin had connected with Lisa. They could become friends. "Great. When I come pick up the painting, maybe we could go for lunch?"

Kalin left the store feeling more light-hearted than she'd been since McKenzie's murder.

In the hallway of the administration building, Kalin tromped to her office. The threadbare carpet needed replacing, and the walls could use a coat of paint. The floor creaked with each step. Compared to the recently constructed staff housing building, the office building was starting to look like a dump. At least her new painting would liven up her office. She turned on her heels and backtracked to Monica's desk in the HR reception area.

"When's the last time you did a staff housing check?" Kalin asked.

"Two days ago."

"I'd like you to do another one today. I want you to pressure the staff to keep the new building in good condition before they start taking it for granted." Kalin had worked with the decorators on the last phase of the project, ensuring every penny went to the best use, and she intended to make sure the building was respected.

"I'm on it."

Confident Monica would do as asked, Kalin left and strode toward her office.

"Any news on the German skier?" Monica called after her.

Kalin kept walking. "Nothing."

"Call me if you find out anything," Monica yelled just as Kalin turned through her doorway.

Kalin found an envelope on her chair and tossed it onto her desk, sat and dialed. She waited to be transferred to Constable Miller's private line.

"Was it an accident?" Kalin asked.

"Hi. I'm fine. Thanks for asking."

"Sorry. Do you know yet?"

"We're still investigating."

"Is there anything I can do to help?"

"Actually, there is. I have a present for Becky, and I'd like to leave it in her office as a surprise. Can you unlock her door for me?"

Although not the type of request Kalin had expected, she was happy to help him with a personal matter. Miller dated Becky Stewart, the resort's cash office manager, and her office was down the hall from Kalin's. "Sure. When are you coming up the mountain?"

"Tonight. I thought I could drop off her gift before I pick her up for dinner. Then she'll find it in the morning."

Romantic. "I can meet you at six. She'll be gone by then. Will you call me when you know anything more about Edwin's crash?"

Miller hesitated, and then said, "If I can."

Kalin opened the envelope she'd found on her chair and discovered printed emails and Facebook messages Ben had sent Vicky when they'd been dating. When Kalin realized what they were, she stopped reading. *Bitch.*

She glanced at the clock on her phone. The Holden team had the run for the next two hours. She decided to go to the base of the hill where she could watch the training. On her way, she stopped at the shredder and took great satisfaction in watching the messages turn to confetti. *Nice try, but these are old.*

Kalin reached the bottom of the run just as Ian Reed flew through the finish line and skied to a stop beside a woman wearing a designer ski jacket and fur hat. With the way she was dressed, she should be standing in a five star European ski resort, not Stone Mountain during race training, but in spite of her clothing, the scowl on her face hid her beauty.

"Mother," Ian said. "What are you doing here?"

Kalin's curiosity piqued. She'd never met her boss's wife, and she moved a few steps closer.

Susan Reed stood with her hands on her hips, glaring at her son. "I came to watch you. Your time is off."

"That was my warm up run," Ian said in a quiet voice.

"Warm up or not, I expect faster runs out of you."

"I'll ski faster next run."

"Just because McKenzie's out of the way doesn't mean you can slack off."

"I'm not."

Susan scanned the hill. "Jeff Morley's skiing well."

"He's a good skier, but I can beat him."

"I should think so. Sunday we'll pray together that your time improves." Susan turned and left her son standing alone.

Kalin watched Ian's face. He rolled his eyes the second his mother turned her back to him.

Ian confronted Kalin. "What?"

He'd caught her staring, and she pretended she wasn't looking at him. "Nothing."

"That's my mother at her best," Ian said.

"I heard you asked for Nora not to tune your skis anymore. Wasn't she doing a good job?"

"You're friends with her. What did she tell you?"

"Nothing. Charlie told me."

"McKenzie died because someone tampered with his binding. Maybe it was Nora."

"Are you serious?"

"I know she's your friend, but maybe you don't know everything that's been going on with her. McKenzie dumped her the night before he died. She hates me. I don't want her touching my gear."

CHAPTER TWENTY-FOUR

Reed shut his office door and motioned for his son to sit at the table. He preferred to keep his home and business life separate, so Ian didn't often come to his office. His wife was unpredictable, and he didn't want her embarrassing him. He wanted Ian around more often, but he couldn't exclude his wife and not Ian. Even though they never spoke about it, he hoped Ian understood.

Susan used to be happy, fun loving even. When their daughter ran away at sixteen, Susan turned bitter. She'd been edging that way since his affair, but their daughter's drug use had pushed Susan to a dark place. Occasionally Melanie would call, but never say where she was, and he never asked. The threadlike connection could snap at any moment. He didn't judge or criticize his daughter, hoping she would come to trust him again. He missed having a family that had fun together, and he missed his wife's smile. "How'd you do today?"

The shine in Ian's eyes told Reed the answer before Ian spoke. Ian wore his red and yellow race suit, and he clomped in his ski boots to the nearest chair. He'd come straight from racing and must have skied fast.

"One minute thirty-three thirty-nine."

Reed took in his son's muscled body, knowing Ian worked hard to be strong, and ignored his body odor. "That's great. Did you beat Morley?"

"I did, but my first training run was slow."

"Don't worry about that."

"Mom was watching."

Reed winced. "Was it bad?"

"No, just embarrassing. Everyone could hear her. She never lowers her voice. Can't you talk to her?"

"Sure. Although, I don't know if it will help."

"Can you get me out of church on Sunday? She's the one into religion, not me. We have a training session."

"I'll try, but you know there's more than one service."

"Why do you stay with her?"

Ian had asked the same question before, and Reed's biggest fear was that he'd have to choose between Ian and Susan. "We used to be happy before she changed. She gave me you and Melanie. Your mother isn't dealing well with Melanie taking off."

"That's not my fault."

"I know, but your mother's having a hard time with it. I think it's easier for me because Melanie calls me."

"She might call Mom too if Mom wasn't so hard on her."

"When's the last time you heard from her?" Reed asked.

Ian drummed his fingers on the table. "You know she doesn't like me to tell."

"Sorry."

"Yesterday," Ian said softly. "She's okay. She's worried about me. She read about McKenzie and Bucher in the paper."

For the first time, the thought of Ian crashing, the way either skier had, frightened Reed. He'd never been afraid for Ian before, and he didn't like the feeling now. "I'm glad she cares about you."

Ian studied the top of the table, telling Reed he had something else on his mind. "Ian, just tell me."

Ian cleared his throat. "Man, I don't hide things well from you. I did something stupid, but I don't want Mom to know."

So there was the reason Ian came to see him. Susan was an excuse. "I won't tell her."

"I want to start bringing my skis home at night."

"Why?"

"I'm worried about someone tampering with them. What if the same person who killed McKenzie has access to my skis?"

"I don't think you need to worry about that. The room is secure." Reed watched his son carefully. Ian was slipping around something.

"Not if one of the tuners killed McKenzie. How am I supposed to ski fast with that hanging out there?"

"Who are you thinking of?" When Ian didn't answer, Reed pressed harder. "Do you know something you're not telling?"

"It's so embarrassing. Mom will kill me."

A knot tightened in the back of Reed's neck, and he twisted his head from side to side. "Your mom won't find out, but you have to tell me."

"McKenzie broke up with Nora, and the next day he's murdered."

Reed exhaled patiently. "Can you get to the point?"

"Nora's pregnant."

"I assume, because you're mentioning it, the baby is yours."

Ian pressed his lips between his teeth and studied the table again. "She says it is."

Reed didn't want to believe Ian had repeated his mistake from Fernie. "Could it be McKenzie's?"

"It could." The anguish was clear on Ian's face. "It was just one time. I didn't mean to fuck up again."

"Did you tell the RCMP all this?"

"I did. I'm sorry, Dad."

Reed had the fleeting thought that he shouldn't have called Kalin at home and hassled her about the RCMP interviewing Ian, then dismissed the thought. She still shouldn't have left Ian's name on the list.

Amber entered her staff housing unit and dropped her toque and mitts onto the counter. She placed her notebook, the one where she kept the list of names of anyone entering or exiting the tuning room who wasn't authorized, beside her toque and turned to face Cheryl Wallace. "You can't stay here much longer."

Cheryl sat at Amber's kitchen table having lunch. Her girl-next-door image didn't fit with the trouble she'd caused at the resort. She wore an argyle sweater and clean blue jeans, and if Amber didn't already know what Cheryl had done, she wouldn't have suspected she had a mean streak.

"Don't be such a wimp. No one's going to rat you out."

"How do you know?"

"If my stupid ex hadn't been such a chicken, no one would have known I threw a rock through his window. If I'd known he was such a baby, I would have dumped him long before he had a chance to cheat on me."

"Security evicted you. If they see you here, they'll know you're not supposed to be here. We agreed on one night."

"So what's with you and Donny Morley?"

Amber frowned at the intrusion into her personal life. "Nothing."

"It's not nothing. I can tell you have a wicked crush on him. Your face turns pink every time he looks at you. You should do something about it."

A triple knock vibrated on the door. "Are you expecting anyone?" Cheryl asked.

Amber shook her head. She opened the door to her staff-housing unit and discovered Monica standing in the hallway. She wished she hadn't come home for lunch and that she still stood outside the tuning room scanning passes. Now Monica would check her unit, and she wouldn't like what she found.

"I'm doing staff checks today," Monica said.

Amber couldn't do anything but let her enter.

"What are you doing here?" Monica asked Cheryl.

"Visiting." Cheryl continued to chew her toast, talking with her mouth full, showing off a set of braces wrapped with blue elastic. "Figures you'd come looking for me."

"You know you've been banned from housing," Monica said.

"So what. I'm just hanging."

Monica walked around Amber and checked each of the five single bedrooms. She stuck her head into the bathroom but didn't enter.

Amber sat at the kitchen table eating peanut butter on toast, but the peanut butter stuck in her throat when she swallowed. Monica had to have seen Cheryl's suitcase and clothes scattered in the third bedroom.

"Cheryl is doing more than having lunch here. She's moved in." Monica joined Amber at the table. "Tell me that's not pot on your counter."

"We're not doing anything. Please don't make a big deal about it," Amber said. Why had she let Cheryl sleep over? The drugs belonged to Cheryl, and she wasn't saying anything. She hadn't even known Cheryl that long, and now she was about to get evicted because of her. So not fair.

"You know the rules. Even if I hadn't found the pot, you can't have someone who's been banned in your unit."

"We're just having lunch," Amber pleaded.

"It doesn't matter what you're doing. She can't be here. Unfortunately, that means you have to move out."

"Please don't evict me." Amber hoped Cheryl would admit the pot was hers, but no luck.

Cheryl chewed on a thumbnail and spat the remnants on the floor.

"It's policy. You have until five tomorrow to move out."

"You can't do this," Amber said. "I've nowhere to go."

"It's not what I want to do, but I have to be consistent with the rules."

"We won't tell anyone if you let this slide. She'll leave right now."

Amber suspected Monica wanted to let her off the hook but couldn't. Monica was the manager now, not just the assistant. She probably had to prove herself or something.

Monica pushed her chair back and stood. With kindness in her voice, she said, "I'd love to help you out, but I can't."

A pit grew tight in Amber's stomach. One part fear. One part anger. What if Monica reported the pot to the cops? She wouldn't do that, would she? And where the fuck was she supposed to live?

Constable Miller knocked on Kalin's office door at five minutes to six holding a box in his hand. He must have come from work because he wore his RCMP uniform.

"Can I ask what's in the box?"

"Sure." Miller smiled. "I bought Becky new cross country ski gloves. Hers are a mess."

"Nice. She'll like that." Kalin grabbed her keys. "Come on. I'll open her door for you."

Becky's office was at the end of the hallway to the right of the stairs leading to the ground floor of the administration building.

"Any news on Edwin Bucher?"

Miller waited a moment before answering. "His prognosis isn't good. He's paralyzed from the waist down. There's a large amount of swelling and once that goes down there is some chance he might get the use of his legs back, but it's unlikely."

"What about his fall?" Maybe Donny could talk with Edwin. Maybe he could help him since he'd been paralyzed himself.

"We're still investigating."

"That's what you said last time I asked."

"Aren't you observant."

"Can't you tell me anything?"

"We haven't gotten the bindings back from analysis yet, so there's nothing to tell."

Kalin didn't want to believe the person who caused McKenzie to fall also made an attempt on Edwin Bucher's life. If that were true, she wondered if there would be another *accident*. She tried not to think about it as she led Miller to Becky's office and slid her key in the lock.

"Do you have keys to all the offices and buildings?"

"I do. I got them when I took over security."

"Was that before or after McKenzie died?"

"Before. Why?" Not even for a second could Miller stop himself from being suspicious. Had Becky's gift been an excuse for finding out if she had keys?

"Does anyone else have the same keys?"

"As far as I know, Fred Morgan. Also, the locksmith, Ted Brightman. Gavin Reed might, but I don't know. I'll confirm that tomorrow."

Miller followed Kalin into Becky's office. He placed the box and a card on top of her chair.

"Did you hear that?" Kalin asked.

Miller listened. "It sounds like someone pounding on something."

"It's coming from downstairs." Kalin and Miller ran to the stairwell and jogged down the steps. They discovered Ian Reed ramming his shoulder into the tuning room door.

Miller stopped and placed himself between Ian and Kalin. "What are you doing?"

"My key isn't working."

How could Ian have a key, not mention that important little fact and be using it to access the tuning room after hours? *Idiot*. None of the tuners or skiers seemed to be taking the security issue seriously. Was Ian the only tuner to have a key or did others? She had no idea how complete her key list was. Kalin moved from behind Miller. "I had the locks changed. No one is allowed in the room after hours."

Ian rubbed his shoulder but didn't move away from the door. "How come no one told me? I need to get in there."

Miller relaxed his stance. "Why?"

"Why'd you bring the cops after me? How did you know I was here?" Ian asked Kalin.

"I think you should tell us why you need in the room," Kalin said.

"I want my skis."

"Badly enough to break the door down?" Miller asked.

"You don't understand," Ian whined.

"Try to explain."

"Am I under arrest?"

Miller spoke before Kalin had a chance to answer. "Of course not. Kalin's job is to secure this room, and she needs to know why you want in after hours. If you have a good reason, she can open the door for you."

"Really?" Ian glanced at Kalin. "There's usually someone in the room until seven. I don't know why it's empty early today. I'm going to take my skis home at the end of each day after Charlie tunes them. I don't want them tampered with."

"You're that worried?" Miller asked.

"McKenzie was killed and you haven't arrested anyone, even after what I told you. You know why I'm worried. I'm not taking any chances."

"Take it easy," Kalin said. "I asked security to close the room since the tuners were done for the day. You might want to keep in mind the room's not always open until seven."

Kalin and Miller escorted Ian to his skis and let him take them from the room. Kalin held the door as Ian departed. Maybe he had just wanted his skis. Or maybe he was up to something else entirely. And what had Ian told Miller?

CHAPTER TWENTY-FIVE

Kalin was not a morning person, and five a.m. was a ridiculous hour to be at work. Yet there she stood, freezing her tush, waiting for the snowmakers' shift change.

Chica stood guard beside her, making her feel secure in the isolated area outside the mountain operations building. Wind whistled through the lodge pole pine trees and stung Kalin's skin. In the darkness, she couldn't see the trees but could imagine them bending with the wind's pressure. She pulled her toque low, keeping the cold off her forehead. The glow of lights appeared on the horizon, and she counted six headlamp beams as they neared.

Kalin followed the snowmaking crew and the odor of diesel they carried with them into the building and found the replacement team preparing to start the dawn shift. It was convenient that the manager, Jason Tober, was on duty. He was one of Ben's closest friends and that should make asking questions easier.

Jason removed his fur-lined hat. Bits of snow and ice spattered when he tossed it on the table. His curly hair was flattened to his head and, together with his pale skin, he reminded Kalin of an egg.

He assembled the team and reviewed the current snow gun placements, snow conditions, which runs had been completed, and recommended the next gun placements. If there were injuries or equipment failures, he would review those too. The process was repeated at each shift change.

Kalin listened to the information, familiar with the details. Jason often talked about snowmaking when he wasn't working. Wind, temperature and snow conditions were all important in setting the gun flow level.

"I have some questions I'd like to ask the team." Kalin waited for Jason to approve her request. "I'm sure you've all heard Steve McKenzie's bindings were tampered with." Kalin looked each snowmaker in the eye and received a nod in return. She used the pause to ensure she had their full attention. "Gavin Reed asked me to assist with the RCMP investigation. It's possible someone entered the tuning room before operating hours on the day of the murder."

Jason stood in front of his team as if protecting them. "Are you saying one of us killed McKenzie just because we're here early?"

Kalin gave him and the room of snowmakers her friendliest smile. "No. I was thinking one of you might have seen someone enter the admin building. Ben mentioned being able to see the door closest to the tuning room when snowmakers change shift. I'd like each of you to think back to the morning Steve died and see what you can remember."

There was head shaking and shoulder shrugging around the room, and no one offered any information.

"Did anyone see anything at all unusual?" Kalin asked.

"I saw Nora Cummings get out of her car, but I didn't see her go into the building," one of the snowmakers said.

Kalin's heart picked up speed. This was not what she'd been expecting to hear. "What time was that?"

"Around five thirty." While he had the floor, the snowmaker asked, "Did someone tamper with the German skier's gear too?"

She should have expected the question, but it caught her off guard. "The RCMP's investigating. I don't have any information." Her eyes travelled across the room, searching each face. "Anything else?"

When no one spoke, she let the room clear and asked to meet with Jason privately.

"Do you have a list of everyone who was on duty that night?"

"Sure." Jason picked up a blue binder and flipped through time sheets. He snapped the rings open and placed the relevant pages in the photocopier.

"Was there anyone on duty that night who isn't here today?"

"I'll check." He waited until the photocopier spit out the final pages. "One person. Mark Gardner."

"Where is he today?"

"He went home. Vancouver I think. He received a call during the shift before McKenzie died. His dad passed away. He signed out at four."

"Do you know when he's coming back?"

"In a couple of days."

Kalin walked home from the early morning meeting and let Chica bound in front of her. She kicked her feet through the snow, using her headlamp to light the way, meandering and giving herself time to think. The path rose and fell between the forest and the golf course and, even at the slow speed, her legs strained in effort.

During her first winter at the resort, Kalin had avoided being in the forest in the dark, but she'd gotten used to living in the wilderness. She carried bear spray and a whistle. She also had her cell. Any animal in the area would smell Chica and probably stay clear. At least that's what she told herself.

She mulled over how to approach Nora. She must have had a reason for arriving at work at five thirty on the day of the murder. She couldn't bring herself to believe Nora killed McKenzie, but she'd only known Nora since the previous summer. If Nora had wanted to hurt McKenzie, she couldn't have done it face to face. She was too petite, and he'd been strong.

Chica caught a scent and bolted into the forest.

"Chica. Come," Kalin yelled, and of course, Chica was too focused to obey. Her rump disappeared behind a lodge pole pine, one that hadn't fallen victim to pine beetle infestation and morphed from green to rusty red, and she was gone.

Minutes later, Chica returned with a dead rabbit between her jaws. She pranced toward Kalin, tail high, and dropped the white rabbit at Kalin's feet.

"Gross." If she left the rabbit on the ground, Chica would run back for the dead animal. The rabbit looked as if it slept, not a drop of blood spilled, meaning Chica had shaken the poor creature until its neck broke. She picked up the rabbit and placed it in the joint of two branches a foot above Chica's reach.

McKenzie's neck had snapped just like the rabbit's. He might have been scared for a second, but he couldn't have known he was going to die. What if Nora tampered with the binding but only meant to injure him or ruin a training run? Kalin needed to confront her and see her eyes when she asked about her early arrival at work on the day McKenzie died.

She returned home, showered, ate and waited until it was late enough to visit Nora. She did all this without waking Ben. At seven, she knocked on Nora's door. When Nora didn't answer, she rang the doorbell several times. A light within brightened the hallway and streamed onto the porch.

"Who is it?" Nora asked from behind the closed door.

"Kalin. I need to talk to you."

Nora opened the door. "Has something happened?"

"Not really. I wanted to catch you before you went to work."

Nora led Kalin into the kitchen, shuffling her feet along the floor as she walked. "Coffee?" Nora asked in a voice deep with sleep.

Kalin sat at the kitchen table. "Sure."

Nora opened a fresh bag of coffee beans, and the aroma spread through the kitchen. She placed a quarter cup of beans in the grinder and hit the button until the beans were finely ground. She poured the fresh ground beans into the coffee maker, and the machine gurgled when the brewing process started.

Nora shouldn't be drinking coffee in her condition, and then it occurred to her she didn't know if Nora was still pregnant. "I talked to Charlie. He thinks you're going to work hung over."

"He said that about me? What a jerk."

"Does he know you're pregnant?"

Nora shook her head, and Kalin took that as confirmation she still carried the baby.

"Then it might look like you're hung over. Do you trust him enough to tell him?"

"I guess. I don't want to get fired."

"I need to ask you a question, and I'm hoping you won't be offended. I found something out today."

"You look serious. Is everything okay?"

"On the morning Steve died, you were seen in the parking lot beside the mountain ops building."

"So? There's nothing unusual about that."

"At five thirty in the morning." Kalin watched Nora's face and was disappointed when Nora stood, turned her back to Kalin and fussed with the coffee pot.

"What are you saying?" Nora asked.

"I'm not saying anything, but I would like to know why you were there so early."

"When I asked you to help find out who killed Steve, I didn't expect you'd think I was the murderer."

"I don't think you killed him, but the police are going to want to know what you were doing, and I wanted to talk with you first."

Nora whirled on Kalin. "You're going to tell the cops?"

"Hang on a sec. I only want to talk to you. You know I have to tell Miller. He'll find out anyway, and it's better if he hears it from me."

As if trying to control herself, Nora breathed slowly. "I'm sorry. I don't know what's wrong with me these days. I can't seem to control my temper." She poured one mug of coffee and handed it to Kalin.

Kalin added milk and sugar and took a sip. "This is good. You're not having anything?"

Nora rubbed her hand across her belly. "I can't eat or drink this early. As for that morning, I went in early to work in the rental shop. I told you I didn't get time off, but I have flexible hours. I can't afford to lose the job or my benefits."

"Did you go in early any other day?"

"No. Steve broke up with me the night before. I couldn't sleep. I went to work because it was better than lying in the dark feeling shitty."

"Did you tell the RCMP that when they interviewed you?"

"No. They didn't ask, and it's none of their business."

Kalin placed her mug on the table and looked Nora in her eyes. "Did you see anyone else that morning? If you did—"

"Nope."

The abruptness of the answer made Kalin wonder if Nora was hiding something, but how could she accuse Nora of that without risking their friendship. "Did anyone see you in the rental shop?"

"I doubt it. I was working in the back room."

"This doesn't look good."

"I think I've had enough of this conversation."

"Please don't be mad. You know I have to tell Miller. Really, I'll position it better than if he hears it from someone else."

Nora's emotions bounced around like a skier on a mogul run. Must be hormones. Kalin had pushed too hard again. Somehow, she had to find a balance between her job and her friends. Kalin eased her chair away from the table.

Kalin left Nora's and headed in the direction of her office. Nora had a reasonable explanation for being in the parking lot at five thirty, but she'd hidden her actions from the RCMP. A guilty person would do that. She could have snuck into the tuning room, altered the binding and then gone to the rental shop. Or she could have gone straight to the rental shop. Or she could have seen someone else go into the tuning room and didn't want to say. Kalin didn't know what to believe, but she did know she'd better call Miller and update him. She slipped her hand from her mitt and dialed.

"It's Kalin," she said.

Miller chuckled. "You're calling me early. What's happened?"

Was he laughing at her, or was something else going on wherever he was? "Nothing happened, but there's something I want to talk to you about."

"I'm sure this will be interesting. It always is with you."

"Hey, that's not fair. I'm trying to help."

"I know you are. I'm teasing. What's on your mind?"

Miller came across as strong, ethical and fun to be around. She understood why Becky had fallen for him. She was sure other women were attracted to him, but thought Becky would look further than his appearance. They made a good couple.

"I met with the snowmaking team this morning. They get off duty between five and five thirty every day and walk by the tuning room on their way from the hill to the mountain ops building. No one saw anyone in or around the tuning room on the morning McKenzie died, but one of them saw Nora Cummings in the parking lot at five thirty but not anywhere near the tuning room."

"That was good thinking, but you shouldn't be investigating on your own. I'll take it from here."

"There's something else."

Miller sighed. "Of course there is."

"I talked to Nora."

"You have to stop interfering. My job is to question her, not yours. Now she'll be able to prepare herself before I talk to her."

"Sorry. I hadn't thought of that. I don't think it matters. She told me she went straight to the rental shop and didn't go in the tuning room. She's not the murderer. I thought she might have seen someone or something if she was there that early."

"Please don't talk to her again or tell anyone else about this. I'll get up there when I can."

"I hear you, but the snowmakers all know. Any news on Edwin Bucher?" Kalin listened to silence for a moment and thought Miller had hung up on her. "Hello?"

"I'm still here. I wanted to speak with your boss before talking to you."

"What's happened? Come on, I shared with you, and you know you can trust me."

"Alright. We received news that Edwin's bindings were not tampered with. The DIN setting was set to his usual number, and the display unit hadn't been touched."

Kalin felt a rush of relief. She hadn't realized how tense she'd been, thinking someone might be killing skiers. The motive for McKenzie's murder had to be personal. "So it wasn't attempted murder?"

"It doesn't look like it."

"And it's not related to McKenzie's death?"

"We don't think so."

Kalin skirted the edge of the mountain operations parking lot. At seven forty-five, the street lamps lit the lot but not the path to the buildings, leaving Kalin in the shadows.

A car drove across the hard packed snow of the parking lot and parked beside the mountain operations building. Amber jumped out of the driver's side, slammed the door and skipped around to the back. She pulled a wheelchair from the hatch, opened the front door and Donny lifted himself from the car to the chair.

Amber wasn't due to move out of staff housing until five, and Donny lived in town. Either Amber had driven to town to pick up Donny, which she didn't believe, or he'd slept up on the resort. Another budding romance.

"Come on, Amber, I need to see him." Jeff stood at the entrance to the tuning room, glaring at her.

"I can't let you in. You're not on the list." Amber placed herself mid-doorway, giving Jeff no room to slide around her. "I'll go get him. Wait here."

"Fine." Jeff watched her ass as she walked away. Too round for his tastes. He liked smaller women, like Nora.

Donny returned a few moments later, grinning at Amber, and asked Jeff, "What's up?"

"Come outside for a minute."

"I'm busy. Charlie will get pissed if I'm gone too long."

Jeff glanced at Amber and back to Donny. "Just for a sec."

"Okay. Let me tell Charlie."

Jeff waited awkwardly beside Amber.

"Your bruises are fading," Amber said.

Jeff touched his cheek, remembering the fight with Edwin—Edwin, who was living every skier's nightmare, the one Donny lived with and couldn't wake up from—and Jeff wished he hadn't hit the guy.

The wheels of Donny's chair created narrow tracks in the snow as Jeff followed him outside.

Donny stopped rolling and let out a sigh. "What is it?"

"Dad's pissed off."

"You brought me out here to tell me that. When is he not?"

Jeff blew into cupped hands to warm his fingers. "Where were you last night?"

Donny shot a glance over his shoulder and grinned.

"You were with Amber?" Jeff smiled. "It's about time."

"She seems to like me despite the chair. What's up with Dad?" Donny slapped his hand on his legs.

"When he noticed you hadn't slept in your bed, he panicked. He yelled at Mom and me. I think he was actually worried about you. I don't think it occurred to him that you were with a girl. That ought to make him happy."

"Did he hit you?"

The cold seeped through Jeff's Spyder suit, and he stomped his feet. "Mom was standing beside me. Have you heard any more about the investigation?"

Donny cocked his head to one side. "Kalin Thompson and Fred Morgan nose around a lot, but they don't say anything in front of me. I think I'm a suspect."

"You?"

"I had access to his skis. And there's the car accident."

Jeff laughed but felt the bitterness of bile rise in his throat. "Yeah right. Like I believe that bullshit."

"Nora was upset when she came in this morning. Have you talked to her lately?"

"Not really."

"You should. She needs a friend right now. She gets lunch at noon."

"What are you? Matchmakers dot com? There's Jenkinson. Gotta go." With his canary-yellow ski boots dangling over one shoulder and skis resting on the other, Jeff trotted to his coach. "What's the schedule today? I thought we were on the mountain first."

"It's been rearranged. We're up right after lunch. It's weight training this morning. We'll be done by eleven thirty."

Jeff headed toward the gym. He left his ski gear in a locker and changed into shorts and a sleeveless T-shirt. His teammates crowded the gym, alternating between free weights and weight machines. No matter what gym he entered, they all smelled the same, and the odor wasn't pleasant, but the sounds motivated him to work as hard as the others in the room.

Focusing on his workout just wasn't happening. He couldn't get Nora off his mind. He used to think he'd marry her. He wasn't sure how he felt about her being pregnant with McKenzie's baby, but it's not as if the guy were around to make a claim. McKenzie should have died weeks earlier, before Nora got herself pregnant.

Jeff clanged the bar into the slats and did a set of crunches on the bench before getting up. He moved to the free weights but couldn't shake the thoughts of Nora. He couldn't understand her. He wanted her back.

After his unsatisfying weight training session, he lingered outside the tuning room and waited for Nora.

Constable Miller approached him. "Just the man I need to see." He pulled a photo from the inside pocket of his RCMP issued jacket, giving Jeff a glimpse of his navy Kevlar vest. He held the photo in front of Jeff but didn't give it to him. "Any comment?"

"Obviously that's me."

"Do you want to tell me why you're smiling?"

"That's your big question?"

"You can drop the attitude any time. It won't help you. I'd like to know why you're smiling considering this is a photo of you looking at Steve McKenzie right after he crashed."

"Now you think I killed him?"

"I didn't say that. It's an odd time for smiling."

"I thought he was hurt. I thought it would knock him off the team for the season. I didn't know he was dead."

"Interesting motive you have." Miller turned and left Jeff standing by himself.

Jeff was still staring at Miller's back when Nora exited the tuning room. He pretended to bump into her by accident and asked if he could join her for lunch. They walked to the cafeteria, collected their food from the buffet and sat at a table by the entrance to the hallway as far from others as possible. Day after day, the same odors wafted from the buffet and the smell was starting to annoy Jeff. Couldn't the cooks change the menu?

"I remember that face. You look mad," Jeff said.

Nora pushed lettuce from one side of her plate to the other. "I didn't get mad at you a lot."

"No. That's true. I didn't mean it that way."

"Kalin thinks I killed Steve," Nora said.

Jeff placed his fork beside his plate. Suddenly, he didn't feel like eating. What's with Kalin? "Donny said Kalin thinks he's the murderer."

"She came over this morning and asked me why I was at the resort at five thirty on the day Steve died."

Kalin had no right to interfere. As if they hadn't suffered enough without that bitch poking holes in their family like a pine beetle decimating a lodge pole. "How'd she know that? Why were you in that early?"

"Are you suspicious too? I was working, and one of the snowmakers saw me."

"Did he see anyone else?"

"I don't know."

Jeff studied Nora's pert nose, her hair sticking out in tufts and her angled cheeks. He almost reached out and touched her but stopped himself in time. He'd have to move slowly with her. Nora didn't like to feel pressured.

CHAPTER TWENTY-SIX

Nora spotted Constable Miller through the floor-to-ceiling windows of the cafeteria. She didn't want to see him. As if Jeff pressuring her to get back together wasn't enough of an issue. He tried to hide his feelings from her, and if it wasn't for Donny and Lisa, she wouldn't have had lunch with him. For their sakes, she needed to stay friends with Jeff. First Kalin, then Jeff and now Miller. She wanted the day to end.

Miller hadn't spotted her yet. Nora hadn't lied when answering his direct questions, but she'd left out important details, and she didn't want to face his inquiring eyes.

She darted out of the cafeteria, hoping to avoid him.

"Nora," Miller called. "I'd like to speak with you."

Nora stopped mid-step, almost tripping but recovering before she fell. Her face flushed. "I have to get to work."

"And I am working. I'll walk you back to the tuning room." He slid in beside her and escorted her along the path. "I spoke with Kalin Thompson this morning."

"That figures. If you've already talked to her, what's the point of talking to me?"

"I'd like you to tell me why you were in the mountain ops parking lot on the morning Steve died."

Nora moaned. "I have two jobs. During the day, I tune skis. During the season, I work in the rental shop. Before the season opens, I prep the shop. My manager lets me set my own hours."

"Do you usually work at the rental shop at five thirty? That seems early."

"I couldn't sleep. Since I was up, I decided to go in."

Miller flipped through his notebook, stopping about midway through the pages. "That was the morning after Steve broke up with you. Is that why you couldn't sleep?"

"Do you have to get this personal?"

Miller waited and waited some more.

Nora couldn't stand the tension and said, "I didn't want to lie in bed thinking about him. There's nothing wrong with that."

"Not in itself. Why did Steve break up with you?"

Nora stepped to the side and let a guy with a snow blower clear the walking path. The snow banks were already three feet high. She was about to miss a great season. She couldn't go snowboarding much longer, so how the hell would she spend her spare time? She turned back to Miller. "What does that have to do with anything?"

"You have a fiery temper. Was that the reason?"

She relaxed her shoulders and told herself to get a grip on her emotions. "I don't have a temper. You're flustering me. Steve died the day after we had a big fight. How do you think that makes me feel?"

"What did you fight about?"

They walked past the lift line. The Holden team started their training session, and Nora caught a glimpse of Jeff getting on the chair. They didn't have a future, and she wished Jeff would accept that. Her relationship with both Jeff and Steve had ended in a brutal argument. What did that say about her? "Really, I have to tell you that?"

"You do."

"We had different ideas of where our relationship should go." *As in, he wanted to break up, and I wanted to get married. Nothing big, really.*

"Because you're pregnant?"

"Who told you that?"

"Is that why he broke up with you?"

Nora put her hands in her ski jacket pockets and dug her nails into her palms. "It had to be Kalin. She's always telling you things."

"Nora, I'm going to keep asking you until you answer me."

"Fine. That's the reason. He was a jerk about it if you ask me."

Miller made a note in his book. "You were angry with Steve."

Nora picked up her pace, trying to shorten the length of time she had to spend with Miller. She noticed he lengthened his stride to match her speed. He even kept writing in his notebook. "I was angry and scared. That doesn't mean I killed him."

"Did you see anyone else that morning?"

"No."

"You're blushing. Are you lying?"

"No. I didn't see anyone. I swear."

They reached the outer door of the tuning room, and he let her go.

"I thought we were friends," Nora said to Kalin the moment she barged into Kalin's office.

Kalin was working on the orientation plan for the upcoming crop of winter employees, but clearly Nora needed to talk to her, so she placed her pen on her desk and swiveled to face her.

Nora hovered.

"We are friends." Kalin stood and shut the door. She had a feeling she knew what Nora was about to say. "Can we talk about this?"

"Does Ben know how horrible you've been to me?"

"This has nothing to do with Ben. I haven't told him what's going on."

"You won't tell your boyfriend, but you'll tell the cops?"

"I told you I had to tell the RCMP you were at the resort, but I talked to you first. I can't hide information from them."

"You're always spouting about privacy and working in HR. I've heard you tell your employees the only thing you'd fire them for was leaking private information. I guess that doesn't apply to you."

"What I told Constable Miller wasn't private."

"You told him I'm pregnant after you swore to me you wouldn't tell anyone."

"I didn't tell him that."

A knock at the door interrupted them. Ben poked his head in. "I can hear you two in the hallway. What's going on?"

"Your girlfriend's a shit." Nora pushed past Ben and disappeared.

Ben's ski boots squeaked as he stepped toward Kalin and kissed her. "What was that about?"

"It's been a weird day. She thinks I told Miller something about her, but I didn't." Kalin filled Ben in on what she'd told Miller but not about Nora's pregnancy.

Kalin's desk phone rang, and she checked the caller display. Monica.

"Amber Cristelli is here to see you. Can I tell her when you'll be free?"

Kalin heard the stiffness in Monica's voice and figured Amber wanted to talk about her eviction and plead with Kalin to go against Monica's order. Amber had to be out of her unit by five. If she refused to leave, the next step in the process was to have security escort her out, but Kalin didn't think Amber was the type.

"Right now." The orientation plan would have to wait. Kalin looked at Ben. "Amber is here to see me. Can we talk later?"

"I was hoping to have lunch. Did you eat?"

"I haven't had time."

"I'll pick up something for you." Ben snuck a quick kiss on her lips before he opened the door.

"You're so nice to me."

He nodded at Amber as he left and she arrived.

Kalin offered Amber her guest chair and acknowledged Monica behind Amber's back before shutting out the workplace.

"Did you hear what Monica did to me yesterday?"

Kalin tilted her head to one side and smiled at Amber. "I don't think Monica did anything to you. She followed policy."

"Well, the policy sucks. I didn't do anything wrong. I can't believe I'd be kicked out for helping a friend."

"The rules are clear. We can't apply them to some people and not others just because we like them. Monica was doing her job. Don't make it personal."

"It is personal. I have nowhere to live now."

"There are still places with vacancies. There's a list on the board outside my office. Don't you have a friend, one that's not in staff housing, you can stay with until you find somewhere?"

"I was trying to help a friend, and now I'm being punished."

"You might want to reassess who you call a friend. Cheryl knew the rules and that you'd get evicted if she was caught there."

"First I don't get the tuning job and then I get kicked out of housing. Why does this place have it in for me?"

"This place, as you put it, doesn't have it in for you. Monica was lenient and left the pot she found in your unit out of the report. It could be worse. I don't remember you applying for a tuning job. Do you mean at the rental shop?"

"Yes. As if you didn't know. You're in charge of hiring."

"I don't keep track of every decision. Who didn't hire you?"

"Nora Cummings told the manager I wasn't experienced enough."

"Nora's been working in the shop for a long time. She knows what level of experience is required to operate efficiently. I'm sure she did what she thought was right for the shop." Kalin guessed Nora hadn't hired Amber because she slept with McKenzie, and she couldn't blame her. "Have you moved out yet?"

"No. I was hoping to get another chance."

"I can't do that. Finish your shift. I'll extend your time till seven."

"Figures you'd take Monica's side. I don't know why I thought you'd do anything for me."

The door bounced off the wall after Amber stormed out, and Kalin wondered if she'd ever get used to employees leaving her office in a snit. She took a deep breath and reminded herself how young Amber was.

Amber's job guarding the tuning room was visible. The HR group kept staff housing issues separate from workplace issues. To fire an employee because of something that happened in housing was unusual, but Amber was doing one of the most important jobs at the resort over the next five days. Kalin couldn't justify firing her for a minor staff housing violation, but how could she continue to trust her?

Kalin tucked into the corner of her living room couch and listened to the fire crackle. She didn't know what to do about Amber. What she did know was McKenzie's murder needed to be solved before her life would settle down again.

A wild storm dumped snowflakes in a kaleidoscope of activity. Snow stuck to the corners of the windows, building small piles in the shape of white anthills. She felt a chill despite her wool socks, folded down at her ankles, sweat pants and fleece hoodie. Chica lay with her nose pressed against the sliding glass door as if pining to go outside. "Not in this weather, girl."

Balancing her laptop on her legs, Kalin clicked on the browser icon. She googled Donny Morley. There were newspaper articles about races he'd won. Alpine Canada logs recorded his results for numerous junior and regional events. Jeff's name also appeared but always lower in rank than Donny's name. Donny's career had been promising before his injury stole that from him, and yet he'd chosen to stay in the industry.

A newspaper heading grabbed her attention, and she clicked the link to *Holden Ski Team Tragedy*.

Kalin knew the story but read the article anyway. The town of Holden was relieved their local ski hero, Steve McKenzie, wasn't injured in the accident even though he was driving the car. Rachel Hudson escaped with minor injuries. The car slid into a tree with the rear door on the passenger side taking the impact. McKenzie walked away from the crash. Donny never walked again.

Next she found an article about Jeff Morley and Steve McKenzie that left Kalin with the impression Jeff had a temper. Jeff and McKenzie were arrested for fighting in public. They'd been outside a bar in Holden.

The article put McKenzie in a positive light. Jeff, not so much.

"Did you know that?" Kalin asked Ben.

He glanced up from the Texas Hold 'Em game he'd been playing on his laptop. "What?"

"That McKenzie and Jeff were arrested last year for fighting in public."

"Everybody knows that."

"How come no one told me?"

Ben sipped his beer and placed the bottle beside his computer. "I don't know. I guess it never came up."

"Don't you think that gives Jeff a motive?"

"It happened a year ago. Why would he wait until now to get revenge? And besides, what's the motive? That he lost a fight with McKenzie?"

"Maybe watching McKenzie race year after year when Donny can't finally got to him. Do you know why Rachel Hudson was in the car too?"

"She was McKenzie's girlfriend."

Nora rarely spoke to Kalin about her adoptive sister. Rachel died not long after Donny was paralyzed, but that's all Kalin knew. "How did Nora end up dating the guy who paralyzed Donny and dated her sister?"

"Don't know. You'll have to ask Nora." Ben turned back to his poker game.

Ben didn't gossip, so Kalin wasn't surprised by his short answer. "I don't think she wants to talk to me right now."

CHAPTER TWENTY-SEVEN

Not long after eleven that evening, Amber stumbled her way across the bar, weaving through the throng. Every chair hosted a person. The dance floor was alive with people thrusting and grinding, oblivious to anyone else. No one would notice if she was gone for a bit. She'd crash later at her friend's place. Before that, she had things to do. She'd had enough of this resort taking advantage of her. She was nice to people, always trying to do the right thing, so what was up? No matter what she did, she ended up getting screwed.

Her public face was sweet. McKenzie, the cocky bastard, had been one to notice. He probably never even questioned whether he could have her or not. Just taken for granted she'd be available. He slept with her and scurried right back to that Nora bitch. Nora probably knew and that's why she badmouthed Amber to the rental manager.

And Kalin. Kalin had been friendly, joked with her about Donny, and then turned on her as if she were shit on bare feet. Kalin didn't even stick up for her when McKenzie pushed her. She'd let the jerk keep on skiing without his pass. Well, she'd show her.

Amber trudged through the snow using the edge of the path to guide her to staff housing. With wind slapping flakes in every direction, she had two feet of visibility. She'd worn skin-tight jeans to the bar without a layer of thermal underwear, or any underwear for that matter, not wanting to look fat, and now she wished she hadn't been so vain. At least her boots kept the bottom half of her legs warm.

Earlier, she'd moved out of her housing unit but hadn't turned in her key. After business hours, no one was in the HR office to collect it.

She'd innocently bring it back to Monica tomorrow.

She reached the staff-housing parking lot and stood in the shadows. The blinding snowstorm kept her hidden, even so, she wanted to make sure no one was there, especially security guards doing their rounds. While she waited, she dug through the snow, found a rock the size of a baseball and worked the edges loose with the toe of her boot. She checked the area one more time, and when she didn't see anyone, she wobbled across the lot. In her drunken state, she needed three tries to unlock the front door. She bolted through the lobby, turned to the back stairs and ran up four flights.

The water system had an outlet for a fire hose on each floor. A small lock secured the wheel that opened the water flow. Amber hesitated. She almost turned and ran, but then convinced herself the resort deserved to be punished. What's a little water anyway?

She bashed the rock against the lock, breaking the shackle with the first hit. She lifted the safety catch, opened the valve and turned the wheel. Water burst from the pipe, spreading across the floor. Within a minute water cascaded down the steps. She took off in front of the river, laughing the entire way down the staircase, listening to the water rush behind her.

The alarm from Ben's two-way radio blasted him awake. Midnight. A first responder call paged into their bedroom. Kalin groaned and rolled over. Ben reacted instantly. He could be at the fire station in five minutes. Jumping into a pair of boots, he grabbed his truck keys and took off. The last to arrive would have to work dispatch, and he didn't intend to be stuck at the station.

Knowing the other volunteer firefighters were rushing to get in, he didn't waste a minute. He was the deputy chief, and he could pull rank and order someone else to remain at the station, but that never went over well. He wanted to be chief, and when the time came, he would need the support of the rest of the firefighters.

His wipers brushed snow off the windshield, but didn't help with the drifts accumulating on the road. Ben adeptly drove around them, avoiding the largest piles, and kept his speed.

At the outskirts of Stone Mountain, he turned left into the lit fire station in front of two other cars. Both garage doors were open, and the trucks sat prepared for use. He hoped the call was something more exciting than a false alarm.

Three other firefighters were already in their yellow fire pants, held up with suspenders that covered navy T-shirts. They were at the ready with their jackets and helmets.

Jason waited for Ben near the front door of the truck. Ben had persuaded Jason to join the fire department. Like most employees working at the resort, he needed extra cash. Even though it was a volunteer position, the municipality paid each member when they were called in.

Jason's experience dealing with high-pressure water systems in snowmaking made him a good fit. He'd finished his custom fire-training certificate at the College of the Rockies and could easily become a senior firefighter. "What's up?" Ben asked.

"An employee called in. There's a flood in the new staff housing building," Jason said.

"Shit." Staff housing was HR's big deal. As Kalin repeatedly told him, the resort had spent over four million constructing the building. Kalin had used the new accommodations for recruiting, boasting the best staff housing in the province, trying to lure employees. A minor flood wouldn't be so bad, but a major flood would be chaos for Kalin and her team. They'd have to find somewhere else for employees to live. Ben hated adding more stress to Kalin's life. She already worked too many hours.

"Hey, Ben." Vicky sauntered toward the fire truck, fully geared up, and ran her fingers through his hair.

"Stop," Ben said.

"I know. You have a girlfriend."

Laughter circulated among the firefighters, but when Ben glared at them, they all pretended they were more interested in getting in the truck than in Vicky and Ben.

The last of the volunteers arrived, and the fire truck took off, reaching staff housing within minutes. Ben and Jason ran into the building to assess the scene. Vicky followed close behind. Ben opened the ground floor door to the stairwell, and water spread into the main area.

"We need to evacuate. Call Kalin and get a list of occupied units. She has it on her computer at home," Ben directed Jason. "Ask her to email it to me."

Vicky beat Jason and called Kalin.

"Stay away from him," Jason said to Vicky once she was off the phone. "He doesn't need the hassle from you."

Vicky put her standard pout on her face. "How come you never liked me?"

Jason shook his head. "Grow up."

Ben pulled the fire alarm. He ran to the side stairway and took the steps two at a time, reaching the top floor within a minute. He crossed the hallway back to the flooded stairway and discovered water gushing from the stand pipe. He turned the wheel, cutting the supply, and caught his breath.

The broken lock was pinned in one corner, jammed under the edge of a rock. He held the lock between his thumb and index finger, examining the damage. The rock shouldn't be there. He didn't need to be a detective to figure out the rock had been used to smash the lock. Vandalism. Someone was pissed at the resort again.

Ben returned to the ground floor and found a group of staff milling around with the members of the fire department. He checked his phone for the list from Kalin and motioned for Jason to follow him.

They entered each unit that had employees assigned, confirming no one remained in the building. Now they had to decide if the building was safe. There might be structural damage caused by the flow of water. Ben took in the ruined carpet, installed a mere month ago, and the water stained walls and ceiling and felt bad for Kalin. He'd watched her excitement while the building came together, piece by piece, over the last year.

Ben called Kalin, and she answered on the first ring.

"How bad is it?" she asked.

"Hard to tell. I'm concerned about the building structure."

Kalin groaned. "It's brand new."

"To be safe, I don't think the staff should sleep there tonight. Can you call the front desk and authorize an allotment of guest rooms?"

"That'll be expensive. We don't get those for free."

Stone Mountain managed the privately owned condos and paid a rental fee if they used them. "Take it easy. Insurance should cover the cost."

"You're right. I should have thought of that. I'm just uptight. Is it safe enough for staff to get some things for the night?"

"I think so. I'll get anyone affected organized and then send them to the front desk."

"I'll meet the staff there to make sure they get settled," Kalin said. "By the way, thanks for having your girlfriend call me."

"I asked Jason, she just—"

"Relax. I'm kidding. Did you take Chica with you?"

"No."

"She's not here. She must have snuck out when you left. I've been calling, but she's not coming. I'll look for her on my way back from the front desk."

"Not at this time of night. I'll go when I get home. She'll come back. Don't worry."

The front desk agents assigned each employee a room. Once confident there were no issues, Kalin drove through the resort looking for Chica, using the search as an excuse to drive by the fire station to see if Vicky and Ben were both there. The fire station stood ominously dark.

Chica didn't answer her calls as she drove around the resort, but with the noise from the wind and visibility diminished by the storm, she wasn't surprised. She arrived home without Chica, without Ben and felt defeated. She plopped on the living room couch and watched the snow fall. Every few minutes she checked outside for her beautiful dog.

The second Ben entered their place, Kalin asked, "Did you find her?"

"No. I asked security to keep an eye out for her. They'll bring her home if they see her."

"She could get lost in this storm. Shouldn't we go looking?"

"She'll be fine." Ben took Chica's leash from Kalin and set it on the coffee table. "Let's go to bed. She'll bark when she comes home."

Kalin followed Ben but didn't feel right going to bed without Chica in the room. "How bad is the building?"

"It's hard to tell. The carpet and walls in the east stairwell are ruined."

She flipped the heavy quilt off her pillow and eased in. "Do you think there's structural damage?"

Ben got in the other side of the bed and shifted until he pressed against her. "We'll need an expert to check. It could go either way."

"How did it happen?"

Ben hesitated. "It was vandalism."

"No."

"Someone broke the lock on the stand pipe and opened the water flow."

Kalin's eyes moistened with tears. "What am I going to do if we don't have rooms for the new employees? Most of them accepted their jobs based on having housing. If they have nowhere to live, they won't come. They'll be here in two weeks."

"We'll know more in the morning." Ben pulled Kalin close, and she rested her head on his shoulder. "There was housing in town before the new building was built. Monica must know how to find rooms."

"I'm not looking forward to telling her this."

"She'll figure something out if she has to."

"Are you sure we shouldn't look for Chica?" Kalin asked.

"She could be anywhere."

"Is Vicky going to be a problem for us?"

Ben reached over Kalin and turned off the bedside lamp. "Never. You're my girl."

Kalin pressed her cheek against Ben's bare chest and closed her eyes as his chest hair tickled her skin. Sleep took its time in coming.

As Ben predicted, barking woke them when Chica returned at dawn.

"See. I told you she'd come home," Ben said.

Kalin whipped off the quilt and ran to the door before Ben rolled over. The storm had subsided, leaving a blanket of white snow. The outdoor light reflected off the snow's surface, giving the illusion of tiny jewels scattered over the driveway.

Without greeting Kalin, Chica trotted straight to her bowl and lapped the water. Kalin stepped on the clumps of snow dropping off Chica and followed her to the kitchen.

She turned on the light and gasped. "Ben. She's hurt."

Blood spattered the floor where Chica had crossed the tiles, and the water in her bowl turned pink.

After she finished drinking, Ben examined her. Blood stained her mouth and throat but nowhere else. "I can't find a wound. She must have killed something."

"What?"

Ben shrugged. "I don't know. Let's get her washed." He dragged Chica into the bathroom and turned on the taps. "Don't tell anyone about this."

Not liking a bath, Chica bolted backward, but Kalin expected the move and shut the door. They wrestled her into the tub. After cleaning her, Kalin threw the blood stained towels into the washer.

"Hand me the new collar you bought her," Ben said.

"I didn't get her a new collar."

Ben winked at her. "The one with her name embroidered on the outside and 'I Love Ben' on the inside."

"What are you talking about?"

Ben's neck reddened. "The pink collar in the front hall."

"You're kidding me. I would never buy anything pink." Kalin went to the front hall and lifted the collar off a peg. She examined the writing on the inside. "How did she get in here?"

"Who?"

"This has to be from Vicky. Is she stalking you?"

Ben rubbed his hand across his forehead. "We've been slack about locking the house. We don't know it's her for sure."

"Really? Is there someone else out there who you expect to get 'I Love You' messages from?"

"I'll talk to her."

"What if she let Chica out?"

"I can't see her doing that, but I'll talk to her and tell her to stay out of my life."

Screw the Blonde Goddess. She can't have Ben. Kalin lifted her pajama top over her head and let it flutter to the floor. She gave Ben her best seductive smile. "We've got half an hour before the alarm is set to go off. Any ideas on what to do with the time?"

CHAPTER TWENTY-EIGHT

At eight thirty that morning, Kalin waited for Reed in his office. There she was again, bringing him bad news. To kill that thought, she wandered along the edge of his desk taking in the photographs. The theme covering the desktop shifted from the wall photos of Ian skiing to photos of family, and if the display was any indication, Reed was proud of his peeps. She stopped at a framed snapshot of a young woman wearing a seventies ski outfit, holding a ski trophy and beaming at the camera.

Reed cleared his throat.

Embarrassed Reed caught her snooping, she said, "Sorry. I didn't mean to pry."

"That's my wife, Susan. She raced when she was a teenager."

Reed's heart-warming smile was the one Kalin remembered from the first time she met him. She guessed that was his usual look but stress turned him serious. "I love the outfit." Kalin smiled back at him. "Looks like she was good."

"She was." Reed dropped his gloves and toque in a basket and hung his ski jacket on a hook. "You're here early. Something must be going on."

"The new staff housing building was vandalized last night. Someone opened the fire hydrant tap on the fourth floor and flooded the building."

"How bad is it?"

"We evacuated last night, just to be safe, and the fire department called in a construction company to assess the structure. We should know later today. I put the staff in private units for now."

"Wasn't the tap secured?"

"It was. Ben found a rock beside the stand pipe and thinks it was used to break the lock."

"I think you need to spend some time evaluating the security situation around the resort. You've made a few errors since your promotion. I know it's not your fault someone vandalized a building, but it looks like it was easy to do. Have you been spending more time on HR issues than on security?"

"No. The other way around. I've let Monica handle most of HR while I focus on the McKenzie situation."

"I see. That tells me you should be asking for more help from Fred. I'd like to meet with you more often and review what you're working on. Ask Gertrude to schedule two weekly meetings for the next couple of months."

"Okay." Kalin didn't want to explain her awkward relationship with Fred, but she didn't want to take the blame for everything that went wrong either. She'd have to figure out how to get Fred on board.

"Do we know who did it?" Reed asked.

"No. I think it's a spiteful act. Whoever did this was angry at the resort."

"You have someone in mind?"

Kalin hesitated, but it had to be said. "Two days ago, Monica evicted Amber Cristelli, and she had until last night to move out. She's the employee who's been checking people at the entrance to the tuning room. I can't think of anyone else."

"How did she get in the building? Wasn't it locked?"

"It was. Amber still has her keys and will return them to Monica this morning." From the length of the wrinkle lines formed by Reed's frown, Kalin could see the answer made him unhappy.

Reed shook his head several times. "You evicted an employee and didn't take her keys away from her."

"She left the building after HR closed for the night. It's our procedure for the employee to return the keys the next day unless we think they're a risk."

"That policy needs to be changed. Did you report the flood to the RCMP?"

"Ben called them last night when the fire department was on scene. I'll call Constable Miller about Amber this morning."

"Did you inform the insurance company?"

"I just talked to them. They're sending someone this afternoon. I've turned this over to the maintenance department."

"Okay. Follow up later today and let me know the status."

On her way through Reed's outer office, Kalin stopped at Gertrude's desk and explained what she needed.

"I can give you Tuesdays at noon and Fridays at five thirty." Gertrude looked apologetic and shrugged her shoulders. "He doesn't have any other regular times open."

Ben was not going to be happy. He already thought she was spending too much time at work. Now she'd be home late every Friday night.

Kalin returned to her office and to a flashing message waiting light. She stared at the blinking square. Sometimes her boss was a jerk. How could he expect her to know about every lock on the resort? The light demanded her attention, and Kalin jabbed it with her thumb. Monica had left her a voicemail saying Mark Gardner was waiting in the HR reception area. Not sure who he was, she called Monica.

"He's a snowmaker. He said you asked to see him when he returned from Vancouver."

"Of course. Send him over."

Kalin's phone rang.

"Your painting is ready," Lisa Hudson said. "Are you still interested in coming down for lunch?"

"Yes. Hang on a sec." Kalin opened her calendar and checked her schedule. "Oh, I don't think I can make it. Lunch is a bit tight, but I'd like to get together. Could we meet later?"

"Sure. I close at five thirty."

"Great. I'll be there."

Nineteen-year-old Mark Gardner stood in Kalin's doorway. His black hair, wet from hard physical labor of the dawn shift, sat plastered against his scalp. He had a skier's raccoon tan and a toothy smile. "You wanted to see me?"

"Come in." Kalin guided him to her guest chair. "I'm sorry about your father."

He gave a slight nod. "Thanks."

"I'm sure you know about Steve McKenzie."

"Yes."

"I'm interested in the morning you were called home. Did you see anyone in or around the tuning room on your way out?"

"Actually I did."

His answer surprised her. "Who?"

"I don't know. I was running to the mountain ops building. I saw the door to the tuning room open and close. You can see it through the glass door at the back of the administration building."

"What time was that?"

"It had to be a little after four."

"You didn't think that was odd?"

"I didn't think about it at all. Not until my boss said you wanted to see me. I'd just gotten a call my dad had a heart attack. Anyway, it was before the crash, so there was nothing to be suspicious about."

"I'm sorry. That was insensitive. Of course you were focused on your dad. Can you describe anything about the person?"

"Tall and thin, but I'm not sure whether it was a man or a woman."

"Can you remember what the person was wearing?"

"I'm sorry. I know this is important, but I just wasn't paying attention."

"That's okay. It's enough that we know someone entered the tuning room. Would you mind calling Constable Miller with the RCMP and telling him what you told me?" Kalin wrote Miller's number on a yellow sticky and handed it to Mark. If only he'd been able to describe the person, but at least Mark had seen someone, someone to blame other than Nora. Donny still came in first as a suspect. Now another person entered the race.

Fred entered her office minutes after Mark left. "You've got a problem."

"I know. If the building is closed for more than two weeks, I'll have to find rooms in town for the staff. You and I need to interview Amber Cristelli. Monica can guard the tuning room in about an hour."

"I'm not talking about the flood. Security found a dead deer early this morning. Killed in front of the Alpine Tracks lift."

Kalin sucked her lips between her teeth.

"Something ripped its neck apart. The guys spent over half an hour moving the body and shoveling bloody snow away from the front of the lift."

"What did they do with the deer?"

"They used a front end loader and moved the carcass behind the maintenance shed. The security reports from last night said your dog was missing and they were keeping an eye out for her."

"That's true."

"If the conservation officer finds out a dog killed a deer, he'll put the dog down."

"How would he know a deer's been killed?"

"I followed protocol and reported the incident. He's coming up later to have a look at the deer. He'll remove the body from the resort."

"Chica came home by herself last night. It couldn't have been her."

"Did she have any blood on her?"

Kalin's heart thudded. She didn't like to lie, but she loved Chica and intended to protect her. "No."

Fred waited a couple of heartbeats. "I'll let you get back to work. I'll return in an hour to interview Amber."

Kalin called Ben and left a message.

Amber dangled the scanning gun at her side and leaned against the wall outside the tuning room. Her head pounded, reminding her of what an idiot she'd been. Booze made her mean, but she'd been so pissed off last night. The problem was after she had one drink, she could never convince herself another would be an issue. All she had to do now was stay quiet. With the snowstorm last night, she couldn't have been seen. When she'd returned to the bar, none of her friends commented on her absence. She'd gone straight onto the dance floor and danced with her pals, feeling awfully smart.

She'd finally met someone decent. After their first night together, Amber knew she could be serious about Donny. Now, she'd gone and done something stupid. Something he wouldn't like. Why she had risked her relationship with him, she couldn't explain to herself. No more assholes for her and no more dumb moves.

Her hangover would get worse during the day. She closed her eyes and took a few deep breaths, staving off the nausea. Cool air crossed her face, and she opened her eyes. Kalin, Fred and Monica headed toward her. They couldn't know.

"We need to speak with you," Fred said. "Monica will monitor the door."

"Sure. What's up?" Amber said with forced cheeriness.

"Let's go to my office. We can talk there." Kalin took the scanning gun from Amber and handed the unit to Monica. "Thanks. We shouldn't be long."

The walk to Kalin's office felt like an eternity, giving stress time to build inside her as if snow were piling up before an avalanche. She blew into her palm, sniffed for any left over beer stench and breathed in the scent of mint toothpaste. She wanted to go home and hide. She didn't want to face Fred and Kalin together. All she had to do was deny, deny, deny.

Kalin began the questioning as soon as she closed her office door.

"Do you know what happened in staff housing last night?"

"Everybody's talking about it." Amber sat in a guest chair and waited for Kalin and Fred to sit. They weren't going to intimidate her. Fred sat in the second guest chair.

Kalin lowered herself into the swivel chair in front of her desk. "Did you see anything?"

"No. I wasn't there. I had to be out by seven." Amber should have known they'd suspect her. She'd been evicted the day before and stomped out of Kalin's office. If she'd been chill about the eviction or if she'd waited a few days, she might not be on their list of criminals. They couldn't have proof, but she found the way Fred stared at her unnerving.

Fred shifted, and his chair squeaked. "Where did you spend last night?"

Amber raised her eyebrows in mock surprise. "Like how is that your business?"

"Someone flooded the building on purpose. From what I hear, you left Kalin's office angry yesterday. I'd like to know where you were," Fred said.

"I was in the bar with friends from ten thirty until two. After that, it's none of your business."

"I'd like a list of those friends."

"No way. I don't have to tell you anything."

"We need someone to verify you were in the bar."

"Like I'd give you my friends' names. Then they'll know you think I flooded the building."

The discussion followed a tortuous path, never getting anywhere, and Kalin and Fred finally gave up and let her leave. Amber hoped she left them believing she had nothing to do with the flood, but she doubted it. She'd stick to the same story if the cops came around. In the meantime, back to work, hangover and all. Time to cut back on drinking.

CHAPTER TWENTY-NINE

Kalin and Lisa relaxed in a corner booth of the Happy Hound pub at the south end of Main Street, Holden drinking chilled white wine. After meeting Lisa at her gallery and picking up her painting, they'd decided to go for a drink.

The server placed a bowl of peanuts on the table and Kalin pushed them toward Lisa.

"You don't like nuts?"

"I'm allergic." Kalin shook her medical alert bracelet at Lisa. "Nora's never said how you ended up adopting her."

"There's not much to tell. Rachel, my daughter, was the same age as Nora, and when Nora's mom died, adopting her seemed like the right thing to do. The girls spent most of their time together in day care, and Nora's mom had no other family."

"You must have been close with her mom."

"I was." Lisa picked up a menu. "Are you hungry?"

Kalin got the impression Lisa wanted to change the subject, so she read a menu. After they ordered, Lisa seemed subdued as they waited for their food to arrive.

The pub owner's wife ran a pet adoption organization in the valley, which explained the pub's name. One wall boasted photos of hundreds of dogs and cats that had been adopted over the last ten years. The other wall displayed the local ski successes and early photos of Stone Mountain, chronicling its history.

"The painting looks perfect in the frame." Kalin poked her fork into a spear of grilled asparagus. "I can't wait to hang it. It'll liven up my office."

"If you'd like another one, let me know. I can custom make one for you."

Susan Reed entered the pub, nodded hello to Kalin and sat at the next table with the owner's wife. Kalin overheard their discussion about cats needing adoption, Susan's role in delivering cats around the valley and the list of cats in her care. Susan appeared friendly and animated, nothing like the day Kalin had seen her talking with Ian at the bottom of the ski run.

"Do you know Amber Cristelli?" Lisa asked, pulling Kalin back to their conversation.

"Sure. She works at the resort. Why?"

Lisa topped up their wine glasses from the bottle of Chardonnay. "She's dating Donny. He seems smitten."

"I'm not surprised. I've seen them flirting with each other." Kalin felt a pit grow in her stomach. She couldn't tell Lisa about her suspicion Amber had flooded staff housing.

"Any idea what she's like? It's been a long time since Donny's had a girlfriend."

Lisa was being a protective aunt, and Kalin wanted to help her but couldn't. "I've only talked with her a few times. She's a ticket checker. I know she has an interest in tuning." She stuck to the truth but still felt as if she'd lied.

"Well, at least they have something in common. Jeff will be happy for him, but I'm sure he'll have an opinion on Amber. He's always looking out for Donny. Especially since his accident."

"The accident must have been hard for both of them. I read a little about Donny's ski career. It's great he tunes for Holden. If he's that close to the sport, I'm surprised he doesn't ski."

"Whenever I ask him why, he changes the subject. He was so good. It's a shame he won't try the sit-ski."

"Does Jeff ever encourage him?"

"I'm not sure. In some ways, the accident was worse for Jeff than Donny. He was supposed to drive Donny home that night. They were at a party, and he wanted to stay later, so Donny caught a ride with a friend. Jeff's been trying to make it up to him ever since."

Kalin knew the so-called friend had been Steve McKenzie.

"Is there anything new in the investigation?" Lisa asked, taking the conversation in a different direction.

Kalin had hoped to avoid the topic, but understood, that like many in town, Lisa had known McKenzie and would be curious. "I don't know. The RCMP is pretty quiet about what they're doing."

"What about you? Are you looking into it too?"

Kalin wasn't sure how candid she should be in answering Lisa's questions. "Not really. I've been asked to secure the racers' equipment and let the RCMP know if I find out anything useful."

"I would have thought your boss would want his own investigation."

"He has a good relationship with the RCMP. He trusts them." Kalin sipped her wine. "Jeff's skiing well. I watched a couple of his training runs. Donny told me the coach is focusing more on Jeff than he used to and Jeff's times are getting faster."

And there was the look of a proud aunt.

On her way out, Susan Reed stopped in front of Kalin and Lisa. "You're Kalin, right?"

"I am." Kalin shook Susan's hand.

"I met with the conservation officer this morning to discuss stray pets in the area and wildlife. Your dog came up in the conversation."

"How come?" Kalin asked even though she knew the answer.

"He said a deer was killed at the resort and suspects your dog."

"Is there going to be a problem?"

"I put in a good word for you. He's going to come and see you. The best thing for you to do is convince him she won't be out loose again. He doesn't know for sure it was your dog, so you should be okay."

"Can I ask why you'd help me?"

Susan smiled and her face lit up. "I like animals. Even dogs. Sometimes I like them more than people."

Kalin left the pub, walked along Main Street and enjoyed the Christmas lights. The town had the festive feel of a community getting ready for a celebration. Every store showed off its talent for hanging Christmas decorations. A Santa, eight feet tall, waved at her as she walked by the bookstore, using a motion sensor to set off the hand. Kalin waved back.

Kalin and Ben hadn't decorated their place yet, but tomorrow she'd make time. This was their first Christmas together, and she wanted the holidays to be special. This was also her first Christmas away from her family in Ottawa. She missed her parents and even her brother. Being estranged didn't mean she'd stopped caring about him.

She waited at the rear corner of her Jeep for the traffic to clear before she opened her door. Donny drove by and beeped his horn. She hopped into her driver's seat and on impulse followed him. He turned into a subdivision not far from the town center and then into a driveway of a bungalow. She wondered if his family had moved there after his accident to make life easier for him.

The garage door opened, and Donny drove in. Kalin pulled up to the side of the snow-covered road, guessing where the curb might be, and got out.

"Hey," she called to Donny before he shut the garage door.

He turned his chair around to face her. "Kalin?"

She didn't have a plan, but the simplest thing would be to come straight to the point. Donny was smart, and she suspected he'd see through her if she bullshitted him.

"I want to talk to you about Nora. Can you spare a minute?"

"I've got to take care of Jeff's equipment."

Kalin examined the garage. High tech tuning equipment filled half of the space. Except where snow plopped off Donny's van, the floor was spotless. A seemingly impossible task in a garage that housed vehicles used to drive up the mountain and back every day.

"You tune all day and then come home and do Jeff's skis?"

"Yes. Jeff likes keeping his gear here."

"I'm surprised Nora doesn't tune them."

"She used to, but you know…"

"I'm worried about her," Kalin said.

Donny pulled off his mitts and dropped them on a shelf. "I don't like gossiping."

"I don't want to gossip about her. I want to help her."

Donny waited for her to speak.

"Do you remember a couple of weeks ago, you were in the drugstore at the same time as Nora?"

Donny remained silent.

"I think you know what I'm talking about."

He blew a bubble with his gum. "I'm not going to talk about Nora's private life."

"I'm Nora's friend, and I'm worried about her."

"You said that." Donny opened the mini fridge that rested in the corner of the garage and pulled out two bottles of beer. "Want one?"

She took the offered beer and searched for the Sasquatch hidden on the Kokanee label. "I don't think Nora killed McKenzie, but she's mad at me right now, and I don't know how to help her."

Donny spit his gum into the garbage can. He placed one of Jeff's skis in clamps and fussed with the tightness.

"Donny, please. Nora is in way over her head."

He took a deep breath, his back to Kalin, and spoke quietly. "How do I know you're not trying to trick me?"

"I don't know. All I can say is she's my friend."

"I've known Nora a long time."

Kalin took this for a good sign. Maybe he would talk. She waited.

"Nora dated Jeff all through high school, and I was the tag-along little brother. She never minded I was there."

"Your aunt told me how close you were."

"Really? How do you know Lisa?"

"I bought one of her paintings, and we hit it off."

"That's good. My aunt needs a friend."

Kalin didn't understand what he meant. Lisa seemed happy, settled in her life, with a thriving business. She sipped her beer and meandered around the garage. She was cold but didn't want to complain. "Did Nora tell you why she was at the drugstore last week?"

Donny hunched his shoulders and bit his lip. "I guess we both know."

"Do you know if she's going to keep the baby?"

To fill the silence, Kalin took another sip of beer, and the cool liquid travelled down her throat. She picked up a scraping tool and feigned an interest in the blade.

Finally, Donny said, "I'm not sure. I haven't asked her, and she hasn't said."

The rays from the ceiling light bounced off Donny's blond hair, and it was uncanny how much he reminded her of her late husband. She loved Ben but still missed Jack.

"I don't know if she's going to be okay," he said.

"Why do you say that?"

"You don't know about my cousin, Rachel?"

The importance of the moment struck Kalin. The air sizzled, and she shook her head, not wanting to break Donny's will to talk by interrupting him.

"She committed suicide. I thought, for a while, Aunt Lisa might do the same."

Kalin knew Rachel died, but Nora had never said she killed herself. She wanted Donny to open up and felt a bit guilty getting him to talk about something that was obviously painful, but her drive to find out who killed McKenzie trumped the guilt. "I've enjoyed spending time with Lisa. She seems solid."

A cynical laugh burst from his throat, sounding a bit like a bark. "She puts on a good front. She has a knack for hiding her feelings, and she can't exactly run a business and attract customers if she's moping around all the time."

Kalin decided to follow his lead. "Do you spend much time with her?"

"I do. Since the accident, I've been closer to her than to my parents."

"She sounds like a good aunt."

"She is."

The side door to the house opened with a bang and a man stood, glaring, with his fists clenched at his sides. "What's taking you so long?"

Donny flinched. "Dad. This is Kalin Thompson. She's a director at the resort."

Morley turned slowly and faced Kalin.

She stepped forward and stretched her hand toward him. He didn't move from the doorstep, and she let her hand drop.

"What's she doing here?" he asked Donny.

"We're just talking."

"Is this the girl you've been shacking up with?"

"Dad! She works at the resort. Please…"

"Make sure the floor's clean before you come in." Morley stood for a second longer, then turned and slammed the door.

"I'm sorry about that. He's not exactly sociable."

Kalin cleared her throat. "That's an understatement."

Donny caught her humor and laughed bitterly.

Kalin turned her Jeep into the resort, and in the darkness, the Christmas decorations made a festive statement as she passed through the lower village and onto Black Bear Drive. A few houses displayed the old fashioned blue, green and red lights, the multitude of colors reflecting off the snow, but most had hung white LED bulbs, showing off a muted but tasteful atmosphere. Kalin preferred the colors and the reminder of her childhood.

The lights from inside Nora's living room glowed, and Kalin decided she should talk with her. Maybe she could smooth things out between them.

Like most employees who lived on Black Bear Drive, Nora rented an in-law suite tucked into the ground floor of an expansive ski chalet. The Jeep's tires crunched over the mound at the end of the driveway, flattening two paths. Kalin trudged through the foot deep snow, knocked and was mildly surprised Nora opened the door.

"What now?" Nora asked.

"I'd really like to talk with you. As a friend."

Nora hesitated, and Kalin jumped at the chance. "Just for a minute. I'd like to explain."

Nora stepped backward. "Fine. Come in."

Once in the living room, Nora turned and faced Kalin, put her hands on her bony hips with her elbows pointed outward and waited.

"I didn't tell Miller you're pregnant."

Nora blew air through her lips and looked away from Kalin.

"Maybe Ian told Miller. I wouldn't do that to you. I'm sorry about telling him you were at the resort early. I'm under pressure from Reed. He expects me to find out who killed Steve. Then I had to tell him staff housing was flooded. He wants me to find out who did that too. I have to report to him about everyone I talk to. I can't not mention you because we're friends. When I gave the RCMP a list of everyone who had keys to the tuning room, Ben was on that list. I didn't take his name off."

"You gave the cops Ben's name as a suspect?"

"No. Just that he had a key. No one suspects Ben. I want you to know I have to treat everyone the same. It's my job. All I did was tell Constable Miller you were at the resort early. He'd have found out eventually, and at least this way he heard from someone who believes you didn't kill Steve."

"Slow down. I understand all that. I don't blame you," Nora paused, "as much."

"Really?"

Kalin's surprise must have shown because Nora scrunched her face at Kalin with an expression that implied, "duh."

"Sit down. Let's have some tea."

Kalin flopped on the couch, relieved Nora wanted to remain friends.

Nora filled a kettle with water and placed it on the stove.

While Kalin waited, she stared at the digital picture frame resting on the mantelpiece. The photos flashing on the screen were of Nora's teenage years. Numerous pictures of Nora and Jeff displayed, one after the other.

Nora returned to see a photo of four smiling faces. Jeff, Donny, Nora and another woman. They were all standing, arms laced, laughing at the camera. Whoever took the photo caught it at the perfect moment of genuine happiness, and Kalin's skin tingled.

Nora carried two mugs of tea. "Happier times."

"Who's the woman?"

"Rachel."

"She's beautiful."

"Just like Lisa."

Kalin accepted a mug and settled farther into the couch, tucking her feet underneath herself. "That's a good photo. There are a lot of Jeff."

"It's probably not good for us, but Jeff and I were looking at the photos last night. I put in the memory card of our teenage years."

"Isn't that hard? Spending time with him."

"Sometimes. Our relationship is confusing. We both work at it for Donny's sake. I didn't want to lose Donny after I stopped seeing Jeff."

"It must not have been a bad breakup."

"It was the worst. At the prom I caught Jeff kissing the class big boob bimbo, and I dumped him on the spot."

An unwanted vision of Ben kissing the Goddess floated around Kalin's head. "That sucks."

"That's not even the worst part. I wouldn't talk to him, and to get even, he slept with the bimbo at a party. He must have known I'd find out."

"Ouch."

"More than ouch. He was with her when Donny and Rachel were in the accident. He never forgave himself, but I forgave him. I think that's why we can be friends."

Kalin wanted to ask about Rachel but couldn't bring herself to form the words. She wanted her friend back, and if she started to question her, she might piss off Nora again. Curbing her curiosity, she changed the subject, and they spent the next half hour chatting about skiing and snowboarding.

Kalin left Nora's and drove along the snow-covered road, looking forward to spending the evening with Ben. She hadn't seen enough of him over the last couple of weeks. They needed an evening in front of the fireplace, naked, drinking wine, naked. Okay, naked was the theme, and she smiled to herself.

He was unhappy with her involvement in the investigation and he'd never interfere, but she wanted to make it up to him. Plus she needed to keep ahead of the Goddess. She couldn't back off her job because her boyfriend didn't like what she did. Reed had made it clear he wanted her assistance. Ben would have to understand.

When she arrived at the front of her place, an SUV filled the driveway, forcing her to park her Jeep on the road. The label on the driver's side door identified the driver as the conservation officer, and Kalin's chest tightened. Chica was part of who they were.

She didn't want to face him, but leaving Ben to deal with the situation alone wasn't right. She opened the door to their suite and picked up on the tension. Ben sat ramrod straight, with Chica at his feet, facing the conservation officer.

Kalin introduced herself, and let him do the same. Chica shifted to Kalin's feet and rested her head on Kalin's knee. "What's going on?"

"A deer was killed on the resort last night," the conservation officer said.

"I know. Fred Morgan told me."

The conservation officer motioned to Chica. "Fred said your dog was loose."

"She was," Kalin acknowledged.

"She came home—" Ben tried to interject, but their visitor cut him off.

"I'd like to hear what Kalin has to say."

Kalin rubbed Chica's head while trying to get a vibe from Ben. "About what?"

"Your dog. I need to know if she killed the deer."

"I don't think so. She came home on her own."

"Was there any blood on her?"

"No." Again with the lying. Not a trait Kalin admired, but she was willing to do it for Chica.

"Are you aware that if a dog kills wildlife, then it gets put down?"

Kalin's heart pounded. "I am, but she didn't."

"Make sure she doesn't." The conservation officer departed, leaving the ominous warning hanging in the room.

Kalin shut the door behind him, and Ben put his hands over her shaking ones.

"Shit, that was tense," Ben said.

"Did I say the same thing you did?"

"Almost word for word. I can't believe Fred called him about Chica." Kalin told Ben about Susan Reed sticking up for them and her advice on how to handle the conservation officer.

"I thought you said she wasn't friendly."

"I know, but I guess she has a soft spot for animals. She told me for Chica's sake, not ours, I think." Kalin thought about the towels in the washer and was glad they'd cleaned up. "What if Chica does it again?"

CHAPTER THIRTY

Jeff and Donny packed Jeff's gear into the van. Because the RCMP declared Edwin Bucher's crash an accident, Reed had allowed injection for the first time since McKenzie's death. The snowmaking team injected the run during the overnight hours, and along with a temperature of minus eighteen degrees Celsius, Jeff expected fast conditions. Even though racing wasn't his dream, Jeff hoped for a personal best.

He wanted to end the training day with fireworks. He'd show his dad and Coach Jenkinson he was talented. Coach had been favoring him and giving him more attention than the others. That meant he had faith, and Jeff owed it to his coach to ski to the extreme.

By keeping his plans secret, Jeff could get Donny out of here, and they'd be set up in Vancouver before their dad figured out what happened. He'd used Aunt Lisa's address for his correspondence with the university, and she said she'd help them move. Once they were relocated, he'd offer for his mom to follow. If she wanted.

Jeff pulled ski pants over his race suit—no point in being cold on the drive up—and Donny said, "Tough guy on the mountain, sissy off the hill."

Footsteps pounded toward the garage's inner door, and Jeff groaned. "I thought he'd gone already."

The door opened with a bang. No one could accuse their father of being subtle.

"What was that woman doing here?"

Jeff looked at Donny. "What woman?"

"I told you she works at Stone Mountain," Donny said.

Their father stood, flashing hot looks between Jeff and Donny. "I asked what she was doing here."

"She came to talk."

"What could a high class broad like her have to say to you?"

Donny scratched the back of his reddening neck and didn't answer.

Jeff didn't know whom they were talking about but kept quiet. His dad was focused on Donny, and if interrupted it could set him off.

"Answer me."

"She's a friend."

"Bullshit."

"It's not bullshit."

Their father's face burned with building rage, and he leaned over Donny. "Don't lie to me."

Jeff tensed.

"Dad, I'm not. I met her this year. She's a friend of Nora's."

"Huh." He turned his attention to Jeff. "Figures you couldn't hang on to a girl like Nora."

Jeff remained silent. What could he say to that? His dad was right.

"What a pair. I'm sick of the sight of you." He stomped out of the garage, and the air left the room with him as if he'd sucked it out.

Jeff opened the door to the van. "Let's go before he comes back."

Packed in the van, Donny drove and Jeff rode shotgun.

Jeff turned the vents to blow toward the floor and put his feet close to them. He hated being cold. When he finished school, he'd move somewhere warm. "What a bastard."

"Don't let him get to you. He'll never change."

"Who was he talking about?"

"Kalin."

Jeff ran his fingers in circles, wiping frost off the window and then breathing on the glass to fog the surface again. "Why was she at our house?"

"She wanted to talk about Nora. She's worried about her."

"Did she ask anything about McKenzie's murder?"

"Not really. She talked mostly about Nora."

"What did you tell her?"

"Nothing bad." Donny grinned. "You're worried about Nora. How sweet."

"Shut up." Jeff cuffed the back of Donny's head. "Really, what did you tell her?"

"It's odd, but we got talking about Rachel. I haven't talked about her in a long time."

"Who brought up Rachel? You or Kalin?" It irked Jeff that Donny was naive. He had no sense.

"I don't remember. We got on the topic of Aunt Lisa and—"

"What would you talk about her for?"

"Dude, you're being over sensitive. Kalin's okay, so what's the issue?"

"I wish you wouldn't trust everybody," Jeff pleaded, his voice tight in his throat.

"I don't."

"Yes, you do. Kalin's snooping around about McKenzie. She's the head of security, and you know we both have to be suspects. She's pretending to be your friend."

"Don't turn into Dad."

"I'm not. I'm just…Christ, I'm just trying to keep everyone safe."

"What does that mean?"

"Nothing."

A few minutes after seven thirty a.m., Kalin dropped her Jeep at the service station in Holden for an oil change.

Ben had followed her to town and waited while she talked to the mechanic. She got in his truck and slid to the middle of the bench seat, leaning her head on his shoulder. Halfway up the mountain, Kalin reached over the seat and grabbed empty air instead of her backpack. "Crap, I left my pack in the Jeep."

"Do you want to go get it?"

"Not really, but my keys are in the outside pocket. If no one's in the admin building already, I'll wait. It's almost eight. Someone should be in soon."

"The front desk keeps a spare to each building."

"You're kidding. I didn't know that. I haven't secured those keys. Damn, I can't believe I missed that too."

Ben squeezed Kalin's hand. "You've been the director of security for two weeks. Don't be so hard on yourself. Can you get into your office even if you get in the building?"

"Monica keeps an extra key for me. Don't turn around, you'll be late."

Ben dropped Kalin at the front desk. "You sure you don't want me to wait?"

"No. It's a good chance for me to talk with the staff. I don't get down here much." She let Chica out of the back seat, attached her leash and entered the building.

Cindy Tober, the front desk agent on duty, was speaking with a guest. While Kalin waited, she admired the mock-up of the resort. An artist had carved a model of Stone Mountain to scale, and Kalin found her house. She traced her finger along the path she walked to work. On the mock-up, the path looked isolated, with dense forest on one side and the golf course on the other. She laughed at herself for being afraid to walk along the trail in the dark last year.

When Cindy finished with the guest, Kalin told her she needed a key.

"Come in back. You have to sign for it," Cindy said.

Kalin opened the half door and strode behind the counter. A small room off to the side contained the employee kitchen and lounge area. Ski and snowboard magazines were strewn across the coffee table. "You look tired."

"I am. I go off shift in half an hour. Jason's coming to get me as soon as he finishes his shift."

"Shouldn't he have been off shift hours ago?"

"You are such an HR geek. Always worried about employees. One of the snowmaking guns busted, and he stayed to fix it." Cindy handed Kalin a logbook, asking her to put the date, the time and her signature on the next free line.

"How old are the keys to the admin building and tuning room?" Kalin asked.

"Don't worry. The key will work. The locksmith dropped off new ones to both doors."

Kalin's gut clenched. One more employee who'd kept the full truth from her.

"I heard Vicky's in town," Cindy said.

"Yup. She's trying to get Ben back."

"Jason told me. He told her to leave Ben alone, not that she'll listen."

"She broke into our house and left a new collar for Chica. She had 'I Love Ben' embroidered on the inside."

Cindy grabbed Kalin's arm. "You're kidding. What are you going to do?"

"I don't know. Do you know her well?"

"I used to, but I never liked her."

"Chica got out the night we found the collar in our place. Do you think she'd let Chica go free just to get at me?"

Cindy removed a key from a locked cabinet and handed it to Kalin. "Maybe. I'm thinking she's stalking Ben."

"Ben said he's going to tell her to leave us alone."

"She's not the type to listen. Good luck, though."

Kalin put her hand on the exit door, about to push when an idea hit her, and she turned back to Cindy. "How do you decide who gets a key?"

Cindy looked up from the computer she'd already focused on. "What do you mean?"

"Did you give me a key because I'm a director and you know me?"

"No. I give one to anyone who asks. The person just has to sign the logbook."

"Do you record when the key is returned?"

"No. Usually the person brings it back at the end of the day. It's for when staff forget their own key."

"Does anyone review the list?"

Cindy winced as if she didn't like the answer she was about to give. "You'll have to ask my manager."

"Can I see the logbook again?"

"Sure."

Kalin flipped back one page and found the date she was looking for. Her heart thudded as she read a name written beside five fifteen a.m. and thought about what the signature meant.

She stood outside the front desk building, called Miller and kept her voice low. "I've found something."

"Didn't I tell you to stay out of this? I don't think you realize the danger you could be putting yourself in."

"I can't help it. I stumbled across something. Do you want to know or not?"

"Of course I do."

"I took my Jeep to town for an oil change and forgot my keys in it."

Miller chuckled. "You want me to bring your keys up?"

"No. I don't know why you think I'm funny. You're always laughing at me." Kalin liked the way he teased her but wasn't going to admit that to him. Their banter had become their style. "I want you to understand I discovered this by accident. I stopped at the front desk to get a key to the admin building. They have a logbook, and I signed out a key. Then I had a thought."

"You would."

"That's because I'm smart. I checked the log for the day McKenzie died."

Silence.

"Are you still there?" Kalin asked.

"I'm waiting for the bomb to explode."

"Two keys had been signed out at five fifteen. One for the admin building and the other for the tuning room."

"Are you going to tell me by who, or are you going to make me sweat?"

CHAPTER THIRTY-ONE

Reed was on the phone when his estranged daughter walked into his office. He didn't say a word, and sweat beaded on the back of his neck.

Melanie stared at him with eyes overpowered by black mascara and black eyeliner.

Reed's mind emptied. He should be listening to the call, and he had to excuse himself from the phone conference. He was confident in his role as the president of the resort but not in his role as Melanie's father. He swallowed and said, "Hello."

"Dad."

He wanted to get up and hug her, but he held back. He suppressed a grin. "Melanie." She'd gained back some of the weight she'd lost. She still didn't look healthy, but she did look better than before. Her black hair, black T-shirt and black jeans made her pale skin even paler. Somehow, the band of freckles across her nose took away from the Goth image she tried so hard to portray. Was it too much to hope she'd made it through the worst?

"Can I come in?"

He let out a breath and realized he hadn't inhaled since she walked into his office. "Of course you can." He pulled a chair away from his table and offered her a seat. "How long can you stay?"

Melanie clasped her hands on her lap, hesitating. "I was thinking of moving here. Not home but here to Stone Mountain."

Reed allowed himself a hint of a smile. *Don't come on too strong.* "That would be great."

"The thing is…I need a job."

"Sure. What do you want to do?"

"Maybe I could waitress. I got some experience in the last six months."

She looked young and innocent, and he wondered how she'd lost control of her life. He'd thought a lot about what he could have done differently. Maybe giving her time to sort things out for herself had been enough. He hadn't judged or hassled her when she'd phoned. He'd hated hiding the rare calls from his wife even though it had to be done. "I'll introduce you to our HR director and get that set up. Do you have somewhere to live?"

"Not yet."

"Do you want to move into staff housing? It's nothing fancy, or I could rent you another place."

Her eyes darkened, matching her eyeliner, and Reed understood he'd overstepped.

"I don't want charity."

"Sorry. You're right."

"Staff housing would be sweet. Do you have to tell Mom I'm here?"

"I'd like to, but I won't until you're ready. She'll want to see you."

"I know, but I can't face her yet."

Reed flipped his phone and read the time. "Do you want to watch Ian ski?"

Her lip ring twisted at an angle when she smiled. "I'd like that. It's been a long time."

"He's training right now. We can watch from the bottom or from the side of the run. Whatever you like."

They stood together at the base of the Alpine Tracks run, father and daughter watching the Holden racers ski. Immense happiness swallowed him. His two kids within range. He stepped to his left, and his arm touched Melanie's. She didn't move away.

Reed pointed midway down the race course. "There he is."

Ian's arm smacked the last gate as he turned around the pole. He skied fast, his form perfect as he held his tuck across the finish line. He slid to a stop with his skis bumping sideways against the snow, his knees bent, and his body full of confidence. He shoved his goggles over his helmet. "Dad. Did you see?"

"I did. Looks like you had a good run." Reed caught the second Ian's eyes recognized Melanie.

"Hey, you." Ian's chest heaved, his cheeks reddened from exertion, and his eyes smiled at Melanie.

"Hey, back."

Ian leaned on his poles, taking the pressure off his knees, and slid his skis back and forth across the snow. "You decided to come. I'm glad."

Reed looked from Ian to Melanie, understanding the tightness of their relationship for the first time. Melanie held herself still, and Ian could never stop moving. Both were his kids, but they were opposites.

Over Melanie's shoulder, Reed saw his wife stomping toward them, her face full of sour juice, and the vision of having a future with his kids blurred.

"What are you standing around for?" Susan asked. "You're supposed to be training." With her anger focused at Ian, she hadn't noticed Melanie.

Reed and Melanie's eyes locked. "Sorry," he mouthed at her.

"Mom," Melanie said.

Susan snapped at Reed, "How long has she been here?"

"How about saying hello to your daughter," Reed said.

"I asked you a question." Susan's voice pierced the air and crossed the snow-covered surface in seconds.

The ticket checkers and lifties turned to watch. Even Kalin Thompson was within hearing range. "Please lower your voice," Reed said.

Susan held a wide stance, her hands on her hips, her chin jutted. She was in fight mode. "What? You're embarrassed? Some of your precious staff might overhear us and find out you're not perfect."

"Why don't we all go inside to talk?" Reed gently held Susan's elbow, but she swatted his hand.

"Mom, please. Melanie just got here. Dad and I didn't know she was coming."

"Don't lie. The three of you have always been against me." She turned to Melanie. "Why are you here? Do you want money?"

"Enough," Reed said. He turned to Ian and spoke softly. "Finish training. I'll take care of Melanie."

Ian hesitated but obeyed his dad.

"Susan, go home. Melanie, can I take you to lunch and then the HR department?"

Susan took one step toward Reed, and he held up his hand in front of her. "Don't."

She looked as if she might fight him, but the menace in his tone must have told her he was serious. He saw the tension leave her stance, and he nodded once at her, acknowledging she was backing down.

Reed and Melanie left Susan standing alone, abandoned by her family. Something inside him crashed over a precipice. One second he loved Susan, the next he didn't.

Kalin ate a spoonful of bean salad marinated in balsamic vinegar and olive oil and pursed her lips. She always over did the vinegar. Maybe next time she'd get the portions right.

"Not any good?" Miller asked.

Kalin ran her tongue over her front teeth searching for bits of basil. "Don't sneak up on a girl when she's eating. I almost spat on you."

"It wouldn't be the first time I've been spit on."

"Ew. Not a job perk I want."

Miller closed her office door and sat in the guest chair. "I interviewed Donny this morning."

Kalin pushed her salad to the side and set down her fork. "It's too weird he didn't have his keys on him the day McKenzie died. What did he say?"

"He said he keeps his keys in the center console of his van and didn't notice they were missing until he arrived at the mountain. That's why he signed out keys at the front desk."

"Lucky for him, it's open twenty-four-seven. Where were his keys?"

"He found them later that day on a counter in his garage."

Kalin laughed. "I guess I got over enthusiastic about my big discovery. I'm sorry I wasted your time."

"I don't think it was wasted."

She shook her head slightly indicating she didn't get what he meant.

"What if someone knew where Donny kept his keys?"

Kalin liked the way Miller's quick mind worked. He was suspicious, not a believer in coincidences, and she had to work hard to keep up with him. "You think the killer borrowed the keys and put them back later."

"Donny said he didn't remember taking them out of his van. The killer couldn't have known Donny was going to work early that day. The plan could have been to use the keys during the night and get them back before Donny left for work. He wouldn't have known they were missing."

"Why was Donny in so early?"

"He said he left work early the night before and had to catch up."

"Do you think Jeff could've taken the keys?"

Miller leaned forward and put his elbows on his knees. "Anyone who'd been in his van could easily see a set of keys in the center console. It's not like he kept them hidden."

The list of possibilities included Kalin's friends. "Any of Donny's friends. Nora. I don't think Donny had started dating Amber Cristelli before McKenzie died, but she might be worth checking."

"You think Amber had a motive?"

"I heard she slept with McKenzie. I don't know if it's true. You know how gossip travels. Maybe she had access to Donny's keys."

Miller wrote in his ever-present notebook. "Anyone else?"

"Donny's dad. Have you investigated him?"

"No."

"I met him the other day. He's nasty."

"Nasty how?"

Kalin described her conversation with Donny the night she met him in his garage and how his father had been angry for no reason.

"Tell me again why you followed Donny. I asked you to be careful."

"Donny's not a threat to me. I wanted to talk to him about Nora. I'm worried about her."

Miller put his pen in his pocket and held eye contact with Kalin. "You do realize it's still possible either Donny or Nora killed McKenzie, or that they planned it together. It's an interesting coincidence Donny and Nora were at the resort around the same time on the morning McKenzie died and they both hid the fact until they were caught. Donny could have left his keys on purpose to throw us in a different direction. He would have known it would make him look innocent."

"What about the person the snowmaker saw? You're forgetting about that."

Miller clenched his jaw. "Putting yourself in a position where you're alone with either Donny or Nora is dangerous. You have to stop."

"I can't believe Nora would harm me. We're friends."

"So you think."

CHAPTER THIRTY-TWO

"Are you kidding me?" Jeff said. "What the hell did Miller want?"

Donny and Jeff sat in the cafeteria. Jeff had come off a high, having had the fastest time race training that morning. He should be ecstatic right now, not worrying about Donny. They'd put their plastic trays and Jeff's ski helmet beside them on the table, deterring anyone else from sitting too close.

"He only asked questions. Why are you so uptight?"

Donny had kept his voice low, and Jeff had to lean over his overflowing plate of spaghetti Bolognese to hear him. The aroma wafting toward his nose made his stomach growl.

"He already interviewed you. Twice. Why did he have to come around again?"

"He's doing his job," Donny said between bites of his burger. "Stop worrying. This is your season. Focus on skiing instead of what Miller's doing. He's going to snoop around until he finds out who killed McKenzie. What's the big deal?"

"The big deal is he thinks *you* killed him. He's coming around again because you're a suspect. I keep telling you to stop trusting everyone."

"He can't touch me. I didn't murder McKenzie."

Jeff's hand clamped his fork with such force he bent the tines with his thumb.

"I don't believe it," Donny said. "You actually think I killed him. Why would I do that?"

The anger in Donny's voice surprised Jeff. Donny rarely lost his temper. Even after he'd been paralyzed, he'd been rational. No blaming

McKenzie because he'd been driving. Nothing. Jeff couldn't understand. He hated McKenzie for what he'd done to Donny, for stealing Nora and for Rachel. The idea that Donny kept anger brewing inside him worried Jeff. "Tell me exactly what Miller asked."

Donny sipped his cola, and ice clinked against the glass when he set it back on the table. "He wanted to know why I had to get temporary keys from the front desk on the morning McKenzie died. I said they weren't in my van like usual, and I found them later in the garage."

"How did he know?"

"He said it was written in the front desk logbook."

"Who told him about the log?"

"I don't know."

"Did he say anything else?"

"He asked questions about where the keys were. Who knew they were in my truck. Why I went in early. How often I went in early. Did I see anyone else at the resort that morning." Donny took a breath. "I think you're making way too much of this. Miller will find out who killed McKenzie. He's a good cop."

"Don't be so gullible. He's a cop. He'll go after whoever he thinks is guilty. What if he had enough to convict on reasonable doubt or whatever they call it?" Donny had so much of Mom in him. She believed in their dad—talk about gullible—and sure, Dad took care of her but not anyone else. Donny could get trapped just by being like her and being too trusting. Jeff would never let that happen.

Donny frowned at him. "You watch too much TV. It doesn't work like that in real life. He won't want just any conviction. He'll want the right one."

"I wish I could think like you. Not everyone is straight forward. I can't believe you don't get that. Wake up."

"What if Dad did it?"

"He couldn't have. He doesn't have the brains to alter a binding," Jeff said.

"Anyone, even someone as stupid as him, could figure out how. All the tools are in our garage. How many times has he stood yelling at me while I tuned your skis? Maybe he paid attention. Miller kept pounding on who knew where I stored my keys. Dad knew."

A malicious thought made Jeff smile. "Maybe you're on to something. I'd have thought the bastard's too blunt. That if he was going to do it, he would have beat McKenzie to death, and he would have done it a long time ago."

"He's good with his hands."

"You think it's possible?"

"I do. There's no way we can move out until this is settled. He might take it out on Mom, blame her somehow for us moving out. If he killed McKenzie, he's crazy. Who knows what he'd do to her."

"Agreed. No moving out until we know who killed McKenzie." Jeff didn't know how much longer he could take living with his dad. The rage inside him was starting to gnaw at him, and once that slab of snow let go, it wouldn't stop barreling down the mountain until he buried his dad, and he didn't want to be that person.

Kalin's desk was buried in paperwork, and she tidied the cluttered surface as she talked with Ben.

Kalin angled her mouth toward the speaker on her phone. "Can you meet me at the tuning room, and we'll go from there? I need to lock up. Security is busy with a traffic accident."

"Sure. Ten minutes?"

Kalin pressed the disconnect button, picked up the file resting on her desk and opened the top drawer. Inside the drawer, she found a photo. Ben standing behind the Goddess with his arms wrapped around her and a great big fucking smile on his face. His eyes laughed. The Goddess held his hands across her voluptuous boobs, and her blue eyes sparkled at the camera.

Kalin flipped over the photo. In red ink, circled with a heart, she found *Ben and Vicky forever* written on the back. At least the handwriting wasn't Ben's. How juvenile. Kalin ripped the photo in half and tossed the remnants into the garbage can. The Goddess would not get the better of her. She locked her office when she left, thinking she'd have to start locking the door during the workday too.

Kalin arrived at the tuning room and found Ben standing with Amber. He had an odd look on his face.

"That's a unique hair clip," Ben said.

Amber touched the clip at the side of her head. "My mom sent them to me. I thought I was going to get the tuning job, and she thought clips designed in the shape of skis were cute. She's forgotten how old I am."

"How come she only gave you one?" Ben asked.

Kalin raised her eyebrows at him.

"I lost one." Amber folded her tongue and rolled her tongue stud between her lips.

"I'll lock up." Kalin took the scanning gun from Amber, told her she could go and left the gun inside the tuning room. McKenzie's ski jacket still hung in the corner, and she decided it was time to return it to his family. She folded the jacket over her arm and an envelope slipped to the floor. *Not gonna happen* was scrawled on the outside. She should call Constable Miller, but instead she opened the envelope. The first piece of paper had information about getting an abortion. The second was a note to Nora. *I'll pay whatever you need. But that's it. We're done.*

Kalin put the note back in the envelope and the envelope back in the pocket. She returned the jacket to the hook. She rubbed her fingers over her eyes, wondering what she should do now. The writing on the outside of the envelope had to be from Nora. The words could be taken as a threat, or they could mean she thought there was hope for her and McKenzie. Kalin had to believe the latter. She called Miller and told him what she'd found and where she'd left the jacket.

"I think this proves Nora didn't kill McKenzie," she said to Miller.

"How do you figure that?"

"She must have put the note in his pocket after he got on the mountain. She'd be expecting him to read it when he finished training."

"Or she put it there the night before. McKenzie rarely wore his team jacket home. She could have had a change of heart and forgotten she put the note there."

"I don't believe that. The timing was too tight. I think McKenzie gave her the abortion information the morning he died, and after he left for the hill, she wrote *not gonna happen* and put the envelope in his pocket."

After the call with Miller, Kalin checked the tuning room was empty and locked the door. "Ready?" she asked Ben.

She snuggled against Ben's arm and walked at his side. Her winter boots sunk into the top layer of snow. The air felt clean and carried the soft scent of pine. "What were you asking Amber about her hair clips for? You thinking of starting a hair clip design business?"

Ben didn't smile at her joke. "I think I know where she lost her clip."

"What's the big deal?"

"The morning after the flood, I helped maintenance clean up. I found a similar clip on the ground floor stairwell. I only noticed it because of the shape."

Kalin frowned. "Do you think she did it?"

"Maybe. But I like her. I don't want it to have been her."

"What'd you do with the clip?"

"Nothing."

"It could still be in the stairwell. Let's go look."

Kalin and Ben entered the stairwell in staff housing. With the drywall repaired but not yet painted, the building appeared run down. She tapped a note into her phone to call maintenance and ask for the painting schedule. The hair clip was nowhere to be seen.

"Are you sure it was the matching clip."

"I think so. Call Miller and see if he'll interview her again. He might be able to get her to admit she flooded the building."

Snowflakes the size of cotton balls floated onto Kalin while she stood on Nora's stoop. How should she bring up the note she'd found in McKenzie's jacket? And would Nora talk to her about it?

After a minute, Nora opened the door. "Come in."

Before Kalin stepped over the threshold, she shook snow off her head and wiped her shoulders. "I thought I'd surprise you." She held a box of herbal tea and a bag of microwave popcorn. "Ben's out with his buddies, and I didn't feel like sitting at home."

Lisa stepped into the foyer, holding a glass of red wine, and leaned elegantly against the wall. "Hi. Looks like a girls' night." She wore a shimmering turtleneck sweater and a sleek black skirt that reached her ankles. Her hair was twirled into a clip on the back of her head.

Kalin wanted to talk to Nora about the note but not with Lisa there. "I didn't mean to interrupt. I'll go."

"That's silly," Nora said. "You know Lisa."

"Are you sure?" Kalin asked.

"We're having wine and cheese." Nora laughed. "Well, Lisa's having wine. I'm off that for a while." Nora grabbed Kalin by her hand and pulled her in.

The fireplace threw shards of light across the room. Candles filled the mantel and windowsills.

Nora sat inches from Lisa on the couch, and Kalin flopped into the armchair. She'd brought tea, thinking of Nora's pregnancy, but really, she'd rather join Lisa in a glass of wine.

"I've told Lisa I'm keeping the baby."

"You seem excited." Kalin looked at Nora over the top of her wine glass. "Have you told Ian?"

"Ian?" Lisa asked.

"Sorry," Kalin said to Nora. "I thought…"

Nora held Lisa's hand and explained what had happened with Ian.

"The baby's not Steve's. Are you sure?" Lisa asked.

"I hope Steve's the father, but I can't be sure. Ian talked to me yesterday. He stopped and chatted about skiing. He didn't mention the baby and neither did I, but it's an improvement. Maybe he'll want some involvement if it turns out he's the father. I can't believe I'll be a mom." Nora turned to Lisa. "That makes you a grandmother. Are you ready?"

"The important question is are you? You don't have to keep the baby."

"What if Steve is the father and I didn't have the baby? I don't think I could live with that. Not after what's happened."

Kalin remembered the fight she'd read about between Jeff and McKenzie, and that it happened around the same time Nora and McKenzie had gotten together last February. Maybe Jeff had been building resentment for him. A man didn't stay friends with a woman after a breakup unless he wanted back together.

"I want to ask you something about the investigation," Lisa said to Kalin.

"I'll tell you what I can."

"Do you think the RCMP really suspects Donny? I know he was interviewed again today."

"I don't know what they think. Constable Miller talks to me, but he just asks questions." Again with the secrets, but she couldn't repeat Miller's words.

"I can't help worrying. Donny's been through enough without being a murder suspect," Lisa said.

"It's going to turn out okay." Nora reached for Lisa's hand. "Miller thinks I did it, not Donny. And I know I didn't, so what can happen?"

"Did he accuse you?" Lisa asked.

"He interviewed me again today. It was dumb, but I left a note in Steve's ski jacket about the baby, and Miller found it. The note doesn't prove anything."

Kalin felt uneasy not mentioning she found the note and called Miller. She sipped her wine to hide her burning cheeks. Maybe she wasn't cut out to be a mini police chief, except that she wanted to be one. Why couldn't someone else have been McKenzie's girlfriend? Why did it have to be one of her friends? She knew in her heart Nora didn't kill McKenzie, so she wasn't hurting her by sharing information with Miller, but she still felt like a traitor.

Nora rubbed her hand over her stomach. "This baby will come into a happy family, whatever that might be, so enough of this depressing talk. Did you see Jeff's times from today?"

A wide smile crossed Lisa's face, filled with laughter.

The doorbell rang, and Nora scooted to the front hall. The weariness of the last couple of weeks had left her, and her perkiness was back.

Kalin hoped that meant she'd come to terms with her situation.

Nora returned with Jeff at her heels. He stopped short when he saw Kalin.

"What?" Nora asked.

"Nothing." He unzipped his fleece and flopped beside his aunt, slouching with his knees spread apart and resting an elbow on the side arm of the couch. "I didn't know this was a girl's party."

Nora moved to the hearth. "It's not. Quit being so sensitive." She curled her back, warming herself. "Ben's out with friends, and Kalin wanted some company."

"I'm sure she did," Jeff said.

"What's with you?" Nora asked.

"What's with you?" Jeff bounced back at Nora with a smile that took the harshness out of his words. "I'm getting a beer." He pushed himself off the couch and sauntered to the kitchen. The fridge door opened and a glass clinked against the counter.

"Should I go?" Kalin asked.

"No. He's fine. I think he wanted to talk about Steve and the investigation. He probably thinks he can't do that if you're here. He'll get over it. Let's play euchre. That'll distract him."

Kalin and Nora teamed up against Lisa and Jeff.

"Donny's usually my partner," Nora said. "And we usually win."

"You do not," Lisa teased.

"Sometimes we let you win. You know, since you're not that good," Jeff said.

Nora punched Jeff's shoulder. "Shut up. I'm better than you any day."

Lisa caught Kalin's eye. "When Donny was first in the hospital, the four of us played this a lot. Jeff and Nora always squabbled."

Kalin sipped her wine and tried to concentrate on the rules, but she couldn't stop herself from thinking about Nora and the note, and Jeff and his history of violence.

CHAPTER THIRTY-THREE

"Melanie Reed is waiting in your office for you. She says she has a meeting," Monica said when Kalin entered the HR reception area.

"She does. She wants to work as a server."

Monica grimaced. "Hiring Reed's daughter is a bad idea. If she has any issues, how are we going to deal with her?"

"I don't think we have a choice. He asked me to hire her."

"She's had problems."

"Maybe she's over them." Kalin hesitated. "I know where you're coming from, but she's his daughter. What could I say?"

Kalin's cell rang.

"I've got good news for you," the maintenance manager said. "Staff housing has been cleared. It's structurally sound. Once the cleanup is finished, you can move the employees back in."

Kalin winked at Monica. "You can drop your plan to house staff in town. We're getting the building back. I'll go speak with Melanie."

"Um, before you do. I was wondering if you've had any luck finding a replacement for me."

Monica looked uncomfortable asking, but she'd been doing her new role as manager as well as her old role.

"Not yet. I'm working on it."

"I was wondering if I could move into your old office. I mean, now that I'm the manager."

"As soon as we find someone. Until then, I need you to cover the desk." Kalin better start focusing on a replacement before Monica timed out and decided she didn't want to perform two jobs. "I'll get on it. Right now, I've got to see Melanie."

Melanie stood with her hands clasped in front of her waist, waiting for Kalin. She wore black dress pants and a white blouse. Her hair was pulled tight into a ponytail. Even if Kalin hadn't heard about her problems, she would have picked up on the look. She'd seen more than one recovering drug addict at the resort. The skinny frame, acne-damaged skin and sunken eyes were a giveaway.

Melanie handed Kalin her résumé. She had six months experience as a server in Vancouver. She'd listed the restaurant manager as her reference. Kalin would call, just out of protocol, but she'd hire Melanie regardless of what she found out. "Have a seat."

"I know this is awkward for you, but I'm an excellent waitress. I've been clean for nine months. My reference is good. I didn't want to come here without being ready."

Raised voices outside of her office grabbed her attention, and Kalin glanced in the direction of her door. "Hang on a sec. I need to see what the problem is." She stood and opened her door.

"I know she's in there, and I want to see her."

"That's my mom," Melanie said.

"Do you want to talk to her?" Kalin asked.

Melanie pinched her lips into a thin line and shook her head.

"Okay. Stay here. I'll deal with her."

Kalin returned to the HR receptionist desk and found Susan Reed standing in front of Monica, demanding to be let into Kalin's office.

"How can I help?"

Susan removed brown leather gloves, taking her time pulling each finger free, and set them on the reception desk. Her fingers were perfectly manicured, her fingernails covered with a subdued red polish that matched her lipstick. "I know my daughter is in there. I want to see her."

"I'm interviewing her for a job right now. Maybe you could meet her later?"

Susan glared at Kalin.

Reed entered the reception area. "Susan, not here. Okay?"

"Get away from me. You can't dump me just because your precious daughter comes home and then think there won't be repercussions. If none of you will see me at home, then I have to come here."

"Please don't drag Melanie into this. This is about us. Can we go to my office? Please."

"No."

"We can talk about this, but not here. If you want to see Melanie,

I'll help you do that."

Susan softened but only slightly. "She's my daughter. I missed her too, you know."

"I know. Let her finish interviewing. She'd like to live near us, and to do that, she needs a job."

When she didn't argue, Reed added, "We'll work things out with her. We have a chance now that she's home."

It was enough, and Susan followed Reed out of the HR office.

Kalin returned to Melanie. "Okay, where were we?"

Reed led Susan into his office and closed the door. She settled herself across from him. He found it disturbing that love existed one moment and not the next. The emotion physically left his body. He never realized that's how love died. He'd seen friends fall out of love, but no one had mentioned the suddenness. He'd been married twenty-one years and failed.

"So you'll come home now," Susan said.

Why did she have to use her authoritative tone? Couldn't she back down for one second? "We need to talk about what's best for Ian and Melanie."

"What's best for them is to have a stable family."

"I'm not so sure." He examined her face. He used to think she was beautiful. She drove to Calgary every six weeks to have her hair styled and dyed at a high-end salon. She plastered herself with every anti-aging cream that came on the market. She mail-ordered her makeup from the States, but without her smile, the effort was wasted.

"You're not serious. We've been through tough times before. What's different now?"

"Melanie needs to know she's loved. Unconditionally. I don't think you can do that."

"How dare you. Don't even think about criticizing me. I was a good mother to her. She started the drugs. Not me."

Reed's phone rang, but he left it unanswered. The four rings until the call switched to voicemail felt like an hour. "I'm not criticizing you. We need to be realistic. Melanie has to come first right now."

"If it wasn't for the drugs, we wouldn't be having this conversation," Susan said.

"I know that, but I think Melanie is better. I don't want her to slide downhill."

"So let's work together and figure out what to do."

After a quick knock, Gertrude opened the door. "The director's meeting has started. Should I tell them to wait?"

Susan glared at Gertrude, and Gertrude smiled politely.

"I won't be long. Tell them to start."

Once the door shut, Susan turned on Reed. "All I get is a quick meeting with you. You can't postpone your other meeting? This is our marriage we're talking about."

Reed ignored her outburst. "I've already figured out what to do. I'm going to be available for Melanie. I'm not going to push her, but I am going to help her when I can."

"We can do that together."

"I don't think so."

Susan twisted her gloves as if she were wringing water out of them. "I love Melanie and Ian."

"I know you do."

"With McKenzie gone, Ian has a shot at the Olympic team. Melanie wants to live here and get her life in order. Now's the time for us to stick together."

"I can't do that."

"Are you asking for a divorce?"

Was he? He didn't want to live with Susan right now. He wanted to be with Ian and Melanie. "I'm not sure."

"What an inadequate answer."

"Susan, please. Give me some time."

"How much?"

"You know what's sad? I can't remember the last time you smiled at me. The affair was years ago. Do you even like me anymore?"

"What kind of question is that?"

Reed looked around his office at the photos displaying his history together with Susan, Ian and Melanie. Most of the photos were taken on some ski hill. They used to ski together, Susan full of life, her eyes sparkling with excitement. He'd destroyed something in her when he cheated on her, and he regretted that the most. The photos showed an active family who did things together. They didn't show how fractured they'd become. They didn't show he'd taken her beautiful smile and thrown it away. He shook his head slowly and sadness built inside him. "You're unhappy. Anyone can see that. Why do you want to stay married?"

Susan remained silent.

"Until you can answer that, I think we should live apart."

Amber and Donny drove to the base of the Kidz Zone, a bunny hill hidden on the backside of the resort. The street lamps from a small subdivision bracketing the run illuminated the area. Amber had persuaded him to try the sit-ski, and she hoped it was the right move. Donny said he wanted to try skiing before anyone else, especially Jeff, got excited, so she couldn't tell anyone. She thought that meant he trusted her.

He parked at the base of the hill and joined Amber at the back of the van.

"You ready?" she asked. "I spent last night reading up on how to do this. I bet you're great."

Donny transferred himself from the wheelchair to the sit-ski, and Amber handed him the outriggers.

"Here, I think the Velcro adjusts to your wrist like this." Amber fiddled with the straps until they felt tight. "Do they feel okay?"

"How would I know?" Donny grabbed her arm and pulled her down. He pressed his cold lips onto hers. "Let's try this thing."

"Slow down, cowboy. You need to learn how to fall first."

"That's dumb."

"No, it isn't. I read that's what you do first. Then you get to ski."

"So you're an expert?"

Amber laughed. Donny made her feel good about herself, and she was glad she'd talked him into coming out here. "No, but at least I did some research."

"Okay, we'll do this your way."

Donny used his outriggers to push himself to the hill.

"Remember not to fight it when you fall. You could jar your shoulder." Amber pushed him up the slope to a spot with a steep enough descent to pick up a bit of speed and fall over, which he did within seconds.

Donny oriented himself so the sit-ski was facing downhill. He followed Amber's instructions and propped himself up with his fist and an outrigger. Halfway up and straining to stay balanced, he whipped the second outrigger into position and pushed himself the rest of the way.

"Good thing I go to the gym. This is hard."

They practiced several more times until Donny couldn't wait any longer.

"Come on, Amber. I want to try this thing. I've fallen enough."

Amber pulled a sheet of paper from her pocket and used her flashlight to read the instructions.

Donny nudged her hip. "What are you doing?"

"I'm reading through the steps. I don't want to get this wrong. You need to start with small radius turns before you learn to carve."

"No problem." Donny pushed forward, picked up a little speed and pressed against the side cut of the ski, causing him to carve and pick up more speed. He fell within a couple of meters.

Amber ran after him.

He was laughing so hard he couldn't speak. He got himself up without help from her. "Let's go again."

Amber pushed him back up the hill, getting her own workout, and let him go. This time he rotated his shoulders and brought the ski around without jamming the edge too hard, but he still picked up too much speed and fell.

On the third try, he shoved his bum out at the bottom of the turn. The motion wasn't graceful, but he skidded around and completed one turn. Amber felt excitement radiate from Donny, giving her a thrill of pleasure. They practiced together for another hour, and he completed three linked turns.

The moment brought them tighter, and the strength of her feelings for him frightened her. If only she hadn't flooded staff housing. Donny would dump her for sure if he found out.

CHAPTER THIRTY-FOUR

Kalin listened to Nora chatter during the entire drive to Holden. Now that Nora had decided she was keeping her baby and she didn't mind sharing with Ben, she couldn't seem to stop talking about her pregnancy.

Nora's phone rang. "What's up?" She paused, then said, "I'm on my way to a movie with Ben and Kalin. Wanna come?" She tapped Ben on the shoulder, cupped her hand over her phone and whispered, "Turn around."

"We'll be there soon," Nora said and punched the end button. "Donny wants us to pick him up."

Ten minutes later, Ben turned his Ford into Donny's driveway, sweeping the headlamps across the front door.

Nora pointed toward the house. "Look, Lisa's here."

Lisa stood on the front stoop with her finger pressing the doorbell.

The garage door hummed open, and Donny appeared.

Nora bounced out of the truck. "Hey, Lisa. We're going to a movie. Wanna join us?"

Lisa shook her head. "Thanks, but I'm picking up your mother. We're having dinner tonight."

Donny flashed Nora a look but didn't say anything.

"It'll be fine," Lisa said. "Go on and have fun."

When the four fastened their seat belts, Ben drove expertly over a mound of snow. The ploughs had come and gone, but snow had refilled the road.

"Kinda weird Aunt Lisa's having dinner with Mom," Donny said.

Nora shifted sideways to look at Donny. "I know. I can't remember the last time that happened."

"Unfortunately, I can. Maybe this is a good thing," Donny said. "Tell me again why we're going to this movie."

Kalin craned her neck toward the backseat. The film was the black and white classic *Casablanca* starring Humphrey Bogart and Ingrid Bergman. "Because I love old movies, and it's classic week at the theatre."

"So what's up with you and Amber," Nora asked. "Is she your new girlfriend?"

"I just started seeing her. She's amazing... She took me out on the sit-ski yesterday."

Everyone in the car went silent. Nora grabbed Donny's hand and squeezed.

"It was incredible. I made three turns in a row, but did I mention it was incredible?"

"What made you change your mind about skiing?" Nora asked.

"Amber. There's just something about her."

Like she flooded staff housing? Kalin hoped not, or Donny was going to be one hurt dude. Then she remembered Amber had slept with McKenzie and wondered if Nora would tell Donny that awful little fact. Sometimes small town living drove her crazy. Too many close relationships, and eventually someone she knew was going to get hurt.

Donny turned serious. "Have you heard how Edwin Bucher is doing?" he asked Ben.

Donny and Ben locked eyes in the rear view mirror.

"He's back in Germany."

"Is he paralyzed?"

"Yes."

Donny was silent for a moment. "Does anyone at the resort have his contact information?"

"I have it in the office," Kalin said.

Donny shrugged. "I was thinking about calling him. I don't know. It might help him if we talked. I know what he's going through."

"You're such a sweet guy," Nora said.

The movie theatre in Holden was a vision from the fifties. Velvet cushions on top of wooden chairs filled the auditorium. Every second row had a double seat, known as lovers' seats.

The chairs were removable, and Ben hoisted an end seat and placed it at the back of the theatre, leaving a spot for Donny's wheelchair. Nora sat next to Donny, and Kalin and Ben took a lovers' seat. Kalin's fingers intertwined with Ben's, and their thighs pressed together. She saw The Goddess staring at them from the other side of the aisle. Kalin grinned at her, more of a smirk really, but it telegraphed the "he's mine" message. The lights dimmed, and the movie began.

Engrossed in the film, Kalin flinched when it stopped midway for an intermission and the lights brightened.

"Beer? Popcorn?" Ben asked. Donny and Kalin nodded. Nora asked for a ginger ale.

"I'll go with you," Kalin said.

The owners closed the canteen during the movie, but opened again during intermission. Popcorn was popped fresh and topped with real butter.

She entered the foyer, and Constable Miller waved her over. She excused herself from Ben.

"What are you doing?" Miller asked.

"Watching a movie. Same as you and Becky." Kalin waved at Becky, who was standing in line with Ben.

"I saw who you're sitting with."

Kalin bit her bottom lip. "Nora's my friend, and Donny's her cousin. Sort of."

"What does *sort of* mean?"

"Donny's aunt adopted Nora when Nora's mom died."

"I told you I thought you should stay away from them. Until we know who killed McKenzie, you need to be careful."

Kalin tilted her head to one side and smiled. "I'm here with Ben too. Nothing's going to happen."

"Okay. Let me know if you find out anything relevant."

"I shouldn't interfere or investigate, but if I happen to learn something…" Kalin laughed. "Did you talk to Amber?"

Miller scanned the area around them. "I did. She refused to admit she started the flood. There's not much I can do. She lived in the building, and her hair clip could have fallen at any time. It doesn't prove she's guilty."

"Do you believe her?"

"It's not relevant what I believe. Kalin, I'm serious about you being more careful. You don't know everything there is to know about Nora."

"What does that mean?"

Becky arrived at Miller's side. "Is he giving you a hard time?"

Why did Becky have to interrupt them at that moment? A few more seconds. That's all she'd needed. "You know him. All business."

"Well, not tonight." Becky grabbed Miller's hand and pulled him to the auditorium.

Kalin joined Ben in the beer line. "Here, give me that." She took the popcorn, and Ben accepted three beers and a ginger ale from the bartender.

"What did Miller want?"

"He told me not to end up alone with either Donny or Nora. That I should stay with you."

"Excellent advice." Ben nudged her with his hip, guiding her back to the movie.

Jeff had lost count of the number of times his dad had waited for him, pacing the garage floor, building anger with each step. And now he was doing the same thing, waiting for Donny. That he might be heading the same way as his dad frightened him to his core. His temper showed more often, and Donny didn't understand his behavior. His training had been great. Nora was available again, and given time, she might come around. He still loved her. He had plans to go to university. So what was his problem?

Jeff spoke as soon as Donny rolled into the garage. "What are you doing?"

Donny pulled his phone from his pocket and hit the power button. "Coming home from a movie."

"I saw Kalin in the truck. Why would you go to a movie with her? I told you not to trust her."

"I didn't go with her. I called Nora, and she asked me to come along. She was going with Ben and Kalin. What are you, my chaperone?"

"What were you calling Nora about?"

"What's wrong with you? Nora and I have always hung out. It's never bothered you."

Their mom walked with the quietness of a cat trying not to be noticed, so the footsteps stomping along the hallway inside could only belong to their dad. "Is Mom home?" Donny asked in a lowered voice.

"She is." They stayed quiet until they could no longer hear him.

Donny grabbed a mop and wiped the tracks from his wheelchair. "Did Mom say how dinner with Aunt Lisa was?"

"No, but she didn't look happy when she got home. She took some aspirin and went to bed. Where's Kalin now?"

Donny swished the mop, making sure he didn't miss a spot. "She went home. She said she had to work early, like before seven or something."

"Kalin's investigating McKenzie's murder. She's got her own motives for going to a movie with you."

Donny leaned the mop against the wall. "I think you've got it wrong. I called Nora. Kalin couldn't have planned that. How long have you been waiting in the garage for me?"

"I wasn't waiting. I saw Timlin's truck pull in."

"Did Dad see it?"

"I don't think so. Why?"

"I told him I was on a date."

Donny's phone interrupted them. "Where are you?" He grinned a Jeff while he listened. "I had my phone off. I went to a movie." He paused. "Do you want me to come over?" His grin turned into a look of concern. "Give me half an hour." Donny tapped disconnect.

"What's going on?" Jeff asked.

"Miller interviewed Amber about the flood in staff accom. She's upset." Donny turned toward his van. "I'm going to see her."

"Does Miller think she's guilty?"

"I guess someone found a hair clip that matches Amber's in the same stairwell that had the flood."

"So?"

"She was evicted that day."

"Let me guess. Kalin ratted her out." Donny didn't confirm Kalin gave Amber's name to the cops, but Jeff knew it was true. "I told you Kalin's after you. She's picking on Amber to get at you."

"That's crap. I gotta go. I won't be home tonight."

Amber waited in her living room for Donny to arrive. Tonight would be a turning point for them. Time to grow up. Maybe Donny would understand, at least she hoped he would. Starting their relationship based on a lie sucked. What if he was the one and he found out later she'd lied? She had to choose between letting him believe she wasn't guilty and being honest with him. He said he'd be half an hour, which gave her time to decide.

She put on three outfits before settling on a wool sweater and skinny jeans. She put her hair in a ponytail, changed her mind, pulled off the scrunchy and let her curls hang loose on her shoulders. She feathered blue eye shadow over her lids, removed it, and put on a more subtle shade of ecru. She brushed her teeth, adorned her lips with a pale pink lip-gloss that matched her nail polish and waited.

When the doorbell rang, she almost didn't answer. *Why did I call him?*

Amber's housemate had built a wooden ramp that angled up the one step to the porch, and Donny wheeled his way in. He reached up and pulled her in for a kiss. "You okay?"

"I don't know why I was such a drama queen."

Amber offered Donny a beer, and they moved to the living room. The room exuded a hotel atmosphere, decorated by the owners with generic furniture and artwork. Inoffensive but also uninspiring.

"Tell me what happened."

"Fred and Kalin questioned me about the flood, and I guess they didn't believe me when I said I didn't do it. I didn't think they'd call the cops on me." Her moment was now. Either she lied to him or she told him the truth. She grabbed a cushion and hugged it to her chest. "I want to tell you something."

"Sure."

"It's hard. I know we haven't been dating long, but…"

"But?"

"I really like you." Amber loved that he blushed at her comment.

Donny smiled. "I like you too, a lot."

"I think we might have something together."

"Have I done something?"

It figured his first thought would be that he'd done something wrong, not her. She didn't deserve someone as good as him. "No. Nothing like that. I have, and I don't know how to tell you."

"But you want to."

"I don't want to start our relationship with a lie. I want you to know who I am, but I don't want to lose you because of this."

"Tell me, and we can talk."

"I started the flood."

Donny remained silent for a moment, and then quietly asked, "Why?"

She hadn't expected the question, and a teeny bit of hope crept inside her. She thought he would tell her how horrible she was and then leave. Instead, he was going to give her a chance to explain. "I was mad. It was stupid."

"What were you mad at?"

"I'd been evicted and blamed the resort, but it was my fault. I was mad I didn't get a job in the rental shop. I drank too much at the bar. I know that's not an excuse, but I wasn't thinking right. I snuck out, opened the water main and went back to the bar like nothing happened." Amber's eyes filled with tears, and she let them roll down her cheeks.

"Tell me again why you're confessing."

"I like you, and I want this to work."

"That's the good part of the story."

"Don't joke. I'm serious."

"I know you are." Donny pulled her to his lap and kissed her.

Amber tilted her head away and removed his hands from her cheeks. "Do you think I should tell Kalin? Maybe I could make it up to the resort somehow."

"No. You'll put her in the position where she either has to report you or keep it to herself. That's not fair."

"I need to do something."

"We'll figure it out. What about volunteer work for the resort?"

Amber would never again settle for a guy who wasn't nice. Donny was going to help her make this right, and whatever they came up with, as long as it was together, she'd deal with it. "That might be okay. You're not mad?"

"A little bit of water is nothing."

CHAPTER THIRTY-FIVE

Kalin left home for her office before sunrise, wanting to catch up on some of her regular work. Between the investigation into McKenzie's death and the flood, she'd been ignoring her day-to-day job. Arriving before anyone else should give her a chance for some uninterrupted work time.

Her snowshoes helped her cover ground quickly by preventing her from sinking into the new snow. The beam from her headlamp bumped and jiggled across the path in front of her. By the time dawn arrived, she'd be at work and hopefully fully awake. This getting up early stuff wasn't her strength.

She wished she could've brought Chica with her, but snowshoeing with the dog on a leash was difficult. Chica kept stepping on her shoes, tripping her, and she was too nervous to let Chica run off leash. They'd been lucky there'd been no proof Chica killed the deer. Next time, well, she didn't want to think about next time.

Kalin reached the darkest part of the path, halfway between her house and the resort, when she heard a snowmobile approaching from behind. Wanting to make sure the driver saw her, she turned and faced the machine. The snowmobile's headlamp grew larger until the machine whipped past her, inches from her side. Her first thought was the driver hadn't seen her.

The realization that McKenzie's murderer was still on the loose slammed into her. Why hadn't she listened to Ben and Miller and been more careful? She never should have come out alone in the dark. She stood erect, facing the direction the snowmobile had driven, dropped her mitt, slipped her hand into her pocket and wrapped her fingers around her bear spray.

The powerful machine looped around and skidded to a stop. The driver revved the engine a couple of times, jerking toward her in small movements. After several terrifying seconds, the snowmobile leapt forward and drove straight at her. She jumped backward, landing on her back in a snow bank at the side of the path.

She struggled to stand, but each time she pressed her hand to push herself up, she sunk deeper. The snowmobile slowed, turned and picked up speed again. She rolled to her side, shoving herself against the base of a tree. She grabbed a branch and pulled herself upright.

The snowmobile slid to a stop a couple of feet in front of her.

A man wearing a black jacket and black helmet pressed his gloved hand on the throttle, revving the engine. She stared at him, knowing she couldn't outrun him, and waited. Her heart pounded, and her eyes stung with tears.

The driver of the snowmobile ceased revving the engine and removed his helmet. "I want to talk to you," Jeff Morley said.

The evidence pointed to Jeff being the killer. He'd proven himself to be violent. McKenzie had paralyzed his brother and stolen his girlfriend. She should have seen this coming. Fear pressed inside her, underneath her breastbone. "Did you follow me?"

"No. But now that you're here, I've a few things to say."

Kalin didn't believe him. He must have waited for her to leave her house. She'd told Donny and Nora she couldn't go out after the movie because she was working early. Donny could have mentioned it to Jeff. He'd timed his outing on the snowmobile so he'd catch her in the middle of the path, farthest from any help. She'd been stupid, and she hated being stupid. Anger bubbled up her throat, and she exhaled a violent breath. "I'm not talking to you here. Meet me in my office at a decent hour."

Jeff laughed an ugly laugh. "What I have to say is private."

If she could knock him off the snowmobile, she could use it to get away. Even wearing snowshoes, she could drive the sled.

"What were you doing hanging around my family last night?"

Kalin held her bear spray at her side. "I've been friends with Nora all summer. You know that. We decided to go to a movie, and she asked Donny. What's the big deal?" Kalin dropped her other mitt, slipped her left hand into her ski jacket pocket and found her cell.

"It's more than that. You've glued yourself to my aunt."

"I bought a painting from Lisa. Then I met her by accident at

Nora's. I didn't know she was going to be there."

"You're lying. I know you met her at the pub too. You're trying to figure out who killed McKenzie, and you're going after Donny."

Kalin hadn't meant to lie. She'd forgotten the drinks with Lisa. "I think you're misunderstanding the situation."

"What do you have against Donny? You accused Amber of starting the flood just to get at him."

"Why would I do that?"

"How the fuck do I know? I just know you're going at him from all directions. My dad had a fit finding you in the garage with him." Jeff stared off into the forest and after a moment shrugged. "I won't let anyone hurt him, you know."

Icicles of fear cracked along Kalin's skin as if she stood naked in the winter air. "What does that mean?"

"There's nothing I won't do for him. I want you to stay away from all three of them."

Inside her pocket, Kalin oriented her phone, finding the top end. She slid her phone out of her pocket and glanced at the display. She tapped the phone icon, then recent calls. It was all she dared for now. "What do I tell Nora?"

"Figure something out."

"You know Nora better. If you want me to dump her, tell me what to say. Help me with this." She risked another glance at her phone and tapped Ben's number. The second she thought the call connected, she whipped the phone to her mouth. "I'm with Jeff Morley."

"What the fuck?" Jeff slapped her hand, and the phone flew off the path into a mound of snow.

In response to light tapping on the front door, Ben rubbed sleep out of his eyes, walked barefoot along the hallway, thinking Kalin must have forgotten something and maybe he'd get another hug out of her. Maybe she'd decided she wouldn't go to work so early and come back to bed with him.

He opened the front door, only half surprised to find Vicky standing on the doorstep wearing her ski jacket open over a blood red negligee. The necklace he'd given her for her birthday hung between her breasts, and Ben remembered how he'd played with the pendant. Christ, she could make him feel good. He wiped the thought from his mind, pissed at himself for falling for her tricks.

Chica pushed her way past Ben, wagging her tail, trying to greet Vicky. Ben grabbed her collar and pulled her into the foyer.

"Why isn't she wearing the new collar I bought her?"

Her perfume entered the foyer before she did. She'd chosen his favorite on purpose, probably just to get at him.

"Are you crazy coming here?"

Vicky's eyes hovered on his bare chest, making it clear what she wanted from him. "Kalin's not home, so what are you worried about?"

"It's seven in the morning. Where else would she be?"

"I overheard her telling Donny she was going to work at seven today. Seems like a good time for us to talk."

"I told you, I don't want to talk. There's nothing to say."

Vicky fingered her low neckline. "I'm kinda chilly here. Can I come in?"

Ben watched her breath form clouds in front of her face and forced himself not to worry about her. She could zip up her jacket if she was cold. "You're not welcome here. This is my home with Kalin."

"If you won't let me in—"

"Stop this." Ben started to close the door. He'd had enough of her trying to get between him and Kalin.

Vicky put her palm on the door and held it open. "I still love you. Can't you understand that?"

Ben's phone rang. Kalin's name appeared on call display. "I gotta go." He stepped backward into the hallway, slowed his breathing and debated whether he should answer.

Kalin pressed the nozzle on the bear spray, aiming at Jeff, but the wind took some of the spray in her direction. She held the nozzle until the can emptied. Jeff backed away from her, holding his palms to his eyes.

Kalin hoped the phone was still connected, but even if it wasn't, Jeff had no way of knowing. "I'm on the path halfway between work and home. I need help."

"You bitch." Jeff wiped his eyes, and tears dripped over his cheeks. "Stay away from my family." He shoved his helmet on and took off in the direction of Kalin's office.

Kalin didn't hesitate. Running in snowshoes wasn't easy. Her eyes burned, and she couldn't see much through tears that filled them. She ran toward her home, hoping Ben was heading toward her.

Dawn crept through the trees, improving visibility, and despite her tear filled eyes, she picked up speed. She saw Chica before she saw Ben. Chica galloped toward her, and Kalin suppressed a sob.

"Ben," she yelled.

"I'm here."

An instant later, she saw him sprint around a curve in the path. Kalin ran until she thumped into his chest, wrapping her arms around him.

"Are you okay?" He ran his hands over Kalin, rough and urgent, searching for wounds. "Are you okay?" His voice trembled.

Kalin pressed her face into his chest. "I need to rinse my eyes."

"What happened?"

"I pepper sprayed Jeff." Kalin stepped back from Ben. He wore pajama bottoms stuffed into winter boots and his ski jacket open over his bare chest. He hadn't taken the time to get dressed, and she loved him for it.

"Let's get some snow on your eyes. That'll ease the burning." Ben sat Kalin down and held cold snow against her eyelids. "What was he doing?"

"He followed me. He told me to stay away from Nora, Donny and his Aunt Lisa."

"If he touched you—"

"He didn't. He took off after I sprayed him. I think he believes Donny killed McKenzie and I'm trying to prove it."

"We have to call Miller."

"Kalin, wait," Nora called between breaths.

Kalin wanted to ignore her and almost kept walking. It was one thirty, and Fred said he had a meeting at two. She was heading to his office in the lower village to talk about Jeff Morley. Her shoulders dropped in acceptance that she had to face Nora, and she might as well get it over with and let Nora defend Jeff. She slowed her pace so Nora could catch up. Forcing a pregnant woman to chase her along the street seemed petty.

Nora reached for Kalin's arm and held her elbow. "I'm really sorry. I don't know what Jeff was thinking."

Taken aback, Kalin wondered why Nora was sorry. She hadn't done anything.

"I just talked to Jeff. Constable Miller dragged him in and spent half the morning interviewing him. I think it was pretty intense."

"What did Jeff say?"

"He said he'd been really, really dumb. He got all worked up thinking you were going after Donny. He didn't think it through. You're not going to press charges, are you?"

They reached the top of the metal stairs connecting the upper and lower village. From there, Kalin could see the river, mostly frozen, on the other side of the lower village. The ice looked peaceful on top, but the river raged below. Maybe that's what Donny was like. Maybe one big chunk of ice let go, freed his rage, and he'd gone after McKenzie. Maybe Jeff believed that too. "For what? He just talked to me."

"You're being understanding. I've seen Jeff when he's mad, and he can be scary. It's like he's a different person."

"Like his father?" Kalin remembered the anger she'd picked up from Mr. Morley when she'd met him in the garage. Donny had laughed it off, but Kalin had seen the mean streak.

"Oh no. Never like that. His dad's awful. Have you met him?"

"Once. He wasn't what I'd call friendly."

"I hope he doesn't find out about this morning. He'll kill Jeff."

Kalin stopped at the bottom of the stairs and faced Nora. "Are you seriously worried or was that a figure of speech?"

"I don't mean he'd kill him, but his temper is so bad. I think, sometimes…"

"Sometimes what?" Kalin asked softly.

"I think he might hit Jeff. I'm not sure. Donny and Jeff have never said anything, but I get a vibe."

Once in a while Nora sounded younger than her age. "Have you talked about this with Lisa?"

Nora shook her head. "Lisa has enough to deal with without worrying about the guys. They can take care of themselves."

Kalin checked the time on her watch. "I gotta go. I have a meeting."

Ian Reed strolled toward them. He looked as if he had something to say. When he was within a few feet of them, he smiled at Nora, said, "Hi," and kept moving.

"What's that about?" Kalin asked.

"I don't know. Why?"

"It doesn't look like he's trying to avoid you anymore. Have you guys worked things out?"

"Not that I know of," Nora said. "One more thing?"

"Sure."

"If Jeff called to apologize, would you talk to him?"

"Is that what he wants?"

Nora leaned forward and hugged Kalin. "It is."

Kalin hugged Nora back. What the heck? For Nora, she could manage a conversation with Jeff. "Sure. Does he have my cell? Forget that. I lost it this morning. Tell him to call my office."

Ben loitered in the parking lot beside Jeff Morley's truck, his anger growing with each passing moment. The Holden training session had ended at four, and Ben had been waiting for Jeff since then. The bastard had frightened Kalin. Ben couldn't control her actions, but he could protect her. He watched Jeff approach and saw his back go rigid when he recognized Ben.

Jeff raised his hands in submission. "Dude, I'm sorry."

Ben pushed himself off the truck and blocked Jeff's way. "You think that's good enough?"

Jeff walked around him and opened the tailgate. He shoved his skis and boots inside. "I didn't mean anything."

"Are you crazy? You chased Kalin in the dark on your snowmobile. Do you have any idea what that made her feel like?"

"I said I was sorry."

"I don't fucking care how sorry you are. I want you to stay away from her."

Jeff sneered. "Tell her to stay away from my family." He opened the front door and grabbed a snow scraper. A thin layer of ice covered the windshield, and he turned his back to Ben as if he were too insignificant to face.

"She's doing her job. Leave her alone."

"Or what?" Jeff turned and laughed at Ben.

Ben's anger burst inside him, and he swung at Jeff. His hand crunched against Jeff's cheek, landing in the same place Edwin Bucher had pummeled him.

Jeff grabbed Ben's wrist and twisted his arm behind his back. He shoved the scraper against Ben's neck.

"Stop it," Kalin screamed.

Jeff turned in her direction. Ben landed a punch on the side of his shoulder, knocking him to the ground. He kicked Jeff in the ribs, and Jeff rolled into a ball.

Kalin grabbed Ben's arm. "Stop it. What's wrong with you?"

Ben backed away. "If you go near her again, I'll kill you."

Jeff rolled onto his hands and knees and pushed himself to standing. "Take it easy."

"Get out of here," Kalin said to Jeff.

Jeff glared at her and then at Ben. He stooped and picked up his scraper. With the driver's side of the windshield clear, he stepped into the truck and sped away.

"Are you hurt?" Kalin asked Ben.

"No. I'm fine." And he was, but Kalin seemed shaken.

"What the hell was that?"

Ben didn't say anything.

"You're going to make things worse by fighting."

He stepped away from Kalin. "You're mad at *me*? After what he did this morning, someone has to protect you."

"I don't need protection."

"Yes, you do. What if he'd hurt you?"

"He didn't."

"I don't want to fight with you," Ben said.

"Me neither, but what you do reflects on me. I can't be the director of security if every time something happens, you come to my rescue."

"Your safety is more important than what people think."

"This job's important to me. You know that."

"I don't get how you always muddle your way into the center of drama. You're so bull headed." Sometimes she infuriated him, but the look of her standing in front of him, with her hands on her hips, defiantly staring at him, filled him with pride. She was courageous. "I love you."

She lowered her head and looked at her feet.

"Are you hiding a smile?" he asked.

"I'm not."

"Yes, you are."

Kalin leaned into him.

"I'm sorry," he said. "I can't let that asshole get away with what he did. He needs to know I'll come after him if he goes near you." Ben fumbled in his pocket. He handed Kalin her phone and her mitts. "I went back for your cell. It's toast though. You'll have to order a new one."

CHAPTER THIRTY-SIX

Ian accepted the soda water his sister served him. Melanie had done the undoable. She'd dragged herself back from a drug-induced haze and was trying to make something of herself. He could learn from her.

"What time do you get off work?" He sat at a table in the Mountain Side Restaurant, emitting heat generated during his training session. His times were faster than Morley's, and Coach Jenkinson had winked at him, telling him he was on his way.

"Five. I've been working all day."

"Do you want to eat together?" The restaurant didn't have many customers, which was usual during pre-season, and he could hold a table as long as needed.

She flipped her black ponytail off her shoulder. She'd tied her hair so the purple streak didn't show. She'd transformed her black eye makeup into a light shade of grey. After a slight hesitation, she said, "Sure."

Eating together was a start. Dad had made the big move. Leaving Mom must have been hard, but Ian thought he'd made the change for Melanie and for him. The three of them could be a family. Ian slipped off his boots, leaving them askew on the slate tile, and rested his feet on the next chair, stretching his calves. He faced the fireplace and watched the flames.

While he waited, he reread Melanie's note for the hundredth time. He'd found it stuffed into his ski jacket pocket the first day she'd returned. She'd apologized without making excuses. The note made him think about his own behavior. He'd hurt people too. Especially women.

Melanie had made a big change. Maybe he could too.

After her shift, they ordered burgers and fries. Both drank soda water. With her addiction problems, he wasn't going to drink alcohol in front of her.

"Who's staying at the house?" Melanie asked.

"Mom. Dad and I stayed in a motel. He found a place on the hill to rent, and we moved in today. You could move in too."

Melanie shook her hair loose from her ponytail and raked her fingers through it. "I'm not ready for that. Have you talked to Mom?"

"No. You?"

"No. Maybe you should," Melanie said.

"You're worried about her?"

"I have my issues with her, but I want her to be okay."

"You could call her," Ian suggested.

"I don't think so. Maybe sometime, but not yet."

Ian shoved fries around his plate. "I'll go see her. I'm going to stick with Dad, but I can't cut her off completely."

Ian wanted to talk about her note but wouldn't bring up the topic unless she did. He told her about his disgrace in Fernie. He wanted her to know he had problems too. That she wasn't the only one who screwed up. He admired her for what she'd done to get better. He admired his dad for standing up to his mom. It was time he did something himself that could be admired.

He didn't know why, but he said, "I've done it again."

"Done what?"

"Have you met Nora Cummings?"

"Your freckles are turning orange. Why are you blushing?" Melanie squinted her eyes at him. "You didn't. Is she your girlfriend?"

"She was dating Steve McKenzie, but we had a night."

Melanie put her burger down and looked at him with sympathetic eyes. "She's pregnant?"

Ian lowered his head into his hands. "Yes."

"How do you know you're the father?"

He rested his elbows on the table and put his chin in his palms. "She said I am."

Melanie laughed. "Not to be cynical, but you believe her?"

"Yes. The thing is I like her."

"Then tell her."

"I don't want a baby, and I don't want a serious relationship."

"If it's yours, it doesn't matter what you want. You have a responsibility."

"When did you grow up?" Ian swallowed the last of his burger. No matter how upset he was, he was always hungry and could eat. He reached across the table and shoved a few of Melanie's fries into his mouth.

She swatted him. "Hey."

He grabbed her hand and held tight. "I've missed you. I'm glad you're back."

"Me too. Now go make things right with Nora."

Nora was about to open her front door when Constable Miller pulled his RCMP SUV into her driveway. *Go away and find a real criminal.*

Miller approached her. He pulled his notebook from his jacket pocket and held a pen between gloved fingers. "You know I spoke with Jeff this morning?"

The metal from her earrings made her ears cold, and Nora wished she'd worn a hat. "Yes. He didn't mean anything."

"Did you ask him to frighten Kalin?"

Nora put her hands over her ears, trying to warm them. "Why would I do that?"

Miller wrote in his notebook, but his eyes never left Nora's. "You tell me."

Without meaning to, Nora stepped away from Miller, but the door blocked her path. She had nowhere to go. "I haven't done anything. Jeff got mad at Kalin because he thinks she's going after Donny for Steve's murder. It has nothing to do with me."

"Do you think Donny killed Steve?"

"No."

"Did you see Donny at the resort on the morning of Steve's murder?"

Nora couldn't stop the heat rising into her cheeks. She jutted her chin and straightened her legs. "No."

"I think that's twice you've lied to me about that. What time did you see him?"

"I didn't."

"Things seem complicated with you, Donny and Jeff. You've quite a past together. Is there anything you know that might help me with the investigation?"

"I told you, I don't know anything."

"When was the last time you had contact with your mother?"

"With Lisa?"

"No. Your biological mother."

What the fuck? How did he know about her? Cold air blew inside the material of her green and black cargo pants, but it was the icy fear that made her freeze in place. "My mother died before I was two."

"Nora, you've lied enough to me. It's time for you to be honest."

Nora took a deep breath. "I'm telling you my mother is dead."

"How did she die?"

His jacket sleeve rustled against his side when he shifted position. Too bad it wasn't loud enough to drown out his voice. She'd never questioned how her mother died. She'd taken it for granted what Lisa said was true. She put her hand on the doorknob, thinking if she could just get inside, she could slam the door in his face.

"Nora?"

"In a car accident."

"How did you end up with Lisa Hudson?"

Nora's cell vibrated in her pocket, and she ignored the caller. "Lisa was my mother's best friend. She adopted me."

"So you've known Jeff and Donny since you were adopted. That must make you pretty close to them. Close enough to make sure they aren't charged with murder."

"You don't know what you're talking about."

"Are you trying to protect them so they'll keep your secret?"

"What secret?"

"Since Lisa and your mother were best friends, Lisa must know your mother's family. Where are they?"

Nora remained silent, her face flushed. She was breathing hard. *Something isn't right here.* "I have no idea."

"Who told you your mother died?"

"Lisa, of course. Why are you asking me about her?"

"I think it's time to end the lies. You know your mother is alive, and since you're lying about that, I'd like to know what else you're lying about."

CHAPTER THIRTY-SEVEN

Kalin was still shaking after the encounter in the parking lot. She left Ben waiting outside and returned to close her office. She needed a few moments away from him. Fighting with Jeff was not the answer.

Dusk was a short experience in the mountains, and she missed Ottawa's long transition from daylight to darkness. She tested the light on her headlamp, satisfied the battery was charged enough for their walk home, and began to tidy her office for the night. They'd agreed to meet in fifteen minutes. Ben shouldn't interfere, but how could she be mad at him for standing up for her?

The sound of someone clomping up the steps to the second floor disturbed the silence of the empty offices, and Kalin waited to see who was entering after hours. Her security team wouldn't lock the outer doors until seven. She reached for her cell, remembered it was broken and called Ben using her desk phone. She was talking with him when Lisa Hudson walked in.

"Hi, Lisa," she said and then to Ben, "It's okay. It's Lisa."

"I've brought my snowshoes. Do you have time for a loop? I'd planned to go with Nora, but she's not answering her phone. Something must have come up," Lisa said.

Kalin hesitated and cupped her hand over the phone. "I'm meeting Ben. We usually snowshoe home together."

"I was hoping we could talk. Do you think Ben would mind?"

"You can come with us, and I could drive you back to the resort later for your car."

Lisa shook her head. "I want to talk with you alone. About Jeff."

Kalin said to Ben, "Do you mind if I do the loop with Lisa? I'll be home in an hour and a half."

"Are you sure that's a good idea?"

"It's fine. I won't be alone, and Lisa can drive me home after."

"He's worried about you," Lisa said.

"Typical guy." Kalin pulled a pair of snow pants on top of her jeans and stepped into her winter boots.

Outside the administration building, they each strapped on snowshoes. Kalin checked the metal blade on the bottoms of the shoes by stomping backward and feeling the blade grip the snow. The loop she wanted to take meandered around the village, starting at the Alpine lift station, circling through the forest and ending at the edge of the parking lot. It would take an hour and fifteen minutes of steady snowshoeing to complete the beginner trail. The advanced trails ascended the mountain, covered rugged terrain and were meant for hardy athletes.

Lisa put on a silver hat with a fur border. Combined with her tailored ski jacket and shapely ski pants, she exuded elegance. Kalin laughed at her own pants, more like what a snowboarder would wear, and guessed she looked like a jock. Maybe she should dress more like Lisa. Then she could compete with the Goddess. She laughed out loud. Who was she kidding?

"What's so funny?" Lisa asked.

"I was just thinking about Ben."

Forest surrounded them by the time Lisa brought up Jeff. "I talked with Jeff earlier. Did he call you today and apologize? He promised me he would."

"I haven't heard from him, but I don't have a cell right now."

"Why not?"

"I dropped it in the snow this morning and was too frightened to search for it." Kalin didn't mention Ben had found the soaking and now useless phone.

"I'm sorry about Jeff's behavior. I don't know what he was thinking."

Kalin stepped over a tree that had fallen across the path and pointed her headlamp at the obstruction to show Lisa.

"Jeff's overprotective when it comes to Donny," Lisa said. "Maybe a bit like Ben is with you."

"Why does he think I'm a threat?"

"Donny didn't kill McKenzie."

"I don't think he did. Is that what Jeff's worried about?"

"I think so. There are some things you should know about Jeff. I'm not excusing his behavior, but—"

"There's really no excuse for what he did." Kalin figured Jeff hadn't had a chance to tell Lisa about the fight he'd had with Ben, and she didn't want to bring it up.

"I know that. I want you to understand where he's coming from. He's under a tremendous amount of pressure."

"I don't see how scaring me will help him."

The two trudged in silence for a few moments.

"Jeff's family situation is not the greatest," Lisa finally said.

"I met his dad the other day. I gather he's got a mean streak."

"Jeff's been protecting Donny for a long time. It's second nature to him."

"Is he violent?"

"Jeff? No. His dad can be. I worry sometimes he'll push Jeff too hard one day."

"Are you worried that Jeff killed McKenzie?"

"No. I know he's my nephew and I'm biased, but he doesn't have it in him. He's not vengeful. I think if you understood what happened, you wouldn't think either of the boys killed McKenzie."

"What I think doesn't matter. The RCMP will find out who did."

"You can influence them."

"I don't think so. I give Constable Miller information when he asks. He doesn't ask for opinions, only facts. Wasn't Jeff angry that Nora and McKenzie dated?"

"That happened gradually. They spent time together after Rachel died. I think he wanted to ease his guilt about her, and he grew on Nora. A year had gone by before they started dating."

Lisa had to know about Jeff and McKenzie fighting. The incident had been in the local paper, so why was she lying about Jeff's feelings now? Maybe Lisa believed Jeff killed McKenzie and wanted to downplay his emotions. "I'm not sure I'd be as understanding if I were Jeff."

"I love all the kids. They worked things out. I had to accept their relationships too, whether I understood it all or not."

"How did Nora deal with what McKenzie did to Donny?"

"The car crash? It was an accident. Nora knew that. It almost destroyed all of them. I'm amazed they came through so well. Especially Donny. I don't know who killed McKenzie. I do know it wasn't Nora or the boys. Their home life is a mess, and you're making things worse for them by questioning Donny and Nora all the time. Can't you leave them alone?"

"Do you want me to talk with Jeff and tell him I don't think Donny's the murderer?" It was the only thing Kalin could think to offer that might ease Lisa's burden. She didn't care what Jeff thought or what his problems were.

"That would help."

They came to a split in the path. One direction led to the parking lot by the administration building and the other kept going on the loop. They'd only been out for fifteen minutes, but the snowshoe outing hadn't turned out to be much fun. If they stopped now, Ben would just be getting home, and she could surprise him. "I'm a bit tired. Let's head back."

They reached the parking lot just as the security SUV parked in front of the mountain operations building. Kalin indicated she wanted to speak to the driver and asked for a ride home, relieving Lisa of the responsibility.

The SUV stopped in front of Kalin's home, she said thank you for the lift and hustled up her driveway, eager to be with Ben. She opened her front door and heard muffled voices coming from the back of the suite.

She turned the corner from the hallway toward their bedroom, and her heart fumbled. Ben had his back to her, with his long-sleeved T-shirt hanging loose over his jeans and his brown hair messy.

The Goddess stood in their bedroom doorway. The problem was she wore only a bed sheet, draped elegantly off one shoulder. Her hair hung loose around her face. Her bare feet showed off a fresh pedicure.

Jeff parked in his driveway and stared at the garage. His dad must have opened the door, waiting for him to come home. He hated the garage, the spot his dad had chosen to corner him. An easy place to clean up blood. A place his mom never entered. His dad was careful, knowing when his mom was out of the house, hiding his rage until he was alone with Jeff.

Anger was growing inside Jeff the way a snow mound grew at the side of a road when a plough went by, getting harder on the inside with each passing sweep of the blade. The interview with Miller played repeatedly in his head, the scene unfolding the same way each time.

He'd thought Miller would be aggressive, come at him full on about hassling Kalin. Instead Miller had been relaxed, talking about how stressful life was and the difficulties he must face taking care of Donny. How Jeff must feel guilty about skiing so well when his brother couldn't ski at all.

The interview was almost over by the time Jeff understood Miller thought Donny killed McKenzie and Jeff was protecting him. His gut burned at the thought. If he had to, he'd confess before letting Donny go to jail.

He slammed his hand onto the steering wheel, accidentally hitting the horn. He closed his eyes with regret. Talk about announcing to his dad he was home. The inside door to the garage opened.

Jeff slid his butt sideways across the truck seat, dropped his feet onto the concrete floor and faced his dad. Sometimes he was so stupid.

"Well?" his father said.

"Is Mom home?"

A wicked grin smeared across his father's face. "She's not here to protect you. What happened to your cheek? Just like your old man, getting into fights, eh?"

"I'm not like you." Jeff clenched his fists and swallowed hard. Fighting Timlin had been an annoyance, nothing more. He wanted to do more than punch his dad. He wanted to bash his head in, but that would make him the same. He'd rather be beaten than be the beast.

"You relax your fists, boy. I just want to talk to you."

Jeff wondered if his dad had sensed his desire to kill him and if some basic instinct had warned him to back down. He dropped his shoulders and let his arms drop loose by his sides, hands un-fisted and unthreatening. "What's up?"

"My buddy, Don, has a son who works at the police station. He was on duty this morning."

So his dad knew. "I can explain."

"You better."

"Kalin Thompson was fingering Donny for McKenzie's murder. I told her to back off. She needed to be put in her place." Jeff caught what might be a look of pride in his father's expression, and it embarrassed him how much that meant to him. What he'd done to Kalin was wrong, but Donny had to be protected. If he played this right, his dad would approve. Being a bully to protect the family would be something his dad could support.

"Did you scare the piss out of her?"

He forced a laugh, showing his dad he'd enjoyed toying with her. "I don't think she'll go near Donny again."

Donny drove his van into the open spot in the garage. They waited for the automatic ramp to slide to the floor and for him to join them.

"Am I interrupting something?"

"You know what happened this morning?" his father asked.

Donny flexed his biceps and clenched his fists. "Nora told me."

"You can relax. Jeff did a good thing, protecting the family."

"I didn't kill McKenzie, and both of you need to get that." Donny turned his back to them and wheeled away.

"Get back here and clean the floor."

"No." Donny wheeled into the house and let the door slam.

Jeff felt the shift as if something had fundamentally changed in the power structure. Donny had never stood up to their old man before. Their old man had never backed down before. Maybe he could pin the murder on him. If Jeff could do that, his dad would go to jail and be out of their lives.

Nora sat on Lisa's front porch, waiting for her so-called adoptive mother to come home. She had a key, but it wasn't her home anymore. Miller had shattered that illusion. How could Lisa have done this?

Janet Wood. Miller had at least shared her birth mother's name. He'd looked as if he felt bad about telling her something so big once he realized she hadn't known. She used his guilt to force him to tell her Janet Wood was in prison for killing her infant son.

After Miller left, Nora had driven to Lisa's, wanting to confront her. Lisa arrived and invited Nora in.

Nora backed away from her. She shook all over, and her stomach performed somersaults. "How could you lie to me all my life?"

"What's wrong?"

"I know about my mother. You had no right to hide her from me."

Lisa sank into the nearest chair on her porch and lowered her eyes. She sat still for a moment, picked ice off the wicker armrest and then squared her shoulders and faced Nora. "Tell me what you found out."

"I know I had a brother. I know my mother killed him. I know she's still alive and rotting away in prison. How could you tell me she died?" Tears streamed down Nora's cheeks. She was lost. She stepped farther away from Lisa.

"Who told you this?"

"So it's true?"

"Yes. How did you find out?"

"Constable Miller. He thought I knew."

"Oh, Nora. I'm so sorry. Can you let me explain?"

Nora's throat closed, causing a pressure that made it difficult for her to speak. Her life's foundation cracked underneath her. "I can't deal with this. It's too big a lie."

"Please…"

Nora ran to her car, and without looking at Lisa again, shoved the car into reverse and peeled away.

CHAPTER THIRTY-EIGHT

Kalin eyed The Goddess, resisted the urge to bolt, and even through angry eyes, she could see the woman's beauty, could see what Ben saw in her. Chica pushed at her legs, but Kalin ignored her.

"Well, hello," The Goddess said from her place at their bedroom door.

Kalin held her breath.

Ben swiveled and faced Kalin.

Time stopped.

An ache started at the bottom of her stomach and exploded into full out pain by the time the sensation reached her chest. She might die on the spot from a broken heart.

Ben took one step toward her. "It's not what you think."

Kalin raised her hand with her palm facing Ben. Her arm trembled. "Don't."

"Get dressed and get out of here," Ben said to The Goddess.

The Goddess pouted, but Ben wasn't looking at her. His eyes focused on Kalin. "Please listen, just for a minute. Please."

Kalin heard the panic in his voice and lowered her hand. She didn't trust herself to speak, so she remained silent.

"I've only been home for a minute. Vicky was waiting when I got here. Nothing happened."

"She's almost naked." Kalin heard the anger in her voice but didn't care.

"That's how I found her. She's trying to break us up."

The Goddess leaned against the doorframe and put one hand on her curved hip. "You don't think she's going to buy that, do you?"

Ben didn't answer her. "Kalin, I'm not lying. I love you. I would never do anything to risk us."

Kalin wanted to believe him but couldn't. She let tears fall, not caring if The Goddess saw. She could have Ben. They deserved each other. Kalin turned to leave.

Ben dropped to his knees. "Kalin, don't go."

Kalin's throat closed, and she couldn't speak.

Ben's jacket lay on top of Chica's leash, and Kalin stooped to move it out of the way. She was going to take her dog. Ben couldn't have Chica. Kalin's stomach cramped, and she wanted to throw up. How could Ben do this to her? She loved him. Her brain didn't want to believe, but her eyes told her what had happened. A band tightened across her chest, and if she didn't get out of the room soon, the sob that was building would burst out.

And then a smile crossed her lips. His jacket was cold. He couldn't have been inside for long. Ben had told the truth.

She walked past Ben and put her nose inches from The Goddess's. "You can't have him." She leaned a little closer and felt The Fallen Goddess's breath on her cheek. "You heard him. Get. Out."

Jeff held his fist inches from Nora's front door. He was jittery, and he shouldn't be. They had a past together. She used to love him. She could love him again. So what was he worried about?

Before he worked up his courage to knock, Nora opened the door.

She wasn't wearing her usual cargo pants and black boots. Instead, she wore black jeans and a peach sweater. He didn't know she owned anything peach. If anyone had asked him, he would have said she wouldn't wear that color. She was all darks. Even her hair looked under control. He wanted to reach up and pull a strand wayward. Somehow, she looked terribly sad.

"Oh," she said.

"Are you going somewhere?"

Nora glanced over his shoulder. "I am. What's up?"

"Can I come in?"

She shook her head and stepped outside beside him. "I'm meeting someone in town."

"Can I tag along? I've got nothing to do."

"I, um, I'm going out for dinner."

Jeff's temper started to build. McKenzie died two weeks ago, and she was already going out with someone else. "Who with?"

"No one you know."

"You need to stop this," he said.

"Stop what?"

"Why do you keep trying to push me away?"

"We're friends. I'm not pushing you away."

"Yes, you are."

"Don't yell at me. I've had a bad day. I need to think about my future, and there's nothing wrong with me going out for dinner." Nora pulled the door closed and twisted the key in the lock.

"We're meant to be together. I am your future. Please don't go on a date tonight. I need you."

Nora lowered her head and spoke softly. "It's never going to happen between us. We were high school sweethearts. That doesn't mean we're meant to be together. I think you should find someone else."

"I don't want someone else. I want you."

Nora walked to the side of her car and hesitated.

Jeff followed her. "Don't go."

"You'll be okay." She touched his cheek and smiled. "Really, you will."

Jeff watched her car fade down the road. He could chase her, but what would that do? The bastard McKenzie had started all this. The guy was dead, and Jeff still hated him.

On his way home, he drove through Holden and by the Irish pub. Nora sat at a window table with Ian Reed. She'd lied to him when she said he didn't know the person she was having dinner with. He pulled to the curb, left his motor running and got out. He stood on the sidewalk until he was sure Nora had seen him and then returned to his truck. He slammed the gear shift into drive and took off. Ian Reed. What the hell did she see in him?

Jeff returned to a dark house and was glad he didn't have to face anyone. He left his truck in the driveway. With no one home, he could use the front door.

Once inside, he noticed Donny's bedroom light on at the back of the house. He hovered in the hallway and listened to yelling.

"You brought this on us," his dad said.

"I didn't do anything," Donny said.

"You killed McKenzie, you dumb fuck. If you were going to do it, you should have been smarter."

"I didn't kill him."

"How do you think I felt when Miller came to my place of work? In front of the guys. He came there to question me. Like a criminal. That's what I felt like."

"It's not my fault," Donny said.

"Yeah, it is. Miller wouldn't have come there if you hadn't killed McKenzie. He asked about your keys. Who had our garage door combination. Blah, blah, blah. He couldn't hide that he thought you did it."

"But I didn't."

"He went to see your mother at the hospital. You've embarrassed her in front of the other nurses. Can't you do anything right?"

"I told you, I didn't kill him."

"Stop lying to me."

A fist crunched against bone. Jeff scrambled into the room and grabbed his dad's forearm before he could hit Donny a second time. His dad turned on him.

"Stay out of this. It's between your brother and me."

"Say his name, you bastard. His name is Donny. Say it," Jeff shouted.

His dad raised his fist. "You watch your language."

Jeff took in Donny's bleeding nose. He saw his dad's fist. The darkness of rage took over. He released the first punch. He kept punching until his mother's screaming penetrated his haze filled brain.

His dad lay in a heap, his blood soaking into the carpet.

Donny remained in his wheelchair and cupped his hand underneath his nose, trying to contain his blood.

His mom stood in the doorway, eyes wide, holding onto the doorframe as if she might fall over if she let go.

CHAPTER THIRTY-NINE

"Ian?" Nora said when she opened her front door. Her smile turned to a frown when she saw Donny's face. "What happened to your nose?"

"Nothing. Have you talked to Jeff tonight?"

"Yeah. He's in a state."

"Then you know what happened." Donny followed Nora into her living room. The fireplace crackled.

Nora slumped onto her couch and pressed her fingers into her forehead. "I didn't expect Jeff to show up here."

"Something happened here?"

"He arrived right before I went to dinner with Ian."

"Why were you having dinner with him?"

Nora gave him an exasperated glare. "I needed to talk to him about something."

"What time did Jeff show up?"

"Around six thirty. I told him we would never be a couple and then he followed me to the restaurant and found me there with Ian."

Donny closed his eyes. "Jeff's had a bad night."

"Did something else happen?"

"He beat the shit out of our dad."

"Because of me? I don't get it. Jeff was upset with me, but—"

"I guess he came home angry, and then when he saw my dad punch me, he snapped."

"Your nose," Nora said.

"It's the first time my dad's hit me, and Jeff walked in right when he landed the punch. After the fight, Jeff took off, and I went to the hospital.

I've left him a bunch of messages, but he's not answering."

"This has been a horrible day."

"I need to find him. I don't know where else to look."

"What about Lisa's?"

"I went there already. The house was dark, and she's not answering." Donny paused before asking, "Are you dating Ian now?"

"We went to dinner. That's all."

"Why do you have to pick guys that would upset Jeff the most?"

"What does that mean?"

"You dated McKenzie. I know he's dead, but he was an asshole. Did you know my dad beat Jeff every time McKenzie got a faster time?"

Nora recoiled into the couch. This was a Donny she'd never seen before. He gripped the arms of his wheelchair with such force she thought he might bend the metal.

"First you choose the guy who paralyzed me. He's the reason Rachel killed herself. I don't understand why him. And now Ian. He's not much better than McKenzie. He treats girls like crap. Jeff's a good guy. Are you the type who likes nasty men? Is that what you've turned into?"

"What are you talking about? Steve had nothing to do with Rachel dying."

"Are you kidding me?"

"You're not making sense."

"He dumped her at the party. Right before the car crashed, they were fighting. It was like they'd forgotten I was there. McKenzie wanted nothing to do with her or her baby. She pleaded with him and grabbed his arm. He shoved her away, and she yanked him back. He lost control and crashed into the tree. And Rachel lost her baby."

Nora felt as if Donny had punched her in the stomach. She moved away from him and backed into the hearth. "Rachel was pregnant? Why didn't you ever tell me? I had a right to know."

"I had my own problems, and Rachel asked me not to. I promised her."

"You and your family are all liars. You deserve each other." Nora chose her favorite photo of Donny from the mantel, tore it from the frame and tossed it into the fireplace.

The veins on Donny's neck expanded and turned a gruesome red. "I've never lied to you. I kept Rachel's secret. That's different."

"No, it's not. You hurt me by hiding that. Just like Lisa hiding what happened to my mom. I hate all of you."

"What does this have to do with Aunt Lisa?"

"You're lying about Rachel. She would have told me if she'd been pregnant. I can't believe not one person in my life is honest. My life has turned into one big lie."

"Rachel didn't want me to tell anyone. McKenzie humiliated her. She blamed herself for the accident. She thought it was her fault I would never walk again. She killed herself because of me and because she lost the baby. How could I repeat her secret?"

"Because it would have helped me."

"Not everything is about you. Why can't you love Jeff? Ian is nothing."

"Ian is the father of my baby."

"I thought McKenzie—"

Nora was being cruel, but couldn't stop herself. "You thought wrong."

After Donny left, Nora spent half an hour trying to decide what to do. She'd never seen Donny lose his temper before. He could barely speak after he found out Ian was the baby's father. Spit sprayed from his mouth as he yelled at her. The conversation had gotten out of control.

She shouldn't have been so positive about Ian being the father. She could have said it was only a possibility, explained what happened with Ian, but she'd been too angry to think about Donny's feelings.

If she'd known about Rachel, she never would have gotten together with Steve. Donny should have told her. Just like Lisa should have told her about her birth mother.

Nora called Donny and left a message. Somewhere in her mind, she became aware that she was shaking. She needed to calm herself. The turmoil inside her couldn't be good for the baby.

She went to her kitchen, opened the fridge and found the dark chocolate. She began her ritual of making hot chocolate from scratch. The acrid stench of burnt milk filled the kitchen. *This isn't going to work.* She tossed the burnt pan into the sink. She was desperate to talk to someone, and she'd lost Lisa tonight.

"Kalin. It's Nora. I'm sorry to call so late. I need to talk." Nora had started smoking when she'd smashed her knee and had quit two years ago, but now she would have given almost anything to have a cigarette.

"Hang on a sec." Kalin sounded as if she'd been asleep.

Nora heard muffled sounds and could imagine Kalin getting out of bed and moving to another room. Ben was probably asleep beside her, and Nora felt a spasm of jealousy that Kalin was in a great relationship while her own family was falling apart. She paced from the kitchen to the bedroom, waiting for Kalin to come back on the phone.

"You sound odd. What's wrong?" Kalin asked.

"Donny was just here. We had a big argument." A sob burst from Nora before she could control it. She held the phone away from her mouth, not wanting Kalin to hear.

"Do you want me to come over?"

"No. I'm fine. I just need to talk."

Nora told Kalin about Jeff showing up at her house, her dinner with Ian, the fight between Jeff and his dad, and her argument with Donny. She left out that her birth mother was alive and in prison. That she'd walked out on Lisa without letting her explain. That she had no idea if she should contact her birth mother or not. That her heart was broken from so many sides, she didn't know if she'd ever feel anything again.

"I can't believe I fought with both Donny and Jeff in one night. I've ruined everything."

"I'm sure that's not true. Jeff will have to accept you're not in love with him. It's not your fault he came over uninvited. Give him some time and then explain what happened with Ian."

"I'm more worried about Donny. It was like someone else was sitting in front of me. If you'd asked me yesterday, I'd have told you Donny would never yell at me."

"Maybe being hit by his dad set him off," Kalin said.

"I don't know. He lost it when I told him Steve wasn't the father."

"Why would that make him mad?"

"That's the weird part. You'd think he'd be happy the baby wasn't Steve's."

"Maybe he's just upset it's not Jeff's baby," Kalin said.

"That doesn't make sense. I don't understand it. He totally scared me."

Jeff sat with his Aunt Lisa in the atrium at the back of her house. She couldn't seem to sit still and watered flowers while Jeff told her what happened. Snow sat heavy on the glass roof, making the room feel as if it were closing in on him, and he understood her need to move.

The doorbell rang, and Lisa dropped the watering can, letting the contents spill onto the tiled floor.

Jeff grabbed a cloth and wiped the spill. He hoped Nora hadn't come over too. He didn't want to talk to her in front of Lisa.

"I'll see who it is." Lisa poked her head out of the atrium and looked through the window that framed the front door. "It's Donny."

"I thought he might come looking for me. I shouldn't have left him there." Jeff took a long swallow of his beer and rested the bottle on the side table.

"Your mom was there. I don't think your dad would touch him again."

"I hope you're right."

Lisa let Donny in and led him into the atrium. He glanced at Jeff without saying anything.

"How's your nose?" Jeff asked.

Donny touched the bandage on his face. "Broken. It'll heal."

"Beer?" Lisa offered, and Donny shook his head.

"What happened after I left?" Jeff asked.

"Mom went right to his side. Crying. She didn't even ask if I was okay."

"You're kidding."

"Nope. She glared at me, and then helped him get to the bathroom. I left them there."

"She'll never leave him," Jeff said.

"Maybe she will." Lisa set her glass of white wine beside a potted cactus. She'd poured the drink but hadn't taken a sip. "Remember the night you went to a movie with Ben, Kalin and Nora, and you asked me to go with you? I had a long talk with your mom. I offered for her to move in here. With both of you, if you want."

Jeff smiled. "You're the best."

"She's my sister, and I can't stand watching this anymore. I would do anything for you. You deserve some sanity in your life."

Jeff picked at the label on his beer bottle. "If she wouldn't walk out on him tonight, I can't believe she ever will. She deserves what she gets."

"You don't mean that. Try to understand from your mom's point of view."

"Are you kidding? Donny's her son. How could she side with that bastard?"

"Did she see Donny get hit?"

"What?"

"Maybe she thought you hit him. From what you told me, your dad was worse off than Donny. At least give her the chance to explain."

"I'll think about it," Jeff said.

"She'd be embarrassed to take him to the hospital. How could she face the other nurses and explain what happened? She might have felt she had to treat your dad at home."

"Were you at the hospital this whole time?" Jeff asked Donny.

"I went to Nora's looking for you."

Jeff's head began to throb. "I don't want to talk about her."

Lisa looked from one nephew to the other. "What's going on?"

"I made an idiot of myself. I asked Nora to get back together right when she was getting ready to go out on a date. What a moron."

"You weren't the moron," Donny said. "I was."

"I doubt it," Jeff said.

"I lost my temper. When she told me Ian is the baby's father—"

"What?" Jeff shouted.

"You didn't know." Donny reached for Jeff's hand, but Jeff snapped it away. "I'm sorry. I shouldn't have blurted that out."

"I don't know if she's sure," Lisa said.

Jeff and Donny stared at her.

"The night Steve broke up with her, she called and told me it was because he didn't want the baby. She'd told him it was his. Days later she told me it might be Ian's."

Jeff looked at Lisa. "You knew she was pregnant and didn't tell me?"

"How could I say anything? Nora's my daughter. I couldn't betray her."

"She's angry with you," Donny said to Lisa. "She said you lied to her. What's going on?"

"It's just a misunderstanding. I'll set it right with her tomorrow."

CHAPTER FORTY

Disturbing dreams had kept Kalin from getting a good night's sleep, so she'd felt sluggish all morning. After talking with Nora the previous night, she'd lain awake dwelling on Steve McKenzie's murder. She thought she knew who killed him, but without solid proof, she needed to talk with Nora before she called Constable Miller. Nora had confided in her as a friend and not as the head of security. No matter how much she wanted to, Kalin couldn't keep her work and her private life separate.

She hadn't discussed her thoughts with Ben. They had their own issues to overcome, and she didn't want to complicate their relationship. She smiled at the thought of The Fallen Goddess slinking out of their bedroom, down the hallway and out the front door. Kalin had won the war.

Kalin spent half the day organizing employee orientation. She chased Monica down and grilled her about the hiring numbers. But each time a lull occurred, her mind returned to Nora. Finally she gave in and found Nora in the rental shop.

New snowboards had arrived that morning and Nora was unpacking, getting them organized. A stack of snowshoes rested in the corner, needing unpacking too, but Nora focused on the boards. She was dressed for behind-the-scenes work and wore loose pants, black boots and a baggy sweatshirt. Kalin noticed her hand shake as she slid a box cutter along a seam of tape and opened the flaps.

"I brought you an herbal tea."

Nora reached for the cup. "Thanks."

Kalin persuaded Nora to take a break and get some fresh air. Without race training filling the hill, the pristine ski run glistened in the sunlight. The dull thrum of the chairlift was absent, leaving no hint of the tragedies that had occurred. The chairlift would remain silent until opening day, but the groomers and snowmakers would continue to ready the mountain.

"I've been thinking about everything you told me last night," Kalin said.

"I shouldn't have dragged you into my mess."

"I don't mind." They strolled across the courtyard in front of the empty cafeteria, keeping to the sunlit areas. Nora's face glossed over with a false cheeriness, and Kalin sensed her closing off as if last night's conversation never happened. "Have you seen Donny today?"

"No. We closed the tuning room yesterday."

Kalin blew steam from her tea. "Have you talked to him?"

Nora shook her head. "I don't know what I'd say."

"I've thought a lot about what you said last night."

"There's nothing you can do. I've known Donny like forever, and it's the first time we've fought. We've been friends for too long not to get over it. He was just venting."

"I think it was more than venting."

"What do you mean?"

"You told me he lost it when you said the baby was Ian's."

"He's mad for Jeff, I think."

"What if it's something else?"

Nora stopped walking and faced Kalin. "I don't like where you're going with this."

Kalin held Nora lightly by the wrist and felt how delicate she was. "Donny had a big reason to hate Steve."

Nora removed her arm from Kalin's hand and resumed walking. "I told you, it's not Donny's style to be violent."

Kalin had to pick up her pace to keep up with Nora. "Think about it. Steve paralyzed him. Then Steve dumps you because you're pregnant."

"Donny didn't know Steve dumped me or that I was pregnant."

"Lisa did. Could she have told him?"

"I doubt it." Nora stopped walking again and stared at Kalin.

"What are you thinking?" Kalin asked.

"Jeff could have. I saw him when I was walking home from Steve's that night. He didn't know why Steve dumped me, only that I was upset about it."

"Donny saw you in the drugstore. After he found out you were pregnant for sure, he could have assumed Steve was the father. There's a record of him picking up keys early at front desk that morning."

"I know. I saw him go into the tuning room when I was walking to the rental shop."

"But you never told anyone."

"Of course not. There's something else you don't know. Donny said their dad hit Jeff every time Steve got a better time racing."

"See. Donny had more than one reason to resent Steve."

"Oh, God. Donny told me last night he thinks Rachel committed suicide because Steve dumped her right before the car crashed. He said she lost her baby in the accident. He thinks she felt guilty, that it was her fault he would never walk again."

"Who else knew that?"

"No one. Rachel made Donny promise not to tell about the baby. I didn't even know she'd been pregnant. I never would have gotten together with Steve."

"Donny must have felt horrible after she died. You said he snapped last night. What if it wasn't the first time?"

Nora shook her head repeatedly. "Not Donny."

"I need to tell Miller."

"Please don't. Let me think about it. If it was Donny, it'd be better if he went to the police himself. Can't you give me some time to talk to him? What harm can it do?"

Late afternoon, Jeff returned to his aunt's house. He hadn't spoken to his parents since last night, and he hadn't seen Donny all day. He entered Lisa's den and flopped face down on the pullout couch. He buried his face in the pillow. Exhaustion settled throughout his body, yet sleep wouldn't come.

He rolled over and examined the photos and paintings hanging on the wall. His aunt was talented. Her paintings were cheery. Considering what had happened in her life, he didn't know how she kept that up. He'd thought her art would take a dark turn after Rachel died, but it hadn't. She liked bright colors and scenes of action. She must have the same coping mechanism as Donny.

He couldn't count the number of times he'd hidden at her place over the years. She didn't interfere often in their family life, but she was a stable force behind it. She was his mom's sister, but they were so different. Lisa was strong whereas his mom was weak. Maybe he should give his mom a chance. At least find out if she knew their dad hit Donny. He owed her that much.

He stared at the painting hanging over Lisa's desk. She'd modeled it after a photo taken in his garage. After the accident, Donny had decided to tune Jeff's skis and maybe make a career of tuning. Lisa was teaching him, and they were practicing on her skis. Jeff had taken the photo, and she'd liked the composition. She'd changed the dull grey of the garage into vibrant blues and greens. She painted her skis bright red with flashes of yellow. She captured joy in Donny's face and in her own while she looked at him.

"I would do anything for you," she'd said last night, and he wondered what "anything" meant.

He stared at her painting. She was tuning skis.

"Anything."

Tuning skis.

And he knew.

The doorbell rang. He groaned and shoved himself upright.

Nora stood on the front porch. She looked forlorn and beautiful, but he wasn't sure he wanted to talk to her. After last night, he was embarrassed. Not only had he acted like an idiot, it sounded like Donny had been worse. She stared at him through the glass window that framed the front door, and he couldn't tell if she was happy to see him or not. He guessed not.

She used her key and entered the front hall. "I'm looking for Donny."

Jeff loved Nora, but he didn't know how to reach her anymore.

Nora pointed to the living room. "Can I come in?"

"Whatever. It's your place as much as mine." He stepped to the side and allowed her to pass. He was about to explode. She was so close, and yet he couldn't touch her. "Can we talk?"

"Sure."

"I know about Ian." Jeff saw her hesitate. "The baby."

Nora lowered her eyes and picked at a fingernail. "I don't know what to say. I made a mistake, but if the baby's his, he has a right to be involved."

"You don't love him?"

"I don't. It's not like that."

A feather landed on his heart. She didn't love Ian and that was something.

"I'm sorry about your dad. Donny came to see me after it happened. I'm frightened for him."

"Why?"

Nora's green eyes blurred behind tears. "I think Donny killed

Steve," she whispered. "I've been trying to call him, but he's not answering his phone. I thought he might be here."

"He didn't kill Steve."

"I want to believe that, but you should have seen him last night. He completely lost control. I've never seen him angry like that."

"My dad broke Donny's nose. He watched me kick the shit out of the bastard and then he watched Mom take Dad's side."

"I think he was more upset for you than himself, but that's not when he lost it. It was when I told him Ian was the baby's father."

"That doesn't make sense."

"Donny thought I was pregnant with Steve's baby and Steve dumped me because of it. Maybe it was too much for him and after everything Steve had done, he killed him. Last night he lost his temper because he killed the wrong guy, thinking Steve was the father."

"You're wrong."

"I know he's your brother and you love him. I love him too. We have to do something to help him. Kalin's going to tell Miller."

"Does Aunt Lisa know?"

"I phoned her when I couldn't find Donny. I didn't want to talk to her. We had a big fight, but I thought Donny might answer if she called him. She got really upset when I said I suspected Donny. I think Donny should turn himself in, and I wanted her to convince him it's the best thing. If he confesses before the cops figure out he's guilty, they might go easier on him."

"Do you know where she went?"

"To see Kalin. She wants to talk to her and see if she can change her mind."

"Fuck. This is bad."

Nora reached forward and grabbed Jeff's hand. "What's wrong?"

"Where are they?"

"Lisa was going to ask her to go snowshoeing. She wanted to talk with her in private."

"Did she say which trail?"

"I didn't ask. What's wrong with you?"

"Nothing. I gotta go. Stay here in case she comes back, and don't say anything about Donny to anyone." Jeff grabbed his truck keys and took off running.

CHAPTER FORTY-ONE

A light breeze carried snow flurries gently to the ground. At minus five degrees Celsius, the temperature was perfect for snowshoeing. When Lisa had called, even though she was tired, Kalin hadn't hesitated in accepting her invitation.

Lisa was becoming her friend, and she hoped the mess with McKenzie and Donny wouldn't interfere with that. Although she knew it was a wild hope, maybe if they came up with a plan together, their friendship wouldn't be ruined.

Lisa hadn't said anything about Donny when she'd phoned, and Kalin didn't know if Nora had spoken to her about him.

She walked from her office and met Lisa at the entrance to the trails. Twenty centimeters of snow rested on top of the sign that announced the beginner, intermediate and advanced trails. Snowshoe traffic flattened the beginner trail, but the intermediate and advanced were pristine.

"Where's your dog?" Lisa asked.

"At home. She needs to be on a leash right now, and she steps on my snowshoes when she's close to me."

"Does she run away?"

"No, but she has a thing for wildlife."

"My car's right there if you want me to lock your stuff inside," Lisa said.

"Sure." Kalin handed Lisa her backpack full of work files. No need to carry the heavy load.

When Lisa returned from the car, she said, "Let's do Extreme Dream."

"I'm up for it." Kalin loved the Extreme Dream loop, and the exercise might wake her up. Rated for advanced snowshoers, the trail ascended through the forest, paralleling the Alpine Tracks ski run, and then traversed along the ridge on the south side of the resort. The sheer drop from the highest point along the ridge met a kilometer wide valley hundreds of meters below, hosting one of the best views on the mountain.

Kalin plopped her snowshoes in the snow. She tightened the straps and tested the holding. The sharp claws on the bottom of the snowshoes grabbed the surface and held. She clamped her headlamp over her toque and turned on the light. Lisa went through the same process. They started the steep incline, working their way to the top of the Alpine lift station, taking thirty minutes to reach the summit.

"What's Ben doing tonight?" Lisa asked between breaths.

"He's at fire practice. I didn't get a chance to call him, but we'll be back before he is. Maybe the three of us could have dinner together later. We can have something ready by the time he gets home."

"That sounds good. He won't mind the extra company?"

Kalin laughed. "Ben likes everyone."

"Except Steve, I heard."

"True. He had issues with him," Kalin said. "Not many people liked Steve."

"I don't think he cared about anyone other than himself."

"I didn't know him well. Nora was the only person I met who liked him."

"And look where that got her," Lisa said.

They followed the trail as it turned toward the ridge. Several meters ahead of Lisa, Kalin stopped to catch her breath and slow her heart rate.

Her headlamp dimmed. She removed it and shook it, giving the battery a bit more life. Her spare batteries sat in her backpack stored in Lisa's car. Hitting the trails without backup gear was stupid, really stupid, but her mind had been too focused on Donny killing Steve.

Lisa caught up, and they continued to traverse the path. "At least with Steve dead, he can't hurt Nora anymore."

Jeff drove like a race car driver, trying to get to Stone Mountain in record time. He didn't know what his aunt was planning, but he needed to get to her before she met with Kalin. He called her several times during the drive. No answer. He banged the phone on the passenger seat more than once and threw it on the floor.

There were four parking lots with trail access. He drove to the one closest to the resort entrance, looking for either Lisa or Kalin's truck. Lampposts planted around the empty lot created a festive atmosphere. The light snowfall made the scene postcard perfect for a Christmas vacation and not for the nightmare he was living.

He spun out of the lot and sped to the next trailhead. Again, he had no luck. On his third try, he found his aunt's truck. He slipped into the adjacent spot. He retrieved a flashlight from his glove compartment, phoned his aunt one more time and got out of his truck.

He needed snowshoes. He couldn't catch up to them with boots alone. He checked Lisa's truck for a spare pair and instead saw Kalin's backpack in the front seat.

The rental shop had snowshoes, and he took off in its direction. At a full run, he reached the shop in a couple of minutes. The lights were out. He pushed on the door. Locked. Without hesitating, he kicked the window beside the door and smashed the glass. He crawled through the small opening and grabbed the closest pair of snowshoes.

Jeff ran back to the trails, strapped on the snowshoes and raced forward. He stopped and stared at the three trailheads. The beginner trail was trampled. There were no markings on the intermediate trail. Two sets of shoes left imprints on the advanced trail.

He decided they would have chosen a fresh path and hoped the tracks belonged to Lisa and Kalin. He kept his flashlight beam on the trail, picking up the tracks. The falling snow hadn't covered them yet. The trail branched off in several places, and as long as the snow didn't come down harder, he should be able to find them.

CHAPTER FORTY-TWO

"Are you saying Steve deserved to die?" Kalin asked.

The light flakes transitioned into heavy snow, and the wind picked up. Kalin and Lisa were midway through the loop. No point in turning around if the weather got worse. Sudden weather changes were as common as they were unpredictable on the mountain, making it easy for people to get caught in a storm. "Did you hear me? I asked if you think Steve deserved to die."

"Yes," Lisa said with commitment.

"You don't mean that."

"When I lost Rachel, I didn't think I'd ever get over it."

"I know what it's like to lose someone you love."

"I miss her every day. Nora said she told you about Rachel. I wish I could have done something for her. I didn't see it coming."

"Maybe she hid her troubles from you. Sometimes people are good at pretending."

They stomped forward a few steps, and Kalin surveyed the path ahead. They were close to the precipice that ran along the resort's property line. Between her fading headlamp and wind whipping snow sideways, she could barely make out the fence that bordered the edge. The temperature drop that came with the wind froze her cheeks. The weather made her nervous, but she didn't want to say anything to Lisa. She kept her moving in the same direction instead of turning back toward the trailhead.

"I'd been focused on Donny, and I didn't notice Rachel declining into a depression. The changes were subtle, and we were all struggling.

Steve didn't even try to contact her after the accident. At the time, I thought it was a good thing. That she could put him behind her. Now I don't know. I second guess everything I did."

"It wasn't your fault."

"It was Steve's. Rachel died, Donny can't walk and Nora is about to be a single mom, all because of Steve. I'm glad he's dead."

"Lisa, this is making me uncomfortable. If you have something to say, please just say it." Kalin guessed Lisa was trying to convince her Steve's death was acceptable. Nora must have told her what Kalin said about Donny. Kalin stood at the edge of the ridge, deciding how to handle Lisa. She had to tell her why she thought Donny killed Steve. She wanted her to understand. Lisa may not forgive her, but she had to do what was right. "Nora told you what I think."

"Donny didn't kill Steve."

Kalin wasn't sure if Lisa had raised her voice to be heard over the wind or because she was angry. "I know it's hard to believe, but all the evidence points to him. I think it's better if he tells Constable Miller himself. Miller's a good man. He'll help Donny if he can."

"You don't know what you're talking about. Donny's not spiteful. He's not mean. Suggesting he could kill someone is outrageous."

"After Nora and I talked, I think she believes it too."

"Only because you're good with words and confused her."

"Nora loves him like a brother. She can't see a way out of this either and wants to help him."

"I can't let you do this."

"I wish things were different, but I have to do what's right."

"Donny doesn't deserve this. I didn't mean for him to be blamed."

"Please stop being so hard on yourself. Donny's an adult and made his own decisions."

Lisa buried her face in her mitts and sobbed. When she got herself under control, she lifted her face and said, "I killed Steve."

Kalin's headlamp dimmed and faded to nothing. "I don't believe you and neither will the RCMP. You can't protect him that way."

Lisa turned away from Kalin, and her headlamp illuminated a two-foot gap in the fence, a gate to nowhere. "You don't get it. Why couldn't you just stay out of this? Steve McKenzie ruined my family. Look what he did to Donny and then to my beautiful Rachel. He destroyed her. Nora was already in love with him by the time I found out they were dating. When I thought he'd gotten Nora pregnant and dumped her, I couldn't take anymore. He'd done enough to us, and he had to be stopped."

Kalin's heart thumped. She remembered Nora saying she'd called

Lisa the night Steve left her. Kalin backed a couple of steps away from Lisa. The second half of the trail was downhill, and she could run the whole way. She snuck her hand in her pocket and remembered she no longer had a phone or her bear spray. Jeff had seen to that.

Before she had time to react, Lisa launched at her. Caught off balance, Kalin stumbled sideways. Lisa pushed her toward the edge, toward the opening in the fence. Kalin grabbed her sleeve and hung on.

"Stop! Think about what you're doing." Kalin wrenched Lisa's arm but didn't slow her movement. She jammed the claw on the bottom of her snowshoe into Lisa's calf.

Lisa cried out in pain, but the pain made her more ferocious. She swung her arm into Kalin's face and knocked her sideways.

Kalin's elbow buried in the snow, hitting ice beneath the surface and jarring her neck. Her temple hit the ground. She rolled onto her stomach and pushed hard to get up.

Lisa jammed her knee into Kalin's back, shoving her face into the snow. "I can't let anything happen to Donny."

Kalin twisted and shoved Lisa sideways. The women lay side-by-side facing each other. Lisa's headlamp had fallen off and lit her face, and Kalin recognized craziness in her eyes.

Kalin was the first to get up. Lisa, seconds behind her, grabbed Kalin's jacket. She used her entire body to push Kalin toward the cliff's edge.

Kalin grasped Lisa's hands, trying to rip them from her jacket. "Stop!"

Lisa was beyond hearing and shoved Kalin again.

Kalin jammed her snowshoe claw in Lisa's leg a second time, aiming for the spot she'd already hit. Lisa's hands slackened, and Kalin used all her strength and shoved her shoulder into Lisa's chest. Lisa stumbled backward, letting go of Kalin's arms, and stopped inches from the edge.

Kalin stepped away from her.

Lisa stepped closer to the cliff, her intent clear.

"Don't jump. We can work this out."

Jeff arrived and tripped as he got close. He scrambled forward on his hands and knees, reaching for his dropped flashlight. He lit the anguish in Lisa's face. He rose and ran forward. "Aunt Lisa, wait."

"Go away," Lisa said. "This isn't your problem."

"Aunt Lisa, please. I can help you."

"I had to kill him. He deserved to die...Tell Nora I love her. I love you too."

"I know. It's okay." Jeff reached for his aunt's hand, but she shook her head.

"It will never be okay." Lisa took one more step. Backward.

Jeff lunged, throwing his arms toward Lisa, but came up empty. He grabbed a fence post, stopping himself inches before he went over. He screamed and screamed Lisa's name.

Kalin crept toward the cliff, aware of the icy slope near the edge. She searched the void for any sign of Lisa. She hadn't been able to save Tom Bennett, and now she'd failed Lisa.

The wind blew upward over the precipice, shooting sharp snow into her face. She closed her eyes to everything—to the snow; to Lisa stepping over the edge and into death; to Jeff repeating Lisa's name in an endless chant. She wanted to keep her eyes closed and pretend the nightmare never happened.

CHAPTER FORTY-THREE

Kalin returned from Lisa's funeral and took refuge in her office. The afternoon closed in on five o'clock, but she couldn't face going home until Ben collected her.

The week since Lisa's death had been hectic.

Ben had been with the search and rescue team when the avalanche dogs found Lisa's crumpled body. They'd used a helicopter to remove her remains from the steep terrain and carry her to Holden.

Lisa was buried beside her daughter in a small cemetery overlooking the lake. Donny and Nora welcomed Kalin and Ben. Jeff, although distant, was polite when Kalin thanked him for trying to help her and for talking to the RCMP on her behalf.

Miller interviewed her and Jeff separately, and they both told the same story. The RCMP declared Lisa's death a suicide. Miller had been generous and let Kalin in on some details of the investigation. He'd been much busier investigating than she'd been aware. Kalin told him about Lisa's confession. Miller disclosed that a hair had been found on the inside of the binding, and with DNA testing, the lab results confirmed the strand belonged to Lisa. She had access to Donny's keys, and she had motive. Donny's name was cleared.

Nora and her baby were a concern. With Lisa gone, Kalin promised Nora she'd be there for her. They'd know soon enough who the father was. Nora had been distant since Lisa died, and Kalin suspected the loss was too much but that Nora would come out of the mess okay.

Kalin studied the painting on her office wall. She decided to leave the canvas hanging in a prominent position as a tribute to Lisa. She understood Lisa's motive. Lisa loved the children in her extended family, and Steve McKenzie had done too much to them.

Ben poked his head around her door. "I have somewhere I want to take you."

"Where?"

"It's a surprise. Get geared up."

Kalin shrugged into her ski jacket and grabbed her toque and mitts.

"You'll need ski pants."

She locked her office and followed Ben to the snowmobile waiting for them outside the administration building. Kalin hopped on and snuggled into him, wrapping her arms around his chest, straddling him and pressing her legs against his. Ben traversed along the snowshoe trail and crossed onto the Alpine Tracks run. The snowmobile angled sharply once the skis hit the steep ascent of the ski run, and Kalin tightened her grip.

Ben drove to the top of the Alpine Tracks run and stopped at the deck overlooking the resort. Two Muskoka chairs were cleared of snow and positioned for the best view. Between the chairs, a table was set with champagne and glasses. Flashlights planted face up in a ring around the chairs lit the area.

"Are we celebrating?" Kalin asked.

"I hope so."

Ben popped the cork and poured two glasses. He handed one to Kalin and clinked his glass against hers. "To you. To us. To our future."

They sipped champagne and watched stars glitter above them across the moonless night.

Ben broke the silence. "I bought you a present." He handed her a box.

She slipped off the red bow and removed the red paper, careful not to rip it. Inside, she found a pair of gloves. With the romantic atmosphere, the ordinary gift puzzled her. Why all this effort for a pair of gloves?

"Try them on."

She removed her mitts and slid her left hand into the matching glove. "There's something in the finger."

Ben had a goofy smile on his face. "See what it is."

Kalin shook the glove.

"Careful," Ben said.

Kalin poked her finger into the glove's ring finger. Her fingernail snagged something, and she dragged out a diamond ring, letting the jewelry slide onto her palm.

"I want my life to be with you. Not just living together, but committed." Ben lowered himself to one knee, held Kalin's hand and said, "I love you. Marry me?"

~ * ~

If you enjoyed this book, please consider writing a short review and posting it on your favorite review site. Reviews are very helpful to other readers and are greatly appreciated by authors, especially me. When you post a review, drop me an email and let me know and I may feature part of it on my blog/site. Thank you.

Kristina

KMStanleyWriter@gmail.com

Message from the Author

Dear Reader,

Life as the director of security at a ski resort is exciting. Oddly enough, most mishaps occur at night. Each day I arose and read my email, assuming I hadn't already been awoken in the dark hours to deal with an emergency, and checked whether there was fall out from the previous night's adventures on the resort. A road collapsing, an ice storm that shut off access to the resort, a full out brawl in the bar, medical emergencies, and a flooded building were all events I've been called to work for.

The Stone Mountain Series exists because I moved away from my home in the mountains of British Columbia, and I missed her terribly. I left for an adventure on the seas, and my past life of living in a ski resort became my muse.

Stone Mountain and Holden do not exist on the British Columbian map. I made them up. For those of you from the area, you may see a resemblance to Panorama and Invermere. I love the area and wanted to write about it, but didn't want to be restricted by an actual place. My imagination needed more freedom to get the story out. The positions at the resort exist in some form, but the characters are fictitious.

If you'd like to connect, send me tweet @StanleyKMS telling me you've read DESCENT, and I'll follow you back. I can also be found at http:\\www.KristinaStanley.com.

Soon to be published, BLAZE will take you on a Stone Mountain journey of arson and betrayal. How far can you be pushed before you want revenge?

With all my heart, I thank you for reading DESCENT.

Kristina Stanley

Novels by Kristina Stanley

Descent

Blaze
(Coming this fall)

About the Author

Kristina Stanley is the author of the *Stone Mountain Mystery Series*. Her books have garnered the attention of prestigious crime writing organizations in Canada and England. Crime Writers of Canada nominated her first novel for the Unhanged Arthur award. The Crime Writers' Association nominated her second novel for the Debut Dagger. She is published in the Ellery Queen Mystery Magazine.

Before writing her series, Kristina was the director of security, human resources and guest services at a resort in the depths of the British Columbian mountains. The job and lifestyle captured her heart, and she decided to write mysteries about life in an isolated resort. While writing the first four novels, she spent five years living aboard a sailboat in the US and the Bahamas.

Find out more about her at www.KristinaStanley.com.

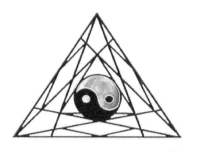

IMAJIN BOOKS ™

Quality fiction beyond your wildest dreams

For your next eBook or paperback purchase, please visit:

www.imajinbooks.com

www.imajinbooks.blogspot.com

www.twitter.com/imajinbooks

www.facebook.com/imajinbooks

IMAJIN QWICKIES ™
www.ImajinQwickies.com